Not a Friend

Cover Art by Liz Parkes

ISBNs
Paperback: 979-8-9929903-1-7
Ebook: 979-8-9929903-0-0

Maybe I'll dedicate future books to my friends or family, but this one? This one is just for me.

Trigger Warnings

While *Not a Friend* is an emotional journey full of delicious banter, fun friend groups, and hot musicians, it's important to me that every reader knows what to expect.

Please be aware that *Not a Friend* includes the following:

Situationships

Smoking, alcohol consumption, and intoxication

Mild body shaming (not from the love interest)

Miscommunication (situationships, remember?)

Questionable cheating (it's complicated)

Actual cheating (off-page, not the love interest)

Mentions of child neglect (off-page)

Anxiety (with on-page anxiety attacks)

Open door, 18+, explicit sex scenes (with enthusiastic consent)

Enjoy!

Contents

CHAPTER 1

Now

You'd think I was someone who didn't
get nervous anymore.
You'd be wrong.

The leather interior of the fancy two-door rental car clung to the backs of my thighs from my spot in the passenger seat. I kept my eyes fixed out the window as we made our way through the turns and dips in the country road. Rows and rows of grape vines and olive trees—some freshly harvested, others plump and ripe for the picking—filled the expanse of green hills. Early autumn had begun to make its mark on Northern California.

The late afternoon was gorgeous from our vantage point, the sky barely fading from clear blue with puffy clouds to luxurious shades of purple, amber, and blood orange. Golden hour would settle perfectly by the time we arrived.

Perfect for photos. Perfect for wedding festivities.

According to Gemma, my best friend and bride-to-be, destination weddings in wine country were making a "huge comeback." It also didn't hurt that Gemma's wealthy uncle was the co-owner of a five-star resort-slash-vineyard in the heart of the Californian countryside, making for the perfect wedding venue.

Kieran drove the car up the steep, winding road that led to Moncleith Mountain Resort, my stomach rolling in time with each dip and twist. I released a slow exhale, mentally counting to ten along with it.

Kieran's hand came to rest easily above my knee, his pinky finger sliding ever so slightly under the hem of my sundress. I smiled at the contact, loving the way his tanned hand looked against the freckled skin on my thigh, but I was grateful his eyes never left the road. I didn't want him to see the nerves bubbling just under the surface of my façade.

The flight from Boston yesterday was spent oscillating between excitement for my best friend's big day, relief I had a few days away from work, and absolute dread at the mere possibility of seeing *him.*

Kieran squeezed my exposed thigh gently. "Whatcha thinkin' about, Olive?" he asked, the soft timbre of his voice easing me out of my own head.

"Nothing," I answered a bit too quickly. I gave him a tight smile and covered my hand with his, lacing our fingers together. "Just not looking forward to the crowd is all. I heard Gemma and Grant invited practically everyone they've ever known."

"Hmm," he hummed, giving me a look as he nodded.

Hmm, a classic Kieran-ism, also known as his way of saying he thought something was stupid, or boring, or sounded generally uninteresting and unimpressive, but he was too nice to say it directly. Or, in this case, *Hmm* meant *Of course, Gemma invited everyone under the sun to her lavish wedding.*

He'd never been impressed by her success on social media or her influencer status, but he knew better than to vocalize his complaints to me.

Gemma Clark, my fabulously beautiful, magnetic best friend, was getting married to the love of her life and one of our grad-school friends, Grant Christensen. He was perfect for her, of course. She would have never in a million years agreed to marry someone who treated her even a fraction less than exactly what she deserved.

He complemented her in every way possible. Where Gemma was always the life of the party, the deserving star of the show, the natural influencer who was always down to go out, Grant was her *Star Wars*-loving, house plant-growing, boy-next-door fiancé with an aeronautical engineering degree. They couldn't be more different, but they fit together like a glove. They had since the very beginning.

I turned back to the window and resisted the urge to chew on my bottom lip for fear of ripping the skin and making it bleed. Again.

Is he going to be there?

My thoughts had been constantly, uncontrollably, flashing to *him* in the six months since we received the save the date for the wedding, but more so in the last handful of days. Memories. Some I'd all but forgotten about until I had the sickening realization there was no way *he* didn't get an invitation to the wedding. Since then, the memories lit up my mind like lightning in the night sky at the most inopportune moments.

Am I going to have to face him again?

I thought about the last time I saw him nearly two years before, how everything had ended.

Well, "ended" wasn't the right word when things never really, truly began in the first place. As much as I tried not to think about it, I couldn't stop my thoughts from drifting, mentally preparing myself for what I would do if I saw him.

Or worse, if he saw me.

Or worse than that, if he saw me first and I didn't see him at all until *boom,* he was right in front of me, giving me no time to think before reacting. *What would I do? What would I say?*

Is there even anything *to* say?

Kieran turned onto a freshly paved drive lined with pristine land-scaping. Resort amenities passed as we ascended the hill—pickleball and tennis courts, private access pools, and hot tubs.

"This place has everything," Kieran said, his eyes wide. "Wanna play pickleball sometime this weekend? It's a great workout."

"Maybe," I mumbled, keeping my eyes trained out the window. "I'll be pretty busy helping Gemma with wedding stuff, remember?"

Even though the actual wedding wasn't for another two days, it was incredibly on-brand for Gemma to ask all her friends and family to *"Make the trip worth your while!"* by hosting an entire weekend-long wedding extravaganza at the venue.

Air conditioning blasted across my face despite the balmy autumn breeze outside, but the sting of nervous sweat still gathered under my arms the closer we got. Tonight was just the welcome party.

It'll be fun, I reminded myself, *everyone will be there.*

Well, hopefully, not everyone.

When the road evened out to a wide drive that led to a towering, Italian-style stone and terracotta building, a breathtaking expanse of vineyards came into sight just behind it.

Before I could even open my mouth to gawk, the view was obstruct-ed by two valets hustling to open our car doors. As quickly as we could get our bags out of the trunk of the rental, a third valet pulled up next to us in a golf cart, promptly loading our things into the back. Beyond, the resort grounds were full of bricked trails leading to rows and rows of private, cabin-like suites.

I guess that explains the escort.

"I'll go get us checked in," Kieran murmured with a kiss to my temple. "Be right back."

October air caught my hair as it whipped through the gentle hills and valleys of the property. I admired the vineyard's sheer beauty and breathed in the smell of freshly harvested sweet grapes and autumn leaves while I waited. Distant, acoustic music swelled from the far side of the building, out of view.

Must be where the welcome party is.

Is he here?

The thought involuntarily jumped to the front of my mind. I couldn't resist it if I tried.

What does it matter if he's here or not? He might not have even come. The likelihood of him being able to make the trip is slim to none with how busy he must be now. Gemma said so herself, his RSVP was still very much TBD.

I shook my head as the familiar anxiety I'd been battling crept up again. No, I refused to allow myself to fall down a mental rabbit hole thinking about him. This weekend was about supporting my best friend.

No drama.

"Okay, all set!" Kieran jogged over, handing me a heavy-looking canvas bag—welcome gifts for the friends and family of the bride and groom as they checked in. Only this bag was considerably heavier than welcome gifts I'd received at any other weddings I'd attended.

"What the hell?" I snorted. Peeking inside, I found an arsenal of goodies preparing us for the weekend ahead, along with the source of the hefty weight. In addition to some wedding weekend essentials, there was also a bottle of expensive-looking white wine and a Polaroid photo of Gemma and Grant smiling broadly at the camera with the words *Let's Get Ready To Party!* printed on the bottom.

"I'm glad they're taking such an understated, *demure* approach," Kieran grumbled, guiding me to the waiting golf cart with a hand on my waist.

The cart hauled us up a shallow, winding path to a circle of cabins that resembled a cul-de-sac. Snagging the room key from Kieran, I let myself in while he and the valet ushered our bags inside.

The suite was ginormous, with high ceilings and wide French doors that led out to a balcony at the back of the bedroom. A California king bed took up most of the space; the fluffy white duvet beckoned me to curl up and take a nap after our long drive.

I turned in place to explore and gasped when my eyes landed on the bathroom. It was breathtaking. White marble countertops, lights lining the giant vanity, and a glass shower with one of those hanging rainwater showerheads. I sighed with bathroom envy.

The door closed with a *thud*, followed by a whistle as Kieran took in the suite for himself.

"Damn," he whispered, though probably more to himself than to me.

"Not too shabby," I confirmed.

He appeared in the bathroom doorway and leaned against the frame.

"What?" I asked, already reading the look in his eye.

"That's an awfully big bed in there."

"Is it?" I leaned close to the mirror to splash water on my face.

He watched my reflection. "Should we test it out before the party?"

I laughed and nudged him in the ribs as he drew closer to guide his hands around my middle.

"We have to get ready!" I tried to ease away from him, but he only backed me into the vanity, humming his protest against my neck. "Kieran, the party starts in less than an hour, and I still need to shower."

"That's plenty of time."

"No, it isn't." I craned my neck away. With a kiss on the lips and a pat on the shoulder, I shooed him away. "Now go."

He brought my bag of toiletries from the bedroom and left me to take a shower, but as soon as the door closed and I was left again to my thoughts, my lingering smile faded.

Is he here?

The scalding water was glorious against my back, gently massaging the tension out of my shoulders. When I finished, I grabbed my phone and turned on some music, cranking up the volume in an effort to drown out my thoughts as I styled my hair.

Is he here?

Forty-five minutes later, my brown hair hung in loose curls around my shoulders. My makeup wasn't great, but it was great for me. Freckles still peeked out from under the foundation, no matter how much I tried to cover them.

"I thought you were going to wear the yellow one," Kieran said as he finished tying up the back of my dress—a mid-length milkmaid-style sundress with little purple flowers that made me feel pretty. I was already anxious, but at least I didn't feel insecure on top of it.

"I planned to wear it on Saturday." I packed five dresses for the weekend, knowing my selections would be a game-time decision depending on how I was feeling in the moment.

"Hmm," he said.

"What, you don't like this one?" I teased, doing a half-twirl.

Kieran pulled me toward him. "It's hot. They're all hot. But the yellow one is…" He gave me a heated look, to which I rolled my eyes and opened the suite door.

He looked downright mouthwatering. Was it the way his perfectly tailored suit pants hugged his muscular thighs? How great his toned arms looked with his sleeves rolled up to the elbow? His dirty-blond hair pushed back out of his face, highlighting his light green eyes? Whatever it was, it was irresistible. Part of me regretted saying no to trying out the California king.

"Will there be a lot of people you know here?" he asked as we made our way, hand in hand, down the brick path from our suite.

"A few. Gemma's mom and brother. Some friends from grad school, too." I didn't offer any names.

The distant music grew louder with each step. Soft string instruments and an acoustic guitar added to the romantic ambiance of the property.

I tried to keep my face neutrally happy as we continued down the path to the welcome party, but I couldn't stop my eyes from impatiently darting over every face we passed, as though *he* was going to suddenly spawn right in front of me.

Relax, McLaren, I chided myself. *Act like a normal fucking human and not like a nervous Chihuahua. So what if he's here? What difference does it make? Absolutely none.*

The illuminated pathway led to the winery side of the resort behind the main building. We made our way deeper into the property, following a steady stream of well-dressed partygoers, and were greeted by the smell of sweet, fermented wine and wood barrels. At the end of the walkway, our view opened to a breathtaking courtyard situated between two buildings, with the countryside beyond a picture-perfect backdrop.

Twinkling string lights hung overhead, bridging the gap between the two buildings and vining down Roman-style columns bordering the courtyard. A quartet of musicians sat poised in the corner, surrounded by lush greenery, like muses in a garden. The photos Gemma sent me months ago didn't do the place justice. For a second, I was convinced we were in Tuscany rather than Napa County.

"Jesus," Kieran whispered.

High-top tables with tiny candles peppered the space, already partially occupied by other guests carrying glasses of wine. Waiters weaved between them, offering champagne and various wines balanced on serving trays. I snagged a glass of red as soon as they were within reach and gave the crowd another once over.

Maybe it was a form of self-preservation, the itching need to know if he was there or not. Or maybe it was a deep-seated trauma response. Either way, the lack of control made me fidgety.

The way I saw it, the more information I could take in—in this case, the more faces I could mentally inventory—the better I could gauge the situation and recalibrate possibilities of what might happen. The better I could anticipate possible interactions, the better sense of control I had, and the more grounded I felt. Which would explain why I felt like I was orbiting somewhere in the sky instead of standing on solid ground.

On the surface, maybe that logic was flawed, but it was a process I'd used my entire life. A way to keep myself prepared for any outcome. Reasonable as it was or not, I wasn't going to lie to myself: the biggest variable in predicting how the weekend would go depended on whether *he* was there or not.

So yes, I scanned the crowd again.

"Babe?"

My head snapped to Kieran, who was looking at me with an adorably confused expression, like he was waiting for my answer to something.

I shook my head. "I'm sorry, I wasn't listening. What did you say?"

He laughed, the corners of his eyes crinkling. "I said I'm going to head to the bar and get a drink before it gets too busy. Want anything?"

"Oh, uh…" My head involuntarily swept left, then right again. I was still holding the nearly full glass of red wine I'd gotten from the server when we walked in. "No, I'm fine for now. You go ahead; I'm going to look for Gemma."

"Have fun with that," he said with a lilt in his tone, bending to kiss my temple before turning toward the bar. "I'll find you after."

I took a long swig of my wine, which was way too dry for my liking. The aftertaste reminded me of what I imagined fresh asphalt to taste like. Or a tire. Or the inside of a leather boot.

I recognized a few faces as the crowd grew. Gemma's mother chatted with an older gentleman whom I assumed must be her newish husband as of a few years ago. In the corner, I spotted Martinez, one of our old friends from grad school. I hadn't seen him since a few days after graduation, at Grant's last game night he hosted with all of us before we went our separate ways. It was the last time the whole friend group was together at once.

Well, *almost* the whole group.

I wandered through the crowd, passing a towering champagne wall and a mall-style photo booth Gemma's mom begged her not to rent. She thought it would be tacky, but Gemma convinced her it was "actually retro," thus making it a must-have.

A huge, printed engagement photo of Gemma and Grant caught my eye. It wasn't until I took a few steps closer, and the image faded to another, that I realized it wasn't just an engagement photo. It was the slideshow Gemma had told me about—a television screen displaying pictures of the happy couple throughout the years.

My face split into a grin as I moved to the screen. A gap-toothed Gemma, no older than seven or eight years old, smiled back at me, proudly holding up loot from the Tooth Fairy. Naturally, she was the cutest kid in the world.

The photo faded to the next—a teenage Grant, standing outside of a driver's education school, holding his freshly printed driver's permit in the air. An embarrassed expression contorted his youthful baby face, and I imagined him saying, "Mom, that's enough. No more pictures," while the photo was taken.

The image faded. Gemma, on Halloween, dressed up like a princess. Then, Grant and his younger brother, Jared, in a swimming pool. Then, side-by-side pictures of Gemma and Grant at their respective high school proms, their dates strategically cropped out of the photos. I watched and laughed at each photo as they faded into and out of view, the two getting gradually older with each one.

Finally, the image faded into a photo of the happy couple together. They stood cheek to cheek in the middle of a crowd, arms wrapped around each other as they smiled at the camera.

It reminded me of the night they met. There was something so special about the way Grant, for being so completely different from Gemma, clicked instantaneously with her. He somehow kept up with her, with the ease of someone who had known her forever. As if he saw her for the force of nature she was and wanted to hop on her moving train and take it wherever it would go. I remembered how closely they huddled together in the deafening club, how loudly she laughed at his jokes.

If I believed in love at first sight, I would believe it for them.

Then, my smile slowly receded back again, replaced by a hollowness in my gut as I thought about *him.*

For over a year, I'd done so well at keeping him wrapped up, sealed tight in a box in the corner of my mind. But not knowing if he would be at the wedding was cracking my resolve. The Unknown was never a friend of mine. And it was never good for my anxiety.

I trained my eyes on the corner of the image, knowing what I would find.

A tall figure with dark hair that was perpetually an inch too long stood showing off his profile: a straight nose, strong jaw, and a ghost of a smirk playing with the edges of his mouth. His arm was loosely wrapped around a girl next to him, hand resting ever so lightly on the small of her back, barely making contact. He leaned in close, towering over her to hear something she was saying to him.

Anyone else looking at the photo displayed would never have been able to tell the girl was me. Her face wasn't visible at all. Only the back of her head, her long brown hair, and the palpable sense she liked that boy *way* more than he liked her.

The memories of the night Gemma and Grant met flared again. Only this time, they weren't of my best friend falling in love right in front of me. They were of *him.* His knee bumping into mine under the sticky table, his hands ghosting around my waist as we danced, his tentative smile on the drive back to his apartment.

Heat climbed high on my cheeks.

To think about Gemma and Grant was to also think about *him.* Because the night my best friend found the love of her life was also the night I met Nate Cassidy.

CHAPTER 2

Five Years Ago, December

*This kind of thing is getting boring, but I have a
hard time saying no.*

"Shots! Shots! Shots! Shots!" Gemma chanted, fists pumping in the
air. The waitress shook her head as if debating whether or not
to cut us off, but she set the tray of small glasses on the table between us
anyway. Music blared in my ears through the club speakers as rhythmic
basslines bumped through the soles of my shoes. The place was packed
to the brim with drunk twenty-somethings dancing in the crowd not
ten feet away from where we sat. Half of them wore typical nightclub
attire; the other half wore heinous Christmas sweaters.

"Oh god," I groaned loudly. Grabbing a vial of the clear liquid, I took
a sniff and immediately regretted it. "Why are there so many?" There
was only me and Gemma, but the tray held ten tiny glasses of what I
now knew was tequila.

"Because," Gemma replied, eyeing me as she grabbed a lime wedge
from the little paper bowl in the middle of the tray, "we're celebrating."

"Ten shots is a little more than celebrating."

Gemma sighed dramatically. "Fine. If you must know, I do have a hidden agenda. It's my personal mission to finally get you laid. Tonight. Honestly, Olive, how long has it been?" She loved to point out the painfully long dry spell I was in.

"It hasn't been that long," I lied. It'd been over a year, but who's counting?

She raised her perfectly-plucked eyebrows at me.

"Okay, fine," I relented. "It's been a while, but we're *not* taking all of these. You're trying to get me laid, not give me alcohol poisoning."

We were only on our second round of drinks, but I was already feeling that lovely warmth of being just tipsy enough to have fun but not quite enough to make stupid decisions.

"They aren't all for you, dummy. But you are going to take at least one." She handed me a lime wedge, giving me her I Know You Better Than You Know Yourself face.

"What?"

"I'm just trying to help make sure you have fun. You always over-think and clam up before you get the chance to make a move, Oli. You need to loosen up."

Easy for you to say.

Gemma was accustomed to guys approaching her anytime we went anywhere. It was an inevitability. Her blonde hair and dimples that could be seen from across the room made them moths to a flame. I was the friend who—in the eyes of men in their twenties—didn't hold a candle to their much hotter friend. The backup friend, in case it didn't work out with the hotter one. Second string.

It was almost comical how many times men looked *through* me to get a good view of Gemma. Or better yet, ignored me altogether as if I wasn't *right there.* As if they genuinely didn't register another human standing next to The Hot One.

Gemma was the definition of The Hot One.

I didn't blame guys for being drawn to her. She possessed a level of charisma and likeability that I could never.

Which meant she was never alone or without a free drink at a bar for more than twenty seconds.

I played my part of "Gemma's friend" dutifully. Stepping aside as guys tried their luck with her was one thing. However, exchanging painfully awkward small talk with their creepy wingman friends was another. It was the *worst* part. Especially because it was usually an obvious plan for the wingman to "do his friend a solid" and "distract" me so his buddy could swoop in for the kill.

Gross.

Sure, there had been times when rejection stung a little harder, and my ego took a hit. Sure, it was embarrassing and dehumanizing at times, but I didn't pity myself. Nor did I blame Gemma for it. I mean, how could anyone stand out when they were right next to someone like *her*? Hell, I probably would've flirted with her, too, were it not for my unfortunate heterosexuality.

The way I saw it, I was painfully plain in every way. Especially compared to her. Thick brown waves next to her straight, bleach blonde locks, extra weight around my middle and thighs next to her model's body, hazel eyes and freckles next to her baby blues and dimples, oversized clothes next to her bodycon dresses.

If I did clam up or overthink any time I talked to men in the wild, it was in part because of my secured position as the backup friend. A response based on past negative experiences.

"Fine, I'll loosen up." I eyed the tray between us skeptically. "This is still way too many shots for us to take by ourselves."

"What if we make some friends and invite them to help out with the extras?" Gemma wiggled her brows at me.

I'd had hookups and boyfriends through the years, but nothing compared to the attention my friends got on the regular. While they were out sowing their wild oats in undergrad, I was more concerned with watching their drinks, saving their seats, and making sure everyone got home safely.

Thanks, anxiety.

Thus began the dry spell Gemma was bound and determined to break by making sure I got a "proper dicking." Her words, not mine. Plus, the end of a shitty first semester of grad school at Sumner University was the perfect excuse to go out. It was the last chance for most students to party before winter break, so everyone was going out in style.

At least, everyone from the ages of twenty-one to thirty in Hartwood, Massachusetts, by the looks of it.

"I don't see anyone jumping at the opportunity to take drinks from two strangers in a club," I reasoned. "Sounds like a really great way to get drugged."

Gemma laughed at a volume that rivaled the music blasting overhead. She propped an elbow on the table, pointing at me. "You forgot one thing, my dear Olive." Her grin spread wider, white teeth bright against her deep red lipstick. "Boys are stupid."

She wasn't wrong there.

With a wink, Gemma sprang into action, throwing herself backward, leaning her barstool back so far she nearly toppled out of it. Reaching a long arm out, she tapped—more like *slapped*—the shoulder of a cute blond guy standing at the table behind her.

He twisted around quickly, his eyes going wide. Probably confused as to why he was being slapped by a stranger. But his confusion turned to concern when he noticed Gemma's barstool leaning precariously on two legs.

"Oh, shit." He sat his beer down on our table and steadied her with a hand at her waist. "Woah—you okay?" he said with a laugh. I saw it in his eyes immediately. The Gemma Effect.

"Yes!" Gemma casually flipped her hair over a shoulder as if she fell into people's arms on a daily basis. "More than okay, thank you!"

The blond kept his arm around Gemma like he was still afraid she might slip off the barstool. Not at all because he wanted to keep his hands on her for a moment longer.

Gemma continued like a well-rehearsed actor.

"My friend and I ordered too many shots," she shouted into his ear. The music transitioned into a zippy electronic beat, somehow even louder than the last one. "Here"—she leaned forward and grabbed two glasses—"we'll never drink them all. Take one with us! Give one to your friend, too!" She placed one glass into his hand and reached behind his shoulder to give the other to his friend.

His incredibly attractive friend.

His dark, messy hair was a stark contrast against the short, neatly styled hair of the blond. The way he kept his head angled downward, even as he stepped closer to our table, gave an air of cool aloofness that opposed the friendly confidence of his friend.

Both men took the shot glasses with zero reservation. I rolled my eyes with a silent laugh. Seeing the Gemma Effect in action never ceased to amaze me. All she had to do was flash a bright smile and start chatting, and she could make people do just about anything.

I watched the dark-haired guy as he shuffled around to stand between his friend and me. He eyed the shot glass silently before bringing it up to his nose. Then, he sniffed, ticked his eyebrows together, and promptly placed it back on the table, sliding it a few inches away with a finger.

"What are they?" the blond asked Gemma, leaning in close to hear the answer.

The music cut out for a beat drop just as she yelled back, "Tequila!"

The one with dark hair shook his head. "Yeah, I think I'll pass on that," he murmured, shifting his weight from one foot to the other as the rest of us licked the back of our hands and passed the saltshaker around.

He stuck his hands in his front pockets as we clinked our glasses together over the center of the table.

I threw the shot back, feeling the tart, stinging liquid go down my throat and land hotly in my belly, warming me from the inside out.

The dark-haired one watched with mild disgust, cringing as I put the glass back on the table.

"Not a fan of tequila?" I asked, giggling at his expression.

"I used to like it a lot." He gave me a sideways glance as if reliving a horrid memory. "It's the *tequila* that isn't a fan of *me*, I promise you."

I let out a short burst of laughter that surprised me as it came out. His mouth spread to a tentative, close-mouthed smile.

"Sorry." I giggled, feeling heat in my cheeks. I couldn't tell if it was from the alcohol or embarrassment from the snort I'd just let out.

Gemma made quick work of jumping into conversation with the guy she slapped, effortlessly flirting as she ran her long, painted fingernails through her hair. He soaked up her every word.

Fighting the urge to clam up, I gestured to the vacant seat next to me, offering it to the dark-haired guy.

"They'll be in their own world the rest of the night, won't they?" he asked, nodding towards Gemma and his friend.

He maneuvered the stool, scooting it closer to me with one hand before settling down. His long legs filled the space between us.

"Oh, most definitely." I nodded, twisting my body toward him and propping a hand under my chin to truly look at him for the first time.

The first thing I noticed was the sharpness of his jaw. His frame was tall, with that slim musculature swimmers and runners have. His dark brown hair was shorter on the sides but hung lazily on the top as if he made a habit of running his fingers through it a thousand times a day.

"What's your name?" he asked, his knee bumping into mine under the table.

"Oli. Well, Olive," I corrected with a wave of my hand, "but Oli is fine, too…"

"Oli," he repeated as if tasting the name on his tongue. "Nice to meet you. I'm Nate."

CHAPTER 3

Five Years Ago, December

I'm a terrible dancer, but I can pretend for tonight.

Nate offered me a hand, and I shook it once in the cramped space between us. "That's Grant," he said, pointing across the table.

Grant leaned closely to Gemma, head ducked low with a face-splitting grin as she spoke into his ear. She moved her hands animatedly, emphasizing whatever story she was telling.

"That's Gemma," I said. "I think she likes your friend."

He nodded, glancing at the two already enamored with each other. "I think he likes her, too."

I wondered if Nate often found himself in the same position as me. Was Grant his Gemma? It was easy to imagine Grant hopping from table to table, chatting and flirting as he passed with Nate tagging along behind him.

I stole another glance, and it was like my brain and body finally put two and two together.

A really—*really*—hot guy was sitting next to me, inches away, and he wasn't asking me for Gemma's digits.

Oh, shit.

I should say something. Hold conversation. Do something, anything.

I suddenly didn't know what to do with my hands. I debated taking another shot of tequila just to give them something to do.

Thankfully, the music swelled as the DJ mixed in the next song—one of the biggest pop songs of the year. Sweaty college students flooded the dance floor, filling the space.

Nate leaned in closer.

"I'm going to grab another drink," he said into my ear. His shoulder pressed against mine with the slightest pressure, his knee bumping mine again. Not in a drunken, handsy way, but in a comfortable way, like how one would casually lean against a friend. "What are you drinking?"

I grabbed the nearly full vodka soda lime that had been sitting, ice slowly melting, for the last twenty minutes. *God, I can feel the hangover already.* "I already have one, thanks, though," I said, taking a gulp of the watered-down drink.

He nodded before turning his back and lifting from the barstool. Tapping Grant on the shoulder, Nate said something into his ear before disappearing into the crowd.

Well, that was fun while it lasted.

He'd clearly found his excuse and got out of dodge to try his hand at someone else in the crowd.

Was I unapproachable? Awkward? Rude?

Was it the way I gave him two names? Is it pretentious to introduce yourself as your own nickname? No. Lots of people have nicknames. His name is Nate, for crying out loud. What's that short for? Nathan? Nathaniel? I'm not the only one here with a nickname.

Am I just… ugly? No.

At the risk of sounding vain, I knew I wasn't ugly. Maybe dull next to Gemma, sure. But ugly? No, I didn't think I was.

I took a deep breath, pressing the mental reset button. As always, I accepted the loss, shrugged to myself, and ignored the teeny tiny pang of rejection. I could respect the hustle of a single man in a university town. Nobody plays the field harder than them.

Godspeed, Nate.

I abandoned my bar stool when a classmate of mine stopped to chat. Sitting for too long made me restless. We took a round of the leftover tequila shots, which Gemma and Grant paused their conversation to partake in, and for the first time since my last final, I allowed my shoulders to relax.

Alcohol worked its way through my system, easing the tension that had been building all semester and allowing the music to move through me. The bass thumped heavily in my chest as I swayed. Somehow, it'd gotten even busier in the packed club. No longer was the LED dance floor the only crowded space. The entire building was practically shoulder-to-shoulder.

My classmate and I were gabbing about the latest book-turned-movie adaptation when I felt a featherlight touch on my back.

I expected it to be Gemma giving me the low-down on Grant. But when I turned, Nate towered behind me.

He smiled politely and raised a full drink as if to say *cheers* before taking a long swig. I raised my glass in response, mirroring his movement with a sip of my own.

Was I surprised to see him return? Yes. I assumed he would be going home with someone else by now. He was hot enough; he probably could've had his pick of anyone present.

But there he was with a full drink.

Whoops.

Maybe I was an asshole for assuming his intentions when he left the table before, but maybe he just didn't want to ditch Grant.

When my classmate waved goodbye, Nate squeezed closer and ducked his head. "Sorry, that took forever." The top of my head barely reached his chin. "The line was so long." His voice had a smooth, soothing, clear quality to it. The kind of voice meant to narrate audiobooks or host podcasts.

"Yeah, it's crazy in here!" I shouted over the music as a guy dressed as Buddy the Elf pushed by.

My eyes caught Gemma as she left the table and bounced toward the dance floor, Grant trailing closely behind.

Nate closed in tighter to avoid being run over by another rogue elf, his chest bumping my shoulder. He leaned in until his lips were close to my ear. "Do you wanna dance?"

Goosebumps rose over my shoulders, and, for whatever reason, I froze.

Do I want to dance?

We were in a club. Of course, I *wanted* to dance. But did I want to dance with him?

I thought back to earlier that night when Gemma and I were getting ready. She was, of course, giving me shit about my dry spell.

"Meeting someone out can be fun, Olive! You don't even have to like them. If they're cute and don't seem like they're going to murder you, why not have fun for the night? It doesn't have to be that serious, I promise."

To which I responded, *"Fuck it. You're right."*

"Sure," I said and downed the rest of my drink.

When he gave me a crooked smile and held out a hand, I took it. My hand was engulfed by his, warm and soft, save for a callous I vaguely registered against my skin. Nate pushed his way through the packed dance floor until we were near the center, surrounded by dancing bodies.

The music was louder here than on the outskirts of the dance floor. Nate kept hold of one hand as we moved to the beat, but we were quickly forced closer together, my breasts pressed to his chest, his hips firmly against my belly. This close, I smelled his leathery, sweet cologne that mingled with the fabric softener on his black shirt and felt the warmth of his skin.

Our proximity sent a nervous thrill through my body, but I kept moving and didn't let my thoughts wander to how awkward I probably looked while we danced. Nate lacing his fingers through mine helped.

We are half-pickled in a giant room with a bunch of drunk twenty-some-things. Who here doesn't look at least a little bit ridiculous?

Feeling bold, whether by the cover of darkness or by the tequila shots, I let my free hand explore tentatively, pressing it against his abdomen, snaking up his chest, and settling around his shoulder.

When the next song mixed through the speakers, bringing in a new wave of energy, I twisted and pressed my back into Nate, surprising myself by guiding the hand I was holding to my waist and down my hip.

He followed my lead, roaming his hand slowly, curiously as our bodies moved together. He bent over me, lowering his head until the tip of his nose touched my exposed shoulder, grazing it lightly along my nape. I shivered despite the heat of the club.

It had always amazed me how paradoxical crowded places could be. That there, in the middle of a crowd, with so many eyes around us, I still felt concealed. Private, even.

Intimate.

In that kind of environment, even the boldest of touches could feel like a secret.

He must have set his drink down somewhere because a second later, his other hand wrapped around my middle and joined in his hesitant, wandering touches.

When the song changed, I faced him again and he splayed a hand wide across the small of my back to pull me in even tighter. Lowering his head to my shoulder again, he hummed softly along to the deafening music against my neck. The loose ends of his hair tickled my skin, but I leaned into it, dizzy from his closeness, heart thundering in my ears after going so long without being touched.

His hands traveled freely now, no longer tentative and hesitant. They edged on hungry as they traveled down my waist, around my round hips, across my ass. A flush crawled up my chest and painted my cheeks in time with the butterflies in my belly. When they rose lazily up my body and lifted my arms, my fingers laced together with his above my head.

I met his gaze under heavy lids. Earlier, I assumed his eyes were brown. But pressed against him now, they were actually a dark blue. The color of the middle of the ocean—the deep sea. My heart thudded against my ribs when they flicked to my parted lips.

I barely heard him say the words, but I saw them form on his lips.

"Can I kiss you?"

I nodded my consent without a second thought.

It wasn't the hard, sloppy kiss I thought a kiss in the middle of a club would be like. Instead, Nate was gentle yet strong as his full lips moved against mine in a steady, slow rhythm.

He cupped the back of my neck, the tip of his thumb resting under my chin, holding it in place. An involuntary moan sounded from somewhere in my throat, and I felt him smile against my lips. When we finally pulled apart, I was blushing so hard I had to physically look away from him. Had to lower my gaze and take a deep breath to clear the fog.

Nate was biting his lower lip to hold in a grin when I met his eye again.

He glanced over my shoulder. "Your friend is coming over here." I shuffled around the cramped dance floor to follow his gaze. Sure enough, Gemma was parting the crowd with Grant in tow, closely behind her.

"So is yours." I couldn't help but lean back against him while we waited for them to make their way to us. His chest was solid and warm on my back. He snaked a hand around the side of my hip.

"I was looking for you!" Gemma shouted into my ear as she crushed me in an embrace. "We went back to the table, and you were gone."

"You found me! This is Nate, by the way," I said, gesturing to him.

Nate and Grant were giving each other the stereotypical bro-ish high-five-slash-handshake thing all men magically knew how to do as if they took a class on it the second they all turned fifteen.

When Nate smiled at Gemma, I searched his face for that look. The one that said she was clearly the better option out of the two of us. The realization that she was the hot one and he was stuck with the backup friend. But he only gave her a polite smile and a quick handshake before formally introducing me to Grant. At least, as formal as you can get in the middle of a packed dance floor.

Gemma reached across our foursome and pulled me closer by the hands.

"I'm sorry I lost you earlier," she said directly into my ear, her lip gloss sticking to my hair. "Are you good?"

I nodded. "Yeah, I'm actually having a lot of fun. Are you?"

Her baby blue eyes lit up, and a wide smile spread across her face like honey over toast. She then told me as much as she possibly could about Grant within fifteen seconds. About how nice and funny he was, how he and Nate were both second-year grad students, and (arguably the most important bit) she was planning on going home with him.

"I can stay if you want me to." She eyed Nate skeptically before looking back at me with raised eyebrows. If I wasn't comfortable or said I didn't want her to go, I knew she would stay in a heartbeat.

But I couldn't contain my slow grin or the blush on my cheeks.

"That's what I thought," she said, smacking me on the ass before dancing back to where the guys nodded along to the music.

Within minutes, Gemma and Grant left the club hand in hand, but not before Gemma shared her phone location with me.

I shared mine back, just in case.

When I turned to Nate, he had one hand in his pocket, and the other extended, reaching for me.

"Then there were two." He laughed.

"I think I need another drink." More like a distraction from the blaring fact that I felt naked without the safety blanket of Gemma nearby, but hey.

We made our way out of the crowd and to the bar, but not before retrieving the jacket I'd left on my barstool. Nate kept his fingers lightly pressed against the small of my back as we squeezed between tables and groups of drunken dancers.

"You never did tell me what you were drinking earlier," he pointed out as we found a spot to lean against the crowded bar. Colorful string lights hung above our heads, casting his face in red and green, highlighting a shallow dimple on his right cheek. I resisted the urge to poke a finger into it.

"Vodka soda," I told him, "with a lime. I don't always drink it, but tonight it sounded good."

He flagged the bartender down and ordered drinks for both of us.

"So, what do you usually drink then?" He crossed his arms over the top of the bar and leaned closer to me.

I hummed, inching closer until my arm grazed his. "It just depends on my mood, I guess."

Away from the center of the music, his voice, his laugh, was clearer than before and just as soothing. The electricity of flirtation bubbled within me, saturated with apprehension and the fear I was going to ruin the night by saying something stupid.

"So, what kind of mood calls for vodka?" he teased.

"Vodka, soda, *lime*," I corrected, "calls for a *very* different mood than just vodka, Nate."

The bartender returned and placed two identical vodka sodas in front of us, lime wedges poking out of the ice.

"My apologies," he mocked, sliding one glass in front of me and taking the other. "Please elaborate, Oli."

I squeezed the lime into my drink and took a long sip, reveling in the sound of him using my nickname. "I guess tonight I was partly in the mood to celebrate and partly in the mood to say 'fuck it.'" I shrugged, taking another drink.

"Celebrating the end of the semester or something else?" He cocked his head to the side, causing a strand of his dark hair fall over his forehead.

"The end of the semester, of course, like everyone else here." I gestured to the still-packed club. "Gemma decided we both needed a night out since the last few weeks were particularly hellish."

He dropped his lime into his drink. "Makes sense. And what about the 'fuck it' part?"

I paused at that, debating my answer. To be perfectly honest, the 'fuck it' part was the liquid courage Gemma convinced me I needed to break my damn dry spell. The only issue was I never thought it would actually work. But so far, the mental image of how the night might progress with Nate was becoming clearer and clearer, and I was getting more and more nervous.

Don't clam up now, Oli.

"The 'fuck it' part… is just for me."

He nodded like he understood, even though there was literally no way he did. Hell, *I* didn't even fully understand it. There was no way to verbalize my need to just… let go. To stop holding myself to such a ridiculously high standard all the time, stop trying to be perfect, stop feeling like I didn't work as hard as everyone else, stop taking myself so seriously. It was exhausting. I needed to let go, give myself a break, do something purely for me.

"What about you?" I changed the subject. "Do you have a go-to drink? I see you copied my order this round."

He smiled into his vodka soda. "I'm impartial. I'll drink pretty much anything. Except tequila."

"Why not tequila?" I nudged his arm with my elbow. "Who hurt you?"

"Oh, god." He laughed as if remembering a bad memory. "It just never ends well."

A rowdy group of guys all dressed as Santa crowded the bar, making elbow room scarce. To conserve space, Nate put his arm around me and pulled me in close as if he'd done it a million times before.

We talked for the better part of the next hour, with me half-tucked within the circle of his arms, his face so close to mine to hear me that if I were to look up at him, we would be nose to nose. When we finished our drinks, we ordered a round of water. We talked until the crowd thinned out, and after a while, he asked the question that made my heart jump to my throat.

"Do you want to go back to my place?"

CHAPTER 4

Now

Is she here?

"Oli!"

My attention snapped from the slideshow of photos toward the shout. I didn't have to search for the source. Gemma jogged to me in excited, staccato steps punctuated by her stiletto heels, arms spread wide. I met her in a crushing hug, careful to hold my wine glass as far from her skin-tight ivory dress as possible, and breathed her in.

A fraction of my nerves settled. She was the balm that made everything better. Nothing seemed so bad when I was with her, and it'd been too damn long. Sure, we FaceTimed and texted constantly, but it'd been a few months since we'd last hung out in person. We only lived a few hours apart, but between work and my spending weekends with Kieran, we never seemed to find the time.

We still talked about every detail of the wedding weekend, though. Maybe she and Grant weren't having a bridal party, but I still very much had maid-of-honor status when it came to the parts that mattered, like wedding dress shopping and tie-breaking when the two of them couldn't decide on cupcake flavors.

"Thank god you're finally here," Gemma grumbled into my ear. "My mom is already driving me insane."

"Are we surprised?" Her mom meant well, but she tended to overstep wherever she could. She was opinionated, even about the most trivial details, and she *always* voiced them.

"No," she snorted.

Grant emerged from the crowd. Over Gemma's shoulder, I caught his eyes softening when he spotted Gemma and me pulling apart from our embrace.

"There she is," he said with a charming grin, coming to my side and giving my shoulders a squeeze. "You get in alright?"

"Yeah, we got checked in and everything. This place is even more gorgeous in person, Gem. You're gorgeous. Everything is gorgeous."

She really was. From her simple, elegant dress, her tanned skin, her freshly highlighted blonde waves in a trendy half-up style, and her eyes sparkling under the string lights—she looked like Aphrodite incarnate. Or an angel. Or a princess. Or a combination of all three.

"I was just admiring your embarrassing photo display." I pointed a thumb at the slide show behind me. "You had a great haircut on your thirteenth birthday, Grant."

He groaned.

Gemma giggled. "Isn't it precious? I swear there were a thousand more pictures his mom gave me that I wanted to put in there, but he vetoed most of them."

"I would have vetoed all of them if I could have," he said. "You and Mom conspired against me."

Gemma and I shared a look. They *had* conspired. They even enlisted the help of Grant's younger brother, Jared, to scour old Facebook albums for every embarrassing photo of Grant that existed.

My eyes flashed over Gemma's shoulder, involuntarily scanning the crowd again.

Is he here? Would now be a bad time to oh-so-casually ask Gemma about his RSVP?

"Where's your man?" Gemma asked.

"Great question." I craned my neck toward the bar, searching for Kieran, knowing he wouldn't join me if he saw I was talking with Gemma.

Kieran and Gemma didn't exactly get along. Well, *Kieran* didn't really get along well with *Gemma*. Not to her face—he was always perfectly nice to her in person—but he'd made less and less of an effort to conceal his opinions about her in private over the two-ish years we'd been together. He wasn't the most "online" person and had a general distaste for people he perceived were "showy." So, naturally, someone who made their living posting about their life on the internet, like Gemma, wasn't his cup of tea.

When I finally spotted him, he was caught in conversation with Gemma's younger brother, Michael. I immediately rolled my eyes, knowing the two of them were likely already deep in conversation about sports or workout regimens.

I tipped my head in their direction. "Looks like he already met your brother."

"Oh, god." She followed my line of sight. "Yeah, we're doomed. They're going to be best friends before the night is over."

"I'd better get over there before they start arm wrestling or something. You go," I shooed her. "Mingle with your guests. I'll run interference with your mom. We'll talk later." I wrapped an arm around her middle for another quick hug. "You're beautiful. I love you."

"I'm going, I'm going." She kissed me on the cheek before grabbing Grant's hand and disappearing back into the growing crowd.

I threw a glance toward Gemma's mom to double-check that she was still occupied before weaving my way to where Kieran and Michael stood. As I drew closer, the tail end of their conversation confirmed my suspicion.

"I'm telling you, man, that guy is going to be a first-round draft pick next year," Kieran said animatedly. "I'm putting money on it."

"You're kidding!" Michael bellowed. "With the ankle injury he had last season? Not a chance." He shook his head and slugged the last of his beer before noticing me with a double take. "Olive, I like your boyfriend, but he's dead wrong about football."

"I was afraid you two would hit it off a little *too* well," I said breathlessly, eyeing the pair of men as I propped an elbow on a high-top table.

Kieran's laugh was his only response as he pointed to Michael, ready to jump back into conversation. "Hey, what do you think of the new tight end for the Ravens? What's his name?"

"Don't even get me *started* on that lucky son of a—"

And that's my cue.

"Okay," I clapped my hands together. "I'll let you meatheads get back to it. Find me if you need me."

They barely acknowledged my exit as I turned, hoping to spot another friend nearby.

Martinez has to be close.

Gemma's mom was still chatting with a few folks—no need to interfere with anything just yet. I scanned the perimeter where I'd seen Martinez earlier but didn't catch sight of him. I craned further, popping up to my tiptoes the best I could in my heels to check near the string quartet.

My breath caught in my throat. The sheer force of my double take sent a shooting pain up my neck.

He was standing there, leaning casually against a pillar on the edge of the courtyard as if he'd been there the entire night. As if he were a decoration, accenting the space as much as the architecture and the florals. Bathed in the warm glow of the string lights, with one hand in his pocket, the other holding a short glass of amber liquid, was Nate fucking Cassidy.

CHAPTER 5

Five Years Ago, December

In a word? Intrigued.

For the second time that night, I was glad Nate couldn't see my face. I needed a split second to comprehend his question.

Do you want to go back to my place?

The heat of his body against my back as we leaned against the bar was almost dizzying. I waited for my anxiety to kick in and make my decision for me, telling me to bail on the whole night as quickly as possible.

But then I remembered the words Gemma said to me again.

"Why not have fun for the night? It doesn't have to be that serious, I promise."

And she wasn't wrong. Two consenting adults were allowed to do what two consenting adults wanted to do. A one-night stand didn't have to be a high-pressure situation if I didn't want it to be.

He doesn't give off murder vibes, Oli, I told myself, *and you wanted to live a little. So here is your chance. Live.*

"Yes." I nodded, our noses nearly touching when I turned my face toward his.

Nate held my eye for a beat too long, static and tension forming in the air between us. In sync, we each picked up our waters and polished them off. Then, he paid the tab, took my hand, and led me out of the club with long, confident strides.

I was grateful for the slight chill in the air that kept me grounded as we made our way out the front doors, around the side of the building, and down the sidewalk. Something about the brightly illuminated streetlights and the open air of the quiet road around us made me assess Nate all over again. I took him in without the shroud of darkness and strobe lights.

He was still tall, towering over me by an entire head. But now I could see his deep blue eyes had a mischievous look to them, like there was always some smart-ass remark lingering on the tip of his tongue. He combed his dark hair out of his face with long fingers, confirming my suspicion he did that a lot.

He gestured to a black car parallel-parked ahead of us. "This is me," he said, jogging ahead to open the passenger door for me. His eyes caught mine again and I held his gaze, hovering just outside the open door. He leaned in, and my breath hitched when he planted a soft, chaste kiss on my lips before I ducked into the passenger seat.

"Are you cold?" he asked as he pulled out of the parking spot and started down the dark road.

I was cold, but in a way that clears your head and makes you feel refreshed. A much-welcomed reprieve after the alcohol and the stifling heat I didn't realize was suffocating me slowly when we were inside. I took deep, cleansing breaths, letting the crisp air fill my lungs, and rested my head back against the headrest.

"I'm okay."

"I'm only about ten minutes up the road here." He pointed ahead with a wrist atop the steering wheel.

Why are guys so sexy when they drive?

"If you get cold, just let me know." Nate fiddled with the radio, skipping through a playlist that was connected to his phone. My attention focused on the music, noting the artists' names as he flipped through. I only recognized a few of them; the rest I'd never even heard of.

He finally landed on a song he was happy with and let it play. A few notes in, he glanced my way. "What kind of music do you listen to?"

I'd had an interest in music for as long as I could remember. I learned to play piano when I was little and took music theory and music history classes in high school. But it was my minor in music in undergrad that solidified my appreciation at a deeper level. I listened to anything from classical to classic rock, pop to metalcore, and prided myself on having a wide interest in music with a record collection to match. It was my most prized possession.

"A little bit of everything, honestly."

He nodded. "Same. I'm not particular. The only thing I get picky about is country."

I had to agree. My taste was wide enough that having strong opinions one way or another was pretty rare. I could almost always find something to enjoy, no matter the artist.

While some spent their time pretentiously hating anything that wasn't their favorite genre, I liked to look at it as more of a spectrum that shifted with life's seasons. I tended to lean toward classic rock and alternative indie groups personally but could sing along to Taylor Swift or Top 40 Hits like the best of them.

The way I saw it, music was quite literally made to be enjoyed. The beautiful thing about it was there was a genre for everyone.

Nate thrummed the tips of his fingers on the wheel and hummed along to the folksy melody playing.

"This song is good," I nodded along.

"Isn't it?" His wide eyes left the road for a millisecond to smile over at me. "They're some of the most talented people making music right now. And they're just as good live, if not better."

"You've seen them?"

"Yes, and they were amazing." My eyes caught on his sharp jawline as he checked his blind spot. "What's worse is, like, *nobody* outside of New England has heard of them."

"Seriously? That's crazy. They're so good."

I nodded to the rest of the song as it played, enjoying Nate's quiet humming almost as much. When it ended, he turned on another song by the same artist. I loved it, too.

It was hard not to laugh at myself. I'd always imagined what it would be like to leave the club with a guy for a potential one-night stand. I'd watched my friends do it lots of times. They and their prince charmings (sometimes frogs, if I'm honest) would exit through the club doors in a whirlwind, not to be seen until the next morning, severely hungover but somehow looking exhilarated. Sometimes, they would rave about the fun night they had, and other times, they lamented about their ridiculously embarrassing experience over brunch.

But I never thought about what happens in the in-between. After the club doors close, but before the clothes come off. I felt silly for my ignorance.

"You okay?" Nate asked, breaking my unintended silence. He smiled over at me with closed lips, showing off the dimple on his right cheek.

"Yeah," I lied. I was getting more nervous the closer we got to his place. "Just thinking about something Gemma said earlier." I waved dismissively. "So, are you and Grant close?"

Smooth subject change. Not.

"Oh yeah, we've known each other forever."

"Childhood friends?"

"Yeah. Played tee-ball and everything. His brother and I are in a band."

A band? You've got to be kidding me.

Now, I really had to fight the urge to snort a laugh at the ridiculousness. Of course, the mysterious hot stranger I was going to be one-night-standing it with was in a fucking band. How cliché. Did it matter, though? Even if he turned out to be the damaged, woe-is-me, tortured-poet type I was now *certain* he was... he was still very hot and most definitely not a murderer.

"A band?" I played along. "Very cool. What instrument do you play?"

He's going to make me listen to him play "Wonderwall" later, isn't he?

Dry spell, Oli, dry spell.

"It depends on the song. I sing and mostly play guitar, but sometimes I play the piano. Grant's brother, Jared, is mainly on drums."

I noted his use of the word "mainly," implying they all played other instruments, but I chose to protect my peace by not asking him to elaborate.

"What's the band called?"

"Crescent Light."

I nodded. "Cool name. I'll have to check you guys out sometime."

I waited for him to force feed me one of his songs through the speakers while he had a captive audience in his car, but he just kept tapping his thumbs on the steering wheel as the next song played.

My palms turned sweaty when we pulled into a nice-looking apartment complex. My fingers twisted together in my lap. My clothes felt too tight, too itchy, too warm.

Relax, I self-soothed, *just have fun with it.*

Nate led us through a side door of the building and up a set of stairs. I couldn't help but study his movements as he climbed the stairs in front of me and fiddled with his keys to unlock the apartment door, the way his body moved with careless relaxation.

When he opened the door, he walked ahead and leaned against it for me to pass, putting a hand on the small of my back to guide me through.

"So, this is my place," he said, his voice holding an almost imperceptible apprehension.

Glad I'm not the only one.

He flipped on a light, pointing across the open concept space to a floor-to-ceiling window that took up most of the living room wall, and the large cat perched on a cat tree there. "And that's my cat, Billie."

I made a beeline to the cat. Billie was quite possibly the cutest thing I'd ever seen—dusty gray and fluffy with a mostly white face and pink nose. The cat lounged lazily but slowly unrolled from the ball it had been lying in for me to give it a scratch under the chin.

"Oh, hi, Billie," I cooed to the cat as I traced a finger between its eyes, over the top of its head, and around its ear. Billie's head turned, leaning into the touch.

"She's the light of my life," Nate said in an exasperated tone from behind me, "and she's spoiled as all get out."

"As she should be."

Billie let out a low rumble of a purr, closing her eyes against my hand.

Reluctantly, I turned away from her to take in the rest of the apartment. Maybe I had a preconceived notion of what it would look like based on the fact he was a single guy in his twenties who was also in a band, but the place was shockingly nice.

I'd been in some truly heinous bachelor pads before, the kind that shakes you out of a lust-filled stupor and tells you to run for the hills. I half-expected the floor to be littered with dirty laundry and take-out boxes, or worse. But alas, Nate pleasantly surprised me. The apartment was clean and simplistic, with high ceilings, tidy, faux-marble countertops, and sleek furniture. There were even a couple of house plants scattered on the countertops and on floating shelves in the only small hallway.

"Nice place."

"Thanks." He put his hands on his hips and looked around, too, as if he was trying to take it in the same way a first-time visitor would. "It's pretty bare bones. I'm not here all the time, and I don't have that much stuff, so I never have a reason to get settled in." He pivoted in place. "Water?"

"Yes, please."

As he grabbed two glasses out of the white cabinets, I watched his shoulders flex under his shirt, and my stomach fluttered again with a new wave of butterflies.

"Bathroom?" I asked.

He gestured around the corner. I just needed a second to shake out the buzzing nerves in my fingers and toes. Gather my thoughts. Get a grip.

As soon as I was alone in the bathroom, I shut my eyes and wrung my hands violently.

Be cool, Olive, be cool.

I crossed to the sink and ran my hands under the cold water, pressing them to the back of my neck, hoping it would help ground me. It didn't.

The hand towel next to the sink was soft and fluffy against my skin and smelled like dryer sheets. A far, *far* cry from the crusty frat boy towels I'd had to endure before.

Is this a bad idea? Should I turn back now and pretend tonight never happened?

My head was starting to ache as the drunkenness left my body, and the first signs of a mild hangover set in.

When I faced myself in the mirror, my cheeks were flushed. Whether it was from alcohol or rosacea, I had no idea. But it didn't matter because, under the nerves, I recognized something else, too.

Excitement.

Thrilling, eager, anticipatory excitement. Despite the anxiety, I knew what the next step of the night was. Shit, I was blushing at just the *thought* of kissing Nate again. The thought of going further? It made me damn near giddy.

Looking myself in the eye, I mentally repeated the mantra I'd adopted for the evening:

Fuck it.

I'm doing this.

I left the bathroom with newfound confidence, vowing to embrace whatever the rest of the night brings, no matter what.

I am sexy. I am desirable. And damn it, I deserve this.

Nate was still in the kitchen, leaning against the counter with two glasses of water next to him. Soft music played through the apartment; some indie guitar rhythm accompanied by a slow, steady drumbeat. He gave me a soft, close-mouthed smile as I approached him.

"I think I'm going to need a shot for courage," I blurted. We both knew where this was going. No use in trying to be coy about it. "What do you have that's strong?"

His smile spread into an amused grin. "Okay." He let out a low chuckle. "You sure?"

"Yep." I popped the *p* when I said it. "What do you got?"

"Let's see…" He trailed off as he turned to face the cabinets above the sink. He grabbed two shot glasses, handing them to me one at a time. When he reached back up to rifle through the bottles of liquor stashed there, my eyes drifted to the inch of skin that came exposed in a line above the waistline of his pants. "You up for whiskey? I think it's the best I have up here. Or I have red wine if that sounds better."

I made a face. "Hard pass on red wine. Whiskey is perfect."

"Sorry, I don't have any vodka. I know you've been drinking clear liquor all night."

Sweet of him to notice. "Whiskey will do just fine."

He smirked at me over his eyelashes as he poured amber liquid into the shot glasses. "Not in a celebrating-slash-'fuck it' mood anymore, I take it?"

"Nope." I shook my head once. "Just 'fuck it.'"

"Okay, well, we can only take one shot of this stuff. I still need my dick to work."

I guess he doesn't see the point in being coy, either.

Heat rose higher on my cheeks as he handed me one of the shot glasses, then held his own high in the air in a toast. "Fuck it."

I clinked the rim of my glass with his. "Fuck it."

We downed the shots in one go, and before I could even put my glass back on the counter, Nate was plucking it out of my hand and closing the space between us.

CHAPTER 6

Five Years Ago, December

Did I just… knuckle bump?
Jesus fucking Christ.

Nate cupped the sides of my face as he leaned down to kiss me. Just like the first time on the dance floor, I expected the kiss to go in that hurried, messy way so often reserved for nights like this. A one-time thing that had no reason to be graceful or pretty. But he took his time with me as though we'd kissed a thousand times before.

He moved against my mouth with slow, deliberate intensity, gradually parting my lips with his. The whiskey on his tongue tasted sweet as it slipped into my mouth. I couldn't hold back the soft moan I let out against his lips.

A hand traveled from my cheek to the back of my neck, sweeping my hair behind my shoulder so he could make contact with the skin there. Tangling the fingers of one hand into my waves at the root, his other hand settled on my back, his thumb pressing and rubbing against my waist. He gave the hair at the base of my neck a slow tug, encouraging me to tilt my head back, exposing my neck to him.

His lips lazily made their way along my jaw, sprinkling kisses under my ear, down the column of my neck where my pulse thrummed, and into the hollow where my shoulder met sensitive skin.

My mind swam with the heady thrill of being touched, and I breathed in the masculine, leather and fabric softener scent of him, unable to resist. He smelled so *good*.

Fingertips toyed with the opening of my jacket, making to pull it off my shoulders but pausing before they did. His eyes connected with mine, a silent check-in before he proceeded. I responded by pulling the jacket off the rest of the way for him and dropping it on the ground, holding his gaze all the while. The corner of his mouth ticked up as he leaned in for another long kiss, and he closed his hands around mine before taking a step back toward the hall.

Once the door to his bedroom clicked shut, he pulled me close again, inviting me to invade his space and take what I wanted.

His fingers slid beneath the hem of my shirt, sending goosebumps over the soft skin of my tummy as he inched it upward. I lifted my arms as he pulled it off, then greedily returned the favor. Taking his shirt off was a little less graceful, considering our height difference, but I savored the view regardless.

Smooth contours of a broad chest dipped into a toned abdomen. I spied a handful of tattoos—one on his chest over his heart, a few others on his arms—but I didn't slow down to get a good look at them. I wouldn't have had a chance anyway because his mouth was on mine again, more eager than before.

God, I thought as his warm chest pressed against mine, *I'm so touch-starved.*

Hungry, I shot my hands to his waistline and tugged on his belt buckle, maneuvering the leather until it pulled free. He responded in kind, pulling at the button of my jeans and unzipping them. We only broke away to shimmy out of our jeans awkwardly and amid mildly drunken giggles before we stood upright again.

Nate took a beat to let his eyes wander over my body. I felt his white-hot gaze as it traveled from my shoulders, down the curve of my breasts, over my soft tummy, around my rounded thighs, and back up again. My first instinct was to cover my body, but I was distracted by his lips, parted and swollen as he drank me in, and the slight blush along his muscled chest and neck.

He grabbed me and hoisted me up. Shocked as I was at his strength, I wrapped my legs around his waist and hung onto his broad shoulders for dear life.

He undid my bra, letting it fall between our bodies before tossing it to the floor. His lips were all over my neck, my chest, as he laid me on the bed and moved on top of me. Trailing down to my now-exposed breasts in open-mouthed kisses, he took his time acquainting himself with each. He kissed along the soft slopes, tenderly taking each nipple into his mouth and swirling his tongue before continuing his torturous movements. I buried my fingers in his dark hair, trying my damndest not to writhe under him. I failed miserably.

When his lips met mine again, I couldn't resist any longer.

In any other scenario, I might've taken my time and gotten on my knees to tease him with my mouth. In any other scenario, I might've wanted him to do the same to me.

But I didn't just want this. I *needed* this.

I reached between our bodies to palm the impressive erection straining against his boxer briefs. He sighed deeply against my mouth, a shudder running through him at my touch. Delight bloomed within me at his reaction.

Who was this guy? I couldn't remember ever feeling a level of desire like this—*impatience* like this. There wasn't a second to spare. I had to know what it felt like to have him buried deep inside me. I didn't know when I got so bold, only that I surprised myself when I said to him, "I want you to fuck me."

Goosebumps rose over his arms before he locked his deep blue eyes on mine.

Lifting himself to his knees between my thighs, he hooked one finger under the waistline of my panties. I mentally thanked Gemma for convincing me to wear a simple black thong instead of my trusted granny panties.

"This okay?" he asked breathlessly.

I nodded furiously, but he didn't move. He raised his eyebrows as if waiting for a verbal answer.

"Yes," I practically whined. "Yes."

With that, he slid my panties off and discarded them in the same general direction as where he'd thrown my bra. He bent to catch my mouth in another deep kiss. Only this time, I felt a single-digit trace between my legs. He dragged it up and down, opening me, spreading the slickness there before slipping into my core.

"Fuck," he whispered. "You're so wet."

Every nerve in my body lit up like a Christmas tree. I moaned as he worked his finger inside me, hooking it upward, then adding another. A crease formed between his eyebrows as he drank in my needy expression.

If his fingers feel this good…

As if reading my mind, he kissed down my body, removing his fingers as his lips moved across my hips and landed on the sensitive, tender skin of my inner thighs. He disappeared for a moment, and I wanted to protest his absence when he slid off the bed. But he returned soon with a familiar-looking foil packet in hand.

I glanced down to see that he had also discarded his boxers.

Wow.

He took note of my surprised, hungry expression and gave a cocky smirk as he climbed back between my legs and used his teeth to peel away the corner of the packet. I didn't think watching a man roll a condom over his length could be so hot, but holy shit. I was going to come undone before we even started.

He centered himself over me and traced his tip over my clit, teasing me until I wanted to beg for more. He only took mercy on me when I let out an exasperated noise in protest. With a small, cruel huff of a laugh, he lined himself up to slide slowly, so, *so* slowly, into me.

I felt every inch of him as he eased himself farther and farther, deeper with each pump until he was fully seated. After pausing to let me adjust to the pressure, he settled into a steady rhythm over me, hitting me so deliciously that I couldn't help but arch my back in response.

He hooked one of my legs behind the knee and pulled it up, hitching it so high on his hip that it nearly touched his chest, doubling the deep pleasure, making my head spin.

Holy shit.

Already inching toward euphoria, it dawned on me that I was probably never going to see this guy again. Something about that was freeing, a permission I didn't know I was looking for. I wanted to take advantage of the opportunity while it was happening, feel all of him as deeply as possible while I still could.

Mustering the courage to make the move, I pushed at his shoulder until he understood my motive. With an arm supporting under my waist, he flipped us until he was lying on his back beneath me.

I took his length in hand and lowered myself as far as I could go. With a groan, Nate let his head roll back onto the pillows. His eyes shuddered to a close as I began to move.

If I could file away and save mental images forever, I would have saved the image of Nate like this. Undone, uncontrolled, messy, and submitted to the pleasure we both felt.

I was already addicted; I just didn't know it yet.

I savored his chest and abdomen, running my nails down the length of his torso, over the tattoo on his heart—a sunrise over a horizon—as I began my own pace on top of him.

The crease between his brows returned when I swiveled my hips just right. His hands flew to grip me, one at my waist, the other no doubt leaving purplish marks on my thigh. I tightened and fluttered around him, the first signs of my impending orgasm, and I suspected he was getting close, too, with the way he held me.

He flipped us back over with little warning, taking my legs with him, guiding one of my ankles up and over his shoulder. Propping himself up with one hand near my head, he pumped into me so deeply I moaned at the shock of the new pleasure.

I inched toward my peak, driven closer and closer with every thrust, spurred on by the sounds Nate made as he fucked me. Fingers grabbing at his comforter, I begged for some kind of purchase as my approaching release pulled tighter. With one last thrust, it finally snapped. My breaths turned shallow as I came, the shudders of my orgasm wracking through me.

Within a matter of seconds, Nate followed me over the edge with ragged, sloppy movement as he moaned his release.

When we stilled in the darkness, our heavy breaths were the only sounds filling the otherwise silent room. He gingerly wrapped a hand around my ankle, still hooked over his shoulder, and lowered it onto the bed.

As he lay down at my side, the post-orgasm high floated to the ground and faded.

Reality set in.

I suddenly wished I was under a blanket.

"Wow," Nate huffed, breaking the silence and my thoughts.

I turned my head. He did the same, a satisfied smile across his lips. Then, for reasons I will never be able to explain, I burst into laughter.

Uncontrollable, uncomfortable, obnoxious laughter.

I laughed until tears formed in the corners of my eyes. Nate just watched me, mouth agape with amusement and confusion.

"I'm sorry!" I gasped for air, covering my mouth, willing the giggling to stop.

He raised exasperated brows at me. "Wa— Was it that bad?"

This only made me laugh harder because it was so ridiculous. Of course, it wasn't bad. The man made me come so hard I saw stars. "No! No, it was good. Great, in fact. Really, *really* good." Tiny giggles bubbled to the surface. "I'm sorry. I don't know why I'm laughing."

He was starting to laugh, too, each word punctuated by chuckles. "Well, shit. You have a funny way of showing it!"

"I'm sorry," I repeated, my cheeks heating. "I was just so nervous earlier, and I think it's coming out like this now." I gestured to my face.

"Really?" His laughter slowed, brows drawing together. "Why were you nervous? I mean… you seemed to know what you were doing just fine." His eyes drifted over my body for a moment, then came back to my face. The gaze made me itchy, but I supposed I didn't have anything to hide at that point.

"I don't know. I don't normally go home with guys I meet at the club." I chose to leave out the fact that I hadn't had sex in over a year.

"Well, I'm honored to be one of your club guys then," he said, holding up a fist and offering a knuckle bump to me. A knuckle bump.

Fully embarrassed and fighting back another bout of laughter, I quickly bumped his knuckles. *I can't leave him hanging*. Then, I took it as an excuse to climb off the bed and go to the restroom.

I padded back into his bedroom a minute later with a throw blanket I found stretched on the back of his couch wrapped around me and both glasses of water that were left abandoned on the counter. I put one glass in Nate's outstretched hand when I reached him. He was lounging in a pair of boxer briefs with his back against the headboard, aimlessly scrolling through a selection of movies on the TV.

The silence was so loud.

"Well," I said, not meeting his eye. "Thanks for that."

"I could say the same thing." He smiled, patting the mattress beside him.

I hesitated.

Isn't this the part where he's supposed to tell me there's an Uber already on the way while he not-so-gently pushes me out the door? Sitting down to watch TV will only make it that much more awkward.

"I should probably get going." I bent to grab my discarded jeans and top. *Where the heck is my underwear?* "I can call an Uber."

"Do you have work or something in the morning?"

"No," I answered, turning in place.

"And you don't have class either, right? You said you were done with your finals?"

I nodded, scanning the floor again for my fucking underwear.

"It's like 3 AM, Oli," he continued. "Just crash here."

I blinked at him, assessing if the offer was genuine or if he was just being nice. It wasn't until his eyebrows raised that I realized I still hadn't answered. He sat up to face me, swinging his legs over the edge of the bed, the muscles in his abdomen flexing with the movement.

"Look," he continued, "you don't have to stay if you're uncomfortable or if you just don't want to, but I'm not kicking you out either." He held up his hands, gesturing around the bedroom. "I mean, I'd rather not have to spend another lonely night in this big, comfortable bed all by myself. And you're already here, so…" The dimple on his cheek came into view again when he cocked his head to the side, a close-lipped smile playing on his lips as he leaned back on his hands.

"Okay, fine." I rolled my eyes playfully. "I need something to wear, though." The throw blanket still around my shoulders was soft but not preferred over actual clothing.

He clapped once in response as he stood from the bed and strode toward the dresser next to me. His bedroom, like the rest of the apartment, was minimalistic, simple, and clean. It contained a bed (with bed sheets, a comforter, *and* pillowcases, I might add), a short dresser with a TV on top, and a desk. In the corner sat two guitars, one acoustic and one electric, an electric keyboard, and a small amplifier.

I didn't look around the room for long because my gaze was quickly drawn back to him in his tight boxers. I let my eyes take their time traveling down his lean back, his ass, his muscular thighs. He had more tattoos sprinkled all over his body. A bow and arrow on his ribs under his right arm, a tarot card of The Fool on his right triceps, a broken sword from *The Lord of the Rings* on the back of his right calf. The muscles in his shoulder danced as he dug through the dresser drawer, but I stopped gawking when he turned to face me.

"Does this work? They're both clean, I swear."

He handed me a pair of thin cotton boxer briefs and a well-worn T-shirt.

"Well, I *assumed* they were, considering you pulled them out of the dresser, but now I'm questioning…"

He snickered as I turned my back to him, sliding the briefs on while the blanket still dangled over my shoulders. The blanket dropped when I pulled the baggy T-shirt over my head. It was the kind of shirt that had been worn and washed so many times that it had that perfectly soft, broken-in texture against my skin. When I looked down at it, Jim Morrison's face looked back up at me—one of The Doors' album covers.

"Have you ever seen this movie?" Nate asked, taking up his spot again on the bed. It was some newly released action comedy starring a comedian and a former heavyweight champion turned actor. Not my typical kind of movie, but what the hell? I told him I hadn't and settled into the pillows next to him as he pressed play. He scooted closer to me until our shoulders touched.

Considering what had transpired not thirty minutes before, sitting with our legs outstretched in front of us, arms touching from shoulder to elbow, felt so… sweet.

Innocent, even.

The corners of my mouth turned up.

I only got twenty minutes into the movie before I drifted to sleep.

CHAPTER 7

Now

One last hit, just to taste you again.

I almost wish someone was recording me because I'm sure I looked like a fucking idiot.

When I spotted Nate leaning against the column on the other side of the courtyard, my eyes went wide before I snapped my head down, eyes locked on my open-toed heels. A second later, I figured I probably looked odd staring at my feet, so my head shot back up again.

Part of me expected him to disappear in the half-second I looked away because I was somehow shocked all over again to see him still standing there when I looked back up. I blinked, frozen in place as he turned to speak to the other members of Crescent Light—Jared, Leo, and Miles. I didn't want to see him.

I didn't.

So I looked to my left, feigning a casual adjustment of my hair around my shoulder. Then I looked up at the sky, willing there to be a fucking blimp or something just to justify it. I finally settled on keeping my head low as I turned, walking back to where I'd left Kieran and Michael.

"I, uh, I'm going to step outside for a minute and get some air."

Kieran gave me a mildly puzzled expression like he was waiting for the punchline to the joke. "Babe." He took a tiny step forward, throwing an amused glance at Michael. "We *are* outside."

Shit.

"Right, yeah. It's just getting pretty crowded." I scratched my scalp. "Plus, I want to take a look around the property a bit more. See if Gemma needs anything. I'll be back in a few minutes, okay?"

"Want me to come with you?" He was asking to be nice, obviously not wanting to end his riveting football conversation.

"No, it's fine."

I turned on my heel before he could respond.

The problem was that the only exit I knew of was in the direction where Nate was standing. I dared a glance to see if he was still there and found it vacant.

I didn't know if it was a good thing or a bad thing. Keeping eyes on the source of my anxiety felt safer than letting him roam free, but at that point, it wasn't worth the risk to locate him.

I scanned the perimeter until I found a sign pointing to the opposite corner of the building from where we entered. Another exit.

Thankfully, a narrow brick path, similar to the one at the entrance, wrapped around the other side of the building. Following it, I snagged another glass of red wine from a server on my way out. I took a long gulp, wincing at the dry, bitter aftertaste.

I walked the path as quickly as I could without tripping in my heels until the music from the welcome party faded. Until I could find a quiet place to calm my racing heart.

A few other party attendees mingled ahead, huddled together in the designated smoking area. My steps slowed, narrowly avoiding getting close enough to risk any of them talking to me, and I leaned my back against the building, letting my eyes close.

I counted to ten in time with my breathing.

RSVP or not, I knew he was going to be here. I knew it in my bones. Maybe I can hide out here forever. Or at least until I can find another escape route.

Don't be stupid.

I counted to ten a second time. Then, a third.

And as if the universe was laughing at my torment, a phantom, familiar voice sounded from my left.

"You're drinking red wine now?"

I didn't open my eyes. I didn't have to. I knew who was standing there.

I cursed myself, cursed the wine clutched in my hand, cursed the world. As much as I wanted to stand there with my eyes closed until the earth rose and swallowed me whole, there was no escaping it. I had to face him.

When I turned my head and cracked my eyes open, Nate was there, leaning against the brick, mirroring me a few paces away.

How Nate managed to look sheepish while maintaining a fair share of that cool confidence he always carried with him was a mystery to me. He studied me with his head cocked to the side—sizing me up or waiting on an answer; I wasn't sure.

A silent challenge? Or a taunt? An olive branch, perhaps?

Either way, someone had to be the first to fold.

He assessed me, jaw flexing and relaxing like he was focused on controlling his breathing as much as I was. I imagined he was trying to discern if I would talk to him cordially, blow him off, start crying, or rip him a new one.

I didn't know which I would choose, either.

Smoke from the cigarette I only just noticed he was pinching between his first two fingers filled the space between us.

I sighed, dropping my shoulders, and looked down at the glass clutched in my hand. Fighting was pointless. And besides, I didn't have any fight left in me when it came to Nate. Our history, what was said, what was done. It simply was what it was.

"Yeah." I relented. "Red wine."

The corner of his mouth pulled up by a centimeter, though his brows pulled together a fraction, too.

That's how it was with Nate. He was all micro-reactions, small adjustments, subtle changes. If you blinked, you missed it. He said nothing while saying everything, as long as you knew how to read him.

He pushed off the wall, taking a slow pull of his cigarette as he closed the distance between us in two long, tentative strides. I eyed every movement of his long frame, grinding my teeth together in frustration that, even after stewing on the possibility of facing him in the last few days, I still had no clue what to do around him.

When he got close, he held the cigarette out to me, the movement reminding me of a dog handler offering a treat to a feral mutt in return for a modicum of trust.

I wasn't a smoker. Never fell into the habit, except for the few nights a year when I was just drunk enough that it sounded like a good idea.

I wasn't nearly drunk enough. I was barely even buzzed, but something about the cigarette felt inviting, and I wasn't about to turn down an excuse to do something with my hands.

I accepted the cigarette and deliberately met his eyes as I lifted it to my lips and took a long inhale, noting the subtle taste of whiskey on the end. Something in the back of my mind was vaguely aware of the fact that this was the closest I'd been to feeling his lips on mine since...

It doesn't matter.

Nate had always been prone to picking up and doing away with his smoking habit. I remembered going months and months without seeing him with a cigarette, never smelling it on his clothes or tasting it on his mouth. Then, out of the clear blue sky, I would show up at his apartment to see him standing out on his small balcony, having a smoke between writing sessions.

The last I saw him, on that final night when everything went to shit, he told me he'd quit for good.

"I thought you quit," I said, stifling a cough as I handed the dwindling cigarette back to him between pinched fingers.

His deep blue eyes met mine for a fraction of a second as he took it. "I did."

I raised my eyebrows.

He laughed through his nose.

The dimple on the right side of his face appeared.

Yeah, I can't do this.

I wrapped my arms around my middle and turned to make my way back toward the party, hoping that putting distance between us would ease the tightening in my chest. When the unsettled feeling inside me didn't relent, I walked faster.

"You know," he started from behind me, a hint of hesitation in his voice, "nights like this always remind me of the night we met."

Always the one to break the silence. Even when I didn't want him to.

I pivoted on my heel, facing him once more, willing myself not to be distracted by the tendril of smoke rising from his full lips.

"We met in December on the other side of the country," I pointed out. "It's October."

The corners of his mouth pulled tight, stifling a smile, but he continued. "It was December, but it wasn't that bad outside that night. I remember you pretended not to be cold in that useless jacket you were wearing, but you were shivering."

I shifted, my arms still hugging close around my middle to ward off the chill. He offered the cigarette to me again from where he stood. I would have to be the one to bridge the gap this time.

Closing the space between us again, I took it with a defeated sigh and leaned against the brick. We stood in silence as I took another puff and handed the butt back to him. With one last short inhalation, he put it out against the wall and stuffed the extinguished paper into his pocket. I downed the rest of my red wine in one hefty gulp, breathing through the bitter aftertaste.

"You okay?" he asked, all the genuine concern in the world dripping from his words, even as he stared at his booted feet, toeing a few loose pieces of gravel.

I let out an exasperated laugh and leaned my head against the cold stone, staring up at the autumn sky. I couldn't help but shake my head at the sheer surrealism of standing and talking to Nate as though it were normal. As if he was still part of my life. As if we were friends.

"I've never been your fucking friend."

"Yeah," I whispered. "I'm good."

His eyes, deep blue and ever-perceptive, narrowed. "I don't believe you," he whispered back.

All I could do was blink toward the sky and bite my tongue. There were too many feelings flooding my senses and no time to form them all into coherent thoughts, much less words. I met his eye and shook my head—the only answer he was going to get on that particular subject—as if to say, *Drop it.*

He nodded his understanding.

The wordless kind of communication always did work well for us, in more ways than one.

The weighted pause lasted a little too long, so I turned again without a word to walk back to the party.

I wanted to crawl under a big rock and go to sleep. Or maybe walk right into the fucking ocean and disappear under the dark waves. Anything to not be here, exposed in front of so many people, before I had the chance to process my feelings.

When I was far enough from him to feel like I could breathe, Nate spoke again, just loud enough for me to hear.

"Well, you look really pretty, Oli."

I stopped cold in my tracks. As much as I wanted to rebuke the butterflies that still, even now, after everything that had happened, flooded through my core, I would be lying if I said it didn't feel like a caress from a long-gone lover. Because it did.

He always felt like a safety blanket I could lay back down in no matter what happened, no matter how long it had been. It was just *too* easy with him. It always had been. And I'd been bitten in the ass before because of it.

No. I wasn't going to let him make me feel all those feelings again. I wasn't that girl anymore. The one who felt things for him so fully, so completely. The girl who *needed* to feel those feelings reciprocated, whether she knew it or not.

I thought back to the girl I was five years ago and felt so sad for her. Because how could she want someone so badly? How could she crave someone who was never going to be what she needed, no matter how much he was *exactly* what she wanted? How could she see herself with someone who made her feel disposable? Who made it clear he didn't want to share his life?

So, I forced my feet to keep walking.

He didn't get to talk to me like that. He didn't get to give me compliments and tell me sweet nothings like he was oblivious to how they used to make me feel. He didn't get to say the things I used to lie awake at night wishing he would say.

No, that wasn't who he was, and it never would be, even if part of me used to ache that it could.

CHAPTER 8

Four Years Ago, January

Do you know how juvenile it feels to stay awake debating if you should ask your friend's new girlfriend if she can give you her friend's number? What am I? Fifteen?

"Grant and a bunch of his friends are going out tonight, and he invited us," Gemma said as she emerged from the bathroom with her hair wrapped in a towel. "Wanna come?"

Gemma and Grant made their relationship official two weeks after the night they met. While it was unlike Gemma to jump into something so fast, it strangely made perfect sense. *They* made perfect sense. I, on the other hand, hadn't spoken to Nate since the night we spent together.

I glanced over my shoulder from my position on the floor. A small stack of vinyl records sat in my lap, begging to be sorted into their respective places in my collection. I'd gotten a few new additions from my siblings' obligatory gift exchange and treated myself to a few more from the vintage record shop in my hometown when I was there for Christmas. I hadn't had the brainpower to sort them into their new homes until that evening.

I gave Gemma a noncommittal face. "When? Where at?"

"About an hour, and I'm not sure." She threw her body forward, the force alone flipping the towel over her head, and into her hands. "Some low-key bar I've never been to. I guess they go there a lot when they want to chill and drink for cheap. I figured if nothing else, it could give me material for my blog."

I'd planned to spend the evening watching a documentary I'd been saving. My eyes dipped to my sweatpants, the stretched-out cotton riddled with holes from years of wear. "I think I'll stay in. I already have my comfy pants on."

Gemma straightened, finger-combing her blonde locks, sending droplets of water spattering around the living room. I had the vague thought that she would make a terrible serial killer with all the evidence she would likely leave sprayed around the crime scene.

"Come on, Olive! It's just going to be a bunch of dudes. Don't make me go alone. Please?"

I rolled my eyes, already knowing I was going to cave. I could never resist a "please" from her.

An hour later, we walked into the dimly lit bar.

I settled for a pair of jeans and a comfortable lavender-colored sweater after Gemma promised again that the location was low-key and would not require the usual level of Going Out Readiness. She was right. Unlike places close to the heart of Sumner U's campus, Brick Road Bar was downtown and far from the majority of undergrads.

While most bars near campus kept a considerable portion of their floor space open for dancing and standing room, Brick Road was filled with tall, wooden communal tables. Tonight, they were full of patrons hunched together on barstools. A matching wooden bar took up the entire length of the far wall, also occupied by lounging customers engaged in conversation with the two bartenders behind the counter. A jukebox lit up the corner, blaring classic rock through the sound system. I immediately felt more at ease there than I ever had in any campus bar.

At the front of the room was a stage that looked like a permanent fixture, its wood just as worn and stained as the rest of the flooring. It sat only a foot or so off the ground and held a full drum set, a few guitars propped up on stands, and an electric keyboard. I'd heard a few people mention going to gigs and open mic nights around campus throughout the years—this must've been one of the places they were hosted.

"Gemma! Over here!"

Grant perked up like a meerkat from the back of the room near a cluster of pool tables. By the way his table was littered with empty pint glasses, it was clear he and his friend had been there long enough to get comfortable. In the middle of the table sat two pitchers of beer and a faded, flimsy deck of cards.

Gemma and I slid onto stools as Grant introduced us to his friend. Martinez, an athletically built guy with tattooed arms, flashed us a bright smile as he poured us beers.

Grant's eyes followed Gemma as she pulled her stool closer to him and settled in. He leaned in to give her a quick peck on the cheek as if he literally could not resist it.

I bit back a grin.

He's in love already.

"Okay, who wants to deal first?" Martinez asked, clapping his hands together.

Wordlessly, Grant grabbed the deck of cards and began shuffling. Catching my doubtful expression, he simply said, "We'll explain as we go, don't worry."

As it turned out, following the rules of their game—four-handed euchre, which they simply called "four-handed" since it could apparently be played with modifications for four, five, or six players—was like trying to paddle a boat upstream with only one ore while simultaneously juggling flame throwers and reciting Shakespeare. Difficult and nonsensical as hell.

The game consisted of a single deck including only cards of nine and higher, and was played with a partner. To win the game, teams had to win at least three of the five hands per round and the game was over when a team reached ten points.

Its rules also dictated which suits were in power each round and gave some cards more power than others. For example, jacks were stronger than any other card, but only if they were the same color as the suit in power. And in those cases, the jacks were no longer called jacks—but instead were the Right and the Left.

Entirely too confusing, to say the least.

Martinez and Grant remained patient as Gemma and I fumbled over the first few rounds, but after twenty minutes of asking them to repeat the rules, it was getting embarrassing. The fact that I managed not to drop any cards when it was my turn to shuffle the small deck was a miracle in and of itself.

"That's not a spade, remember?" Grant laughed as he slid the Jack of Spades back over to Gemma for the second time that round. "It's a club."

"But it's *literally* a spade!" Gemma shouted, nearly knocking her drink over as she pointed to the black spade in the corner of her card.

"Correct, but it's the Left," Martinez, Gemma's teammate, explained. "So, it's technically a club this round."

"How is anyone supposed to remember all these rules?"

Grant bit back a smile and gave Gemma a precious, pitying look. "Babe, do you have any other spades in your hand right now?"

Gemma studied the three cards in her hand like she was cramming for a final exam. "No."

"Oh. Well, in that case, go ahead and play the Jack of Spades."

Martinez burst into laughter.

Gemma gave the table an incredulous look. "Are you fucking *kidding* me?"

"I think we have time for one more round before the show starts," Grant announced as he dealt the next hand.

"There's a show tonight?" I asked.

"Yeah, my brother's band is playing. That's why we came."

His brother's band. Nate's band. My cheeks heated.

Across the table, Gemma side-eyed me with a sly grin.

The little traitor.

She must've known they were playing tonight and conned me into coming. She'd been dying to hear all about my night with Nate a few weeks ago, to no avail. When she'd spilled the dirty details about her night with Grant, I left my night with Nate to her imagination. The dry spell was broken; that was all she needed to know.

"Maybe *you* came to see your brother's band," Martinez grabbed the pitcher in front of me, "but *I* came for the free beer."

"The beer is *not* free," Grant said, "and you aren't getting out of paying again, asshole."

"But free beer tastes so much better," Martinez reasoned with a long swig.

"Then get another guy to buy one for you."

Martinez let out a groan. "Too much effort."

I laughed and tried to act like I wasn't sitting a little straighter now, like I wasn't sneaking glances at the stage on the other side of the room and the guys who were now doing last-minute instrument and equipment checks.

"Pass or play, Olive?" Martinez asked.

Looking at my pile of cards, I scrambled to grab them and made my decision quickly. "Pass," I said, only realizing I actually should have picked a suit *after* the word left my mouth.

By the time the hand was over, soft cheers and claps resounded through the bar. The crowd nearly doubled in the last twenty minutes, with people who came specifically to see the band, by the looks of it.

The four men on stage fell into position at their instruments. I recognized Jared on the drums immediately. He and Grant could've been twins, except for Jared's shaggier blond waves and the stubble that contrasted his brother's clean-shaven look.

Stage left was a tall guy with thick black curls and a gentle vibe about him. He adjusted the strap of a bass guitar over his shoulders and sent a smile to the opposite side of the stage, where a guy with completely opposite energy stood. The guitarist met the bassist's smile with a stern look, which may have been his version of a smile. He dressed head to toe in black: a black beanie, a black T-shirt under a black denim jacket, black jeans, and black combat boots. He plucked a single key on the electric keyboard next to him, testing its volume. But my gaze settled on the front of the stage, on Nate as he looped an acoustic guitar over his shoulders and took his place at the microphone.

"Thanks for coming out," Nate spoke softly, casually into the microphone. "We're Crescent Light."

The opening song started slowly. With just an acoustic guitar, Nate played so softly that I slid to the edge of my seat and leaned in just to hear.

Every note lingered, the melody full of yearning. When he came in with the first lines, he sang them with such tenderness that it was as if they were private. A secret he wasn't sure he should tell. It was like he was unzipping himself and bearing his soul to the attentive crowd gathered around. The buzzing bar had gone quiet, everyone holding their breath as they listened.

Then, for a moment, Nate fell completely silent. So silent you could hear a pin drop.

A ghost of a smile played on his lips for a split second before the entire bar erupted with sound. In perfect unison, every member of Crescent Light played a resounding chord at full volume, followed by Nate's voice as the chorus cut through the thunderous noise.

The quality of Nate's voice was unlike anything I'd ever heard live before. It was clear and smooth, much like his speaking voice, but held another quality altogether I couldn't quite put my finger on. He was the kind of singer who could captivate every person in a room, regardless of whether he was playing to a crowd of ten people or ten thousand.

One song led into the next, then the next. Aside from the fact this was the band of the guy I'd had an enjoyable night with (understatement of the century), I genuinely loved each song Crescent Light played. They mixed and incorporated genres, melding each song with influences from indie, rock, folk, and pop. The sheer *musicality* they exuded was unbelievable, especially in a tiny hole-in-the-wall like Brick Road Bar. The music lover in me couldn't look away, even if I wanted.

The lead guitarist moved his hands from the guitar to the keyboard positioned in front of him for the bridge of one song, then back on the guitar again for the rest. At one point, the bassist picked up drumsticks and added a layer of percussion, rounding out sounds as he harmonized with backing vocals. Nate also moved to the keyboard for a time, playing there for an entire song while singing. There was even a point where Jared had one hand wrapped around a drumstick, keeping the pulse of the song going, while the other hand played on a synthesizer positioned next to him. They moved effortlessly from instrument to instrument, each song more addicting to witness than the last.

More than anything, though, the four men on stage looked like they were having the time of their lives. Even when they weren't providing backing vocals, the other three members mouthed along to every word, animating the lyrics, smiling at each other, dancing and swaying as they played.

I was entranced.

⇝⇝ ⇜⇜

"Hey guys," a voice behind us greeted. The show had ended twenty minutes earlier, and a fresh round of pitchers appeared on our table shortly after.

I swept my hair over my shoulder to find Nate towering along with his bandmates. The short sides of his hair were slightly damp with sweat, his cheeks still a little flushed.

Was he this pretty a few weeks ago?

"Hey, baby brother!" Grant stood to hug Jared just as he circled the table. "Grab a seat."

We cleared the table of empty glasses as they sat, Nate taking the barstool next to me, Jared filling the spot on the other side of Gemma. She immediately struck up a conversation with the two of them like they'd known each other for years. The other two members of Crescent Light stood at the other side of the table. Miles, the curly-haired bassist with warm brown skin, smiled a boyish smile as he laughed at Martinez.

Leo, the guitarist with dark features who shared piano duties with Nate, stood slightly shorter next to him, stoic as he listened.

Nate and I hadn't spoken since our hookup. I'd left early the morning after, while he was still half-asleep, and we never got around to exchanging phone numbers. Though if he wanted to reach out, he could have gotten mine pretty easily through Grant and Gemma.

I wasn't sure how to handle his proximity.

Should I be friendly? Ignore him? Act like he was any other guy I'd just met?

I'd never been in this situation before. Usually, one-night stands stayed just that—one night and a clean break.

Sleeping together didn't mean we were friends. He didn't owe me his time or attention just because we'd hooked up, nor did I owe him mine. But his looming presence hung in the air like the atmosphere holding its breath before a storm. Pressure building ever so slightly as seconds ticked on.

Relief washed over me when he broke it.

"Hey," Nate murmured, nudging my shoulder.

"Hi," I whispered back.

"I didn't know you were going to be here tonight."

"Grant invited us out. I didn't know you were playing." I wasn't sure why I felt the need to justify my presence. Too scared to seem like I was overly eager, I supposed. "I enjoyed the show. You guys are really good."

"Yeah?" He leaned across me and reached for the pitcher of beer. I didn't lean away when his face came only inches from mine. "I'm glad you came. How've you been?"

He slipped easily into conversation with the casual comfortability of someone I could have known for years. I wondered if he ever felt awkward or out of place.

"Good," I said, playing with the rim of my glass. "Swamped already with pre-work for next semester. It's probably good I got out of the house tonight."

"See?" Gemma cut in, the eavesdropper. "I told you coming out with me tonight would be fun! She's been locking herself in her room to do homework way too fucking much for it technically still being winter break."

"So diligent," Nate teased, passing me a sideways look.

"That's enough," I chastised. "Both of you."

Gemma blew me a kiss from across the table, then turned back to Grant and Miles, who were locked in an animated debate about whether or not Luke Skywalker would have ended up a Sith Lord instead of a Jedi if he and Leia had been raised from birth by Anakin.

Nate's hand bridged the gap between our legs as he absentmindedly ran a fingertip along the outer seam of my jeans. "I'm going to step outside for a minute," he said in a hushed tone. "Wanna join me?"

I nodded, sliding off my stool, and followed him closely.

The wind outside was refreshing compared to the stuffy, stale air inside Brick Road Bar, but it turned frigid after only a few seconds. I pulled the sleeves of my sweater over my hands as Nate took up a spot against the worn brick wall and pulled a pack of cigarettes out of his back pocket.

"I wouldn't have pegged you as a smoker," I said. There had been no detectable evidence of it a few weeks ago. "Does it help your singing voice or hurt it?"

He smirked around the butt of the cigarette. "I have no idea. I'm not a smoker—*wasn't* a smoker." He pulled it out of his mouth, searching for the right words. "I'm smoking, yes, but I'm not a smoker."

I raised my eyebrows at him, stifling a laugh.

A sigh of mock defeat. "I'm trying to quit," he said, placing the end back in his mouth and lighting it.

"Is that how it works?"

He smirked and offered the cigarette to me. "Wanna not be a smoker with me?"

I didn't think twice about plucking it from Nate's fingers and taking a puff.

"What are you studying, by the way?" He leaned a shoulder against the brick. "I don't think we ever got around to that last time we... hung out."

I mirrored his stance. "No, I don't think we did."

He laughed through his nose.

"I'm getting my master's in journalism," I said.

"And undergrad?"

"Mass communications with a minor in music."

His eyebrows rose as he hummed in approval.

"What about you?" I asked, reaching for the cigarette again. "I didn't think they offered a 'rockstar' track."

"Close," he chuckled, running a hand through his dark hair. "Computer science with a music production minor in undergrad. Master's in audio engineering."

"Very impressive."

He shrugged, taking another pull and blowing it away. "I'm a computer nerd under all this bravado. What can I say?"

When we returned to the warmth inside, the group had dealt another round of cards on the table, this time including Nate and Jared.

"Yeah, I don't have enough patience for that fucking game," Leo mumbled when they tried to peer pressure him and Miles into playing, to no avail.

The game was even more complicated with six players, and I had the sudden realization I was going to have to shuffle a larger deck of cards and deal to even more people. I was able to make do with a small deck when it was only four of us, but now there was a double deck in play.

I was horrible at shuffling cards. Monstrously horrible. I always got in my head and fumbled them, or worse, dropped them on the ground. The sounds of my older brothers poking fun at me as a kid attempting to shuffle a *Phase 10* deck rang through my mind, and I was stressing about having to get on my hands and knees in front of Nate and his friends to fish rogue cards from under the table before it was even my turn to deal.

Thankfully, Grant got up for a refill, and Martinez and Jared immediately went into conversation when it was my turn. *Good.* The more distracted they were, the fewer witnesses I had to my embarrassment. I split the flimsy deck and dropped cards from the front to the back of the deck, a few at a time. It was a pathetic attempt and not nearly good enough to make sure they were properly shuffled.

Slow and steady.

A hand dropped by mine, palm up. Nate eyed the sloppily-handled cards before his gaze landed on my face.

"I can do it," he offered softly, "if you want."

I gave him a small, grateful smile and dropped the deck into his hand. One rogue card flew out, but it landed only an inch away. He shuffled quickly—expertly, without a fuss—and placed the deck face-down in front of me to deal.

"Thank you," I mumbled.

"Of course."

Gemma and I opted out of the next game in favor of watching. We had just as much—if not more—fun watching them play and trash-talk each other. I felt strangely at home surrounded by Grant and Nate's group of friends. We fit right in. No questions asked.

As the night drew to a close and bar tabs were paid—Grant covering Martinez's share—Nate rested a hand on my knee and leaned in close so only I could hear.

"Do you want to come back to my place tonight?"

My eyes met his for only a second before I nodded.

He smiled a wide, close-lipped smile. "Don't leave without giving me your number this time."

CHAPTER 9

Now

The game we play, the rules implied, but no one wins.
The words we say, the truth unsaid, it never ends.

When I returned to the welcome party, I tried my best to avoid Nate, but my god, he was *everywhere*. He towered a few spots ahead of me when I got in line for the bar. When I tugged Kieran to the station of finger foods—despite his objections about saving his calories for drinks—Nate stood on the opposite side of the table, sucking cupcake icing off the tip of his thumb. Then, I escaped to the restroom to catch my breath and get a grip, but of course, he was walking into the men's restroom as I walked out.

I could practically feel his eyes every time he glanced my way, his gaze a hot brand on my skin. He tried to keep his distance, too, decidedly honoring my please-don't-fuck-with-me vibe, but we were in each other's magnetic field now. Circling the other whether we wanted to or not.

I heard Martinez before I saw him. It would have been virtually impossible *not* to hear him, actually.

"Olive! Yo, Olive!"

Martinez looked as handsome as always with his rolled sleeves showing off his heavily tattooed arms as he stuck one into the air. I made a show of sarcastically hiding my face, but he kept hollering.

"Oli! Over here!"

"Who's that?" Kieran asked, pulled away from his conversation with Michael by the yelling. Confusion painted his expression, accented by annoyance.

Martinez's frantic waving only worsened.

I giggled and shook my head. "One of my friends from grad school. He won't stop until we go over there."

Grabbing Kieran's hand, I maneuvered through the crowd, my friend's cheering only getting more excited the closer we got. My heart filled at the sight of him. Followed by a strange mixture of shame and sadness when I realized I couldn't even remember the last time I'd spoken to him.

Our friend group had mostly kept in touch via social media when we finished grad school, but I hadn't seen most of them since moving to Boston. I only kept in touch with Gemma and Grant anymore.

As we drew closer to the corner of the courtyard where he was making a fool of himself, I spied the top of Jared's blond mop of hair, followed by Miles's thick curls, Leo's serious expression, and the devil himself.

Nate's eyes flicked from his conversation with his bandmates to me, then to Kieran, and back to me. His lips pulled into a small smirk, like he knew how uncomfortable this was about to be for me and was going to love every second of it.

"There's my girl," Martinez said, spreading his arms wide for me to walk into his embrace. "How have you been, beautiful? Long time no see, Miss Famous Journalist."

"I don't know about famous. How are you?"

"Better now that you're here."

Always such a flirt.

"Martinez, this is my boyfriend, Kieran." I put a hand on Kieran's shoulder, surprised to see such a stern expression on his face.

"Hey, man." Kieran's face shifted into a tight, polite smile as he held out for Martinez to shake. "Kieran. Nice to meet you."

"And this is Miles," I said, giving Miles a quick side hug.

Kieran offered his hand to Miles, introducing himself. Jared held his hand out instinctively next.

It dawned on me that we were making our way around the pseudo-circle with introductions. I hadn't planned on introducing Kieran to Crescent Light, and especially not Nate. In fact, my plan was to keep the two of them entirely separate, if possible. But at this rate, *not* introducing them would be flat-out weird. I sure as hell didn't want the two of them to interact any more than cordially necessary.

From the corner of my eye, I caught Michael joining our group with a fresh beer.

I made my move.

"And this is Grant's brother, Jared," I gestured, meeting no one's eye as I continued down the line. "And this is Leo, andthisisNate. Hey, Martinez, you've met Gemma's brother, right?"

I shot Martinez a frantic warning look over Kieran's shoulder as he leaned in to shake Leo's hand.

Please do something.

While Nate and I kept our "relationship" under wraps back in grad school, it was the worst-kept secret in our friend group. Everyone knew, regardless of whether we advertised it or not. Kieran, on the other hand, did *not* know about my history with Nate. With any luck, it would stay that way.

And god bless Jaden Martinez; he picked up what I was putting down immediately.

"Yeah!" he responded a bit too loud, commanding the attention around our group. "But it's been a while. Michael, how've you been?"

I watched Kieran from the corner of my eye as he extended his hand from Leo to Nate, his bright, toothy smile met by Nate's polite, closed-mouthed one.

"Baby sister's getting married, eh?" Martinez practically screamed at Michael.

"Nice to meet you," Nate's smooth voice murmured. From my periphery, Nate slid his right hand out of his pocket to shake Kieran's outstretched one. I faced Martinez and Michael, partially hoping my body language would urge others to do the same, but also because I couldn't bear to watch Nate and Kieran interact without wanting to dissolve into ash and fade away a la *Infinity War*.

"She's my *older* sister," Michael corrected Martinez. "But, yeah."

Kieran leaned a fraction of an inch closer to Nate, and my heart thundered in my chest like I was at the tippy top of a rollercoaster. "What did you say your name was?"

"Right! Duh!" Martinez continued, shooting me a glance. He was committed to the bit now; nothing left to do but soldier on and keep shouting his half of the conversation in a desperate attempt at distracting Kieran from lingering on Nate for too long. "I always forget she's the older one. You're just so big! Defensive lineman, right?"

Football. Perfect. Jaden Martinez, you are my hero. It might be an open bar, but I owe you a drink.

"It's Nate."

I begged the universe for a black hole to form right where I stood.

"Yeah, defensive lineman," Michael said.

Kieran nodded, then straightened, finally turning his attention to Martinez and Michael. "You doing fantasy football this year, man? We were just talking about our leagues."

Hook, line, and sinker.

I glanced to the high heavens. Nate caught my eye from across the little circle we'd formed, an amused twinkle in his eye that asked, *What was that all about?*

I gave him the stink eye, threatening him in my mind.

Not a fucking word, Cassidy.

He ticked his head to the side as if to say, *Suit yourself,* and turned, suddenly very interested in the fountain behind him.

This weekend is going to suck.

CHAPTER 10

Four Years Ago, April

A laugh like a melody
I can't get out of my head

McLaren Clan

Rion

> Attention siblings. Easter will be at my house. Easter Day, noon, don't be late.

Aspen

> or what

River

> Why not mom and dad's?

Lily

> Because he's trying to do something nice, asshole

Me

> I don't know if I'll be able to make it. I'm swamped with school

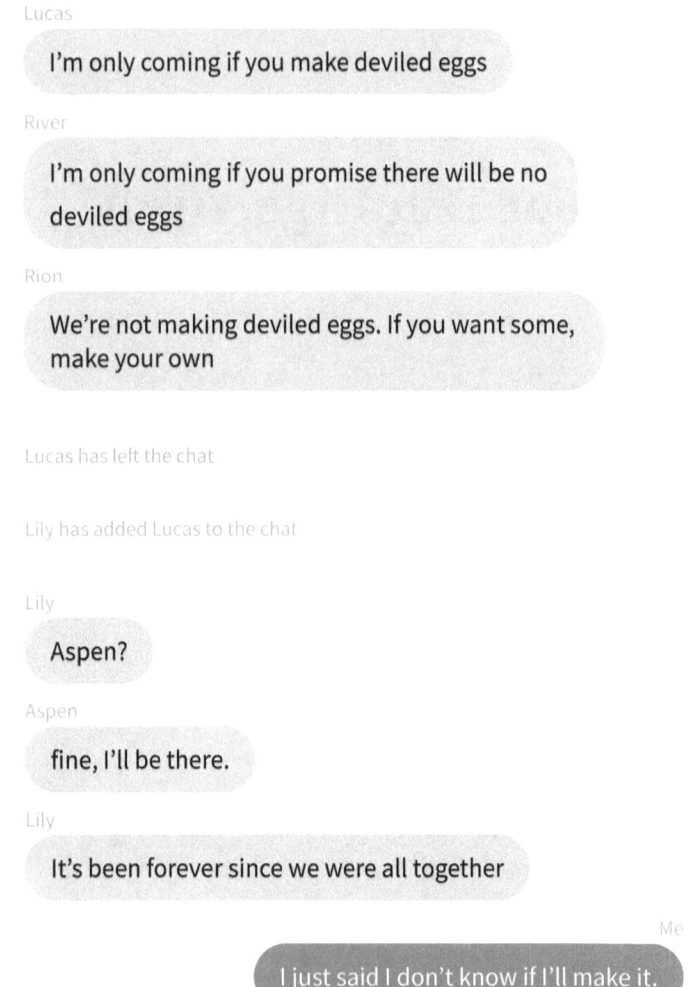

Lucas

I'm only coming if you make deviled eggs

River

I'm only coming if you promise there will be no deviled eggs

Rion

We're not making deviled eggs. If you want some, make your own

Lucas has left the chat

Lily has added Lucas to the chat

Lily

Aspen?

Aspen

fine, I'll be there.

Lily

It's been forever since we were all together

Me

I just said I don't know if I'll make it.

G emma hunched over in her seat, grabbing at the stitch in her side. Considering the bar crawl was on its fourth bar in less than two hours, we were both heading in a direction well beyond our limits. The other bar crawlers in Gemma's classes shared in the irresponsibility as the group of thirty grad students rounded up to walk to the next bar.

Spring semester at Sumner U had gotten off to a busy start. Weeks went by in a flash with the steady stream of homework, reading assignments, projects, quizzes, and exams keeping us slammed around the clock. The Friday before Spring Break was always reserved for certain disciplines' annual bar crawls, with marketing students being some of the rowdiest. We journalists didn't do a bar crawl, but Gemma stated I was an honorary marketing student by proxy and insisted I join. Who was I to argue?

After ordering yet another vodka cranberry at the new location, a hole-in-the-wall dive bar that reeked of cigarette smoke and old leather, I took a seat on a rogue bar stool next to where Gemma and one of her classmates racked up a game of pool. It was a horrible decision. My alcohol-riddled mind swam and began to wander a moment later.

I thought about school, the end of the second semester, how graduation was going to be there before I knew it.

Where would my journalism degree take me? Would I be able to put my music minor to use somehow?

Whenever I spent time perusing the internet for open positions in the area, a sense of dread would wash over me. Nothing stuck out or sounded like a good fit. And anything that sounded half-decent seemed above and beyond what I thought I was capable of. Imposter syndrome blocked any feelings of hope or excitement for my future, like a dark cloud on a sunny day.

Then, my thoughts drifted to Nate. Because of course they did.

We'd grown close throughout the semester, meeting up every few weeks for study dates that sometimes turned into *other* kinds of dates. Okay, more often than not, they turned into other kinds of dates. But outside of hooking up, we'd developed a friendship, too, falling into a rhythm so easy and seamless that it was a little scary.

I spent countless hours over the spring semester curled up on Nate's couch with my laptop resting on its arm while I worked on assignments. Meanwhile, he would be hunched over his electric piano, bulky headphones wrapped around his head as he tapped away on the keys. Sometimes, we chatted while we worked; other times, an hour would go by without saying a word to each other. "Parallel play," he'd jokingly called it.

There were stretches where Nate and I didn't talk for days, sometimes weeks, at a time, but we always seemed to pick up where we left off.

The first time it happened, I resigned myself to the belief that our little fling had run its course. He had inevitably grown bored of whatever we were doing, as guys in their twenties did, and I probably wouldn't see him again, save for the group setting with Gemma and Grant. And I had to be okay with that. I was mildly sad, but I told myself it was fun while it lasted.

Until a week later, when Nate called me out of the blue to tell me he was back in town. Crescent Light had apparently had a few shows in New York and New Jersey, so they'd been on the road playing gigs almost every night. Any spare second during the day was spent catching up on classwork, sleeping, or writing new music.

Another time, we were going on almost a month without talking, but then he texted me.

Nate

What's your favorite candy?

Me

Random. Sour gummies, why?

Nate

I just realized I've never asked you

I giggled at the spontaneous questions, but they slowly became a semi-regular thing. Very rarely did they start a conversation. They were merely thoughts that popped into his head, and he simply had to know the answer right then and there.

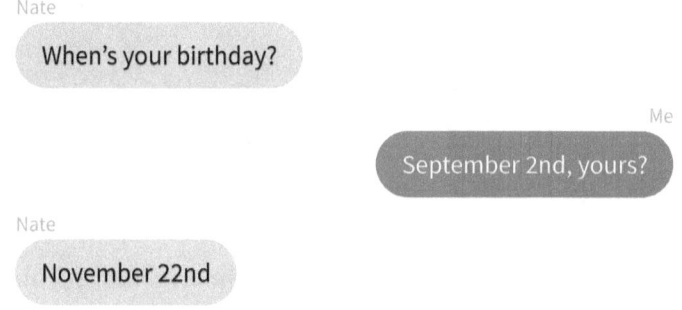

Nate

When's your birthday?

Me

September 2nd, yours?

Nate

November 22nd

End of correspondence for the next week.

The disappearing act was something I grew to expect. It was almost always music-related, or that he'd gone to Connecticut to visit family. Sometimes, he would simply be buried so deeply in music or school-work that nobody would hear from him. I took comfort in the fact it wasn't just me who would be left wondering why he was MIA.

Hell, sometimes I got so busy juggling classes and homework that I didn't have anything left for a social life, either. But when he disappeared, there was no telling how long it would last. Currently, we were around two weeks.

In any "normal" relationship, I might have general knowledge of his schedule, and we might be in regular communication, texting or talking on the phone almost daily. But this wasn't a normal relationship.

It wasn't a relationship at all. I wasn't his girlfriend; he wasn't my boyfriend. We didn't owe each other anything. It was the beauty of whatever we were doing. We were friends. Sure, we usually had sex when we hung out, but "friends" was the closest thing I could call it.

A mutually beneficial situationship.

Crack!

Gemma's pool stick sent the eight-ball careening into a corner pocket. I adjusted on my barstool, stretching each leg out to ease the pins and needles in my feet, but the sensation of swaying back and forth stayed long after I stopped moving.

My thoughts were already on Nate, though, and the vodka cranberry I drank as I spaced out only encouraged them further.

On the night we met, he made me feel alive. Electric. But he was so unlike me. He was careless energy without the irresponsibility one would expect of someone like him. I was all perfectionism, self-doubt, and anxiety. He had a weightlessness I wished I had the capacity to feel.

"I think I'm going to head out," I shouted as I stood, head spinning. Gemma nearly whacked her partner in the head with her pool stick as she swung around to hug me.

"I love you! Thank you for coming with us, okay? I love you so much," she slurred again as she planted a wet kiss on my cheek.

"Mhm," I mumbled back, "love you, too."

I made it a few steps out the front door before I had to rest against the side of the building. The cool stone against my back grounded me as my body swayed.

I wonder if Nate's in town.

No, he's probably not.

Didn't he mention a Crescent Light show? Or something about going to the campus studio to record? Or was that last week?

Before I could think better of it, my fingers typed his name into my phone and pressed the call button.

He picked up on the third ring. "Hey."

"Oh," I stumbled on the uneven concrete but regained my footing before tripping altogether. "Hey."

"What's up?" Amusement and concern mingled in his smooth voice.

"Oh, you know. Just left a bar crawl with Gemma." I pointed with my thumb at the building behind me as if he could see it. "Currently stumbling home. Classic Friday night."

He chuckled, and I imagined him shaking his head. "You aren't stumbling home by yourself, are you?"

Maybe it was the vodka cranberries, but I decided now was an excellent time to flirt. "Well, I wouldn't be by myself if you came to pick me up." I cringed as the words left my mouth.

"Yeah? Where are you?"

Less than ten minutes later, Nate's black car pulled up to where I waited on the sidewalk. When I caught a glimpse of his face through the window, my heart skipped a beat. I never got used to seeing him. It didn't matter how often we hung out—if it'd been three days or three weeks—I still got giddy and nervous from all the happy, lovely feelings. Heat already pooled in my belly as I thought about all the things I wanted him to do to me.

Like clockwork, excitement was quickly replaced by trepidation. All of the same questions flooded my mind. *What are we? What are we doing? What does he want? What do I want?* I was perpetually caught somewhere between *I need him* and *I need answers.* As always, I ignored my doubt in favor of riding the high.

He held a steadying hand out from the driver's seat as I climbed into the passenger seat with what I'm sure was ballerina-like grace. Feeling bold, I leaned across the middle console to kiss him. It took a beat for him to realize what I was doing, but he cupped my cheek in time for our lips to meet, deepening the kiss for the briefest moment.

The second his skin touched mine, I wanted more. Infinitely more. But he pulled away, holding my chin with a featherlight touch.

"What was that for?" he teased.

"Can we go back to your place?"

It was probably a good thing he kept his hands to himself, thrumming his fingers on the wheel as he drove. Who knows what I would have done in that state had he reached over to rest a broad hand on my thigh?

That was another thing about Nate.

He wasn't overly affectionate. At least not in front of other people. When I thought about the times when the whole friend group got together—Gemma, Grant, Martinez, the band—all that came to mind was the flutter in my gut from Nate's lingering glances across the room. I thought of fingertips grazing my knee beneath a table, knuckles against the small of my back as he passed by, him leaning in an inch closer than necessary to talk to me. I thought of all the countless small moments. When we were with the others, we were all light touches and stolen kisses in dark corners.

But his philosophy on affection didn't seem to exist when we were alone. He would tease me all day, throwing fleeting, heated looks my way over Grant's kitchen table at game night, brushing his fingers against mine while passing me a drink, standing so closely I could feel the warmth of his body, but never wrapping me in his arms. Then, the second we stepped foot in his apartment, alone at last, we were something else entirely. In the comfort of privacy, we were all hands and teeth, bruised lips, and heavy breaths. The days were usually innocent enough, but the nights were made for getting tangled together.

By the time Nate parked outside his apartment building and we began the stairwell ascent, I could feel the alcohol catching up to me in full force. With every step, my legs slowly deteriorated into a jelly-like substance. I swear, my feet became leaden, too. Yet despite all this, I felt happy and bubbly, like I could've floated into his bed if I wanted to—were it not for the damn lead blocks attached to my feet.

Nate followed closely behind, which was strange considering he usually led the way up, and he kept a careful hand planted on the small of my back. I glimpsed his other hand stretching toward me, too, as we climbed. Not touching me, but ghosting near my elbow like he thought I might tumble backward, and he was preparing to catch me.

"I won't fall, Nathan. I'm fine." My words sounded a little too slurred to be convincing, even to me.

"I believe you," he mused. "And it's Nathaniel. Eyes ahead."

"What?" I stopped mid-step. His chest collided with my back, his hands gripping the outside of my thighs to steady us both. I twisted to face him, still a step above, so we were nearly eye to eye for a change. "*Nathaniel?*"

His brows rose, a hint of a smile ticking the corner of his mouth upward. "Is there a problem, *Olive?*"

"No." I shook my head, my hair creating a curtain around my face. "S'just I thought *Nate* would be short for *Nathan.*"

He leaned closer, sweeping my hair behind my ears with his middle fingers. "Nope." He planted a soft kiss on my lips, a day's worth of stubble pressing into my chin. "Nathaniel."

I thought on it, letting his full name settle in my system. "I like it," I decided, turning on my heel and definitely not stumbling on the next step.

An exasperated "Jesus Christ" sounded from behind me.

While he fiddled with the keys to his apartment door, my eyes shifted in and out of focus. I swayed where I stood, but all I could think about were his lips on my neck. I craved the feel of his hands traveling up and down my body.

As soon as we were inside, I slung an arm around his neck and pulled him down into another kiss, trying my damndest to deepen it. He wrapped an arm around my waist and held me so closely, so tightly, I was barely standing on my own. He combed his fingers through the hair at the base of my neck with his other hand, pulling gently at my waves.

"Let's slow down," he whispered.

I barely heard him. He smelled so good. *How does he smell so good?* All thought slowed completely to a stop as a wave of overwhelming, drunken desire took over.

I tugged off my jacket with some difficulty, one arm turning inside out. It didn't matter. I needed him, all of him, right then, and I couldn't think of anything else. Not the fact that my face was flushed and burning hot, or that my hands and feet tingled on pins and needles as the alcohol continued to work its way into my system. I didn't think about the dizziness or the faint nausea that was gradually worsening.

I pulled at the button of my jeans and was struggling with it when Nate put a hand over mine to stop the movement. *Does he want to do that part? Fine.*

Abandoning the attempt on my jeans, I reached for his instead. My fingers grazed the skin under the hem of his shirt, the soft trail of hair there, as I fumbled against the button on his pants.

He wrapped a warm hand around each of my wrists and pulled them up to his chest, holding them there with enough gentle force that I looked up to meet his deep sea eyes.

"Let me get you some water, okay?"

I nodded wordlessly as he guided me backward until the back of my knees met his couch. With one last peck, he released my wrists and turned to the kitchen.

I sat in a huff, feeling a little rejected and a lot drowsy. *God, this couch is comfortable.* I closed my eyes and let my head rest against the throw pillow while I waited. My stomach twisted, but I tried to ignore it as I breathed in deeply through my nose and out through my mouth.

Don't puke.

Chapter 11

Four Years Ago, April

I'd like to thank my dad for leaving.
It made me a natural nurturer.

I woke up, groggy and dying of thirst, to Billie perched like a loaf of bread on my stomach. She purred softly, the only sound in the otherwise silent room. My head throbbed as I lifted it and surveyed the room. I was still lying on Nate's couch, only now a thick comforter that wasn't there the last I'd checked was thrown over me. I immediately recognized it as the one from Nate's bed. I blinked, eyes focusing on the coffee table in front of me, and the tall glass of water and two aspirin there.

Dazed and very much confused, I found Nate curled up and asleep on the smaller couch adjacent to mine. Billie hopped off my belly with a chirp as I sat to get a better look at him.

It would have been hilarious had I not had the hangover of a lifetime. He tried his best to fit on the couch—more of a loveseat—but his long limbs couldn't quite manage. He was lying on his back with his arms crossed over his chest and one outstretched leg draped over the arm, a naked foot suspended midair. His chest rose and fell with deep, rhythmic breaths.

He looked so calm, yet there was a seriousness there I'd never seen before. There was usually a hint of a smile that never left his expression, whether it be on his lips or in his eyes. But the drawn look on his face and the small crease between his eyebrows looked foreign on his otherwise relaxed body.

I suddenly felt like an intruder. Embarrassment flooded through me, along with a fresh dizziness. I'd passed out no less than five minutes after getting there.

Why the fuck did I call him while I was drunk off my ass? Why did I agree to that stupid bar crawl? Wait, what time is it?

I patted the blanket, searching for my phone. After fumbling my way up and down the entire thing twice, careful not to wake the sleeping man three feet away, I tried to remember where I'd last seen it.

My jacket pocket. I'd put it there when Nate pulled up to get me.

My eyes shot to where I'd left my jacket crumpled on the floor, but it was now folded in half on the kitchen island. Quiet as a mouse, I got to my feet and tiptoed to it. No phone. Shoulders slumped, I turned in a circle, head spinning with me, and looked for it on the floor, on top of the coffee table, in the cushions of the couch. Finally, I spotted it tucked in the corner of the countertop near the fridge, plugged into a charger.

I shot Nate a mental *thank you* as I reached for it and checked the time. 5:04 AM.

I was asleep for six fucking hours.

My head pounded with every movement, but I was too embarrassed to stay another minute. In a grand show of shame, I grabbed the aspirin off the coffee table, downed them with the entire glass of water, neatly folded Nate's comforter, called an Uber, gave Billie a scratch on the head, and left without further injury to my ego.

→»»⟩ ⟨«««-

It was noon before Nate called me. I debated not answering, still too mortified and not wanting to relive my humiliation, but I picked up anyway.

"You're alive," he said when I answered.

"Unfortunately. Listen, I'm really sorry about last night. I feel like a jerk."

"What? Why?"

I picked up on the sarcastic, teasing tone in his voice, but appreciated his lack of judgment regardless.

"Why? I don't know, because I was drunk off my ass and made you come pick me up in the middle of the night? Then, I gracefully passed out—fully clothed, I might add—on your couch?"

"You didn't *want* to be fully clothed, trust me."

I slapped a hand to my forehead, cheeks burning red in an instant.

Please, god, let me dig myself into a deep hole and stay there forever.

"Yeah, that, too. I'm such an ass. I'm sorry."

He giggled at my horror. "Don't sweat it, okay? I'm glad you called me instead of stumbling home alone. I'm also glad you didn't puke on my couch."

I let my head fall into my hand. "You and me both. How can I make it up to you?"

"You don't have to do anything, Oli. Just keep me in mind next time you make a late-night booty call. Preferably when you're sober enough that I can actually do something about it."

Fuck me. "I'm sure I don't know what you're talking about."

"I'm not just reserved for the late-night shift, you know. I'll take morning booty calls, too. Or even afternoons, if you're lucky."

"Yeah, okay, I'll keep that in mind." I rolled my eyes into next week. "I'm hanging up now."

"Hey, wait!"

"Yeah?"

"I'm having a show next weekend. You should come."

I bit back a grin. "Okay. Maybe I will."

When I hung up, a giddy confusion washed over me. Giddy because Nate was infectious. He had an ease and calmness that didn't come naturally to me, but rubbed off when we spent time together. Sure, I still felt a prickling nervousness with him at times, but the second I got in my head, he'd do something to reassure me or show me there was no pressure.

He'd never given me a reason to worry or question his intentions. He'd never promised me anything, and he'd never asked for anything in return. He had only ever been completely himself, and he accepted me just as I was.

The confusion, on the other hand, was because I'd never been in a relationship like this.

Not a relationship.

Nate didn't seem remotely interested in anything more. Honestly, I didn't know if I wanted anything more, either. Sure, Nate was amazing—sweet and easy to talk to, drop-dead gorgeous, talented as hell—but he had his priorities. He made it no secret that music was the most important thing in his life.

As much as I could easily see myself with him, I also knew daydreaming about it wasn't a good idea. Not with my master's only a year away and my future looming over me.

But for the first time in my life, I felt alright with the uncertainty. This thing with Nate was casual. Low stakes, high reward. While I wasn't looking forward to its inevitable end, I resigned myself to enjoying it anyway.

I can do casual.

CHAPTER 12

Now

*Distracting is an understatement. She is more than distracting.
I'm trying to keep it together, I really am. But I can't think
straight when I look at her.*

After the close call with Nate, I decided to keep my distance from the grad school gang. The less I was forced to be near him, the better, especially with Kieran around. There was absolutely no desire to dredge up the past; therefore, there was no point in giving it another second of attention.

For my emotional safety and sanity, I stuck near Kieran for the remainder of the party.

Saying that he had fun despite not knowing anybody at the beginning of the night would've been a massive understatement. He had lots of fun. More than fun. He had a full-blown blast. Some would say he and Michael had *too* much fun. As the drinks flowed, the two of them took full advantage of the open bar.

He went drink-for-drink with Michael, only Michael was drinking beer, and while Kieran wasn't a small man by any means, Michael was much larger. Kieran didn't drink beer, and he'd barely eaten anything all day, saying he wanted to "save his calories" for drinks instead. He went through gin and tonic faster than I could keep up.

"Good news, Olive. Bartenders let me grab one more drink before they closed." Kieran flashed a bright, lopsided smile my way.

"Look at you." I shook my head, wishing he wouldn't have indulged so much.

The party thinned out quickly once drinks stopped flowing. I didn't complain. My feet ached, and sleep tugged at the edges of my mind.

"Bedtime?" Kieran murmured into my hair once Michael bid us goodnight. A hand snaked down my back to rest on the top of my ass. The murky, watered-down shade of green in his eyes had me thankful the party was over. He was going to have one hell of a hangover.

"Please."

"Olive! Get your ass over here!"

Kieran and I gave each other matching confused expressions—his reaction time a little slower than mine.

"Who was that?" He scanned the nearly empty courtyard.

A quick search revealed Martinez standing at the exit I'd taken earlier in the night to escape. He waved us over, not bothering to look back as we followed him down the brick path toward the designated smoking area.

"He does realize you're my girlfriend, right?" Kieran asked, and for a split second, my heart bottomed out. Was it that obvious I was fidgety around Nate? But then, I realized he was talking about Martinez.

I snorted. "He's gay."

Kieran paused his steps, looking like he was doing mental math. "He doesn't look gay."

"What does being gay look like?"

Martinez was a big guy, strong and muscular with tattoos covering every inch of his arms and chest, including the backs of his hands. Masculine in every sense, sure, but that didn't make him straight.

Kieran shrugged, laughing off the question. "Like him, apparently."

If I'd gone further down the path before, past the smoking area, I would've turned the corner to find picnic tables and what looked like a beer garden tucked away, half-hidden under a group of thick trees.

"Game night," Martinez said simply when we caught up to him.

The space looked like something out of a storybook. The low-hanging tree branches provided enough cover to block most of the stars, and the string lighting overhead cast a warm glow across large picnic tables, and the people sat at them.

In the middle, at the largest picnic table, Jared, Gemma, Miles, and Nate all lounged, surrounded by Grant and Leo on bar stools they'd pulled up.

"Good, you found her!" Gemma beamed in greeting.

"Cards," Jared said, grabbing a grubby deck of cards from the middle of the table and giving them a rough shuffle. "You in?"

Martinez plopped down on Miles's left, meaning the only spot left at the picnic table was—as luck would have it—directly across from Nate.

"Oh, uh…" I crossed my arms. I did want to play, to spend time with my friends—with Gemma—but the precarious heaviness of the situation weighed down on me. Something about all four members of Crescent Light being present made it worse, too. Walking away would be easier.

I was just about to say, *I don't think so,* when Kieran nudged me. "Go ahead. You play."

"Do you want to play instead?" I asked him. "I can teach you."

Kieran grabbed an unoccupied Adirondack chair and settled in. "Nah, I'm not really a fan of card games."

Gemma shot me a look, asking, *What kind of person doesn't like card games?*

Kieran pulled his phone out of his back pocket and lounged back. "I'll just watch." But his eyes were already glued to Thursday Night Football streaming on his phone.

Unconvinced, I glimpsed Nate. Nonchalant as always, he ducked his head to pluck a cigarette from its box and place the end between his lips.

You're letting someone who is completely unbothered dictate what you do and don't do. You have nothing to run from. You have nothing to hide. You belong here. You deserve to play just as much as he does. Kieran doesn't have to know anything. Nobody here will say anything. You are in control. Fucking relax.

"Alright." The wood bench snagged on my dress as I slid into the spot beside Miles, across from Nate.

"Six-handed it is," Jared said as he dealt the thick double deck of cards out to the six of us sitting at the table.

Nate reached a long arm across the table, offering his open pack of cigarettes to his bassist. Miles grabbed one without hesitation, catching Nate's lighter as he threw it over. Martinez snagged the pack from Miles and pulled his own cigarette out.

"I'll share one with you," Gemma whispered to Grant as she took one.

Everyone's just tipsy enough to smoke, I guess.

"Oli?" Nate offered the pack to me a second later.

My stomach fluttered.

If I was going to be around him, I needed to be able to hear him say my name without it feeling so jarring. Without it feeling like a promise. A curse. Something so much more than it was. My eyes flashed to his—golden hazel meeting deep ocean blue—before I shook my head. "No, thanks."

A loud scoff had me turning my head.

"She doesn't smoke," Kieran said, eyeing the pack with a disgusted look.

Gemma snorted, picking up her cards. "Not unless she's good and tipsy."

Nate laughed through his nose, toying with the butt of his cigarette with the tip of his tongue as he sorted his cards.

Kieran's judging look landed on me. "Seriously?"

I shrugged. "Sometimes. I haven't in a long time."

It wasn't until I clocked the uptick of Nate's eyebrow that I remembered our shared cigarette earlier in the evening.

That doesn't count. It was a moment of anxious desperation.

"The bride bids first." Jared elbowed Gemma's shoulder. She'd be his sister-in-law in two days. Crazy. I caught Grant's soft smile from his spot behind Gemma, as though he had the same thought I did. He leaned forward, looping his arms around Gemma's slender waist as she called the first bid of the night.

She sat straighter. "Three spades."

The game was a modified version of the one we used to play, adjusted for six players instead of four. For starters, teams of three. Miles, Jared, and Nate versus Martinez, Gemma, and me. A double deck created twice the power and twice as many opportunities to screw over the other team. Finally, bidding on what you think your team could score determined what the strongest suit of the round was and who went first.

Our team quickly took the lead after Martinez won the first bid.

"I'm going to the bar inside for a beer," Grant announced, rising from his seat after the next hand. "Anyone need one?" Jared and Martinez raised their hands, and Grant took inventory.

"I'm good," said Leo, returning his bar stool to its home and bidding us a quick goodnight.

"Need a refill?" Grant said a little louder, directing the question at Kieran, who was preoccupied with his phone.

I nudged his knee.

"Huh? No, I'm good." He could have left it at that, but then he added, "I'm done with empty calories for the night," to the end. I felt Gemma's eyes as she shot me another look.

In the next round, Jared had the highest bid, but Gemma swept in and upped the bid at the last second. We won that round, too.

Nate dealt the next round, and his team won. Then, it was my turn to shuffle and deal.

Great.

Trying—and failing—to make quick work of it, I shuffled the deck the only way I knew how. None of that fancy bridge stuff, only plopping cards from the front of the deck to the back over and over again. Nobody cared that I was a little slower and sloppier than they were, but I could never shake the distant insecurity that I was being laughed at.

When a few cards slid out of my hand onto the tabletop, I scooped them up, thankful nobody was paying attention.

A hand silently reached across the table, palm up, halting my movements.

I rolled my lips together, debating, before placing the deck in Nate's silent, waiting hand. *Thank you*, I mouthed.

He dipped his chin as if to say, *Don't mention it*, as he split the deck in his hands and shuffled with ease.

"Can you not shuffle?" Kieran asked loudly, leaning forward in his chair.

Nobody else seemed to hear him, but Nate cast a brief, irritated look at Kieran before sliding the deck back across the table to me.

I shook my head as I doled out the cards one by one, ignoring the embarrassment climbing my neck. "I can. I'm just not very good at it."

Round after round, our scores stayed neck and neck. Our competitive natures became more and more apparent as we settled back into the familiarity of being in a big group together, and the shit-talking only increased with each hand. My tongue was no exception to the loosening.

"Oh, fuck off!" I shouted to Jared when he threw a card, beating me in a hand I was winning.

"*Babe*," Kieran murmured behind me, annoyed. I supposed he'd never seen me get competitive before.

"Martinez is cheating," Nate accused a few minutes later, after my teammate won three hands in a row. "Are you printing aces over there?"

"You wish, pretty boy," Martinez retorted with swaggering confidence. He leaned back, taking up a little more space for his ego. "I'm just that good."

Kieran's scoff at Martinez's use of *pretty boy* directed at Nate wasn't lost on me.

"We just need to focus," Jared commanded from across the table. He pointed two fingers at his eyes, flipped them to point at Nate, then to Miles, and back to his own. They were losing, but not by much. The twinkle in Jared's eye reminded me of the same steady, determined look he always got while drumming. "Dial it in. We got this."

Nate and Miles mirrored Jared's movements, flicking their first two fingers from their own eyes to the eyes of their teammates—becoming one with the cards.

They lost the next round. Bad.

When it was my turn to shuffle again, Nate instantly offered a silent palm out. I dropped the deck into his hand without hesitation, the ease of the motion surprising me.

It was like riding a bike. Even if it's been years, the initial shock of your body and mind getting used to the motion wears off swiftly, leaving only muscle memory. Before you know it, it's like you never stopped riding to begin with. Being around him was like that.

He shuffled the deck into an impressive bridge once, twice, thrice before handing it back.

Kieran, who had been mostly distracted by his phone while we played, grabbed my elbow gently, throwing a glance at Nate. "I could've done it for you."

I paused. "Oh." I hadn't even considered asking him. "Sorry, I didn't think about it."

"How much longer do you think you'll be playing?"

"It just depends." I could've asked Grant to take my place at the table if Kieran was sick of watching and wanted us to go, but I didn't want to. "Could be a while."

He nodded and leaned back in his seat.

The game went on, round after round, both teams going forward and back in score. Even though he was sitting on the sidelines with Kieran, Grant remained immersed in the game. Kieran, on the other hand, got progressively more impatient. He changed positions in my periphery, one leg crossing and uncrossing over the other, hands fidgeting with his hair, his scruff, his phone.

"If you want to go back to the suite, you can," I told him quietly after his third audible sigh. The game had gone on longer than it usually did, but I was enjoying everyone's company and finally felt somewhat at ease. Part of me wished he would go to bed without me so I wouldn't have to be distracted by his growing annoyance. Everyone at the table had noticed, and although none of them said anything, I still felt the weighted awkwardness that Kieran's energy gave.

"No. I'll wait."

Eventually, the other team pulled ahead, and the game came down to one final round. Everyone at the table sat a little straighter, knowing the stakes.

As soon as Nate dealt, Jared started shifting in his seat—a tell that he had a killer hand. I studied my own—a split hand between diamonds and clubs. Depending on which suit was the strongest, it would either be a really great hand or a really bad one.

"Three diamonds," I said.

"Four spades!" Miles called.

Martinez grumbled under his breath. "Pass," he sighed. "Sorry, team."

Jared could barely hold back his face-splitting grin when it was his turn to bid. "Gemma, I swear if you up my bid, I'm going to object at the wedding on Saturday."

Grant shot his brother a glare from where he leaned his chin on Gemma's shoulder. "I fucking dare you."

Jared just giggled like a little boy. "Six clubs."

It was a high bid, though not impossible. But looking at my hand again, I had the perfect cards to screw him over. All it would take was Gemma or Martinez winning one hand, and I could do the rest of the work to ultimately win the game.

Jared shifted his eyes to Nate and Miles, a glint of nervous anticipation in his eye as he led the first hand with a king. My eyes widened, but I did my best to keep a stony expression. *He doesn't have the ace. That means—*

Gemma threw down the ace. So far, her point. As long as nobody threw a club, the point was ours.

Nate laid down a heart, and I followed with one of my diamonds. The rest of the table laid hearts, and we won the point.

The next few rounds went as expected. Jared swooped the following three hands. Nate won the next, but his eyebrows pulled together as he leaned over to look at Jared.

They're searching for the missing clubs.

In the next round—Nate's lead—he forced me to reveal one of them. "A-ha!" Jared said. "There's one."

Two points were secured, two hands remained, and it was my lead now. Thank the card gods for my luck. I could've ended it right then, making the last hand a moot point, but I decided to draw out my victory by leading with my last remaining diamond.

Jared gave Miles and Nate a pleading look as if to say, *Please, for the love of god, one of you has to have the last club.*

Gemma scanned everyone's faces. "Who has it?"

"I think he has it," Miles said, pointing a thumb at Martinez.

"Believe me, I wish I did." He tossed a diamond. Useless. "You mean to tell me you don't have it, Mr. Six Clubs?" Martinez teased Jared, folding his hands over the table.

Jared narrowed his eyes.

"Oli has it," Nate retorted, not looking up from his hand.

My head shot up.

He slid his eyes to mine, holding my gaze as he leaned back. "She's flared her nostrils, like, three times this round. Plus, she's picking at her thumbnail." He nodded to where my nail scraped against the cuticle of my left thumb. I tucked my hand into my lap. "She only does that when she's trying to have a poker face." He tossed his last card on the table, not breaking eye contact. "We're fucked. She has it."

A grin tugged at the corners of my mouth. It didn't matter what anyone else had. I had the strongest card left in play.

Victory was mine. The game was over.

"Aw, come on!" Jared whined.

"Yes!" Martinez fisted the air in triumph. "Let's fucking go—that's my girl!"

Gemma high-fived me over the table when I revealed the last club. "Nice job, partner! Suck it, Jared."

I threw my head back and laughed, reveling in our sweet victory and the sounds of defeat from Jared and Miles. As I leaned in to gather the cards strewn about the table, my cheeks straining from smiling so wide, Nate smiled back at me.

Time slowed.

His bottom lip pulled between his teeth as his grin spread wider, with that dimple on full display.

My breath hitched.

For the briefest moment, only one thought flashed through my mind. *He is so pretty.* Then, all brain function came to a screeching halt when his cocky smile faded, and his eyes dipped to my mouth.

Like ice-cold water dumping over my head, I came back to my senses. *I can't do this. Not again.*

CHAPTER 13

Four Years Ago, September

I almost told my mom about you.

Summer stretched slowly. Nate and Grant finished their master's programs in May, and Grant moved. It was only thirty minutes away, but his farewell party could have convinced anyone he was going off to war.

My time with Nate stretched on as well, though our meetings remained irregular as ever. Between my summer courses and internship at a local paper, his post-grad production job, and the time Crescent Light spent at the studio, the stars rarely aligned.

But the more time I spent with him, the more I collected the small details that added up to the sum of who Nate was. The insignificant things only someone who knew him intimately got to see.

Like the crease that would appear between his eyebrows when he was concentrating, trying to make chords fit his musical vision. Or the freckle placed precisely in the middle of his shoulder blades. Or the rare occurrences where he would *really* laugh. He was an observer by nature and tended to quietly grin or let out a breathy sort of laugh through his nose. But occasionally, something would strike him as funny enough that laughter would burst from him, teeth flashing, dimple popping in the process. Those laughs were my favorite because they were rare. A treat few got to see.

He kept a pocket-sized leatherbound notebook on him, just in case inspiration struck, and he scribbled in it constantly. Sometimes, we would be right in the middle of a conversation, and he would suddenly hold up a finger, pull out the notebook, take a few seconds to write his thoughts onto the pages, mumble an apology, and prompt the conversation to continue where it left off.

The first few times it happened, I stared and completely lost my train of thought. But as time went on, my confusion turned into fascination. I found myself wishing I could hover over his shoulder to read the pages he so diligently penned. Or better yet, I wished I could crack open his mind to see the world as he did. A world where the simplest word, sound, or image could conjure up such inspiration that you couldn't help but pause everything for a moment and document it.

In early autumn, just as the trees started to yellow and turn a beautiful burnt orange, Nate called me.

"What are you doing this Saturday?" he asked the second I answered.

"Saturday?" I stretched my arm above my head, alleviating some of the pain from hunching over my laptop for the last three hours. "I was planning on spending the day on my couch, why?"

He laughed as if I was joking. I wasn't.

"Well, as exciting as that sounds, wouldn't a little road trip be so much better?"

"It depends," I lied. "A road trip to where exactly?" I would've happily road-tripped to the middle of nowhere if it meant spending time with Nate, but he didn't need to know that.

"Boston. My little sister's birthday is next week and I need to go pick up her gift. Care to keep me company?"

I loved Boston. Even though I hadn't been there since I was a teenager, I romanticized it enough that it now held a special place in my heart. It represented a long-lived dream, one where I would end up content, comfortable, and fulfilled. But I never dwelled on the dream for long, afraid of the disappointment I'd feel if it never happened.

I hummed, feigning indecision. "What's in it for me?"

"Are you telling me the pleasure of my company isn't enough? That hurts, Oli."

⤳⤳⤳ ⤶⤶⤶

That Saturday, Nate picked me up a smooth ten minutes behind schedule. Sliding into the passenger seat of his car was always a treat. Being suddenly surrounded by the leather and fabric softener scent of him had become my favorite kind of addiction. Only now, there was also the faintest hint of spearmint gum. And under that, lingering cigarette smoke. He hadn't been smoking the last time I saw him, claiming to quit for the second time in six months, but a pack sat snugly in the console under his radio.

"How's quitting going?" I quirked an eyebrow at him.

He sucked on his teeth. "Not great."

The tattoo on the back of his right arm—The Fool—peeked from under the sleeve of his black t-shirt as he pulled out of my apartment complex. The black ink did all the right things against his triceps when his arm flexed. I openly stared at him as he merged onto the highway.

"Enjoying the view?" He smirked.

"Very much so."

Within minutes, his hand came to rest on my knee. So casual. So intimate. The time between our last hangout and now didn't make a difference. It never did.

"So, what are you getting your sister that's so special you have to pick it up two hours away?"

He checked his blind spot, neck stretching to give me a delicious view of his jaw. "Paige's favorite author had an impromptu signing at a bookshop up there, and they signed a bunch of books, including a new one that just came out. I happen to know the bookshop owner. She said she could put a copy of each signed book on hold for me as long as I picked them up by the end of the weekend."

"Books signed by her favorite author?" I sounded more amazed than I probably should've. I didn't know why the level of thoughtfulness he showed for his sister came as a surprise to me. "She'll love that."

"And since it's Paige's twenty-first birthday, I figured I'd get her a fancy bottle of wine or something to go with it."

"Aren't you a good big brother?"

"Try to be." He flashed a crooked smile.

We listened to music from his phone and enjoyed the comfortable silence for a while. He hummed along as he drove, fingertips absent-mindedly drumming on the top of my leg with the beat. Every once in a while, he'd ask me to look up a song to play next, but we mostly kept to his shuffled playlist.

Our music taste was largely the same, with the odd exception of a classic folksy song that he'd request, or a trendy pop song that I'd follow up with. As the drive stretched on, a sort of game began. It started with Nate asking me if I'd ever heard of a particular band he liked. I had. Then, he asked me if I'd heard a specific B-side song he *swore* was their most underrated track. I hadn't.

"You haven't lived until you've heard it," he told me, reciting the title for me to look up.

I pressed play and dutifully listened to the whole thing. He was right.

"Wow," I said as the last chord reverberated through the car.

"Right?" He squeezed my thigh. "It's so good."

"You know what it kind of reminds me of though?" I asked, my fingers already flying across his phone's keyboard, searching for the song on my mind.

"What?"

I pressed play on the title, a single from a little-known indie band and easily one of my top five favorite songs of all time. "This."

We spent the next hour introducing each other to deep-cut artists and even deeper-cut songs, taking turns giving each other's requests a genuine listen. I couldn't say each song was to my taste, necessarily, and I was sure the same was true for him, but we agreed after each track that they were objectively good.

"I'm sending this one to myself," I told him as I hit the share button on the artist profile of the easy-listening singer-songwriter he'd last requested. I'd done the same to a new-age rock group ten minutes prior.

"Can you add the last song you played to my saved music while you're at it?"

"You got it."

I plugged my phone into the sound system when my battery got low, and relished in the fact that he was now at the mercy of my music. The game had died down, so I switched over to a shuffled playlist of all my downloaded songs while we chatted about nothing in particular.

I didn't notice the Crescent Light song that started playing until it was halfway through the first chorus.

Shit.

In the days following seeing Nate's band play at Brick Road Bar, I'd found time to look them up and listen again in private. They were just as good in studio recordings as they were at the bar. It was all I needed to validate I wasn't just caught up in my lust for Nate—Crescent Light was really fucking good. I'd downloaded a few of their songs and added them to my regular rotation, and over time, I became a genuine fan. I'd even caught myself humming their songs while studying, folding laundry, doing dishes. Nate knew I liked his music, but the extent to which I liked it was my little secret.

Apparently, I'd been listening so regularly I'd all but forgotten that the guy who sang them, who *wrote* them, was sitting two feet from me.

Feeling my cheeks turn tomato red, I prayed Nate wasn't paying attention and covertly grabbed my phone to press *Next.*

"Hey, that's a great song!" He glanced at me with a mock-wounded expression as the next song began. His eyes lingered on my flushed cheeks.

"Sorry. It's probably weird to hear your own voice on my playlist." I dismissed my embarrassment with a wave of my hand. "But I agree. It's a great song."

"I do get sick of the sound of my voice sometimes." He shrugged. "Plus, all I hear are the mistakes. Things I wish I would've done differently."

"I can understand that. Sometimes, your worst critic is yourself."

He lifted his eyebrows as if to say, *Damn right* and kept his eyes firmly on the road. The new song filled the car, giving me an excuse to hum along casually.

"I think it's cute you have one of my songs saved on your phone."

"I have more than one song saved, Nate. I have a whole EP on here. I wasn't lying when I told you I liked your music."

"Really?"

I laughed at his disbelief. There was no way he didn't know how talented he was. "Yes, really. I'm a fan."

He shot me a smug look. "Well, I expect you to be in the front row when we play Wembley someday."

"Totally. I'll be right in the front row with a big sign." We were joking, but I meant my promise. "I might even flash you, or have you sign my tits or something."

"Oh, I would *happily* sign your tits."

⇢⇢⇢ ⇠⇠⇠

Twenty minutes later, we pulled in front of a cozy, two-story indie bookstore with the name *NovelB's* printed on the side of the building. Inside, the store was bisected by a spiral staircase that led to what looked like a lounge upstairs. The second level was open, overlooking the first floor and giving a floor-to-ceiling bookshelf effect. Overflowing displays showed off the latest releases and a mix of journals, bookmarks, bookends, and various knickknacks. I fell in love with the charm almost immediately.

I ambled to a table just inside the door and thumbed through a stack of books while Nate pulled out his phone. He didn't have a chance to text whoever he was meeting because a voice from the top of the staircase interrupted the otherwise quiet store.

"I know that's not little Nathaniel Cassidy."

Nate's chin snapped up, and a breathtaking grin spread over his face like honey over bread. A sweet-looking older woman thumped her way down the stairs. The red lipstick she wore was almost unnoticeable as her thin lips split into a wide smile.

"Mrs. B!" Nate greeted the woman when he met her at the landing. She stood a solid foot and a half shorter than him, but that didn't stop her from pulling him down into a big, maternal hug.

"It's good to see you, Natey. Are you staying out of trouble?"

No.

"Of course! Why would I ever be in trouble?" He gave her a crooked, charming smile.

"Oh, you've always been so full of shit, Natey," she said, lovingly patting his cheek.

I snorted, which caught their attention. Mrs. B laughed along as Nate narrowed his eyes, like us women were conspiring against him in some silent way.

"Who's this pretty thing?" Mrs. B asked, reaching out to give me a hug I happily accepted. It was just as warm as I thought it would be. She reminded me of Christmas morning: gingerbread, fireplaces, warm cider.

"This is my friend, Oli. She was nice enough to keep me company on the drive over."

"How nice! Oli, please call me Mrs. B."

"Nice to meet you."

Mrs. B gave Nate a wise, knowing look. "She sure is pretty."

Nate studied me with teasing, narrowed eyes, then turned back to Mrs. B. "You think so?"

"Oh, yeah." Mrs. B nodded once.

Nate gave me another once-over. "I'm inclined to agree."

Mrs. B burst into laughter, making me jump, and smacked Nate on the arm. "Come on, I don't have all day."

She spun in a flourish, waving her hand over her head for us to follow. Nate winked at me as he turned.

"Now," Mrs. B shouted over her shoulder as she bobbed and weaved between tables, displays, and shelves so full of knickknacks they were about to overflow. "I set aside one of each of the Deb Stronghold books she signed for us."

Nate nearly knocked over a carefully balanced tower of thick fantasy novels in the process of trying to keep up with her. For such a small woman, she moved with remarkable speed.

"You'd better be grateful too, Nathaniel." She shot Nate a threatening look. "Deb Stronghold's newest book sold out in a day. I ordered a few extra copies just to have on hand here at the store after pre-orders were picked up, but nope! Everything flew right out the door!"

"Paige talks about her books all the time," he hollered after her, barely missing another display table. "She must be more popular than I thought."

"She is. Trust me." Mrs. B reached the back wall of the shop and disappeared into a staff-only hallway. "Wait here."

Nate ran his fingers through his hair, catching his breath. "She's a tornado, that woman."

He held a hand out, and I took it, feeling the squeeze of his warm, calloused fingers against mine. "She seems fun. How do you know her?"

"She was my neighbor growing up. Lived across the street and babysat from time to time. My mom and Mrs. B got pretty close after my parents split. I don't think she has any kids of her own; she's always been like an aunt to Paige and me. Jared and Grant, too."

"And she has the hookup for all your bookish needs." I picked up a glass figurine of an owl on top of a stack of books. *Cute.* "And your knickknack needs."

"That, too."

Mrs. B emerged with a stack of five books, all with the name Deb Stronghold in metallic gold across the spines. From the looks of them, they were romance novels. In fact, I'd recognized one of them as a book Gemma begged me to read the year before.

She plopped the pile into Nate's waiting hands. "I risked my life smuggling those, you know. Her fans are cutthroat."

He slung an arm around her shoulders, eclipsing the small woman with his tall frame. "Mrs. B, have I told you I loved you lately? You're my hero. Truly."

She let out another deep belly laugh, shoving at his shoulder.

"Oli, I told you he was full of shit, right?"

Nate bought all five books for his sister and another one for himself. I skimmed the shelves a bit and bought one for myself, too—an unsigned copy of one of Deb Stronghold's older books.

"Tell your mom I said hi, Natey," Mrs. B said as we made our way to the front door. He made no effort to wipe away the red lipstick she left on his cheek. "And for chrissake, eat a burger! You're getting too skinny. Oli, make sure that boy stays out of trouble!"

"No promises!" I shouted with a wave.

We dropped our books at the car and walked to a nearby cafe that was somehow even more charming than the bookstore. Its clean yet cozy vibe, paired with the wide bank of windows facing the sidewalk and park beyond, made me want to curl up and spend the entire afternoon there. Nate bought himself an iced Americano and a nitro tea for me before we walked back into the autumn breeze.

An intimate wine bar with an adjoining shop sat on the corner a few blocks away, stocked with rows and rows of locally made and imported wines.

"What do you think?" Nate asked as he studied the labels of every bottle on display.

I stepped forward, scanning the wall. "Red or white?"

He gave me a helpless look. "How should I know?"

I nodded my understanding. "Paige is turning twenty-one?"

He nodded.

"Does she already drink?"

"I'm sure she has, but I doubt it's been a lot. I'm not even sure she likes wine, to be honest."

I stepped away from the reds. The dryness and bitter aftertaste always bothered me, so I doubted she would have a taste for it. "I think white would be a safe bet," I said, pointing to a bottle of Pinot Gris. "Something like this. Sweet, but not too sweet. Not too dry, either. Easy to drink."

He slid the bottle out of its home, nodding intently at it as if he could read the French label. "Sold. I trust your judgment." He reached forward and grabbed a second bottle.

"Two bottles? Man, you *are* a good brother."

He winked. "This one's for us."

CHAPTER 14

Four Years Ago, September

I didn't know it could be like this. It's easy as breathing,
and yet I hold my breath.

I stared out the window on the drive back to Hartwood, savoring the city a few minutes longer.

"Thanks for coming with me today," Nate said with a gentle squeeze on my knee. "It would've been a long, boring-ass day otherwise. Plus, I would have definitely bought the wrong wine."

I covered his hand with mine. It looked comically small in comparison. "Anytime. Besides, I can never say no to a road trip."

"Totally agree. I love a good road trip. They give me so much nostalgia."

"Yeah? Did you do a lot of traveling when you were younger?"

He nodded, fishing out a piece of candy from the bag he bought at a gas station and popping it into his mouth. Sour gummies. My favorite. "When I was a kid, my dad used to take me on these mini-vacations all the time. Long weekends. He'd pick me up from school on a Thursday, and we'd take off. Just me and him. We did all kinds of stuff. Camping, hiking, baseball games, you name it. One summer, he drove us from

Massachusetts to Yellowstone and back. I remember hitting the road at the crack of dawn and listening to music the whole drive. He's the reason I became a musician."

"Really?" Nate didn't talk about his family much. Neither of us did. Other than the fact that he had a sister, I'd learned more about his life in the last four hours than I had in the nine months we'd known each other. But today had shown me a different side of Nate, a softer side. Like he was peeling off a layer and showing part of himself he hardly ever shared.

"Yeah. He'd teach me about classic rock—quiz me on it to pass the time." Nate formed a serious face, deepening his voice to mimic his father's. "'Nathaniel, is this Black Sabbath or Ozzy Osbourne? Which AC/DC singer is this? Did I ever tell you the history behind 'Rooster' by Alice In Chains?'" A small smile played on his lips, but I couldn't make out its meaning. He returned to his normal voice. "So much of my appreciation for music comes from my dad."

"You must be close."

He scoffed dryly. "Not exactly."

When I didn't say anything, Nate looked warily at me and shifted in his seat. "He, uh," he cleared his throat. "He wasn't very good to my mom. Not abusive or anything like that. He just could *not* stay faithful to save his life." He ran a hand through his dark waves and cupped the back of his neck. "He used to do some shady shit to sneak around behind my mom's back. Small things at first, but they got worse over time. Like all those father-son trips we used to take? It wasn't uncommon for him to sneak away when he thought I was asleep. I always just assumed he was going out for a smoke or down to the hotel bar to have a drink or whatever. At the time, I didn't know any better. But as I got older, I figured out he was using our trips as a cover so he could cheat."

I turned to face him, studying his profile as he continued.

"It got to the point where we weren't going to national parks or baseball games anymore. We were driving hours and hours away just to stay in shitty motels so he could sneak out and do whatever he wanted to. But he always made sure to do something fun with me on the last night—go to the movies, order pizza, whatever—and promise that the next trip was going to be more fun. They never were." Nate paused a beat, rolling his tongue over his lip. "One time, he left me pent up, alone, in a motel room with some snacks and cable TV for two days. And when he got back, he asked me to lie to my mom and tell her we had a great time. I knew the whole thing was just… bullshit."

The image of a young Nate sitting alone in a motel room in the middle of the night made me want to pull him to me—to hold him and never let go. I blinked away the stinging in my eyes. "You said earlier your parents weren't together anymore?"

"No. My dad was god awful at hiding the evidence of his cheating, and my mom's a smart woman. When I was thirteen, she asked me point blank about what we did on our trips. I could tell she knew something was up, so I told her the truth about the motels and him leaving overnight. It was all she needed. She called him on his bullshit, kicked him out, and divorced him. I know now that he had a history of cheating—even before I was born. It was only a matter of time before she was fed up. But back then, my thirteen-year-old brain thought it was all my fault they separated.

"And the funny part is, he didn't even put up a fight. When she kicked him out, he just packed a bag and walked out the front door. It was like the part of him that cared about his family slowly faded until there was nothing left. For the first few years after they split, we still saw him on Christmas and birthdays and stuff, but he was nothing like he was before. He just… stopped caring. About everything. Like, fully stopped giving a shit. He started missing baseball games, would forget to pick us up when it was his weekend to have us, stuff like that. He eventually forgot our birthdays, too."

Nate raked a hand through his hair again, deep in his memories.

"I'll never forget when Paige turned ten, my mom threw her a big sleepover party. All of her friends were there. My mom decorated the house; it was a whole thing. I'd just gotten my driver's permit, so I wasn't home a lot at the time. Too busy being a teenager, enjoying freedom. But Paige *begged* me to stay home for her party. There was nothing more she wanted than to have *all* her friends and *all* her family in one place. I can still see her standing at the front door—poofy pink dress, pigtails, party hat, and all—waiting for him. All her friends were running around, dancing, and having a great time, and my sister was just… waiting. And he never showed." Nate shook his head. "I didn't really give a fuck when he forgot my birthday. Whatever, who gives a shit? But when he forgot Paige's, it bothered me. A lot.

"So, ever since that next year when Paige turned eleven, and I was sixteen and could drive her around, I made it a point to always do something nice for her. To give her as many good birthday memories as possible, so she doesn't associate it with heartbreak from that asshole." He paused again, the muscle in his jaw ticking.

I waited.

"The older I get, the more I don't understand it. My mom is a saint. How could someone have something so good and fuck it up so royally? I like to think my dad's not a bad person, that he just makes really stupid decisions. He's tried to make up for some of it over the years, but it doesn't help. His priorities are so fucking out of whack, and they always have been. The way I see it, he should've never tried to be a dad or a husband if we weren't going to be his priority. Hell, people shouldn't be in serious relationships *at all* if they know their priorities are elsewhere. It's just selfish."

Something in his words struck a chord, and suddenly, I understood Nate Cassidy so much better than I had minutes before.

He took a deep breath through his nose. "So, yeah." He loosed the breath, chuckling. "To answer your question—no, I'm not close with my dad anymore." He lifted a hand from the wheel again to run it reflexively through his hair and down the back of his neck. "Enough about me. What about you? Any daddy issues?"

I'd never seen him so uncomfortable before. He'd shown me a level of vulnerability that had to feel foreign to someone as cool, calm, and collected as he was.

I picked at the ends of my hair. "Not 'daddy' issues, specifically. More like 'family' issues."

"Ah." He nodded. "A remix of a classic."

"Yeah." I laughed. "My parents… are good people. They tried their best, and I genuinely think they want what's best for me and my siblings. They got married young—I think they were eighteen and nineteen. They had my oldest brother, Orion, within a year of getting married. Then they had five more kids within ten years."

"Jesus," Nate whispered to himself.

"I know. My parents were kids themselves when they started having kids. If I'm being honest, I don't think they had any business having kids at that time. They didn't exactly make enough money to support a family that size, they didn't have the best living situation, and they *definitely* weren't mature enough. I remember them fighting a lot when I was little. Like teenagers. All-out screaming matches that would end with my dad leaving the house and my mom shutting herself in their room. They loved each other, but they weren't grown up enough to know how to work together rather than against each other.

"I'm the fourth out of six kids. My home growing up was pure chaos. The house was always a cluttered mess, and I just remember it being so *loud*. There were always at least two siblings fighting, especially my two older brothers. Plus, my parents were never home, so there was nobody to mediate when things got out of hand. Rion was left to figure out how to be in charge while my parents worked multiple jobs to make ends meet. My older siblings were forced to grow up fast to raise the younger kids. I'm sure you can guess how well that went." I chewed the skin on my lip.

"Since my oldest siblings were always in charge, I never got a say in anything. My opinions—my feelings—didn't really matter. Looking back, I struggled a lot with the chaos, the disorganization, the lack of stability. I struggled with not being able to have a shred of control over anything in my life. I just didn't realize it until later. I think that's where I started to develop anxious tendencies, which I still struggle with. Therapy helped when my anxiety got out of hand a few years ago, but there's still a long way to go…" My voice trailed off as my thoughts shifted to my siblings.

I liked to think we all would be closer if we had different circumstances growing up. We loved each other, we cared about each other, but we didn't know each other. Not as adults, anyway. We still saw each other as we did when we were kids. Rion with his exacting rule. River, reckless, defying him at every turn. Lily, the one who was *really* in charge. Me, trying to stay out of their way, happy to blend into the background. Lucas, stirring shit up as much as possible just for the laughs. And Aspen, too young and removed to care. It would be great to get to know each other again—now that we'd grown up—but where were we supposed to start?

"My parents did the best they could in their situation, but it's had an effect on all of us. What's sad is my siblings and I aren't even that close anymore. We're all out doing our own things, living our own lives. I talk to my older sister on occasion, but that's about it. We only get together on holidays—sometimes not even then. And, yeah, that's a SparkNotes version of my trauma." I swallowed, suddenly feeling like I shared too much.

Nate raised his eyebrows at me. "Six siblings, huh?"

I laughed, relieved at the broken tension. "Five siblings. Six, including me."

"What are their names?"

"Orion, River, Lily, Lucas, and Aspen."

"And Olive."

My full name sounded funny when he said it. Other people used it interchangeably with my nickname, but never him. "And me."

Nate didn't say anything else. He just laced his fingers through mine and kept them there until I was home.

CHAPTER 15

Now

I thought I could fight it.
Or at least pretend it wasn't there after all this time.
But—shocking to absolutely no one—I was wrong.

I shot up from the picnic table, mumbling something to Kieran about running to the restroom. I barely registered his response over the blood pounding in my ears, the emotions swelling behind my eyes.

My thoughts and feelings muddled together, each more confusing than the last. Annoyance, frustration, anger, insecurity, longing, sadness, desire.

Nate fucking Cassidy.

I burst through the restroom doors and came to a halt, pressing my palm against my forehead. It seemed silly, being so worked up over something as simple as a look. But that look shook something loose within me, something that had been tucked away for a long time, forgotten or ignored long enough that I hoped it was gone for good.

And it took *one look.* His gaze settled on me for a beat too long, I got lost in his deep sea eyes for a time-expanding millisecond; those eyes dipped to my mouth, and the chord was plucked like a symphony cellist tuning before a performance.

I splashed cold water on the back of my neck just to ground myself and closed my eyes. I counted to ten, then counted to ten again before I opened them and stared at myself in the mirror. My brown waves frizzed and curled at the roots from the night's humidity. My dress, wrinkled at my rounded hips from sitting, felt less flattering than it had a few hours prior. And my eyes? They looked as tired and torn as I felt.

How could I go from feeling so good to feeling so… *not* good in a matter of seconds?

Nate Cassidy. That's how.

Fuck him for making me feel this way, I thought. *Fuck him for making things so easy and so fucking hard at the same time. Fuck him for making my brain short-circuit just by saying my name. Fuck him for looking at me with those eyes, smiling with that dimple, laughing that silent laugh, existing with that cool, unbothered confidence. Like nothing ever shakes him, nothing ever gets under his skin. Like he isn't phased by me at all, not even a fraction as much as I am by him. Like none of this matters to him; like I never mattered to him. Does he enjoy messing with me? Just to watch me squirm?*

I wrung my hands to release some of the pent-up, uncomfortable energy.

Just once, I'd like to see him as unsettled as he makes me. Just once, I'd like to see him feel out of control and anxious. Feel the way I feel.

Fuck him for not being honest with me years ago. Fuck him for not being able to be vulnerable without spinning out of control. Fuck him for not talking to me, not telling me how he felt.

Fuck him for making me fall in love with him.

Even thinking it gave me pause. I didn't love him. But I had, once upon a time. I didn't realize it at the time, but I had.

If I could go back, if I would have realized it when it was happening, I would have turned it all off in a heartbeat. Maybe then I wouldn't have to feel this way.

Because the truth was, I fell in love with Nate Cassidy a long time ago. And he never fucking loved me back.

❧❧❧ ❧❧❧

When I finally left the bathroom, Nate was standing a few feet away, half hidden in shadow, leaning against the wall with his hands in his pockets.

Can't I get a moment of peace around here?

Heat still flooded through me, fueled by frustration and confusion and heartsickness and something else I still couldn't discern.

"Why do you keep following me?" I snapped at him, the object of my ire.

Even in the dark, I could make out his quick blinks. His surprise at my words.

Good.

"I'm just making sure you're alright."

"I'm fine, Nate. You don't have to check on me like I'm a little kid." My uncomfortable heels clacked on the stone floor as I passed him.

He pulled his hands out of his pockets and held them out defensively as he pushed off the wall to follow me. "Okay, fine. Jesus."

I whipped around to face him. "Don't."

He dropped his hands, palms slapping against his thighs. "Don't what?"

"Don't do that."

"Don't do what, Oli?" His brows pulled together, and something crossed over his features. Confusion or annoyance, I didn't care.

I pressed the heel of my hand into my forehead before smoothing it over my hair. Over Nate's shoulder, a large bay window overlooked the courtyard where the party had been. It was completely cleared out, devoid of all tables and decorations, and was left looking bare and desolate by comparison. "Just leave me alone, please."

"Alright," his voice softened, so low it was almost a whisper. "I'll go back outside."

"No, Nate." The sharpness in my voice lessened as I met his eye. "I mean, *leave me alone*. This weekend. I— I think it's best if we just steer clear of each other." I chewed on my lip. Nate tracked the movement. I stopped. "Kieran, he… He doesn't know about you, okay? About…" I gestured mutely to the air between us.

He made a face, the crease between his eyebrows deepening, and looked somewhere over my head like he was trying to piece together brand-new information. "He doesn't know about it at all? Or he just doesn't know about the last time?"

Heat climbed up my neck. I tried not to think about the last time. I'd forget it ever happened if I could. It wasn't worth the heartache that followed. "He doesn't know about any of it. We don't really talk about that kind of stuff and—"

Nate swiped a hand in front of him, cutting my words off. "Oli, I'm sorry, but that's not my problem. We're both here. We're both going to be hanging around for two more days." He shook his head and brought his hands to rest on his hips like he didn't know what to make of the situation. "I can't exactly avoid you."

"Yeah, but you can avoid following me when I don't want to be followed." I pinched the bridge of my nose. "You can avoid looking at me. You can avoid smiling at me, like…"

My ridiculous argument slipped away the moment I heard it out loud. *I'm acting like a child.* How was I supposed to articulate something I haven't been able to put words to for five years? "Can you just play it cool? For all he knows, you're just another guy from school, okay?"

Nate's eyebrows shot to his hairline, and he rocked back on his heels. The guy had the nerve to look like I'd wounded him. Me. Wounding him. Laughable.

I continued. "There's no reason to act like we were ever anything but friends." My thoughts hitched on the word.

"I've never been your fucking friend."

How many times had those words rang through my head since the day they were spoken?

"And I know you won't, but please don't say anything to him."

He dropped his head between his shoulders, eyes downcast as if concentrating on his breathing. His hair hung over his forehead, and despite my agitation, my fingers itched to tuck it back into place.

"Please, Nate. I just want to get through this weekend and celebrate our friends. The last thing I want to do is dig up all our shit." I liked to believe I was above begging, but I wasn't.

He nodded, more to himself than to me. "Yeah, okay. Fine."

I released a breath and opened my mouth to thank him, but he'd already brushed past me in a flash, striding into the night.

CHAPTER 16

Four Years Ago, October

My pillowcases smell like your hair. Like lilacs. I have a hard time forcing myself to wash them.

About twice a year since I was fifteen, I'd suffered from fully debilitating migraines. These were beyond the typical migraine, which were still terrible in their own way. I got those once every couple of months. But the fully debilitating migraines—sent straight from Hades himself—were the kind that left me in dark rooms for hours, under heaping piles of blankets with a cold compress held over my eyes. In the past, they'd left me so horrifically nauseated I was unable to keep down food, so disoriented my vision went blurry, so tense my muscles ached.

This was one of those migraines.

What started as a dull pressure behind my left eye progressed to a sharp, stabbing pain in my left temple that shot around the crown of my head, behind my ear, and down the back of my neck.

I tried to get ahead of it, but none of my attempts worked. Nibbling on a piece of toast felt impossible, my jaw was so tight my teeth hurt.

Water made my stomach roil. Moving my tense neck sent bolts of lightning down the top of my spine.

After taking medicine and piddling around my apartment for two hours, hoping I could shake it before it truly set in, I crawled back into bed. Wincing at the shuttered windows that still let entirely too much light in, I closed my eyes and was down for the count.

I dozed on and off through the late morning, willing my body to shut down and sleep the migraine off. When Nate texted me wondering if I wanted to come over to his place, I told him my current state in as few words as possible before rolling back under the covers and closing my eyes.

Gemma checked on me at some point, bringing me a piece of banana bread hot out of the oven and insisting I should eat something. Begrudgingly, I obliged, sitting up in bed long enough to savor the combination of sweet, buttery saltiness. I opened my laptop before slouching back into my pillows, and turned on a documentary I'd been saving for Halloween season, even though I'd probably have to rewatch it. My brain was too heavy to pay attention, synapses moving too fast and too slow all at once.

I didn't realize I'd dozed off again until a soft rapping at my door had my eyes snapping open, refocusing on the laptop balanced on a pillow in front of my face.

Odd for Gemma to knock, but I swallowed and croaked a quiet, "Come in."

When she didn't say anything, I lifted my head and squinted as the door swung open. To my surprise, it was Nate in my doorway, staring at me with a pitying look.

It wasn't the first time he'd been in my apartment. He'd been over for game night before, but it'd always been a pre-planned group setting.

Never out of the blue and never resulting in him seeing the inside of my bedroom.

Pressing pause on my laptop, I propped myself up on an elbow, wincing at the shot of pain down my neck.

"Don't get up," he said as he shut the door with his foot.

"What are you doing here?" I groaned, shielding my eyes.

"My mom gets migraines," he said simply. "Gemma let me in. I brought reinforcements." Only then did I notice the plastic bags in his hand.

I only stared as he took the two steps to my bed and perched at my feet like he'd been there a hundred times. Placing the bags into the crook of my bent knees, he began pulling items out one by one.

"Sometimes caffeine helps her, so I brought this." He revealed a bottle of soda, chilled and sweating drops of condensation onto my quilted comforter. "Or if you're dehydrated." He produced a large bottle of water, but dove back into the bag without pause. "Did you know capsaicin can help with headaches? I couldn't remember if you liked spicy stuff, but I brought this." He produced a jar of spicy salsa and a small bag of tortilla chips. But a second later, he continued. "Oh! And I found these. Figured they'd be worth a shot." He lifted a small bag of ginger hard candies and handed them to me. "Or if all else fails, your favorite." He tossed a small colorful package that landed with a plop next to my laptop. Sour gummies.

I studied the items strewn across my bed in disbelief, my thoughts too slow to take in the impact of his thoughtfulness just yet. When my eyes at last landed back on him, I blinked against his amused expression.

"You're in my room."

He chuckled, eyes darting around the room as if he was just having that realization as well. Rising to his feet, he went to the stack of unsorted vinyl records piled on top of my dresser. Helping himself, he lifted the top one, examining it front and back before rifling through the rest. Shoving his hands in his pockets, he took another glance around my bedroom, studying the succulents with skull shaped pots in my window, yesterday's half-full mug of tea on my bedside table, my thrifted vanity and mirror—complete with a pile of laundry on the matching chair—before settling back on me, lying under a pile of thick blankets.

"Cute. It's very *you*." He settled back at my feet, splaying a hand across my hip. "How are you feeling, McLaren?"

I relaxed back into my pillows and pushed the heels of my hands into my eyes, relieving the pressure there. "Like my head is about to explode, but better than earlier." I peered at him between my fingers. "I can't believe you did all this."

"Don't mention it. I'll let you rest; I just wanted to drop by and check on you."

When he rose, I caught his fingertips with mine. He paused, rubbing a thumb over my knuckles.

"You know, you don't *have* to go," I said. "I mean, I'm not the best company right now, but since you're already here?"

Nate smiled, stealing my breath even as he bent to kiss my hairline. Just as I considered taking my words back, certain he was turning to leave, he steadied himself against the dresser and toed off his sneakers.

A minute later, after tidying all the goodies, he crawled onto the bed. I shuffled and adjusted around his long limbs to give him blankets as he settled behind me, snuggling close with an arm around my middle.

"What are we watching?" he asked.

I adjusted the laptop so we could both see and pressed play. "Murder documentary."

"Relaxing."

Over the next hour, Nate's chest rose and fell against me. His slow, steady breaths in my ear lulled me into a faraway, drifting sort of sleep. I distantly registered his movements, his legs tangling with mine, his body pressing closer, the fading sound of the documentary.

When I woke, it was completely dark outside, and my laptop sat paused with the screen asking *Are You Still There?*

I tested the migraine, rolling my head right and left, noting the dull ache in my muscles. When no punishment came, I twisted around slowly. Nate's arm around my middle constricted, tugging me closer as soon as I was facing him. I snuggled into him, burying my face into the hollow of his neck, breathing in his scent even as he sleepily pulled me tighter.

"How're you feeling?" his gravelly voice mumbled.

"Better. Do you need to get home to Billie?"

He yawned, settling his chin atop my head. "She'll be fine for one night. I'm too comfy."

Sleep tugged again at the corners of my consciousness, unwilling to care about anything but being there, wrapped in his arms. "Me, too."

CHAPTER 17

Four Years Ago, November

*Lyricists have this habit of being known as people who are good
with words. What happens if we're actually
terrible with them?*

I groaned dramatically, falling back onto Nate's couch with a throw
pillow over my eyes.

Nate's computer chair creaked from the corner of his living room as
he turned around. He'd been plucking away at the acoustic guitar in his
lap, bouncing from that to the electric keyboard in front of him for the
last hour. "You good over there?"

I lifted the pillow and lolled my head to stare sidelong at him.
He'd just gotten out of the shower when I got to his apartment, and
his wet hair had dried gradually in all directions, making him look
adorably unkempt. His constant finger-raking didn't help. He blinked
expectantly, hands holding his bulky headphones an inch from his ears
so he could hear.

"I quit."

With a nod, he settled the headphones around his neck, committed
to the bitch-fest that was about to ensue. Fall semester had been tough,

and I felt the pressure of graduation—my future—pressing stronger with each passing day. As he turned the chair to face me fully, my gaze drifted to his bare chest, the sunrise tattoo peeking over the top of his guitar.

"You quit what?"

I pressed the pillow back over my head, pushing on my eyes to dull the blooming headache. "Everything."

"Will you at least let me keep your record collection if you quit everything?"

I hurled the pillow, which he caught with a smirk.

"I feel like my brain is going to melt and pour out of my ears," I groaned. "I seriously cannot look at a laptop or a textbook for another minute, or I will scream."

He shrugged. "So take a break."

Smug asshole.

My eyes narrowed. "Thanks, I didn't think of that. Oh, wait." I swung my legs around until I sat crisscrossed. Billie chirped in protest at the sudden movement and hopped onto her cat tree. "I *can't* take a break because I'm so fucking behind. This assignment is taking forever, and I'm just getting further and further behind."

Nate nodded contemplatively, turning to face his keyboard once again, but left his headphones hanging around his neck.

"This girl in my project group is breathing down everyone's neck to finish their sections because *she* did *her* section the day it was assigned. I can't focus when I see her stupid icon hovering on the shared document. It's like she's watching me. *Menacingly.*"

Nate snorted.

"I'm serious! She's judging my every move, I know it. Someone else in our group already told her to back off." I crossed my arms over my chest and huffed against the cushions, mind reeling. "And while I'm at it, why am I still having to endure group projects in the final year of grad school? Why am I even *in* grad school again? I've lost all reason. Can you remind me?"

As if settling on a debate, Nate nodded once and lifted his guitar from his lap, carefully resting it against the wall. He glanced over his shoulder at me, brows high to accompany his teasing grin.

I stared back. "What?"

"You seem very stressed."

"And?"

"You know I could help with that, right?"

I cackled. "You think you can solve all my problems?"

I imagined his hands—his mouth—on me. It was a constant, unsatisfied craving to want somebody so much.

"No." He ran a hand through his hair as he turned to face me fully, leaning back with a cocky expression. "But it's gotta solve one problem, right? At the very least, it'll give you some dopamine, which you are *clearly* lacking." His gray sweatpants did wonderful things when he adjusted in his seat. He wasn't kidding.

"Are you going to fix that for me, Cassidy?" I challenged, heat pooling in my core.

He stood before I finished my sentence. "Happy to."

Within minutes, his fingers were stroking into me at a slow, lazy pace.

Nate took his time, unhurried as he peppered open-mouthed kisses to the tender skin where my thigh met my pelvis. He curled his fingers up, sliding against my sweet spot with torturous accuracy. Soft hums and sighs tumbled from my lips in response as I enjoyed every second.

"*Fuck*." His forehead dropped to my hip. "The sounds you make."

He peered up at me, studying my face with a cheek pressed to my thigh. Dark hair fell over his forehead, and I ran my fingers through it, sighing again when he sank his fingers deeper. With a languid dip of his head, he licked a circle around my clit, then kissed and sucked on my sensitivity, taking it into his mouth in time with his fingers. My hand gripped his hair, bobbing with the movement.

I was floating and entranced and so, *so* relaxed. Reveling in the feel of his lips against my skin as he savored me, I let my head fall back against his pillows, happy for him to have his way with my body.

When my orgasm washed over me, I hummed my release, my fingers tightening on his brown waves.

Nate kissed his way up my body, teeth grazing over my thighs, my hips, just under my breast. His hard length strained against his sweatpants, tenting the soft cotton.

"Turn over, Oli."

I obeyed, turning on my stomach and lifting to all fours. One of my favorite parts about sleeping with Nate was getting to watch him. Being able to study each micro-expression that painted his brow, watching the pleasure I gave him as it spread through his whole body. Not being able to see him drove me wild in the best way, like he was forcing me to do nothing but *feel*.

He was behind me in an instant, already rolling a condom on. Easing my legs farther apart with his knee, he positioned himself between them, sliding the tip of his cock through my release. I jumped at the sensitivity when he teased my clit, then moaned when he eased inside of me.

Nate pumped into me slowly, letting me take him little by little to adjust. With one hand at my waist, he urged my hips lower, and with the other at my shoulder, guided me into more of an upright position.

The new angle overwhelmed me. Every stroke had his cock pushing against my front wall so deliciously I couldn't help but clench around him.

"You feel so good," he breathed into my neck as he picked up the pace. "You feel... so... good."

He swept my hair out of the way to kiss my neck, the sensation causing all thought to stutter then cease.

My hands gripped the air, begging for purchase but found none. I was practically on his lap, my weight supported by his thighs and chest. He couldn't have been any deeper.

He snaked an arm around my waist, thumb grazing the underside of my breast. "Can I try something?" his breath fanned against my neck.

I nodded, gasping as he slid into me again.

"I need to hear it, Oli."

"Yes, yes, yes." I didn't know what he was going to do, but I was on board. I wanted to take anything, everything he had to give.

His hand rose, pausing to palm my breast before resting at the base of my neck.

Fuck, yes.

Pressing a thumb to my pulse point, Nate used his leverage on my neck to pull me tighter to him, locking me in place. Back flush against his chest, I felt every movement of his body, every breath as his chest rose and fell, every thrust of his strong thighs under me. He increased pressure against my pulse, not too hard, but enough to keep me focused there, to keep my attention zeroed in on his body against mine.

Sooner than I thought possible, I was winding up again, higher and higher with every thrust. He knew it, too, and released his grip on my hip to reach between my legs and draw tight circles around my clit. My head fell back onto his shoulder, eyes fluttering shut against the pleasure.

It was too much. The rhythm of his thrusts, his deft fingers between my legs, the hand wrapped around my throat, his heavy breaths hot against my ear.

"I've got you," he grunted, focused on his steady movements.

I could only manage a whisper. "You're so deep."

He groaned, burying his head into the crook of my neck, but his pace remained unchanged.

"Oh, *fuck*."

"I got you," he repeated.

I clutched at his wrist against my neck, digging my nails into his forearm, holding myself closer to him. He licked a line up my neck, adding another layer to the sensations flooding my body.

Inching to my second release, overwhelmed and oversensitized, I could do nothing but hold on.

"Say my name when you come, Oli."

Oh, god.

I came around him with a shudder, repeating his name over and over again, rolling my hips as I rode out my orgasm.

The hand at my throat crossed around my shoulders as his tempo broke along with his restraint. Clutching me harder, he slammed into me, his other hand palming my breasts, my hips, anything soft and squeezable within reach.

He moaned his release a moment later, the sound like honey in my ears, sending shivers down my arms.

When his movements at last slowed, his body went limp against my back.

Fifteen minutes later, I was back at my spot on his couch.

Nate emerged from the bathroom. "Water?"

"Yes, please." I opened my laptop, balanced it on the arm of the couch, and patted around for my phone. "Your birthday is coming up pretty soon," I said. "Are you planning anything fun?"

"Oh, uh…" His face was hidden by the refrigerator door. "No, probably not. I might go see my mom or something."

When I found my phone, there was one unread text that I had to read over twice.

Austin Guy From Lit

> Hey Olive! Any thoughts on this weekend?

Fuck.

I'd completely forgotten. Austin, the guy who sat behind me in my Lit lecture, was quiet but as sweet as could be. The week before, he'd asked me if I wanted to join him at a new exhibition at the Art History Museum. A celebration of Día de los Muertos during the first week of November.

We'd had a few classes together in previous semesters, and we always got along, but we'd never done anything together outside of class. My first instinct was to turn him down. Whether from platonic disinterest or some kind of loyalty to Nate, I had no idea. Instead, I told him I'd get back to him, and I'd completely forgotten about it until this exact moment.

I must've made a face when I saw the text because Nate gave me a questioning look from the kitchen.

"What?" he asked, handing me a glass of water.

"This guy from one of my classes texted me. He sort of asked me on a date the other day and I totally forgot about it."

"Forgot about when the date was, or forgot that he asked you?" He plopped back down in front of his keyboard and grabbed his trusty leather notebook from the small music stand in front of him.

"I forgot that he even asked me until he texted me about it. It's a thing at the art museum, but I don't think I'm going to go."

Nate glanced back from his chair, a question sprinkled across his features. "Why not?"

What a loaded question from the man who was inside of me not thirty minutes ago.

A familiar ache bloomed in my chest. An uncomfortable mixture of longing, frustration, affection, and rejection came like clockwork every time I let myself think too deeply about the situation with Nate. The complexity of my feelings towards him.

"I don't know," I answer simply. The effort of explaining would be asinine and ultimately pointless. "I've never really talked to him outside of class. He seems nice enough though."

He nodded as he leafed through the pages of his notebook.

There was a palpable sense of an imaginary ball being lobbed into Nate's court. If I was being completely honest, I would have turned Austin down in half a heartbeat had Nate asked me not to go. But we had never had anything close to a conversation about what we were. About where we wanted to go with this weird situationship we had going on. If it would *ever* go anywhere.

My silence was an invitation for him to say something—*anything*—about how he felt. I stared at my phone and counted to ten, willing him to speak. By the time I got to three, I already felt ridiculous. Waiting for him to speak up—to tell me how he felt, that he wanted me all to himself—was useless.

But I couldn't help the question bubbling to the surface. A straight-forward question required a straightforward answer. A telling answer.

"Do you think I should go?"

He hesitated for a beat. "I don't see why not."

The fact that he didn't even look up from his weathered notebook as he continued flipping through the scribbled pages only pissed me off.

"Maybe I will."

I watched the back of his head as he nodded his response. Without another word, he found the page he'd been looking for, secured his headphones back over his ears, and resumed plucking piano keys.

I stared blankly at the freckle between his shoulder blades.

Well, I put the ball in his court, didn't I? I guess I can't get mad when the ball gets firmly thrown out of bounds.

If there was ever a question about what we were, what we had, or what we wanted with each other, the answer was pretty damn clear now.

Nate wanted exactly what we already had going on, and nothing more.

Which I had to be okay with, because having him in my life as my friend, my friend with benefits, my fuck buddy, whatever we were, it felt better than not having him in my life at all.

But damn, it felt like hell in the moment.

Frustration built within me. Did he even care? Did I occupy space in his mind? Did he struggle with trying to figure out how he felt like I did? Did he have feelings for me at all? Or was I just something to keep him company? Pass the time? Blow off steam?

I shook the thoughts out of my head as I quietly gathered my things. I reminded myself again, like a mantra, that we didn't owe each other anything. I had no right to be upset with him without also being upset with myself because I was just as responsible for our status as he was.

As I shut the door to Nate's apartment, I pulled up Austin's text and replied.

Me

Hey Austin! Yes, I'd love to hang out this weekend.

CHAPTER 18

Now

The best part about friends? They see you clearly for who you are, no bullshit. The worst part about friends? They see you clearly for who you are, no bullshit.

"That game took so long," Kieran whined for the third time as we opened the door to our suite.

I nodded, balancing a hand on his shoulder to unclasp the buckles on my heels. He held me steady with a hand at my hip.

"If I knew it would take that long, I wouldn't have told you to play." He undressed swiftly as I gathered my pajamas and padded to the bathroom.

"Oh, come on. I had fun. It was nice to see everyone. We used to sit around and play cards all the time."

"Hmm," he hummed, unimpressed.

I laughed off the whisper of irritation niggling under my skin, setting to work on removing my makeup. "I didn't know you had such a dislike of games."

"I didn't know you had such a like for them."

"Is there a reason why you don't like them?"

"I don't have the patience," he called from the bedroom.

Or you don't want to play something you won't win.

"Help me with my ties?"

His muscled frame took up all the space in the bathroom doorway as he twisted a finger for me to turn around so he could undo the corseted back of my dress.

I gave him a small smile over my shoulder. "Thanks for hanging out with everyone tonight. Even if you didn't have the best time."

"Of course," he said with a kiss to my shoulder, and my smile lingered. He knew tenderness was my weakness.

So what if tonight was a little bumpy? So what if Kieran isn't a perfect fit with the rest of my friends? Does it really matter? No, I thought, *I don't think it does.*

"I also had no idea your friend group was entirely dudes," he said with a chuckle, retreating back into the bedroom.

I guess I'd never thought of it like that before. I was friends with Gemma, Gemma was with Grant, Grant and Jared grew up with Nate, and Miles and Leo were in their band. Martinez was the only oddball, but he'd lived with both Grant and Jared at one point or another throughout college, so he was always part of the crew. The ratio was never intentional.

"And who's that guy again? The one who kept shuffling for you?"

My hands paused on my bottle of face wash. I screwed my eyes shut even as I put on my most convincing casual voice. "Who, Nate?"

"Yeah, the one who looks too cool to be here."

I scoffed. Partially to laugh off Kieran's unwarranted jab at someone he didn't know and partially because of the ridiculousness of the jab itself. Nate would never think he was too cool to be anywhere. It wasn't his style.

Kieran was quiet as I lathered and scrubbed at my face. I hoped that was the end of his probing, but as I rinsed the frothy suds off my hands and patted my face dry, he was in the doorway of the bathroom again, leaning against the frame.

"Is he the one you said was in the band?"

Working in the music industry meant I kept up with all the trends, no matter who was the face of them. Though I made a point not to mention Crescent Light by name unless it was strictly work-related, I did mention that Jared, Nate, Leo, and Miles were in a band when I was giving some context of the old friend group to Kieran. If I left out the small fact that they were one of the best artists on the indie and alternative charts, it was pure coincidence.

"Yeah," I said, squeezing toothpaste onto my toothbrush. Kieran shuffled past, pulling his own toothbrush from his toiletry bag. "He's in the band with Grant's brother, remember?"

"Hmm."

I finished brushing my teeth and left him in the bathroom, allowing myself an eye roll as soon as I was out of his view. I climbed onto the giant bed, not bothering to pull back the covers, and took a long, cleansing breath.

"Why did he keep calling you Oli?"

My head lolled to the side to look at him. His athletic shorts hung low on his hips, abs looking like they were chiseled from a marble slab, and yet I wanted to close my eyes.

"It's just a nickname."

Kieran shrugged a shoulder. "Yeah, but I've never heard it."

I twisted until I was sitting on my knees. "I don't use it much anymore. Haven't used it since school, actually."

"Hmm," he said again. He closed the distance to the bed and bent, fists resting on either side of my folded legs. I leaned into him, willing for him to drop the subject altogether. He kissed me on the lips. "Nobody else used it, though," he said and kissed me again. "Only him."

I rolled my eyes openly. "It's just a nickname," I repeated, laying on my side.

He climbed onto the bed and moved to hover over me, keeping his balance on his hands and knees. He leaned down, scruff pressing against my skin, to kiss me again. I sighed into the kiss, easing him to rest more of his weight over me.

"You didn't, like, date him, did you?" he said it like he was asking about a dead animal on the side of the road.

Jesus Christ.

I sighed again, exasperated this time. "Kieran." We didn't talk about things like this. We never had. It was exactly the reason why I never made a point of talking about Nate, or any of my *actual* ex-boyfriends, with him. I knew nothing about Kieran's exes, not even their names—except for one. I'd debated on telling Kieran about the whole Nate thing before we came to California, spurred by residual guilt of ever having been with someone else, or some other patriarchal bullshit like that. But I hadn't, because what good would it have done? What was the point of dredging up the past when it had never mattered to us? Especially now, when Gemma and Grant were the focus of the weekend, why would I draw attention to anything else?

"What?" He grinned down at me. I could tell by the glossy look in his green eyes that he still had a decent buzz from the open bar. I wished again that he had eaten more before drinking so much. Calories be damned. He leaned in farther, gently pressing me into the bed to kiss my neck. "All I'm saying is I think he wants my girl."

Not the words I wanted to hear. Not only because it was comically untrue but because I needed to snuff out any tiny candle still inside of me that hoped I would ever be what Nate fucking Cassidy wanted.

That ship had sailed.

"Yeah, okay," I said sarcastically. "Can we please move on now?"

"Why?" Kieran asked, kissing down my neck. He hooked a knee between my thighs and settled between them. "You don't want to talk about the bad boy?" he teased.

I laughed because I was supposed to laugh at that. "Because I'm not entertaining this conversation."

"Do you think he has a real job? Or do you think he just plays in coffee shops every day and sleeps at groupie's houses when he needs a place to crash? Do you think he's living the wannabe rockstar dream of 'making it big' someday?" He crooked the fingers of one hand in air quotations. Leave it to Kieran to hear that someone was in a band and assume it also meant they were going nowhere in life, despite my line of work.

There was no point in revealing to him that he knew Nate's band. Most people in New England have at least heard of Crescent Light; I even caught Kieran humming to one of their songs once. They'd been steadily climbing in all the ways that mattered for a band, from opening at Madison Square Garden to joining the Bonnaroo lineup last year. I also bit back the urge to point out that—despite Kieran's assumption that musicians were likely low-lives—all the members of Crescent Light had degrees. Nate and Leo both had their master's degrees, in fact. I never went out of my way to spell out my connection to Crescent Light to Kieran. Defending them would be suspicious at best and would incite a conversation I wasn't interested in having.

No reason to start a pissing match that Kieran probably wouldn't win.

"I don't know, Kier. Can we drop it?"

He let his hips drop more, pressing into me. "You looked so hot tonight."

I unhooked my arms from around his neck, suddenly wanting breathing room. "Thank you."

His affection felt good. Great, even. But as much as I tried to get in the mood, he was drunk, and I wasn't in the right headspace. His weird comments didn't help.

"Kieran, I'm so tired. Can we just go to bed tonight?"

He sloppily kissed down my chest to the tops of my breasts. "I'll go down on you, baby." The magic words to convince me to change my mind. Not that it hadn't worked before—many times—but there was no way it was happening. He was tipsy, horny, and wanted to mess around. That much was evident from his stiff cock against my hip, but my answer was no.

"Thank you for the offer," I huffed a laugh, "but not tonight. I think my social battery is spent. I'm so sleepy."

He paused for a beat before lifting. "Okay, babe." He slid an arm around my waist as he settled next to me.

I'd told a white lie. The comedown after a day of anxiety and socializing left me feeling heavy and wrung out, but I wasn't going to get sleep any time soon. Despite my exhaustion, I lay awake for a long while. Even after Kieran's breathing slowed and deepened as he drifted to sleep, I lay there, replaying the night over and over. Every word, every thought, every flickering, lingering glance.

Like a virus invading my mind, I thought of Nate. His voice, smooth and even. His proximity as he leaned against the brick next to me, so close I could have reached out and touched the hair hanging over his eye. The taste of whiskey on the butt of his cigarette. His eyes, dark and perceptive, dipping to my lips. I thought of what was—memories of what we had been.

When we fell out, I didn't just lose something as silly as a fling, or a fuck buddy, or whatever we were. I'd lost a friend, too.

"I've never been your fucking friend."

All my ire from earlier faded to nothing as I closed my eyes. What was left behind was the true root of my feelings, hiding underneath layers and layers of anger all along.

A deep-seated, gaping, unrelenting sadness at what had become of us.

And what could have been.

CHAPTER 19

Four Years Ago, December

She remembered my birthday.

"I think it's time you talk to Nate," Gemma said as she swung her legs over mine, lounging back against the arm of our couch.

Keeping my eyes on the Christmas movie on our TV, I covered her feet with my blanket, feigning nonchalance. "Talk to Nate about what?"

She eyed me with raised brows.

Like a drawbridge over a moat, my defenses rose. I stared back blankly. "Talk to Nate about what, Gem?"

While I wasn't necessarily avoiding him, things had been funny since our last conversation before Halloween. It was now mid-December, and we'd barely spoken outside of a few inconsequential texts. Was I enjoying it? No, not at all. It sucked. I missed his company, not just the sex, but things were at a standstill. The ball was in his court, and I refused to be the girl who begged for someone's attention.

Gemma shrugged and gave me a small smile, offering comfort against my defensiveness. "You two still avoiding your feelings?"

I laughed incredulously as if to say *Don't ask* and turned back to the TV.

"How long have you been hooking up? Almost a year? I know you. You wouldn't still be giving him the time of day if you didn't have serious feelings for him. And I *also* know casual isn't exactly your strong suit."

"I've been doing casual just fine, thanks," I said, more clipped than I meant.

She straightened, placing a hand on mine. "I'm not trying to pry, babe. I don't know what you've talked about behind closed doors. If you've talked about keeping things casual, fine. Do your thing, girl. But I think it's going to be hard staying casual when you realize you're in love."

My scoff was immediate. "We are not in love."

"Okay, so maybe I'm exaggerating. You know what I'm saying, though."

My feelings towards Nate had been a steadily growing black hole over the last few months. It sucked in all my attention, no matter how much I tried to ignore it. Of course, I had a crush on him from the beginning, and I liked him enough to keep seeing him for a year. But at some point between summer and winter—I wish I knew when—it had taken a sharp turn into something much more than a schoolgirl crush. It was the elephant in every room of my mind, the clown makeup I painted on every morning, and I was doing a horrible job at keeping it at bay.

Gemma, with all the love, support, and sincerity anyone could want in a best friend, was asking me for honesty. Not just with her but with myself, too.

Putting it into the universe made it real, but the words fell woefully short. "I like him," I said softly. When I met her baby blues, I repeated. "I *really* like him."

Her lips spread into a wide grin. "See? I knew it!" When I didn't say anything, she gave my hand a squeeze. "I didn't want to push you. I know you like to figure things out for yourself, but I see the way you two look at each other, even when you think you're being subtle. It's obvious there's more going on than just sex."

I nodded wordlessly, studying the blanket covering us.

"But since we're on the subject," Gemma continued, "how *is* the sex?"

A cackle burst out of me, the sudden levity knocking me out of my thoughts.

"Oh, come on," she pressed. "You've never told me a single dirty detail."

"The sex is…" I searched for the words. "The sex is amazing, okay? It's *beyond* amazing. Like, 'Holy shit, how did I ever settle for boring sex when sex like this exists,' amazing, okay? Is that what you wanted to hear?" I snorted.

"That's not even close to what I wanted! I want to hear it *all*."

So, I told her everything. All the things I'd kept to myself in the months spent with Nate were laid out. I filled in all the blanks for the parts she already knew and gave her all the TMI details she'd waited for patiently. I told her about my conflicting feelings, the mixed signals, and the nagging doubt that clarity would make any difference at all.

"It's not like I didn't give him a chance to talk to me. He could have told me how he felt and he didn't. The way I see it, that means he either completely did not pick up what I was putting down, or he just doesn't feel the same. In which case, I embarrassed myself enough for a lifetime and will now be escaping to the woods to live out the rest of my life in solitude."

There was also a third possibility: We were both afraid to make the first move.

"Not without me, you're not." Gemma lounged back again, tucking her feet under my thigh to keep warm. "There's no way he doesn't feel the same."

I snuggled deeper into the couch. "It's hard to get a read on him when he's so hot and cold. We'll talk every day for a while, then he'll fall off the face of the earth. It's been a month and a half since we've talked." Ever since I'd told him about the date with Austin—which barely constituted as a date after all. Austin and I got along well but the spark wasn't there. We were better as study buddies.

"But that's not uncommon with him, right? Going MIA?"

"Not *uncommon*. Just usually not for this long. I assume he's coming to game night tomorrow, but I have no clue."

"The big question is, what's stopping you guys? I mean, do you see yourself being happy with him if you guys, like, took the next step?"

The flutter in my chest was answer enough. I let myself imagine what it would be like to be with him—*really* be with him. Falling asleep, waking up next to him day after day. Going grocery shopping together, exchanging Christmas gifts, meeting his sister.

It could be great.

Gemma poked my side, looking smug.

"I need to talk to him, don't I?"

"Girl. *Yes*. Like, yesterday."

"Pass or play motherfucker."

Martinez looked comically large sitting at our teeny tiny kitchen table. The wooden hand-me-down table from my oldest brother's first apartment was meant for two people to drink tea at, not for four people to play cards. The usual gang was present and accounted for, with the exception of Leo, who had plans with his girlfriend, and Nate, who had totally flaked. It would've been one thing for him not to make it because he was working on his music, but to say nothing—not even to Jared—was odd.

Martinez and Miles were currently losing at a game of four-handed, and they grew more impatient with Jared and Grant every minute. The brothers were, naturally, using every excuse to draw their victory out for as long as possible.

"I think I need another beer," Jared crooned, sliding off his chair and moseying to the kitchen. He shot me a shit-eating grin as he squeezed past me to get to the refrigerator.

Gemma's and my apartment was the smallest of everyone's, but we'd gotten added to the game night rotation like everyone else. It never ceased to make me smile how easily Gemma and I integrated into their friend group.

Sure, they were a little overwhelming at first—they were loud as all get out and cussed like sailors—but their constant company and noise had become something to look forward to.

There was a comfort in the chaos, I supposed.

"Grab one for me," Grant said. Gemma snickered from her spot on Grant's lap.

"Hell," Miles shouted, "grab me one, too." He slapped his cards face down on the table. "This is painful."

Martinez groaned his agreement. "Christensen, if you don't get your ass over here and finish this game, I'm going to have a bitch fit."

"Relax." Jared returned with the beers and distributed them. He cracked his open, taking a long swig before picking his cards back up. He studied them for a long moment. "Pass."

"I hate you."

Gemma and I subbed in for Martinez and Miles after their terrible loss, but they stayed close to cheer us on against the Christensen brothers.

"If you guys pull that shit again—" Gemma cut Grant a threatening look. "I'm returning your birthday gifts."

"You mean Christmas gifts?" I asked. Christmas was only a handful of days away.

"No. Anakin over here is a January Capricorn."

"He's too lawful-good to be Anakin," Miles quipped from his spot against the doorframe of the kitchen. "He's more Obi-Wan."

Grant clasped his heart, his eyes sparkling. "That might be the best compliment I've ever gotten."

Miles winked.

"Hold up," Martinez straightened. "I forgot about your birthday, Obi-Wan. Are we getting fucked up?"

Grant shook his head and said, "No," at the exact same time his little brother said, "Yes." When their eyes met across the table, Jared just grinned and drummed his fingers on the table.

"No," Grant repeated, shuffling the deck for the new round. "Can't we just hang out and play cards or something?"

"I can make a cake!" Gemma volunteered.

"Absolutely not!" Martinez rejected. "Dude, we aren't doing *this*," he gestured wildly around the room, "for your birthday. I love a low-key night as much as you do, but we are not celebrating by sitting around playing cards like it's a regular old Tuesday." We never played cards on Tuesdays, but his point was made. "Let's go out and get fucked up. We never get fucked up anymore!"

"Hard agree," Miles nodded, tucking a wayward strand of black hair behind his ear.

Grant grimaced. "I feel like my getting fucked up days are behind me, man. The last hangover I had lasted three straight days."

While Martinez continued his begging, reasoning that they never had fun anymore and the group needed a nice outing to maintain morale, I went to the kitchen for a refill. I caught Gemma's eye, motioning to my glass in a, *Do you need a drink?* gesture. Instead of nodding, she rose and followed me.

"So much for talking to Nate," she whisper-shouted when it was just the two of us in the cramped kitchen. "Why didn't he show tonight?"

"No clue." I sighed. "But I think I have a game plan. The next time I see him, I'm going to just come out and say it." I'd tell him I had real feelings for him, and I wanted to see where things would go if we gave it an honest shot. I hated not knowing what the outcome would be—not feeling in control—but I couldn't keep doing what we were doing without knowing how he felt. It was a risk, but he was worth it. *I* was worth it. If he felt the same, great. If he didn't... I would have to be okay with a clean break. I was too far gone. There was no way I could go back to casual.

"Come onnnn," Martinez whined.

"Fine!" Grant groaned. "If I say yes, will you shut up?"

Martinez's grin was audible, even from the next room. "Let's go! That's my man!"

CHAPTER 20

Three Years Ago, January

Is it possible to run toward and away from someone at the same time? I feel like that's what I'm doing. I know it's dumb, but I don't know how to stop.

Two weeks later, Gemma and I piled into the house Martinez, Miles, and Jared shared with armfuls of liquor and cupcakes Gemma had spent the morning making. Children's party hats and an array of even *more* liquor decorated the kitchen counter. We had less than half an hour before Grant was supposed to show up, and time was of the essence, so I set to work.

"Where the fuck is Jared?" Martinez shouted somewhere in the house. "He was supposed to be here an hour ago with the balloons."

I rummaged through the cabinets until I found a large pitcher.

"He said he was finishing with the band and would pick them up after," Gemma called back.

I still hadn't heard from Nate. Even the pointless texts—mostly songs sent back and forth every few days with "check them out" or "sounds like something you'd like"—had stopped. I'd been relieved to get a sign of life from him when he responded in our group chat about Grant's birthday. But other than that? Crickets.

It didn't matter because he was putting a hold on working on Crescent Light's new EP for a night to come out to the bars with everyone, and I was downright giddy to see him. My stomach fluttered at the anticipation of being wrapped in his strong arms, breathing in his familiar, comforting scent, of the likelihood of going home with him once the night was over, and finally telling him how I felt.

The crazy part was that I wasn't anxious at all. Where nerves usually settled in my system, there was only excitement.

I poured an entire bottle of rum into the pitcher in front of me, followed by half a bottle of vodka, orange juice, pineapple juice, and a packet of children's fruit punch mix. I was filling the last few inches of the pitcher with water when Gemma cut the silence.

"Hey, so…" she started, steadily frosting a cupcake until it was covered in a pastel green, "have you heard from Nate lately?"

I smiled. "Other than a few texts last week, not really. I've been busy with classes, and I know he's been busy, too." I pulled my phone out for what felt like the hundredth time and opened my text chain with him. "Why?"

She shrugged, not meeting my eye as she started on another cupcake. "Just curious if you've talked yet. I heard something—"

"What's this?" Martinez asked as he rounded the corner into the kitchen. He pointed at the gallon-sized pitcher, now full of dark orange liquid.

"Hunch punch," I told him, grabbing a red plastic cup and filling it with ice from the bag melting in the sink. "Strong as hell and oh, so delicious."

Jared, who'd finally made his arrival along with Miles and Leo, followed behind, peeking at the pitcher. Bobbing over his shoulder was a giant balloon with the words *Birthday Boy* on display, and next to it, an even bigger balloon of Ewan McGregor as Obi-Wan Kenobi. I poured another cup of the punch without waiting for him to ask.

As Martinez sniffed the concoction, I poked my head around the corner to the living area. I'd hoped to find Nate there with his other bandmates, but only found Miles crossing the apartment toward the bedrooms, and Leo setting down a guitar case in the corner. Unlocking my phone again, I quickly finished typing the text message to Nate and hit send.

Me

Hey stranger! Still coming out for Grant's birthday tonight?

Martinez's eyes lit up as he took a sip. "What's in it?"

"Who cares?" Jared took a huge gulp. "It'll get you fucked up and fast."

"Correct," Gemma added, plopping the icing on the counter and pouring herself a full cup.

"He's here!" Leo shouted from the front room.

I grabbed the stack of *Star Wars* party hats and distributed them quickly as we squeezed into view of the front door in time to yell, *Surprise!* when it swung open. Grant's toothy grin as he took us in was infectious.

"You guys," he droned, clutching his hand to his chest. "You shouldn't have!" He managed to look genuinely shocked despite the "surprise" planned in his presence two weeks prior.

"Here." Jared shuffled ahead and handed a nearly overflowing cup of hunch punch to his brother. "Drink this."

⫸⫷

The gang acted as ridiculously as I'd expected at the bar, and I loved them for it. Grant, as it turned out, was a very popular birthday boy. After being joined by no less than ten of his other friends, we thankfully secured a couple of tables, and I volunteered to babysit our spot while everyone else went wild.

Martinez refused to take the *Star Wars* party hat off and forced Grant to keep his on too. Jared never let go of the Obi-Wan balloon, going as far as explaining to the security guard outside that Obi-Wan didn't have an ID on him, but it's okay because, as a Jedi, he's very responsible. He even took the damn thing onto the dance floor, which wasn't that bad because we never lost sight of his location. All we had to do was look for Ewan McGregor bobbing around.

"Where's Nate?" Grant hollered to Jared between shots about an hour after we arrived.

"I think he's on his way?" he said with a question in his voice. He fished his phone out of his pocket, and I checked mine, too. No response to my earlier text. No responses from him in our group chat with everyone, either.

"Wait, there he is!" Jared yelled over the music. He pointed Ewan McGregor over the small crowd gathered around our table. With a hand cupped over his mouth, he shouted, "Speak of the handsome devil!"

I followed the direction of Jared's shouting and spotted the top of Nate's head on the far side of the crowd. His disheveled hair poked over everyone else's heads like a beacon in the crowded place.

My heart jumped. I missed him.

Holy shit, I missed the guy.

He was sandwiched between some of Grant's other friends I didn't know, and though I could see parts of him, there was no chance he could see me yet.

Two months.

God, has it been that long?

I made to slide off the barstool to work my way toward him when the crowd parted enough for me to catch a real glimpse of him, just in time to see the blood-red nails on a feminine hand reach up to cup the back of Nate's neck and pull him toward her.

In time to see him lean in to plant a lingering kiss on her lips.

I stopped cold, frozen to the spot.

My stomach sank and settled heavily in my gut. Their kiss probably only lasted a second, but it could have been an hour.

I saw it in my head like a scene in a shitty drama show: a girl I'd never seen before wrapping her arm around Nate's neck, kissing him with all the confidence in the world, Nate kissing her back with a hand resting on her waist. And me, stunned on the other side of the crowd, caught like a deer in headlights.

What. The. Fuck.

I came to my senses a second later and settled back into my seat, looking down at my phone as if I were answering a text. As if I didn't just see the man I wanted to confess my feelings for kissing someone in front of me and all our friends.

How many times had I wished he would kiss me out in the open like that?

I wanted so badly to ignore him.

I scanned the crowd, unsure of what to do with my hands, my face, and settled on Gemma as she shot daggers at the back of Nate's head. She had my back, even if she was hammered drunk.

I willed Nate and his *friend* to move further away, but they maneuvered closer, weaving through the packed crowd until they were only a few feet away. I couldn't force my ears to mute the sound of Nate's smooth voice as he spoke.

"Hey, man." He clapped Grant on the shoulder and pulled him into a bro-ish half-hug.

My eyes stayed glued to my phone.

"Sorry I'm late," his voice carried over the music. My elbow came to rest on the tabletop in a ridiculous attempt at hiding my face. The urge to find a quiet place to hide was overwhelming. "I was waiting for her to get off work," Nate went on. "This is my girlfriend, Blair."

My eyes went wide. If he said anything after that, I blocked it out.

I gave myself one heartbeat to absorb the blow of his words.

Girlfriend.

Embarrassment—hot, sticky, weighty embarrassment—sank deep into me. An angry, blotchy flush burned my skin as it rose up my neck, speeding to my face.

I glanced at the time flashing in the upper left corner of my phone.

Ten-thirty is an acceptable time to head out, right? It is now. It has to be. I am so fucking out of here.

I debated an Irish Goodbye, but that probably would've hurt Gemma's feelings, and likely Grant's, too. But Nate was too close. There was absolutely no way I could avoid him if I said goodbye to Gemma.

Whatever. Let him see me.

I squeezed behind Gemma and rested my chin on her shoulder. "I think I'm gonna head out. I'm not feeling well."

She whipped around, her blonde hair arcing behind her, and pulled me into a tight hug. "I'm going to fucking kill him."

I shook my head against her neck. "Nope. It's fine." A lump formed in my throat, but I swallowed it down.

Fuck that. I'm fine. Everything is fine.

"I'm sorry."

"It's *fine*. Have fun, okay?"

"Grant!" she yelled in my ear, swinging her arm back to nudge Grant in the back. "Oli's leaving."

"Olive, no!" Grant pulled me out of Gemma's arms and held my shoulders. "It's my birthday! You can't leave yet. You have to stay here and sing to me." His glossy, bloodshot eyes looked adorably like a sad, drunken puppy dog.

"She isn't feeling well," Gemma reasoned.

Grant's frown deepened. I couldn't help but crack a smile looking at him.

Nate stood in my periphery, running a hand through his dark mop of hair.

"Happy birthday, buddy." I patted Grant's chest. "I'm going home and going to bed." He'd get over it within minutes, or when the next round of shots came.

The fake smile I'd plastered on fell as soon I turned my back to everyone.

I weaved through the crowd, not heading to the main entrance but to a side door I knew led to a quieter side street. It was easier and quicker to get an Uber from that side.

The thoughts I'd staved off came swimming in as I inched closer to the exit.

A girlfriend?

A girlfriend.

I'd caught a glimpse of her—Blair—when I hugged Grant. She was beautiful. Her thick jet-black hair and dark features gave her that kind of timeless, effortless beauty that most women would kill for.

She's so much prettier than me. She's so much skinnier than me.

What was I but plain, frumpy, and undesirable? It was a toxic line of thought, but it flashed through my mind before I could stop it.

No, Oli. We aren't doing that.

None of this was her fault. She didn't know me, and I sure as hell didn't know her. Nate wasn't my boyfriend, nor did he ever hint toward wanting to be. There were plenty of signs that he cared about me, that he liked hooking up with me, that we had a friendship, and still, he'd never made a move toward being anything more. But damn it, I couldn't shake the feeling I was being bamboozled.

Was the chemistry all made up in my head? Was the magnetic pull something my touch-starved body fabricated because I wanted to be wanted *that* badly? Wanted to be chosen *that* desperately?

The sex was one thing. An itch we used each other to scratch. But what about all the times he'd asked me to stay over despite my plans to leave? All the times he'd held me through the night, stroking featherlight lines across my skin? What about the cheeky, boyish smiles he gave me across the table at game nights? The hours we'd spent together, not for hooking up, but simply to occupy the same space?

A part of me always assumed he never made a move because he didn't know how to be in a relationship. I convinced myself that maybe if I made the first move and confessed my feelings for him, it would somehow make him more comfortable taking that step.

I was wrong. It wasn't that he didn't want to be in a relationship. He just didn't want to be in a relationship with *me*.

Cold air blew against my face as I swung the exit door open.

The hot embarrassment in my system quickly transformed into anger. Was I a plaything to him? Someone to string along? Someone to keep him company when he felt lonely? Someone to toss aside when something shinier came around?

The questions didn't stop.

When did this even happen?

Was he sleeping with her while we were sleeping together?

Oh god, do I need to get tested?

Do I know him at all?

I craned my neck down the road, searching for the Uber I'd only just called for amongst the Saturday night traffic as if it would materialize immediately.

I felt icky. The whole situation unsettled me, and I resented the fact that I couldn't pinpoint an exact reason why. If I could've channeled my feelings to a singular source and to be able to say, *This is why I feel the way I feel*, it might've been easier to handle. But it was too convoluted. I felt everything at once, yet nothing at all. I just wanted to go home.

Tapping my foot against the pavement, I checked the Uber's progress again.

I fidgeted, wrung my hands, shifted my weight from side to side, attempting to displace some of the adrenaline coursing through my veins. I turned in place but paused when the exit door swung open again.

Nate.

Visibly cringing, I turned back toward the traffic.

"Oli." He said my name as if it offered some kind of explanation.

I pulled the inside of my cheek between my teeth and chewed, keeping my eyes peeled for my ride.

"Hey," he said tentatively, sounding closer. He stopped beside me, his arm frozen half-outstretched like he wanted to wrap it around my waist but thought better of it.

I sidestepped out of his reach before he could change his mind. The lump in my throat doubled in size.

A long silence followed before he broke it. "Look, I—"

Turning on my heel, I faced him head-on, boring into him with a look I hoped expressed all the incredulity I felt. There was nothing to say. No reason to drag out something that was clearly over—if something could even *be* over when it never really started to begin with.

He blinked back his surprise, hands grasping the air at his sides. "I— Blair, she… y'know, we just—" He bit his bottom lip, searching. "I didn't—"

"Look"—I halted him with a hand—"it's fine. Just drop it." My Uber at last approached the curb, and I waved the driver down. "She's really pretty, Nate. I'm happy for you, okay? We don't have to talk about it."

"But, I—"

"Go enjoy the party," I said as I opened the back door and climbed in.

I slid into the seat and shut the door before he had the chance to respond. I'd meant what I said. I really did *not* want to talk about it.

There was no reason to make it any more painful and awkward than it already was. Never seeing him again wasn't a possibility—we were too connected—but I needed a clean break, at least for the time being.

I wanted answers, and I got them.

Whatever we were, whatever we had, it was over.

Chapter 21

Now

*Foggy memories, clear images. Sometimes it's hazy, but I
remember the good parts.*

The sensation of spinning out of control and falling from a great
height forced me awake. I jolted upright in the bed, heart racing,
hands outstretched in front of me, thoughts swimming as the dream
slowly faded from my mind. I blinked my vision clear as I gulped air
and assessed my surroundings.

Kieran splayed in the bed next to me. He breathed those deep, heavy
breaths that only came from a night of overdrinking—the ones where
your body wills you not to be violently ill with each inhalation. I
watched his bare chest rise and fall and shook my head against the
annoyance of his overindulgent night. How he blew off most of my
friends. The rude comments he made about Nate.

I tried falling back to sleep, but it was no use. Whatever nightmare
I'd been having woke me up so violently that I was wide awake and
fresh as a spring chicken. If that spring chicken looked like it had a fitful
night's sleep full of anxiety-driven nightmares.

The sky was a deep shade of indigo on the other side of the French doors, the first kiss of sunlight still hidden below the horizon. Kieran let out a choked snore. With a huff, I gave up hope of more rest, grabbed my phone from the nightstand, and rose.

Almost immediately, the tightening in my chest returned, a niggling sort of irritation that started at my diaphragm and crawled up my throat. I slipped my arms into a fluffy white resort robe as my bare feet made contact with the cold wood of the balcony and hugged my arms tight against my middle.

Breathe in. Hold for four. Breathe out. Hold for four.

Unsettled. The nagging, uncomfortable, ambiguous feeling that tethered my mind to my gut and made me want to both crawl out of my skin and stand perfectly still at the same time. *Unsettled* was the only way to describe it, like someone reached into the bottom of a sand-filled fish tank and dug up all the sediment.

I closed my eyes and leaned against the balcony railing, attempting to ground myself before the feeling got out of hand and led to an inevitable anxiety attack.

In, two, three, four. Hold, two, three, four. Out, two, three, four, five, six, seven, eight.

Only one thing would help. I needed to peel back the mental layers and pinpoint what was triggering this. There were probably a few culprits, but this felt above and beyond my usual level of anxiety. Until I named whatever was big enough to wake me in my sleep, I would keep spinning out. First, however, I needed to bring myself down to earth and calm my mind. I focused on feeling the cool wood beneath my feet, smelling the damp air, hearing the breeze through the leaves of surrounding trees. It helped little by little. After a few more minutes, the water in the fish tank of my mind was still muddy, but it wasn't swirling and threatening to overflow anymore.

Through the mental haze, the name of the feeling revealed itself: guilt.

I didn't like how I'd handled the night before. As frustrated as I was at the situation this weekend had turned out to be—as frustrated as Nate could make me—I wasn't proud of how I snapped at him. Nate liked to pretend he was aloof, untouchable even, but I knew on some level that it had to be uncomfortable for him, too. And when he came after me to check that I was alright, I thanked him by stomping my foot like a teenager and chewing his head off.

Then there was the matter of how Kieran acted last night.

I didn't like the tense awkwardness of having him insist I hang out with my friends while simultaneously acting like he didn't want to be there. I had no idea if anyone else picked up the subtleties of his unhappiness, but I saw it in each irritated twitch of his legs as he sat waiting for the game to be over. He didn't even attempt to make conversation with my friends, save for the occasional backhanded comment.

Though I would never say it aloud, I wondered if his awkward behavior was insecurity he wasn't used to experiencing that he was covering up with alpha male bravado. Maybe that was why his sarcastic questions when we returned to the suite got under my skin so much. We were in private, and still, he was making offhanded comments about Nate to make himself feel—what? Superior? More manly?

Two days. Two days and we can go home.

I curled up on the balcony's patio furniture and allowed myself a few minutes for a mundane, mind-numbing task. Checking emails was strictly forbidden when on PTO, according to Wren, my coworker and closest friend in Boston. I agreed to a certain extent, but personally preferred to keep an eye on my inbox to make sure it wasn't piling to dangerous levels while I was out. Checking it from time to time was better than returning to a heaping pile of burning shit after a vacation. Thankfully, nothing demanded my immediate attention, so I closed my email and opened the unread texts from the night before.

Wren

So …

Wren

Any news on the hot famous ex?

I rolled my eyes, regretting the day I told her about him, and sent a response.

Me

Not my ex.

Me

But yes he's here.

Me

Unfortunately.

There was no way she was awake yet, even with the time difference between California and Massachusetts, but she would appreciate a dangled carrot of gossip when she woke.

I yawned into my robe.

Caffeine. I need caffeine.

According to the resort website, the coffee shop attached to the main building would open in twenty minutes.

Perfect.

I dressed quietly, careful not to wake Kieran—though a marching band could've stomped through the suite, and he probably wouldn't have stirred—and opted to walk down to the main building instead of calling for a golf cart. The thick knit sweater and leggings I'd pulled on were perfect against the cool autumn breeze as I walked the winding path to the main building.

Crisp, early morning air filled my lungs and cleared my senses, releasing tension slowly from my shoulders. Early morning over the vineyard was breathtaking. Hazy fog hung low, covering everything in a layer of dew. Combined with the purplish light of dawn, the whole spectacle seemed straight out of a fantasy novel.

By the time I had a hot tea in hand from the cafe, the sun had broken the horizon, casting everything in lovely, warm pink and orange light.

The grounds were mostly empty, save for a handful of early risers milling about. An elderly couple not far from me walked hand in hand on the brick pathway toward a narrow dirt path. The path was lined with loose gravel and led directly between rows of freshly harvested grapevines. I blew on my tea and savored the fragrant steam that warmed my nose as I watched them. The couple barely spoke, only lifting their pointed hands in occasional observation as if they didn't need words. The simple joy of the other's company was more than enough. Peaceful, solitary, and alone—but together. Compelled to follow, I fell into step a ways behind them.

The dirt and gravel path spread like veins through the whole vineyard, traveling up one row before splitting to bisect the field between rows and rows of grapes and olive trees and feeding into other paths.

I walked through the vines, careful to give the elderly couple space until we were deep enough that I could veer in a different direction. I wandered up one row for a while, aimless and unhurried and free to let my thoughts clear, before a natural break in the field had me cutting right and following the path in that direction. The rising sun sent the morning fog aloft in a thick, haunting mist, obstructing my vision in pockets the sun had yet to kiss. Humidity clung to my skin, my hair, but I welcomed its touch. It was as if the earth itself was encouraging me to stay grounded, covering me in its mark.

At the next turn, a darkened silhouette up ahead caught my eye. Not the elderly couple; there was only one person in the distance. Another lone patron on an early morning walk.

The figure was too far away to tell if we were both moving in the same direction or moving toward each other, but I continued anyway, keeping my eyes trained on the uneven gravel. Another glance up a minute later confirmed that the other person—a man, by the look of it—and I were walking in the same direction. His back was to me, but he was going at a much slower pace. I'd already closed the distance between us by half. I thought to peel off into another direction, but no other routes would open until we reached the end of this section of the vineyard. Eventually, the narrow path would force me to pass him.

A bit closer now and with the fog nearly gone, I could make out his gait. He walked in a leisurely, almost uneven pattern, like he was distracted by something in his hands. It was as if he was trying to move his arms and upper body as little as possible while still walking. I squinted from a distance, slowing my movements.

A second later, he halted altogether and turned to face the vines next to him, revealing what he was so distracted by.

A small leather notebook and a pen.

CHAPTER 22

Three Years Ago, May

Do you think I can run far enough that
everyone will ~~forgive~~ forget me?

The final semester of grad school was spent focusing on what really mattered: studying, graduating, and lining up a job. The sooner I could start the next chapter of my life, the better.

I set my sights on Boston. If I was going to turn the page on my life, I needed to do it in a place I loved—a place that felt right. As the weeks went on, I picked up the pace on the job hunt, sending applications far and wide to every newspaper, magazine, and publishing house I could find.

Most of the promising job openings were way out of my league and required knock-out resumes in addition to a minimum of ten years of experience, approximately one thousand references, and a bulletproof portfolio to even stand a *chance* at getting an interview.

I kept myself realistic at first and applied to less-than-exciting opportunities I knew I was qualified for just to get my foot in the door. Anything that could get me to Boston and make sure my bills got paid was good enough for the time being.

The most far-fetched and ideal listings, the roles that made my eyes light up and filled my daydreams, lived in bookmarks on my laptop. Untouched. They were a reminder of what the long-term goal was. Of what I wanted to be, even if I wasn't there yet.

If nothing else, they were there for me to torture myself with.

Tired of scrolling through the same listing of open positions for the hundredth time, I opened my bookmarked list with a sigh.

LightFoot Publishing House, *Alto* magazine, and *The Mountain*. All of whom had made a name for themselves not only in the publishing and journalism sphere, but all over the world. Each of them was highly competitive and could open opportunities for a lifetime to anyone who was lucky enough to work with them.

They were a faraway, unattainable dream.

Applying and applying and applying some more had landed me in a vicious cycle of hope and bitterness when weeks passed with few callbacks. Not to mention, the callbacks I *did* get weren't from anywhere I was excited about. When I clicked *Submit* on my twentieth application, self-doubt reared its ugly head.

"What's the harm in applying for the heavy hitters?" Gemma asked as she mixed a bowl of brownie batter.

"Other than the fact that there's no way I'll be selected?" I deadpanned, lowering my record player's turntable needle carefully on the middle of Fleetwood Mac's *Rumours Deluxe* album. The beginning notes of "Gold Dust Woman" filled the apartment.

"The worst that can happen is what, exactly? You never hear anything back from them?"

My eyes settled on the wall in front of me. *Yes.*

She continued without my answer. "So, hypothetically, you apply. A month goes by; you don't hear a word. Guess what? You'll still get a job somewhere, and life will go on." She held the chocolate-covered spoon out to me. Existential crises call for brownie batter.

I took the spoon, saying nothing, but meeting her eyes all the same. She was right. I knew she was. What good was scraping the bottom of the barrel if I had nothing to lose by shooting for the stars?

"Apply for the damn jobs, Olive."

"I hate it when you're right."

⸬≫⸬ ⸬≪⸬

"I sure hope I nail every single one of these interviews because I just signed a lease on an apartment in the city," I told Gemma weeks later during one of our last girls' nights before graduation. Lounging on the couch, I cradled a bag of salt and vinegar chips.

"That's ballsy," she said, hunching to apply ballerina-slipper-pink polish to her toes. "How many interviews do you have lined up?" She'd come from another interview earlier that afternoon. It only took two hours for them to call her to set up a second one.

I sighed. "Three."

The knot in my stomach twisted at the thought of committing to a year-long lease in the city with no actual income secured. My latest job rejection shook me to my core because it should have been a hole-in-one. If I couldn't get an entry-level assistant position, what hope did I have for something better?

"I know it's risky, but the apartment complex wouldn't wait until closer to graduation for me to sign. Plus, it was the only complex with units bigger than an actual shoebox. Or that has a heater. And no roaches of note."

"Who needs heaters in Boston anyway?" she snarked as she carefully rose, closing the cap on the polish. "And none of that matters because you are definitely getting one of those jobs. There's no way you won't."

I rolled my eyes and turned my attention to *The Bachelorette*, our chosen trash entertainment for the evening.

I'd always loved Gemma's optimism, but sometimes it struck a nerve. Some of us weren't as effortlessly good at everything as she was. Besides, she had her budding social media popularity to fall back on if the job hunt went belly-up, paid sponsorships and all. Not to mention perfect grades, a perfect body, and the perfect boyfriend, but who's counting?

My bitterness at my circumstance wasn't her fault, and I knew I was being an asshole by letting her genuine positivity get under my skin. It was an odd feeling, realizing how much of a monster you could become when you weren't in the best mental place, even to those you loved.

Despite telling myself I was fine with how things ended with Nate, I wasn't. I really, *really* wasn't. It wasn't just the heartbreak. It wasn't just the blindside. It wasn't even the jealousy that nagged at me.

It was the utter lack of clarity. It ate at me, whispering in the back of my mind. What was worse were the questions left unanswered because there was no point in seeking them. The resolution I would never get because there was nothing to resolve.

Nate never reached out to me after I left him on the sidewalk, and neither did I. What was there to say? I tried shutting my feelings down by simply not letting myself think about them, but they weighed heavily on my chest regardless of whether I consciously thought them or not.

I scooted closer and leaned against Gemma's shoulder.

"Well"—I popped a chip into my mouth— "there *is* a way I won't get one. But we're not going to think about that."

"Right!" She snapped her fingers. "Positive thoughts. We're manifesting."

"We are manifesting," I repeated.

She closed her eyes in mock-prayer, as if willing my big city job into existence by whispering, "Boston, Boston, Boston," in hushed, serious tones.

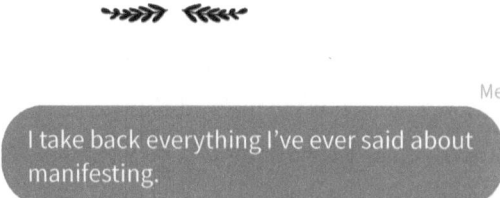

Me

I take back everything I've ever said about manifesting.

I hit send on the message to Gemma, a wide grin splitting my freckled face as I replayed the phone call in my head again.

Against all my wildest expectations, and with no time at all to spare with graduation two days away, I got a phone call from the number one company I was hoping to hear from after interviewing. One of the big opportunities.

The Mountain was a multi-media production conglomerate that was most widely known for its magazines, which had been in print since the 1980s, and its online blog. I'd consumed their content for years, from thumbing through magazines in airports to following their social media profiles and tracking their takes on my favorite new artists.

Their content centered around popular interests in cuisine and lifestyle, but their biggest claim to fame was music. *The Mountain* offered everything from deep-dive historical analyses on long-forgotten artists, to interviews with classic rockers, to album reviews for the latest pop stars, all in one place.

I was shocked when they set up a second interview—I was a nervous wreck for the first and fumbled through the whole thing. For the third interview, they invited me to their office in Boston, right where all the magic happened. I barely kept my jaw off the floor long enough to answer their questions, but somehow, I did it. A copy editor position wasn't too shabby when it was at one of the biggest names in the journalistic *and* music worlds.

Graduation day passed in a blur of smiles and photos and hugs, but all I focused on was packing up and starting anew at *The Mountain*. There were connections to make, dreams to chase, ladders to climb, and I planned to make the most of it.

The sense of relief as I gave Gemma my copy of our apartment key was enough to tell me I was better off moving on from Hartwood—and from Nate. Distance was good. Time was better. With enough of both, maybe I could get him out of my system.

I had a few days to settle into my new place in Boston before my first day at *The Mountain*. Gemma, Grant, and Martinez left quickly after helping me move, but I distracted myself by scrubbing everything in the apartment from top to bottom and hyper-focusing on unpacking as quickly as possible.

The music I kept blaring through my headphones as I unpacked drowned out my thoughts well enough, but didn't stave off the anxiety over my new normal. Each night, I stayed awake entirely too late, tossing and turning, dreading my first day as much as I looked forward to it.

When morning arrived, I wore the most business-professional-while-still-being-trendy outfit I owned and willed my stubborn waves into frizzy submission, ignoring the cartwheels in my stomach.

The other new hires and I were greeted by security in the foyer of *The Mountain* headquarters—a man built like a redwood tree who looked like he had about a million more important things to do than babysit the newbies.

"He looks thrilled," a heavily-freckled girl giggled beside me. She shot me a look out of the corner of her eye, making me roll my lips to stifle a laugh.

"Poor guy got stuck with us today," I whispered back.

"What department are you in?" she asked. Her thick auburn hair sat braided around her head like a crown.

"Online Dailies. Copy editor."

"Really?" Her green eyes widened. "Thank god. I am, too. I think it's me, you, and that guy over there." She pointed to the lanky, nervous-looking guy at the front of the line to get a photo for his new badge. He towered over everyone, but his thin frame made me think he would fall over if there was a strong enough wind.

"His name is Ha-Joon, I met him earlier. I'm Wren, by the way." She extended her hand to me, shiny gold rings adorning every finger, complimenting her freckled skin.

"Olive."

We filed one by one through the line, getting photos taken and waiting on our shiny new badges. A surreal, giddy feeling washed over me when I held my badge in my hands for the first time. I stared down at my smiling face on the shiny plastic—it was a great picture, thankfully—and all I could think was, *I am so proud of her.*

It stole the breath from my lungs. *I did it. Boston, my apartment, The-freaking-Mountain. And I made a friend in the first hour of walking through the door.*

Everything was new and shiny and clean, and the novelty felt easier to embrace than the old. For the first time, I stepped confidently into a fresh version of myself and fully embraced her.

The group of new hires—ten total, spread throughout three different departments—were all ushered into a boardroom to meet our managers. Wren, Ha-Joon, and I were to report directly to Julienne, an impeccably-dressed Black woman whose presence filled the room. The coils of her hair danced over the shoulders of her deep maroon blazer as she shook each of our hands. I could tell within seconds I liked her, but that she was also the type to be selective about who she liked in return. And boy, did I want her to like me back.

"You three better get comfortable with each other," she told us at the end of the meeting, her husky voice making her all the more compelling. "You're going to be spending a lot of time together."

CHAPTER 23
Two Years Ago, March

It's amazing how someone can turn out to be scarily similar to the person they swore they'd never be like. The apple doesn't fall far from the fucking tree. It's me. I'm the apple.

*T*he Mountain had a grueling, three-week orientation where all the copy editors cycled through each primary department—Lifestyle, Cuisine, and Music. The purpose was for employees to have a working knowledge of every branch of the business and build rapport with coworkers outside of their department.

After that, we spent another four weeks writing mock articles using various obscure prompts assigned by the department heads. Then editing, reviewing, and proverbially ripping them to shreds.

"There's your way of doing things, then there's *The Mountain* way," Julienne said in that no-nonsense tone I'd already become accustomed to. "You can't be a good editor if you're a shit writer, and your writing needs to feel like it's coming from *The Mountain*. Not some high school creative writing course."

By our ninety-day mark, we'd settled into our roles with a consistent flow of work.

Wren, Ha-Joon, and I shared a trio of desks separated by paper-thin dividers and worked on a rotating schedule of reviewing and editing articles for the Online Daily blog. Despite our differing personalities, the three of us melded somehow, whether it be by trauma bonding through work stress or by sheer proximity. We had something to prove and felt the same in our positions—challenged to keep up, happy to take on new responsibilities, and desperate to stand out amongst the talent that poured out of *The Mountain*'s doors.

Boston was good for my soul. It gave me the separation I needed to tap into who I was outside of being a student and who I wanted to be in the future, with no distractions. Pouring myself into work provided a sense of place and purpose. Like I could move on, not only from Sumner U and Hartwood, but from the bad habits and immaturities that lingered inside me, too.

They seemed so obvious once I got distance from them. The habit of comparing myself to Gemma, for example. It was born from feeling inadequate compared to her, which she was in no way responsible for. I couldn't have been happier for her next chapter—both with and without Grant—and I felt so lucky to have her full support in my next chapter, too. Living together, though, no matter how much I loved her, had run its course.

I'd also decided I was no longer okay with not knowing where I stood with people.

The ambiguity of Nate's and my relationship—friendship, situation-ship, whatever—and how it ended had done a number on my mental health, more than I'd realized. It struck a painful chord, yes, but it also taught me a lesson. It was easier said than done, and I had no idea how long it would take me to get better at it, but I knew I needed more clarity from the people in my life.

If only it stopped me from thinking about him all the time.

Wren and I became fast friends. Well, *she* became fast friends with *me*. "I can't do small talk forever, so we might as well get right into it," she'd said on our second day at *The Mountain*.

She kept me from isolating myself by dragging me out of my apartment most weekends. Sometimes, it was to go out for drinks, but more often than not, it was to go to local festivals or concerts. Ha-Joon was the most introverted of the three of us, but we peer-pressured him into joining us often enough that we eventually got through his meek exterior. It was refreshing being around people who knew and appreciated music as much as I did and who got the same high from watching live performances.

After six months of working at *The Mountain*, Julienne gave us work-from-home privileges that only required us to come into the office twice a week.

"You've been here long enough, I trust you to do your jobs and do them well. I don't care where you work or what hours," she said, standing almost as tall as Ha-Joon in her power suit and heels. "Work from four to midnight for all I care, just get your shit done, make your deadlines, and don't miss meetings. Cool?"

We knew better than to take advantage of the relaxed schedule. A hundred other people were out there waiting to take our jobs if we fucked up, which meant I was on the hunt for a suitable remote location.

My apartment didn't work. I got restless after a few hours, too distracted by the dishes in the sink and the laundry I'd left dumped on the couch. I experimented with a few other options: alternating between my couch and kitchen table, working from a nearby park on a rare sunny day as the winter snow melted and the first hints of spring arrived.

I kept workshopping new locations until the weather permanently took a turn for the better, and funnily enough, it was a place I'd been before.

It wasn't until I walked in that I realized it was the same cozy little cafe I'd been to with Nate a year and a half prior, the day we picked up Paige's birthday gifts. I craned my neck back outside the door to see the sign overhead: *Full Circle Coffee & Co.*

It was only a few blocks from my apartment, charmingly tucked between an antique store and a bakery. The wide bank of windows overlooking the park beyond let in natural light to warm up the space. The cafe didn't seem too busy, nor was it too slow. There were at least three other patrons camped out at respective tables, working or reading.

It was somehow the perfect fit for my creativity, productivity, and wandering brain. I pushed off the memory of Nate leaning against the counter and the knowledge that NovelB's bookshop was only a short walk away.

For the next few weeks, I unconsciously created a new routine for my days out of the office: wake up, get dressed, go to Full Circle, and order a steaming cup of Earl Grey. Then, I'd sit at the same table every morning, which practically became my property after a week, and work until around two in the afternoon. Then, I'd pack my things, trudge around the block back to my apartment, do a few chores, make an early dinner, and settle back down for another hour or two of work at the kitchen table. I did this over and over again, three times a week for months, letting the pattern wash over me like a steady, cleansing wave.

Before I knew it, I'd been in Boston for a year.

One simple joy of this routine was getting to observe other people's patterns as well. I interacted with the same handful of shop employees, getting to know each of them little by little.

Jade, a barista around my age with short, split-dyed hair, was a fast favorite who worked all the time. I could count on one hand how many times I'd shown up to the cafe to find Jade wasn't already there. Then there was Nolan, a heavily tattooed father of twin toddlers who was also a photographer on the side and made a killer chai latte.

I picked up on the other regular shop patrons, too, and observed them between meetings and edits. My little table sat in the corner along the same wall as the front door, against a window with a perfect view for people watching, conveniently next to a set of power outlets to keep my computer charged.

There was a college-aged girl who speed-walked in every morning with a swinging ponytail of thin braids. There was a florally perfumed older lady who always complained the coffee wasn't hot enough.

But the one who caught my attention a little more than the others was the tall, muscular man with short blond hair and a wide, bright smile. On the days he wore navy medical scrubs, he would dash in and out with his coffee to-go. But other days, he dressed casually and worked from the cafe like me.

He had the vibe of someone who knew they were ridiculously hot, walking into the cafe with a straight back, coiffed hair, and enough self-assurance to fill the room. But he always greeted the baristas with a warm smile and asked, *How are you?* before ordering, something that seemed like common courtesy but was actually pretty rare. I thought it was sweet.

On one occasion, a few months into my favorite new routine, he came in with his scrubs on and caught me looking as he turned to leave with his to-go cup. He did a double take when he caught my eye and flashed a bright smile before rushing through the open door. I smiled back in the awkward way strangers do when they pass each other in a grocery store and ducked my head back to my laptop, embarrassed to have been caught staring.

But from that day on, each time he came in, he would smile or give a boyish upward nod in addition to his friendly interactions with the baristas.

My schoolgirl crush on Scrubs Guy was fed on the rare days he would come in with a laptop, wearing athletic clothes that hugged his broad, muscular frame in all the right places.

Eventually, our interactions became so regular that Scrubs Guy added me to his regular, *How are you?* list. Months passed, smiles and nods and *How are you's* performed like a ritual thrice a week, like a little dance for us regulars at Full Circle Coffee & Co.

"How long are you going to make us fantasize about you two falling in love?" Jade asked one morning. The half of their hair that had once been turquoise was now a soft pink.

"What are you talking about?" I scoffed, genuinely confused, as I spooned honey into my tea at the counter.

"You and Kieran. If we have to watch you make eyes at each other one more day, I might have to force you together *Parent Trap* style."

"Who?"

They leveled a stare at me. "You know. Tall, blond? Usually wears scrubs? Honestly, I wish you would talk already."

Nolan rounded the corner from the back room, his tattooed arms full of cartons of milk to refill the mini fridge behind the counter.

"We have an ongoing bet." Jade folded their arms and scooted closer, leaning in. "We're trying to see how many more days it'll take for one of you to make a move."

"Are we talking about Olive and that doctor guy?" Nolan's head perked up from his crouched position under the counter, suddenly invested.

Jade jutted a thumb at Nolan, eyes wide as if to say, *See?*

"I've never even talked to him," I said, not denying my crush. "What did you say his name was?"

"Kieran." Jade slid my warmed-up blueberry muffin across the counter. "And you two are in love. I don't make the rules."

"I think he does physical therapy?" Nolan rose to full height. "Or sports therapy, or something. I asked him about it once. Seems like a nice guy."

Jade huffed. "I can't be subjected to you ogling at each other one more second before I start playing matchmaker."

"Please don't," I begged, a blush creeping up my cheeks.

The two of them gave me a pointed look, glanced at each other conspiratorially, and went back to work.

CHAPTER 24

Two Years Ago, September

*I remind myself every day that this was what I wanted. My
life is music. I cannot take more than I'm willing to give. I
cannot—will not—make a promise I can't keep.*

I spent the early hours at Full Circle locked into an article that was due
in two days. The re-read was painstakingly slow, but I still managed
to find edits as I went.

I should've gone into the office today.

But I was too locked into the process and too behind schedule to
change the plan.

My last sip of lukewarm Earl Grey did little to keep me warm against
the chilly air as a gust of autumn wind blew through the opening front
door. I fished my arms through the wool sleeves of the cardigan draped
over the back of my chair, never looking up from my screen.

Dammit, another typo.

My fingers snapped back to the keyboard the second they were
through the sleeves, hastily correcting the document. I chewed the
inside of my cheek, eyes scanning slowly for more errors.

I barely registered the man approaching my table, thinking it to be Nolan gathering my empty mug. But when a new mug, heavy and full of brown liquid, clinked right next to the old, my brows pulled together in confusion.

"I guessed English Breakfast," a deep voice said above my head as I stared at the steaming mug, a tea string poking over the side. "I hope that's right."

Scrubs Guy—Kieran—smiled one of his bright smiles down at me.

"Sorry?" I laughed, pulling my lone headphone out of my ear, certain I heard him wrong.

"The tea," he explained, gesturing to the fresh mug. He shifted his weight to his back foot, allowing me to get a full look at him. "I thought English Breakfast would be a safe guess. I hope it's okay I got you a fresh one." He acted politely sheepish, but not an ounce of doubt or trepidation crossed his confident expression.

"Oh!" I smiled down at the mug, then back up at him. "Thank you. That's so sweet." I wasn't drinking English Breakfast. Hardly ever drank English Breakfast, in fact. But the gesture was so kind, I didn't correct him.

"I'm Kieran," he said, ignoring my thanks and holding his hand out to me.

I shook it, debating if I should offer him a seat across from me. But the dark blue scrubs hugging his biceps told me he would be back outside the second his coffee was ready.

"Olive."

"Olive," he repeated back to me, his grin spreading. "I don't mean to be creepy. I just see you here every time I come in and thought I'd introduce myself." His light green eyes sparked along with his thousand-watt smile.

"Don't worry, it's only a little creepy," I teased. "It's nice to officially meet you. Thank you again for the tea."

"Order for Kieran?" Jade called, sliding a to-go cup across the black countertop. They eyed us openly, hair whipping when they snapped their head around to get Nolan's attention. Kieran threw a glance over his shoulder, then turned back to me.

"I'd like to take you out to dinner sometime, Olive."

I wouldn't have been able to hide the surprise on my face if I tried. It was like I short-circuited, blinking twice in quick succession.

He's just… asking me to dinner? Straightforward, just like that? Is this how grown-up men flirt?

I nodded. "Sure, um, yeah. I'd like that."

"Let me get your number." He reached into his pocket, pulling out the latest smartphone on the market.

Nolan did say he was a doctor.

I typed my number into his phone and handed it back, careful not to let it slip through my fingers. He smiled widely once more as he turned on a heel to grab his coffee and head back out into the cool air.

I tracked him out the door and down the sidewalk, mouth no doubt wide open the entire time. My phone buzzed a few seconds later—an unfamiliar number with one word in the text.

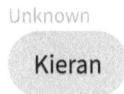

When I gaped at the counter, Jade and Nolan were staring back at me, eyes just as wide as mine, giving each other a sloppy high five.

⟫⟫⟫ ⟪⟪⟪

That weekend, Kieran met me at a steak restaurant that was way too fancy for my usual taste. He'd promised it was the best in Boston, so I put on a tight sweater dress that I would've never worn in Hartwood in an attempt to look steakhouse fancy.

It was clear from the first five minutes of the date that he oozed confidence and charisma. I was honestly surprised at how interested in me he seemed, but more, how interested I was in him.

"So you work for a media company?" he asked over his gin and tonic. I tracked the movement of his tongue as he licked a drop from his bottom lip.

"Yes, technically," I said, sipping my too-dry red wine. When we'd ordered, I was about to tell him I wasn't a red wine girl before he insisted I *had* to try it if I was eating steak. *It's the best pairing,* he grinned, *trust me.* "It's an entertainment and production company, but my focus is primarily on the music industry. New trends, artists on the rise, that kind of thing. I'm mostly editing for the online blog."

"Very cool." He nodded with so much genuine interest that it made me want to sink into my seat. It *was* cool, but he made it feel like the coolest thing since sliced bread.

"It has its perks. Being able to work from a coffee shop, for starters. They encourage us to immerse ourselves in music as much as possible. Concerts and album release parties and all that."

"It must be fun getting to do your hobby for your job. Is that what you want to do forever?"

He was making small talk, but my insecurities caught the edge in his words. I reminded myself that mine was an industry most people didn't know anything about. It wasn't just a hobby; it was hard work.

"I don't know," I answered truthfully. "I love my job. It's the only thing I see myself doing right now, and there's room to climb. So, who knows?"

"Hmm." He nodded.

"What about you?"

"I'm a physical therapist."

Nolan guessed right. "That explains the scrubs." I sipped my wine again and bit back a grimace.

"That it does. And the need for daily mid-morning coffee," he said with a smile.

Kieran did everything right, as if he'd learned it all from a book. He showed up to the date on time, a few minutes early, in fact. He told me I looked beautiful when we were seated, let me order first, held conversation effortlessly, and paid for the meal. It was the first time in my life I could say I'd been wined and dined.

Afterward, he held my hand as we walked the handful of blocks to my car. I'd insisted on meeting him at the restaurant instead of having him pick me up because I wasn't interested in giving my home address to a practical stranger just yet, but I was glad for the few extra minutes to chat as we walked.

"So, how long have you been single?" I asked, surprising myself.

He chuckled. "A while. But honestly, we don't have to do the whole past-relationship breakdown thing. I know most people talk about that kind of stuff on dates, but I'm not interested in who you were before we met. I'm interested in who you are now."

His words stunned me into silence for a beat. And for some reason, though it had been so long, Nate's face flashed through my mind. *I'm interested in who you are now.* How fitting? I was more interested in who I was now, too.

And at my driver's door, Kieran gave me an innocent kiss on the cheek, a blinding smile, and told me to let him know when I made it home safely.

The entire thing was… smooth. Suspiciously smooth.

What's the catch?

Chapter 25

Now

Sometimes I wish I would keep my mouth shut.

I'm not sure what compelled me to keep walking. My feet carried me over the uneven terrain between the rows of vines, closer to Nate as he scribbled away in the notebook I'd seen a thousand times.

His brows drew together as he concentrated. The profile of his familiar, handsome face—his straight nose, the angle of his jaw—took the breath out of my lungs. He eventually closed the leather-bound notebook, shoved it into his back pocket, and raked a hand through his hair. Head bent, he watched his sneakers as he started walking again, instead of the beauty of the vineyard around him.

I chewed the inside of my lip, thinking it better to turn around before that sinking, unsettled feeling from earlier returned, but I didn't. I remembered my guilt and followed, closing our distance in a few short seconds.

"What are you doing up so early, Cassidy?"

He whipped around at the sound, hair falling over his forehead with the movement. As he pushed the locks back into place in that classically

Nate way, I spied a small tattoo of the Crescent Light logo peeking from under the sleeve of his black zip-up. It was new.

He huffed a laugh that was more like a sigh when his eyes focused on me. "Couldn't sleep."

Nodding, I tugged at the sleeves of my sweater. "Me neither." I shifted my weight, thinking I should explain my sudden appearance. "I went out hunting for some tea and saw the paths down here."

"Yeah." He glanced toward the far-away main building. "I was hoping to find some coffee, but the cafe wasn't open yet. Thought a walk would do me some good." His eyes shifted to mine and back to his feet on the path as he tentatively took another step. "Do you... wanna join me?"

I hesitated, knowing I should say no, but felt pulled forward anyway. I fell into a slow pace beside him, the path so narrow, our arms ghosted past each other with each step.

"So, how've you been?" I didn't dare to look at his face but settled on making eye contact with his shoulder. "I guess I didn't ask you last night." My steps slowed to a halt. "I'm sorry, by the way. I know I was being a dick." He mirrored my movements, slowing and half-turning to face me. "I just... I don't know. I didn't expect to see you."

His eyes dropped to his shoes again. "I'm not sure how to respond. I mean, you did tell me I wasn't allowed to look at you or smile at you, and I wouldn't want to break your rules." He lifted his gaze enough that I could see the amusement twinkling in his eyes.

I tsked. "See? What a dickish thing for me to say."

"You don't have to apologize, Oli, it's fine." He chuckled. "I probably deserve it." He took a casual step on the path again. "And I've been good. Really good. The band's doing great. We, uh—" He rubbed the back of his neck. "We have our first European tour coming up soon. So, that's exciting."

I pretended I didn't already know. As a writer for *The Mountain*, it was my job to keep my finger on the pulse for groups on the rise like Crescent Light. Not that my personal tie to the band didn't have me keeping tabs anyway.

"Nate, that's huge—congratulations. You should be really proud of yourself; you guys deserve it."

His lips pressed into a wide, close-lipped smile, and I had a perfect shot of his dimple as it flashed. My eyes lingered there, savoring the familiar sight before it disappeared again.

"Still liking Boston?" he asked.

So much to say, yet so much I didn't *want* to say.

So I settled on, "I love it."

It was weird making small talk with Nate. We'd always somehow been beyond it. Too good for it, even that very first night. He'd always had a knack for jumping right into conversation like we were lifelong friends.

This? This wasn't us.

This felt like we were actors on a stage, dramatically playing the role of two people who'd always been platonic, friendly acquaintances. Not fuck buddies who turned into friends, who fell apart and became strangers who still unfortunately had mutual friends and were forced to be in the same place from time to time.

But there we were.

"So," he began a while later, once we'd turned back in the direction of the main path to the resort. The shift in his tone sent my alarms off, and I knew his words before he said them. "That guy you're here with."

It was bound to come up. Nate could never resist asking the tough questions. I nodded slowly. "Kieran."

"Is that the same guy you were so upset about? Back when—"

"Nate," I warned, my memory flashing to that last night Nate and I spent together. Every time I remembered it, my chest hollowed.

"What?" He huffed a lackadaisical laugh, feigning nonchalance, but his eyes held a lingering seriousness. He wanted his answer.

I halted again to look up into his deep blue eyes. "Let's not do this." It was a stupid request on my part, but it was worth a shot.

He blinked and shifted his feet, the mask of aloof indifference slipping. "I'm just curious if that's him because—"

"Yes," I cut in. "Okay? Yes, that's him."

He pressed his lips into a hard line, recognition painting his brow. "Mmh." He nodded tightly, saying nothing and yet saying *everything.*

The weight of his reaction sat heavily on my chest, but I didn't turn away from it. Instead, I held Nate's gaze for a long minute, unmoving and unblinking.

The space between us filled to the brim with all the things we weren't saying, the things we should have said a long time ago.

I swallowed. "Look, I—"

His eyes flicked over my shoulder and settled on something behind me. "Speak of the devil."

I glanced back before screwing my eyes shut and taking a big step away from Nate, increasing the distance between us. We didn't say another word as we walked the rest of the way to the path's starting point. Kieran loomed on the brick platform there, looking a little worse for wear with his disheveled hair and dark circles, but he waited patiently regardless.

When we neared the end of the trail, Nate hung back a step.

"Hey, you," I said casually, keeping my tone light as I closed in on Kieran. "How are you feeling?"

Kieran held out an arm for me to walk into, circling it around my shoulders as he bent to kiss my temple. He held on a little tighter than usual, his lips on my hairline lingering for an extra beat. Just for Nate to see.

"Like shit," he answered. "I was heading down to get something to eat. Figured I'd find you on the way." He leaned a fraction closer so only I could hear. "Especially since you didn't answer my texts."

"Well, you found me." I laced my fingers with his, which were still draped over my shoulders. I made to turn us away from the field when Kieran spoke again.

"Good to see you, Nathan."

"Nate," Nate and I corrected in unison. I cringed.

Nate's eyes narrowed for a split second before he assumed a carefully relaxed posture, sliding his hands casually into his front pockets. "And it was Kevin, right?"

"Kieran," Kieran said.

Nate nodded, blinking slowly. "Right."

"Breakfast sounds awesome," I said a little too loudly, patting Kieran's side. "I'm starving. Let's go."

Thankfully, the dining hall for breakfast was on the far side of the main building, but Kieran kept his heavy weight against me the whole walk over.

"What were you guys talking about?" Kieran asked when we were out of earshot.

"Not much, just small talk. I ran into him on the trail."

"It didn't look like small talk. I'm telling you," he said, lowering his voice and whispering into my hair, "that guy definitely wants you."

"Har har." I rolled my eyes, but the pit in my stomach tightened all the same.

I hadn't done anything wrong, so why did I feel like I'd just been caught red-handed? Why did simply being around Nate make me feel like I was doing something scandalous? Part of me wondered if I should've told Kieran the full story right then and there, but the other part of me thought it wasn't worth dredging up the past. There was a reason Kieran and I didn't talk about our exes in detail. It wasn't our style. And up until that point, it was never a problem.

It still wasn't a problem.

Kieran shivered against the morning air, having neglected to grab a sweatshirt. "It's cold out here."

"It feels nice!" I argued. "It was much colder earlier when I first came out."

"Good thing you had Mr. Cool Guy to keep you warm, right?" he teased, but the question lingered, mixed with something I couldn't put my finger on.

I elbowed him.

He caught my arm, chuckling. "Careful. I'm still a little queasy. I might hurl."

"Why in the world are we getting breakfast if you're so hungover you might puke?"

"Because—" He waved to Michael when he spotted him sitting alone at a large table in the back of the sunlit dining room. "The best way to get over a hangover is to keep the party going the next morning."

Michael had a comically large pitcher of mimosas already poised in the center of the table as we approached.

"I don't think that's a good idea."

Chapter 26

Two Years Ago, October

No one else comes close. It's no comparison.

At Monday's all-staff meeting, Julienne announced a competition of sorts that *The Mountain* held once a year. It was open to all employees with less than two years at the company who held the position of editorial assistant or below—a rite of passage they lovingly called The Newcomers Competition, or The Newbie Comp.

The rules? Terrifying, to say the least. Not because they were overly strict and unattainable, but because they were so damn open-ended.

The challenge was for all participants to submit an article on anything related to their sector of the company. The article had to be unlike anything currently in print and "personal to the writer." Whatever that meant.

"The Newbie Comp is a tradition at *The Mountain*. It isn't required, but you'd be stupid not to take the opportunity," Julienne said, her black twists falling over her shoulder as she stood. "It's decently low risk and high reward. Find something missing in the content we cover here, look for the blind spots, and shine a light on them. What do you care about? What content do you want more of? What do our readers need to see that they aren't getting?"

Ha-Joon scribbled notes furiously into his notebook, his straight black hair falling over his forehead as he stooped closer to the paper. I shot Wren a look from across the boardroom table.

What are we getting ourselves into?

Her responding look said, *No fucking clue.*

"We don't ask you to participate for no reason," Julienne continued. "The writer of the article we choose to move forward with will have special perks in the future. For one, a callout on the title page of the February cover."

Four months away. Hushed tones spread in the room. Veteran writers nodded as if reminiscing on their experiences in The Newbie Comp.

"For two, the writer selected will have an edge over their peers next time there's a promotion up for grabs. And three"—Julienne smirked—"bragging rights. Being a published writer for *The Mountain* less than two years into the job."

"Holy shit," Wren mused, stars in her eyes.

"Spend some time stewing on what to produce for this," Julienne continued. "Do your research. Dig deep. I want all the applicants to give me something they genuinely care about. I want to feel it in the writing. And I want someone from our sector to win this damn thing. Applications, along with your article, will be due the first Friday after the New Year."

Wren, Ha-Joon, and I glanced at each other. The three of us were the only copy editors in the music sector eligible for the competition. On top of that, we'd been the writers scrambling for more opportunities, and busting our asses doing grunt work in the meantime. This could be a big break for one of us.

The only problem was that while the two of them jotted down ideas, I could think of nothing. How was I drawing such a blank?

"Could they have been any more vague?" Wren hissed as the three of us sat for lunch at our favorite sushi place across the street an hour later.

"Truly," Ha-Joon agreed. "The word 'unique' should be eradicated from the planet. What does that even mean by today's standards? There is nothing left that is truly original. It literally doesn't exist."

"I think they just want it to feel like something more opinion-based?" I spooned my miso soup. "Julienne used the word 'personal' no less than thirty times."

"So, there's only one article getting chosen? I'm so exhausted, I feel like I hallucinated the meeting." Wren rested her freckled face in her hands, her mop of red hair tumbling over her shoulders.

I patted her gently between the shoulders. "I saw you writing ideas down, though."

"I was just doodling to look like I was busy," she mumbled into her hands. "Maybe I could do something about classical music? I didn't spend twelve years learning piano for nothing. But who's going to read about that?"

Ha-Joon sat motionless, contemplating potential topics so fervently that I could practically see the gears turning in his head. He was diving into his mental rabbit hole—who was I to stop him? I needed to prepare as much as everyone else, but the paradox of choice left me gridlocked.

My phone buzzed in my lap.

Kieran

Looking forward to seeing you again this weekend.

It turned out there was no "catch" when it came to Kieran. A handful of dates in, and it was hard not to be smitten by Kieran. It was like dating a real grown-up for the first time. Every time we got together, it was exactly as any person would have hoped a budding relationship would be.

For the first time in a long time, there was someone who gave me butterflies. There had been nobody since Nate, and it felt liberating to be touched like that again. Desired like that again. Only this time, it was out in the open for the world to see, not kept like a secret everyone knew but nobody talked about.

I turned my phone face down, shifting my attention back to Wren and Ha-Joon.

"There's time to figure it out," I reassured them, but it was mostly for myself. "Applications aren't due for months, but we can schedule a spitballing sesh if we need to bounce ideas off each other. For now, let's focus on stuffing our faces with sushi, shall we?"

⋙⋙ ⋘⋘

The last Saturday in October started the best way a Saturday in October *can* start. The cold autumn air pushed through my window, cracked open to let the sound of drizzling rain fill the apartment. It pattered gently against the glass while I made my second cup of tea, turned moody acoustic music on, and settled on the couch to brainstorm my Newbie Comp project.

While my peers tackled the project head-on, I'd spent the last two weeks ruminating on what topic to choose.

It had to be personal. Something we individually cared about. Something substantial enough that it required research, compelled us to "dig deep," and was captivating enough to earn me a promotion when the time came.

After brainstorming with Wren and deciding I hated the ideas, I wound up back at my original topic. It was the only one I kept coming back to, no matter where else I tried to look. The only thing I felt passionate enough about—and held strong enough opinions for—to be able to write a compelling article on: the underground, independent artists in the greater New England area who were severely overlooked in the music industry time and time again.

From my experience, some of the most well-versed musicians and lyricists of the decade were relative nobodies in the industry for the worst reason in the world. They had all the talent and skill to become chart-topping, fandom-inspiring, world-touring artists. The only thing they lacked was the right foot in the right door. It was silly for me not to use the potential platform that would come from winning the Newbie Comp to lift those artists up.

I just had to figure out how I was going to tackle the topic in a way that did it justice.

I'd planned to do that for the majority of the day—researching, listening to records, and taking notes—but in the late morning, I was interrupted by my phone buzzing somewhere in the mountain of blankets wrapped around me. Lifting my laptop, I dug around the fluffy down layers until I finally found the lit-up screen.

Kieran

Movie night tonight? My place?

A stupid grin spread across my face. I'd been secretly waiting for the invitation, knowing it was going to come soon.

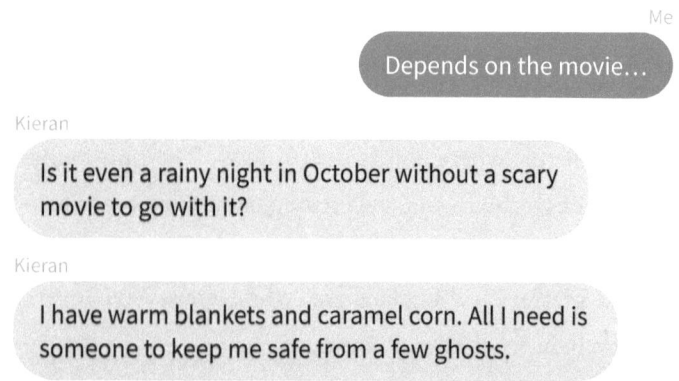

Me

Depends on the movie…

Kieran

Is it even a rainy night in October without a scary movie to go with it?

Kieran

I have warm blankets and caramel corn. All I need is someone to keep me safe from a few ghosts.

I rolled my eyes. *Cheese ball.* And yet, my grin grew.

Me

HA that was terrible.

Me

Okay. You've convinced me

Me

Only because of the caramel corn though

The three dots next to his name appeared, then disappeared. I watched as they appeared and disappeared a second time before I mentally smacked myself for staring at the stupid dots to begin with. Tossing my phone back on the couch, I stood and stretched my cramped legs, but still lunged for it the second his reply buzzed.

Kieran

We may as well make it a sleepover while we're at it.

That night, I drove to Kieran's house with music blaring to drown out my thoughts and the nervous energy crept up my throat.

Not that I was counting, but two years had passed since I'd been intimate with anything that wasn't silicone and lived in my dresser drawer. Not since that last time with Nate, before I found out about his girlfriend. I shook the bitter memory from my thoughts.

It doesn't matter anymore.

If we were talking technicalities, this was my fifth date with Kieran. And spending the night meant exactly one thing.

I attempted to do more project research after his text that morning; then I pretended to read, pretended to watch TV, and pretended to clean, all the while fixating on what the evening promised.

I gave up around three o'clock to take an Everything Shower. The kind where you exit the bathroom as a brand new, fully formed, smooth, exfoliated, moisturized, virtually hairless goddess. Then I went to the store to pick up a bottle of Kieran's favorite red wine—*you can't show up empty-handed, right?*—and ended up also buying a new pair of lacy underwear and a matching pajama set.

Kieran's house was positioned on the corner of a quaint brick road in a beautifully historic side of town. His neighborhood was unsurprisingly picturesque, with tall trees decorating the view, their crunchy orange and yellow leaves floating through the air as the soft evening breeze blew through.

He's living in a Hallmark movie.

I parked on the street, and before I could open the door, Kieran was already striding down the front path, which, of course, was lined with brick and perfectly landscaped.

"Hey," he said, pulling my overnight bag out of my hands despite my objections.

The inside of Kieran's house was as beautiful as the outside. The house itself had so much character that very little decoration was needed, but I had to give him some credit. The hardwood floors in each room were accented by subdued, muted area rugs. The huge leather sectional couch in the living room matched perfectly with the mahogany coffee table and gold lamps throughout the first floor. A fireplace crackled gently, creating an autumnal ambiance that made me want to curl up with a blanket and never leave.

As we rounded the corner into the kitchen, I spied an array of snacks spread across the deep countertop. "What's all this?" I smiled.

"Movie snacks." Kieran grinned.

Dried fruits, mixed nuts, pretzels—not my personal pick for movie snacks, but still sweet—and, *thank god*, the promised caramel corn. Next to the snacks, low-calorie spiked seltzer and all the makings for whatever cocktail I might want to drink.

"You didn't have to do all this."

Will I ever get to a place where I don't feel uncomfortable when someone does something thoughtful for me? Probably not.

"Of course I did." He reached for the bottle of wine in my hands. I stared at the corded muscles in his arms as he inserted the bottle opener and began twisting the cork out of the neck. "I'm trying to impress you, remember?"

I scoffed, reaching for the caramel corn and popping a piece into my mouth. "Consider me impressed."

The sun was setting as we turned on the first movie—a horror film about a secret cult of ancient witches using blood magic to lure young men to their deaths. *Good for them*, I thought, as the first victim unwittingly thought he could violate the supreme witch's sister and get away with it.

Kieran's house was as drafty as it was charming. Halfway through the movie, he retrieved a thick comforter from the hall closet and draped it over the two of us, tucking me close to his side. I didn't mind the chill. In fact, it—combined with the scary movie and the crackling fireplace—only made me want to cuddle up more.

We stayed that way until the end credits snaked menacingly across the screen to an eerie ambient tune. Other than our cuddling, Kieran kept his hands fairly to himself the entire movie, which drove me crazy. Something about the act of having a movie night where we *actually* watched the movie instead of using it as background noise for other nocturnal activities was a turn-on.

"Okay." Kieran's eyes squinted at the TV as he stood, absentmindedly rubbing a hand over the scruff on his chin. After a brief intermission to use the restroom and pour another glass of wine, we debated the next movie. "What's the next vibe we're feeling? Serial killer trying to break into a cabin or a classic possessed doll?"

"Definitely the serial killer," I decided, sipping my red wine, grimacing.

"Exactly what I was thinking."

Joining me again on the couch, we maneuvered and adjusted until we were lying down, my back against his chest, his arms draped under my head and over the curve of my waist. The movie started with an immediate scare, which had me jumping an inch off the couch. He laughed at me as if he didn't jump too.

The movie pressed on, the serial killer stalking his prey from the edge of the woods before the main character realized there was no phone reception and nowhere to go. Kieran idly drew circles on my hip as we watched, fingers pausing only when the anticipation of the movie rose.

My attention drifted halfway through as his circles traveled up my hip and around my waist, playing with the inch of skin showing above my jeans.

The innocent woman on the screen looked out her window to see the serial killer standing just on the other side of the glass, staring at her, and I kept my eyes glued to the screen as Kieran's hands continued their ministrations around the soft skin of my belly. When his fingers inched up at a snail's pace, my breath deepened in anticipatory response.

His lips traveled closer to my neck, his facial hair ticklish and maddening all at once. I tilted my head to give him better access to the sensitive skin and thought, *This is it*, when he planted a lingering kiss to my neck.

"Upstairs?"

I had no idea how Kieran and I happened. One day, we were strangers, and then we weren't. But after that night, he was mine.

CHAPTER 27

Now

*I'm not a violent guy, but what's the resort policy
on hitting someone?*

I recognized other wedding guests filtering into the dining hall as we sat for breakfast. Some of them looked a bit hungover from the welcome party the night before, others were bright-eyed, bushy-tailed, and ready for more festivities.

Most dressed casually, likely in preparation for early activities. As part of Gemma's dream wedding weekend, I'd helped her schedule a down day for folks who traveled to experience the area. Part of that included pre-organized excursions and tours in the surrounding area that guests could opt-in to with their RSVP.

Some were trips to local wineries; some were day trips to San Francisco to see touristy locations like Alcatraz Island and Fisherman's Wharf. At the request of Gemma's mother, there was also a bus to shuttle any interested guests to nearby shops throughout the day.

It was the perfect way for Grant and Gemma to get out of hosting duties all day so they could whittle away at Gemma's last-minute wedding to-do list.

With my help, of course.

Kieran and I joined Michael at the large table he was holding. We wasted no time ordering food. I wasn't lying when I told Kieran I was starving and rejected his offer to split something.

Martinez sauntered up to our table just as my tart mimosa touched my lips.

"Thank fuck," he said, plopping down at my side. "I was hoping you'd have mimosas at the ready."

Behind him, Miles, Leo, and Jared followed. Rounding out the group, to my infinite luck, was Nate.

Maybe it was the hunch of his shoulders or the way he kept his head dipped low, but I got the sense he was hiding behind Jared as they approached. Maybe he was just as at odds with his feelings as I was. His eyes met mine for a split second as if to say, *Sorry,* as he took the last seat on the far side of the table.

Unfortunately, our split-second look wasn't lost on Kieran. He brought his arm around to rest territorially on the back of my chair as a large plate of waffles was plopped in front of me.

While Kieran was a physically affectionate guy by nature, it was usually in sweet, subtle ways: a hand around the waist, a quick kiss on the temple. But this? Clinging to me, hanging heavy arms across my shoulders? It felt forced. Performative.

And I couldn't help but notice that this new habit of his seemed to flare whenever Nate was present.

Who is this guy, and where was my confident boyfriend?

I did my best to keep my eyes glued to the waffles in front of me and not let them drift anywhere near the man at the end of the table, but there was that magnetic pull again. That force of nature that guided my eye to his every time I took a drink of my mimosa, or anxiously adjusted my hair, or leaned in to hear someone speak.

I was once again incredibly grateful for my friend's discretion as they attempted to ignore the tension that could've been cut with a knife. Jared—never one to control his facial expressions—thankfully kept his eyes trained anywhere and everywhere that was not Nate and me.

Martinez, bless him, started nudging my knee under the table any time he caught my eyes lingering for too long. Were it not for Michael and Kieran's general cluelessness and preoccupation with sports talk, this would've been a very different breakfast.

"Who's all going out today?" Leo asked over his mimosa.

"Raise your hand if you're joining the booze cruise!" Michael boomed, his hand shooting high in the air.

Martinez's hand shot up like lightning next to him, and Miles and Leo's hands followed.

"Woah, woah, wait," Kieran perked up. "What's the booze cruise?"

I eyed him incredulously. He knew what the booze cruise was—he'd heard me talk about it with Gemma over multiple FaceTime planning calls. Otherwise known as a sensible, private boat tour of the San Francisco Bay, the "booze cruise" also happened to have a full-service bar on board.

Even if I wasn't going to be preoccupied with assisting Gemma today, I knew the booze cruise was probably the last activity I'd want to join. Spending the whole day outside in the sun, stuck on a boat with no food and a bottomless bar, enduring the choppy San Francisco Bay water? Yeah, no thanks.

"Babe, we're definitely doing that today," Kieran said with finality.

I prickled. "I can't. I'm helping Gemma today." I'd only told him about it five times. "And so are you, remember?"

We'd planned for Kieran to stick around to help us with some of the last-minute tasks in case we found ourselves in need of extra manpower from someone who regularly hit the gym.

"Gemma's got plenty of help," Michael insisted. But what did he know? He was the brother; I was the best friend. He wasn't the one who'd been helping Gemma plan for over a year.

Jared leaned over Martinez. "I'm helping today, too, Olive."

I knew that already. Gemma and I had planned it all out: who would do which tasks, who would help, and who would be on retainer as a backup just in case. Jared would help Grant with some of the heavy lifting, I would help Gemma with decor, and Kieran would be an extra set of hands.

"See?" Kieran pointed to Jared. "He's staying to help so we can go on the booze cruise."

My cheeks flushed. Did we really have to have this conversation in front of a table full of people? Already, an awkward silence descended. From the corner of my eye, Nate adjusted in his seat, stretched his neck.

"I can't," I repeated. "Jared's helping Grant. I'm helping Gemma."

"Well, I'm going," he said, leaning back in his seat, then added as an afterthought, "if that's cool with you."

I nodded tightly, sipping my mimosa. "Have fun."

A little embarrassed and a lot frustrated, I kept my head down for the rest of breakfast and pretended everything was fine.

Nate's gaze prickled my skin with every glance. Even without looking at him, I could feel it like a sixth sense, a hot brand against my skin. I was hyperaware and couldn't shut it off. Every time his voice cut through the din of the dining room, every time he laughed at something ridiculous Martinez said, the sound danced over my senses. Ignoring him was impossible.

When our eyes met again from across the table—just a quick peek over the rim of his glass as he drank—something else lingered there. Instead of the knot in my belly twisting tight, the look gave me a certain... comfort? Relaxation? Like releasing a breath after holding it for too long. It was our silent communication. A look that asked, *You okay?*

I'd be lying if I said part of me wasn't happy we got the chance to talk in the vineyard. I was happy for him. Happy he was finally doing all the things he worked so hard for. Happy Crescent Light was getting the attention they deserved. Maybe I didn't know where we stood—go figure—but I felt like I could finally let go of some of my animosity.

It was nice. Like catching up with an old friend.

Nothing more.

CHAPTER 28

Two Years Ago, November

Days without smoking: ~~23~~ 0

The Newbie Comp effectively took over my life in the best way possible. Once I narrowed down the topic I wanted to focus on, a fire ignited under my creativity.

I spent my days meticulously researching musical artists currently in rotation—solo singer-songwriters and groups alike—in the greater New England area. Artists who were more than deserving of attention but who hadn't been given a proper platform to be heard. I had two groups already in mind that I listened to regularly, one of whom I saw perform live with Gemma during our second year of grad school. It was a good start, but a better sample was needed to research and compare.

The project had me watching live performances and listening to music through a new lens and with a new sense of purpose. I found myself poring over lyrics line by line, dissecting them, stewing on them. I dug into the history of each group and learned who they drew inspiration from and who influenced them. Within a few short weeks of research, I set out to see as many of my chosen artists perform live as I could.

It helped that a lot of them had overlap in their fanbases. So much overlap that some of the artists performed in the same lineups, opening shows for one another.

It was only a matter of time before my research led me to a band that was all too familiar.

I was scrolling through the social media pages of a little-known alternative band when a photo caught my eye. The band's drummer leaned with an arm slung around Jared Christensen's neck, the pair of them holding drumsticks high in the air. The caption confirmed it wasn't a hallucination.

Thank you, Washington, DC! Shoutout to @crescentlightband for letting us share the stage tonight.

Suddenly, my apartment felt too cold.

Crescent Light had been steadily gaining popularity throughout Massachusetts and beyond over the last two years. I shouldn't have been shocked when their name kept popping up in my research, but it was no less jarring each time I saw it. Abandoning my laptop on my couch, I grabbed an oversized hoodie and slipped it on, burying my face under the hood.

If I wanted to be as fair and unbiased in the project as possible, I had a responsibility to exhaust all options that fit my requirements. As much as I wanted to turn a blind eye to Crescent Light, it wouldn't be fair. They belonged with the best.

I tucked my legs under me, returning to my laptop screen.

Thirty minutes. Give them thirty minutes of research. If they're a good fit, they get added to the shortlist. If they aren't, they don't.

It was a stupid thought. I knew they would make the cut before I even typed their name into the search bar.

With embarrassingly shaking hands, I pulled up their discography and pressed play. I found it helped to listen to the music as I did research; it allowed me to fully immerse myself in the feel of the artist I was digging into. I recognized the first song immediately as one of the older tracks I used to have saved on my phone. Well, it was *still* saved to my phone, I just never listened to it. The sound of Nate's voice sent a frisson across my shoulders and down my arms.

God. My eyes closed. *I forgot how good his voice is.*

Crescent Light's popularity wasn't limited to Massachusetts anymore. According to the set of concert dates on one of their posts, they'd played as opening acts for other popular bands in Connecticut, DC, New York, New Jersey, and up to Maine. They even headlined a few shows, selling out one in a decent-sized venue. No longer were they confined to playing in tiny bars and at open mic nights. Their social media also revealed they'd released an EP not long after I moved to Boston. Not surprising. Nate worked on it day and night the last few weeks we were on speaking terms.

They were set to release a full-length album soon and were promoting the hell out of it on their social media pages, which had risen to over ten thousand followers.

Posts were either of updates about their new album, promotions for one of their three EPs, or an aesthetically artsy shot of an instrument: a black and white drum set photo, a microphone in a shabby soundproofed makeshift studio, a close-up shot of hands playing the piano—Leo's, if I had to guess. There were some photos of the members, but almost all were of them on stage, backlit so severely that they were indecipherable.

But there was only one photo of Nate.

I tried not to skim the page with the intention of looking for him, but dammit, my eyes deceived me. The song playing through my laptop speakers shifted to another, one I didn't recognize, but I barely paid attention to it.

The photo was a shot taken from the vantage point of someone standing over him as he sat on a low footstool. He had one long leg splayed out in front of him while the other was bent ninety degrees with an acoustic guitar resting atop it. His small leather notebook balanced open on one knee, and he squinted like he was reading as he played. The photo didn't show his face, just his messy mop of dark brown hair and a hint of his perfect jawline. The caption read, *Fearless leader hard at work*, with a guitar emoji.

I don't know why I sat and stared at the photo for so long. It had been nearly two years since I'd last seen him, since the last time we laughed together, slept together.

Since he made me feel disposable.

I blinked the thought away. Clicking the link at the top of their social media page led me to the band's website. Most of it was the usual: their band's logo at the top, promotions for the EPs, a timer in big, grey lettering counting down the weeks and days until the new album. I clicked on the *Shop* tab in the menu and was led to a page dedicated to their extremely limited merchandise: a few logo t-shirt designs, some enamel pins, signed albums, and a lyric book. I toggled back to the menu and paused for a moment at the tab labeled *Tour* before clicking.

And wouldn't you know it? As luck would have it, Crescent Light was coming right to my backyard. The next fucking weekend. I clicked to view the show info.

Shit.

Not only was Crescent Light headlining the show, there were two opening acts. Of the two, one had already made it to my short list of artists I wanted to research more.

No. I told myself. *Absolutely not. Crescent Light probably doesn't even qualify for my project.*

They did qualify. In fact, they were a perfect candidate based on the parameters I set for my research weeks prior.

Currently, Crescent Light's shows were exclusively in New England and the East Coast, with nothing abroad or nationwide of note.

They had less than five hundred thousand streams on their most popular song and had less than two hundred fifty thousand monthly listeners.

They had never charted on a nationally-recognized music chart, and they had never been nominated for a major music award.

Even their *style* perfectly matched what I was seeking.

Their music was a unique blend of modern indie rock that also pulled inspiration from pop, alternative, and folk. Each member was trained in more than one instrument, making them diverse in their individual talent and in their experimentation with the band's sound. They oozed talent and charisma and were slowly but surely building their platform into something that I knew in my bones could be *big*.

The pieces fell into place too nicely. I couldn't ignore that, try as I might.

My project needed them. And Crescent Light deserved to be in *The Mountain.*

I took a steadying breath as I pressed *Buy* on a set of tickets and braced myself to see Nate Cassidy in the flesh.

>>>>> <<<<<

"What are you doing next weekend?" I asked Wren over lunch the next day.

She stabbed a heaping pile of lettuce onto her fork, fishing for a crouton. "No idea. I don't plan my life that far in advance."

True. "I need a date for this concert I'm going to. It's… for my project."

"Why did you say it like it's an alibi?"

I bit the inside of my cheek. "Well, it's mostly for my project. Like eighty-five percent."

She blinked between chews of her too-big bite of salad.

"But I could also use the moral support?"

Her green eyes narrowed. "Haven't you gone to, like, three shows by yourself so far? What makes this one so special that you need a support buddy?"

I grumbled and pushed strawberries around on my plate. While I'd made a point of leaving my past *firmly* in the past when I moved to Boston, Wren was my closest friend after Gemma, and there was a lot she didn't know about me. If there was anyone I could tell the full truth to, it was her.

"I'm researching this band, Crescent Light, for the Newbie Comp. I used to listen to them a lot. They're… brilliant. Super talented. Definitely a group that deserves to be highlighted, and honestly, my project needs them. But…"

She leaned incrementally, eyebrows raising. "But?"

"I kind of used to be fuck buddies with the singer?" I grimaced, splaying my hands out in front of me as if to say *ta-da!*

Droplets of water splashed on the table as she choked—bad timing on my part—and coughed loudly, eyes bulging.

"Way to bury the lead, Olive!" She coughed again. "Okay. Hang on." She slid her half-empty plate to the edge of the table, wiped a few stray crumbs away, and took another sip of water. Then, she leaned forward, folding her hands in front of her as if in prayer. "Tell me everything."

So I did.

I figured, at the very least, Wren would have a unique, fully non-biased, third-party perspective on everything. We took a long lunch so I could tell her every detail. The good, the bad, the confusing, all of it. I even told her things I'd only ever hinted to Gemma that even *she* didn't get the full scoop on. It was the first time I'd ever let myself look at the full picture of my relationship with Nate with hindsight. The first time I ever said all my feelings out loud.

I used to care so deeply about him, and once upon a time, I thought he cared about me, too. But he was always so caught up in his own orbit, and I deserved better than to sit on the sidelines and wait for him to want me. No matter how much I used to like him.

The weight of those words, ignored and unacknowledged for two years, lifted off my shoulders, and the relief washed through my system.

Wren listened to the whole story, gasping and laughing at all the right times. She interjected for clarification here and there but stayed with me, letting me get the history off my chest.

"So, yeah." I leaned back with a huff. "That's the last time I talked to him."

"You left him on the fucking sidewalk?" She giggled. "God, you're such a badass. I would kill to see his dumb expression when he realized how bad he messed up."

I laughed. "Did he mess up, though? He was single and got a girlfriend. No crime in that."

"No, but he had someone amazing right in front of him and then fumbled the bag. Maybe he isn't a villain, but he's definitely stupid."

Gemma's words from the night I met Nate rang through my mind: *Boys are stupid.*

"Also," Wren continued, "why do men out here have the communication skills of toddlers? He never texted you? Nothing?"

I shook my head, smiling at the ridiculousness. "He probably thought I didn't want to hear from him." I stopped my thoughts before I could consider what would have happened if he had reached out. "So, will you go to the show with me or not?"

"To see the hot singer you used to have sex with? Abso-fucking-lute-ly."

CHAPTER 29

Two Years Ago, November

Delicate as a petal
Hot as a brand
Under my skin
Without, within

The line for the Crescent Light concert was still wrapped around the building twenty minutes after the doors opened. On one hand, that was amazing. Any up-and-coming band should be thrilled to have a line of concert-goers out the door. But on the other hand, on some level, it shocked me to my core.

Crescent Light had gained popularity. Logically, I knew that from my research. But in my mind, I couldn't imagine it. They were stunted. Stuck forever in that place where they only played open mic nights and small gigs in stuffy bars like Brick Road Bar for crowds of no more than forty people.

But my image of them shifted as Wren and I shuffled along in line, surrounded by fans wearing Crescent Light merch. Their logo—a giant crescent moon resembling the letter *C* with a capital *L* tucked inside of it—was everywhere. On the front of shirts, on enamel pins stuck on denim jackets, even on phone cases.

A group of girls who looked to be no older than sixteen stood in front of us wearing shirts that looked custom-made with photos of each band member printed on the back.

What are they, the indie Backstreet Boys?

"Who's that one?" Wren asked, boldly pointing to one of the girls' backs. "He's got that tortured-yet-sexy vibe to him."

I laughed. "That's Leo."

Nate's distorted face stared back at me from one of their shirts. Even *that* proximity was enough to make me nervous.

Finally inside, the venue was abuzz with excited fans pouring to the bars and the restrooms for last-second relief before the show.

"God, this place is packed," Wren shouted over the music and the noise as we filed into the main hall. The concert was for general admission only.

"Let's go up to the mezzanine. We'll get trampled down here." Lacing her fingers with mine, I dragged her to the staircase.

"There better be a bar up there!"

There was. The line was thankfully a little shorter than the one on the ground floor, but still felt miserably long as I fidgeted in place, desperate to get this over with. We got beers and found a decent spot along the front row of the mezzanine level.

House lights dimmed, signaling the show was about to start, and I took in the stage. The drum kit of the opening act sat in the middle, but the Crescent Light one sat upstage, barely concealed and entirely distracting. I was distinctly aware of the knowledge that Nate was in the same building I was standing in.

I peeked down over the edge of the mezzanine to the crowd below, packed in like sardines, only getting more and more squished as the last of the line outside filed in. There had to be at least five hundred of them down there, plus the additional two hundred or so up on the second level that wrapped around the whole hall. I pulled my phone out for the tenth time in twenty minutes, checking the time.

Anxiety fizzled through my blood, knotting up my stomach, making my palms sweaty. I took a purposeful, long breath in through my nose and released it slowly out through my mouth.

Everything's fine.

Anxiety is a funny thing. The fact that I had to frequently remind my brain and body that I was not in imminent danger on a semi-regular basis was silly and nonsensical. But that was just part of living with it. My logical mind knew there was nothing wrong, yet the physical reactions shouted otherwise.

I calmed my racing thoughts by opening the professional part of my brain as the opening band took to the stage.

The Collective Three was, ironically, a five-member group that was known very little in the area, from what I could tell. Yet their style was uniquely their own. I mentally cataloged every detail about them, so deep in my project research that I couldn't help but listen critically. Their music tended to lean heavily into alternative rock, but they consistently used funk-inspired baselines to support their rhythm sections. It was all complemented by their singer, who had an extraordinarily soulful voice that was surprising based on the heavy tattoos and piercings that covered every surface of his body. Overall, I was pleasantly surprised and decided to do a deeper dive on them when I had the time. If not for the Newbie Comp, then for my personal playlists.

The next artist, one I was already researching before discovering tonight's show, took the stage. She was a singer-writer by the name of Leyanna, who had the voice of an angel and a modest backing band. Her black hair hung in long, straight curtains around her narrow face and down her slim shoulders as she sang the most heartbreakingly sad lyrics I'd ever heard. The crowd sang along, swaying to her melodic songs and dancing to her poppier tracks. Throughout my research, I'd become a genuine fan of hers, and I danced right along with the crowd. As her set came to a close, my nerves ramped up again like a tidal wave rushing from my stomach, up my chest, and into my throat.

Leyanna left in a parting of thunderous applause, and as the crew descended on the stage, an excited hum started anew in the venue. The stage crew cleared her band's equipment and made way for Crescent Light, readjusting everything until it was all set and in place.

"You ready?" Wren asked, nudging me in the ribs. She probably noticed I was looking a little green as I stared a hole into the stage like a baby deer caught in headlights.

"Not even a little bit."

I felt her gaze on me, but I didn't meet her eye. After a long second, she leaned closer. "He still gets under your skin, doesn't he?"

It wasn't accusatory. She said it like it was a fact. An observation, and nothing more. I didn't answer, I just nodded.

It was as close as I would get to admitting I missed him. His company. His voice. His laugh. The freckle between his shoulder blades. She wrapped an arm around my shoulders and gave me a reassuring squeeze.

※※※　※※※

My eyes remained glued to the stage when the venue went pitch black. All was quiet for a split second before lights from the back of the stage flooded outward, bathing the crowd in illumination. It reminded me of midnight in the countryside during a full moon when everything shines from the sky alone and leaves a haunting blue haze on the otherwise dark world.

Four shadowy figures emerged, backlit, each indecipherable from the other. The crowd went wild, screaming and pushing closer to the stage, pressing as near as they could to the four men. They took their places—one sitting at the waiting drum set, two dispersing stage left and stage right, and one coming straight forward, looping a guitar strap around his broad shoulders.

I stood frozen, feeling the anticipation of every person in the venue racing through my veins, like any second, my fight or flight might kick in and send me bolting out the door.

An acoustic guitar cut through the noise of the crowd, a soft and simple melody I recognized immediately as the very first Crescent Light song I ever heard. The one from that night at Brick Road Bar, when we all played cards and laughed. When I got to see the musical side of Nate for the first time.

He took me home that night.

It was a song I'd listened to dozens of times and I knew every word. A song that always did, and probably always would, hold a special place in me.

Still shadowed by the lights behind him, the specter I knew was Nate approached the microphone at the front of the stage. Quiet as a secret, he sang the first beautifully haunting lines that I'd heard so many times before.

All the hairs on my arms stood upright, and I couldn't help but lean in because I knew what was going to happen next. I knew that a ghost of a smile would be playing on Nate's lips because it always did at this moment, right before the wall of sound, when the entire band would strike that pounding chord in perfect unison.

At last, Crescent Light was brilliantly lit, all their faces visible for the first time since taking the stage. My heart thumped in my chest at the first glance of his angular face—exactly the same but somehow different. His hair had grown out and skirted his ears, making him look older. More mature. The crowd erupted again, arms waving and heads bobbing to the beat as Nate led them through the first chorus.

"Holy shit," Wren shouted next to me. "You didn't tell me they were this good!"

"Yes, I did!" I didn't peel my eyes away from the stage—from Nate. I couldn't. "Several times!"

"Well yeah, but I thought you were just exaggerating because you were dickmatized by the singer. What's his name again?"

"Nate," I breathed.

"All I gotta say is I get it now. He's fucking hot! *And* a great singer."

All I could do was nod in agreement as I sang along to my favorite Crescent Light song.

The next one was one from their most recent EP, which I never got around to listening to. I didn't exactly want to. Not just because I knew I was going to love it but also because going into the concert with a fresh perspective on some of their songs felt like the least biased approach.

I listened curiously to the unfamiliar song, taking it all in.

It was poppier than most of their others, with cheerful chords that gave me the vision of a young girl listening to it with the windows down in her car on a warm summer night. But as the song went on, the lyrics took on a cheeky, almost antagonistic edge.

Your fake smile lights up the room
So pretty, but it's all untrue
Nobody can see. Nobody but me.
Don't know that love ain't free?
I still remember all the time
I was yours, but you weren't mine
We talked about my daddy issues
And how your family made you cry

I stood stiff as a board, shaking my head at the ridiculous thought that the song could have anything to do with me. But how could it not?

The song faded into the next, a cover of Fleetwood Mac's "The Chain." It was amazing, of course. One of the best covers I'd ever heard. The guys had so much fun while they played, which in turn made them damn near addictive to watch. Song after song, they held the crowd captive.

They played another unfamiliar one from their EP, a sensual, bluesy song that Nate himself played rhythm guitar on. The tempo was slow, unhurried, every word dripping from his lips like thick honey.

You want me like I want you
Oh, babe, I know you do
Nothing to say, nothing to do
Just know it's only me and you
I breathe it in
Your sweet perfume
Let go for me
I'll do it, too
You want me like I want you

Oh, babe, I know you do
You need me like I need you
Honey, what are we to do?

The mental image of Nate and me in his bedroom, illuminated by only the moonlight, wrapped in each other's arms, flashed through my head. A hollowness settled through me. Memories flashed to all the times he sat, hunched over, pen in hand, writing. Writing these songs.

This song.

Wren didn't have to say anything. I felt her side-eye as my cheeks burned and seared. I wasn't naïve enough to think Nate was never going to write about me, about us. The guy wrote about *everything*. He never left the apartment without the leather-bound notebook with all his scribbles and inspirations inside, for crying out loud.

Writing about us was one thing. But writing about us, forming words into lyrics, marrying those lyrics to chords and melodies, creating a demo, recording, putting those records on an album, and then performing those songs live was a very, *very* different thing.

I didn't know whether to be flattered or pissed. More than anything, I felt… exposed? Put on display, naked for the world to see.

It was official; there was no way I would function normally until I looked up the lyrics to every song they'd released in the last two years. All the songs he might have written when we were together or shortly thereafter.

His music was my only chance at ever understanding what went through Nate's head when we were together. It was the only way I might ever get closure because every thought he had, every emotion he felt, had a better chance of going into that leather notebook than being spoken aloud. The temptation to pore over every word was too strong.

Wren and I wasted no time leaving the concert hall after the show was over. She was mostly quiet on the walk back to the car, the silence a comfort to me after the emotional evening, but offered one remark.

"Their music really *is* great, Olive," she said softly. "They'll be perfect for your project."

"I know."

Then, because she couldn't resist. "And, again, he is smoking hot. Congratulations on hitting that, girl." She gave my ass a loud smack, causing me to burst into laughter, effectively breaking the tension in my shoulders and in my heart.

CHAPTER 30

One Year Ago, January

I still miss you.

The final month to work on the Newbie Comp project started with scrambling. Through my months of research, I'd managed to compile a list of eight artists who were all excellent candidates for what I wanted to do. I'd developed an encyclopedic knowledge of each of them, everything from their history, discography, from where they pulled inspiration, the members, and their various skills.

Of those eight, I'd managed to see five of them live, and there were still two more I had tickets to see before my draft deadline. The goal was to narrow down my list to the groups I felt represented what kind of hidden gems the area had to offer. The pure gold yet undiscovered in greater New England.

In a perfect world, I would have had the forethought to try and set up interviews with each of the artists, but the impending deadline made that almost impossible to pull off. I mentally kicked myself, thinking the intimate interviews might've offered the insight I needed to push my project ahead of everyone else's for consideration.

When it came time to put pen to paper and start composing the first draft of my article, I struggled more than I expected. How was I supposed to write about something I personally cared about without letting my personal biases and musical preferences sway the result? Of course, my preferences would play a small role, but the technicalities of the music should shine more than my personal preference.

To succeed at *The Mountain* as a serious writer, I needed to flex the skill of separating *my* taste from acknowledging talent, regardless of whether I personally *liked* it. You don't have to be a fan of metal, hip-hop, or pop to be able to objectively recognize artists in those genres as being outstanding in their craft.

In the end, I tightened my list to five artists who offered something a little different from the other and whose talents I felt I could stand behind when it came time to deliver the final result. Five artists who had the potential to contribute greatly to the music industry if they had the eyes and ears of the right people, and who fans would adore.

Crescent Light was on it.

I practically locked myself in my apartment the final two weeks before the project deadline. I stayed in Boston for Christmas and fleshed out all the criteria I based my research on, and exactly why I chose each of the artists. I explained why each of them was uniquely different than what was already on the market while still maintaining a marketability that would allow them to thrive if given the right platform.

The final version of the project was meant to be fifteen hundred words. My first draft was over three thousand. Thus began edits as I slowly whittled down the resulting document to stay within my required word count.

Kieran helped keep me sane during those weeks when I was just too busy to make time to see him. While he was visiting his family in Maryland for the holidays, I was cooped up at my kitchen table, exhaustively reading and rereading all my research, when my phone pinged. It was a picture. A screenshot from a food delivery service and my address listed as the destination with an order from a protein bowl takeout place a few blocks away. A moment later, I received a text.

Kieran

> Just making sure you're staying fed while you grind away

He even showed up unexpectedly at my apartment when he got back to Boston after New Year's a few days later.

"Put on something warm. We're going on a walk," he demanded with a cheeky smile the second I answered the door.

"Hello to you, too," I laughed.

He crossed the threshold, his cheeks pink and flushed from the cold. "Hi."

The miserable Boston winter had thankfully relented in the last day, offering forty-eight full hours of only mildly-torturous temperatures before the next wave of harsh winter weather was forecasted to hit.

"When did you get back?"

"Late last night." Kieran stooped, giving me a quick peck on the lips. "I mean it, go change your clothes."

I scoffed, holding my arms out to gesture at my sweatpants and the open laptop on the kitchen table. "I can't leave. I told you I have to work on my article."

He stepped forward, crowding me, to put his big hands on my shoulders and give me a supercilious look.

"It's not so important that you can't take an hour to breathe some fresh air, Olive. It'll be good to walk away and clear your head." He jerked his head toward the door. "Come on, let's go. You'll thank me later."

I stood stubbornly still, my chin tilted up. But then I thought about how many days it had been since I'd last left my apartment, seen the sun, felt the wind. Three days, at least. I'd had a sudden bout of self-doubt two nights before and had completely scrapped my draft. I'd been working around the clock to get it back to a comfortable place while maintaining my regular workload. My shoulders sagged, relenting because I knew he had a point.

"It *is* important," I corrected him, "but, fine."

This is what I get for dating a fitness guy.

I stalked to my bedroom and squealed when he pinched my ass to make me hurry up. I changed quickly into a pair of jeans and a thick sweater, slipped my woolen-socked feet into a pair of sneakers, and pulled on a coat hanging by the door.

He was right, of course. The walk was great, not only for my stiff legs and back that suffered from sitting at my computer for days on end, but also for getting out of the mental vacuum I was stuck in. Plus, it was nice to feel Kieran's big hand in mine as we walked side by side through the park near Full Circle Coffee. His hair stuck out from under the beanie he wore, the blue material a stark contrast to his rosy, wind-burnt cheeks. Despite his towering, muscular frame, he reminded me of a little boy who'd been out playing in the snow for too long.

"Don't you feel a little better now?" he asked as we ascended the stairs back up to my apartment, fresh, hot drinks in hand from Full Circle—black coffee for him, tea for me.

I thanked him for his consideration in my bedroom over the next half hour.

The next day, I pored over my new and improved project draft. I'd chipped away at the words little by little to reach the word requirement, paring everything down while still maintaining the integrity, the essence, the soul of the project itself. It felt like an impossible ask—conveying everything I'd learned in the past months while still doing it justice in so few words—but I'd done it.

I had a sense of connection now to these artists. I felt like I owed it to them, to readers of *The Mountain*, and to myself, to make it as meaningful as possible. Even if it never got to see the light of day, I had to try.

It'll never be perfect, I reminded myself.

I knew I was never going to be completely satisfied with it. But I gave myself fleeting moments to be proud.

I rewrote the entire thing again, highlighting what resonated most and reworking bits that could be edited further. I read and reread and reread again a thousand times, finding small edits and fine-tuning until I was, for the most part, happy with what I had.

I spent another two days formatting and titling the thing, battling back and forth in my head how to summarize something that took over my thoughts for over four months into one eye-catching title.

"You can go for something simple?" Kieran suggested from my living room couch as he lounged, watching football. "Maybe you're overthinking it."

"Simple, you say?" I deadpanned, not looking up from my computer.

"Yeah. I mean, a lot of magazine articles I see are pretty straight-forward. Look at this," he leaned up to grab the latest edition of a horrifically patriarchal magazine that also happened to be one of my guiltiest pleasures, which was sitting on the coffee table in front of him. "*Ten Things To Do With Your Tongue That Will Drive Him Nuts... Literally!*" He read in an exaggerated tone. "It's simple, straightforward, and now I'm dying to open this bad boy up and see what exactly those ten things are. And, if I should ask you very nicely to do any of them." He flipped the cover open and leafed through the pages.

"You may be onto something." I laughed.

Taking a deep breath, I tossed the idea around in my head. I typed a few test titles in that format, bobbing my head from side to side, feeling each of them out.

"Okay, please do number six, though," Kieran said over his shoulder. "Like, *please*. I'm begging."

He laughed when I shushed him and went back to perusing the article.

Five Artists You Should Know: A Look Into New England's Underground Music Scene
By Olive McLaren

I didn't hate it. In fact, I kind of loved it. It summed up what the article held without being too self-referential or giving too much away. Just a taste to prompt readers to say *hmm* and hopefully read more, like Kieran did with the weird tongue article. I stared at the title, reading it again and again until I was sure it felt right.

"Okay," I sighed deeply, stretching my arms over my head before rising from my chair. I padded to the back of the couch where Kieran sat and held my hand out. "Let me see what number six is."

"Fuck *yes*."

CHAPTER 31

Now

I never said I was a smart man.

"Are you sure you can't come boating with us today?" Kieran asked for the fifth time that morning as he laced his shoes. We'd come back to the suite to get ready for the day, me bristling the whole time from what happened at breakfast. Now, his insistence that I back out of helping Gemma in favor of getting shit-faced with him was downright irritating.

I sighed. "No, Kieran. For the last time, Gemma needs help, so I'm helping her."

"Haven't you helped her enough, though? I mean, it's *her* wedding. Why has she been making you do all the work?"

Spoken like someone who had only been a groomsman once in his life and had the privilege of simply showing up twenty minutes before the ceremony.

"Because she's my best friend. As a bridesmaid, you help out wherever you're needed. It's what you do."

"But she didn't make you a bridesmaid." He pulled a sweatshirt over his head. "That would take away from her spotlight too much."

I laughed humorlessly as I changed into a pair of jeans. "They don't have a bridal party because they didn't *want* a bridal party. And just because they don't have one doesn't mean I'm any less needed. Look at Jared; he's the best man, whether or not he stands beside Grant tomorrow."

"Whatever you say."

I couldn't wrap my head around why he was being so selfish about the stupid booze cruise. Or why he was pressed about me helping Gemma when I gave him the heads-up weeks ago. Or why he had to bring it up in front of everyone at breakfast.

"I feel like you're pissed at me," he said. "If you don't want me to go on the boat thing, I won't go."

"Just go, it's fine." I didn't have time to debate back and forth with him; I was already running late meeting Gemma. Plus, I didn't want him around if he was just going to complain about helping or make underhanded comments about Gemma the whole time.

"Are you sure?"

"Unless you want to steam dresses and fluff flower arrangements…?"

He made a face, already reaching for the door. "Hard pass."

"Exactly." I turned to him. "You go have fun. There's supposed to be a big group going anyway. You'll have a way better time there than here."

Almost all of Gemma and Grant's college friends were going to be on the boat, in addition to all of Gemma's cousins under the age of forty, her brother, and now Kieran.

With one last goodbye, Kieran left to meet up with Michael and join the bus heading to San Francisco.

I took a brick path to a huge suite overlooking the vineyard, which was being used as Gemma's bridal room. When I let myself in, the first thing I saw was Gemma's wedding dress hanging off the windowsill of the massive circular window that took up most of the far wall.

"There you are!" she sang, crossing the living area to wrap me in a hug.

"Here I am," I muffled into her blonde waves.

"Everything okay?"

Damn her and her ability to see right through me.

"Of course!" I lied. She pulled away to hold me at arm's length, assessing me. I played up my tone. "Why would anything be wrong?"

"No reason." Gemma ran her hands down the length of my arms. Soothing. Petting. "Just checking on you. You just seem a little tense. And, you know…" She hesitated. "Nate made the trip after all. If I knew he was going to be here, I would have told you. Apparently, he told Jared to tell Grant, and, well, you know how that goes. Good thing I had overflow tables built into the seating chart."

I felt my guard slip out of place and pulled the inside of my cheek between my teeth. "I'm fine."

"I didn't say you weren't," she said simply, plopping onto the large white sofa in the middle of the suite. "So… has he said anything to you?"

I sighed deeply and followed. "He found me last night at the party." I curled my legs under me as I got comfortable. "I was caught off guard, so I didn't stick around for much of a conversation. Then after the game, I basically told him to fuck off and leave me alone."

She snorted.

"I felt really bad about it, but then I saw him again this morning, and we talked more. Just pleasantries, mostly. I don't know. I'm trying not to dwell on it. Kieran has been acting weird."

"How so?"

Well, for starters, he doesn't really like you. And I'm not sure he likes anyone else.

"He bailed on helping today; he's on the booze cruise with Michael. There's this possessiveness, this alpha-bro thing he's doing. I've never seen this side of him before."

"Jealousy can be kind of hot in the right context."

"Not this context," I countered, "and it gets worse when Nate's around. I honestly think pissing on my leg would be a more subtle response at this point. It's driving me insane." My usual image of the confident, striking Kieran was morphing gradually into exactly the kind of guy I actively made a point to stay away from. Arrogant. Controlling.

I shook my head. *That's not Kieran. That may be how he's acting right now, but that's not who he is.*

"Does he still not know? About you and Nate?"

I heaved another sigh, dropping my head into my hands. "No," I admitted. "Nothing."

Gemma hummed her acknowledgment. Not a judgmental hum. Just one that said, *Ahh, I see.*

"We don't talk about our exes," I explained, mostly to reassure myself. She already knew the situation. "We never have. He never brought any of his exes up once we became official, so neither did I. And I didn't want to lay it all out for him before coming here on the likely chance that Nate *wouldn't* be here. Crescent Light is prepping for a European tour, for crying out loud! I didn't think airing out all the dirty laundry to Kieran would be worth the trouble because Nate isn't…" I gestured wildly. "He's not… He isn't part of my life! He is someone we hung out with in grad school. The rest doesn't matter anymore."

Gemma laid a hand on my knee. "I hear you. And I'm going to say this next part because I love you, and we don't lie to each other."

My teeth scraped against the skin of my lip.

"And we hold each other accountable. Even if we don't want to hear it."

I nodded, silent.

"You probably should have told Kieran about the Nate stuff."

My shoulders slumped, but she was right—hindsight is 20/20 and all that.

God, the amount of things I would do differently in hindsight.

"I can understand why you didn't tell him. You thought it would be irrelevant. But now?" She held out both hands as if to say, *Look at this mess we're in.*

I groaned.

"Do you still… like… have feelings? For Nate? Like, real feelings? I'm not accusing you of anything—you know I have your back no matter what—but, do you?"

Exhaustion tugged on my senses despite it still being morning. "I don't know. I really don't have a clue, and I don't have the brainpower to think about it right now. Plus, I'm realizing I'm emotionally dumping on you the day before your wedding, and I feel like an asshole."

Gemma laughed, throwing her head back and clapping once. "You aren't an asshole, Oli Bear. I'm here for you."

I groaned again, leaning forward until my forehead thumped against her shoulder. "I'm sorry."

She patted the back of my head. "You don't need to be, but I'll tell you it's okay and that I forgive you because I know that's what you need to hear."

"Enough of the drama," I dismissed, sitting straighter. "I am all yours. Put me to work."

She stood with a flourish and made her way to the walk-in closet, with me closely behind her. "Grant and Jared should be in the courtyard moving the giant arch for the ceremony into the right place, along with some tables and other heavy stuff. He knows his marching orders, but I'll have to quality-check it all here in a bit. First things first, we need to steam my dress and my mom's dress. She's being more of a diva than I am, I swear."

We took turns with the steamer, tackling layer upon layer of chiffon, switching places when our arms ached. Her mom's dress took longer than hers, but we made quick work of the task.

"The florist will be here tomorrow morning to do the bigger installations, like the flowers on the arch and the big centerpieces for dinner, but we're making the smaller centerpieces for cocktail hour and such by ourselves. And by *we,* I mean *you.* I have to meet with the catering team to go over some last-minute changes, but I can help you as soon as I'm done."

"Totally." I nodded. "Not a problem. I'm your girl."

She clapped and forwarded me the floral inspiration photos I'd seen dozens of times. They were to be small, modest bouquets mostly made of roses and greenery in clear, crystal vases of varying shapes and sizes. Easy enough.

"The only thing is, there's a *ton* of them. I have all the vases outside, and buckets of flowers are being delivered in a few minutes. We'll store them overnight in the big walk-in fridge in the reception hall's kitchen once they're all finished. The resort staff is making room for them as we speak."

We left the bridal suite and followed the path to the main building, circling to the grassy clearing where the ceremony would be the next day. Plastic tubs filled with clear vases wrapped in bubble wrap sat stacked in the middle of the makeshift aisleway. Grant and Jared huffed in the distance, barely visible as they struggled to maneuver a large wooden archway toward the end of the aisle.

"I think we should set you up at one of the big tables in the beer garden," Gemma said, hauling the first plastic tub into her arms. I repeated the movement and followed her. "It can be like your little flower shop area!"

"Love it!" I called from behind her retreating blonde head. We set the tubs beside the long picnic table we'd played cards at the night before and made another trip for the remaining vases.

The archway was now centered nicely at the end of the aisle. Grant stood a few feet away, hands on his hips and gasping for air, admiring his work.

"Move your side back a little!" he called to Jared, who was still halfway hidden behind the arch. He bear-hugged his side of the wood and inched it backward, making Gemma cackle as she stooped to grab another tub.

"There!" Grant shouted. "Perfect! Gem, come look at this and tell me the placement is good because I'm about to set the damn thing on fire."

Jared at last emerged from behind the archway, and—it wasn't Jared.

It was Nate, reaching to remove the black baseball cap he'd put on after breakfast. He wiped his sweaty forehead with the back of his hand before turning the cap around and securing it backward on his head. His cheeks were flushed pink, and his lips parted as he caught his breath.

I swallowed and had to blink away creeping memories of him looking that *particular* brand of disheveled in precarious positions.

"I—uh," Gemma started, her stutter telling me I wasn't the only one surprised by Nate's presence. "I think it looks great right there! Great job, guys."

Grant clapped his hands and looked to the heavens, grateful to be done with the heavy arch.

"Where'd Jared get off to?" Gemma asked.

"He's inside helping load in tables," Grant answered, stooping to kiss Gemma on the cheek.

"Gross!" She attempted to push him off but failed since she was still balancing the tub against her hip. "You're all sweaty!"

I grabbed the final tub and caught Nate's eye as I rose. He lifted his chin, the corner of his mouth ticking upward as he silently greeted me. I pressed my lips together and quickly turned to take my tub back to the makeshift flower shop. Gemma followed with her box a second later, plopping hers down with the rest.

"Sorry," she said. "I didn't know he would be here. I thought he was going on the stupid party boat thing."

I waved my hand through the air, dismissing her. "Don't worry about it! It's fine, promise."

When the flower delivery arrived, Gemma set me up with everything I would need to make the arrangements—gloves, clippers, floral tape, water—and set me to work as she left to meet with the caterer.

I was grateful for the solitude. Being surrounded by sweet-smelling flowers and having nothing to do but focus on my assignment was exactly the kind of mind-numbing work I needed to unwind.

Peace and quiet, at last.

CHAPTER 32

One Year Ago, January

Time goes by, we move on
We move on, we move on
When do we move on?

I took a deep breath and gave the article one last look. One last chance for edits on the completed application, the pages of supporting research, the article itself. I chewed my thumbnail to the quick as I roved over everything. Saving it all in one file, packaged nice and pretty for Julienne and the judging committee, I held my breath and hit *Submit*.

I think the relief of having the weight of the project off my shoulders sent my body into a tailspin. Completing and submitting the damned thing had somehow switched a flip inside of me. No more than an hour after submitting, a dull, concentrated headache bloomed behind my left eye.

I knew immediately it was not going to stay that way.

Within the hour, despite my efforts to get ahead of it, the headache progressed into a full-blown migraine, sending me back to bed, where I stayed for the majority of the day.

In the early evening, when the worst of it had subsided and I could keep food down, I checked my phone.

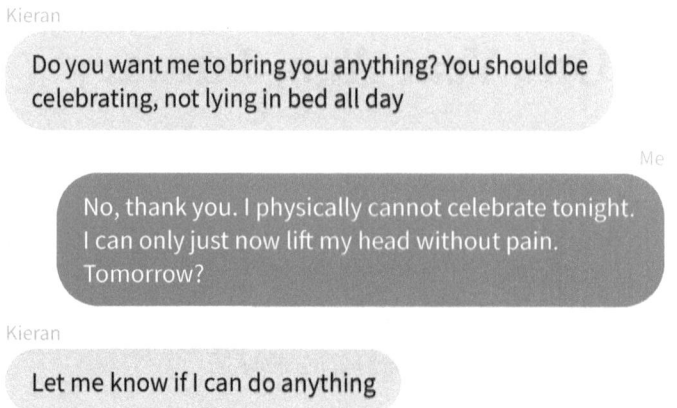

Kieran

Do you want me to bring you anything? You should be celebrating, not lying in bed all day

Me

No, thank you. I physically cannot celebrate tonight. I can only just now lift my head without pain. Tomorrow?

Kieran

Let me know if I can do anything

The knots in my stomach twisted the entire night, not just from the migraine but from nerves about my project submission. Being first in line for promotion considerations in the future would be amazing, yes. But more than that, a published shoutout in *The Mountain* could be life-changing for the artists I featured. I wanted so desperately to do something for them, anything at all that might make a difference because, dammit, they deserved it. Julienne asked us to dig deep, and I had. I just hoped it was enough.

By the next morning, I felt well enough to check my phone again.

Gemma

Sending you good vibes, babes!! You got this!

Kieran

You should come over later if you're feeling up to it

I opened my email and refreshed the inbox no less than fourteen times. Nothing pressing or important. Definitely nothing about my submission other than the confirmation that they'd received it. I opened the group chat I had with Wren and Ha-Joon and typed out my message.

Me

Do we know when we're going to hear anything back about the Newbie Comp?

Wren

I have no idea, but surely 24 hours was enough time for them to decide, right?? How long do they need?

Wren

I'm a nervous wreck

Ha-Joon

Julienne said they were taking the weekend to deliberate. There are only nine submissions. I assume we should know before Monday?

Wren

I swear if that jerk from Lifestyle gets chosen, I will riot.

Wren

Not really, but still. One of us deserves it.

Ha-Joon

LMAO

I shot back a laughing emoji and crawled out of bed very, very slowly, assessing every sensation. No pain. A good sign, even though the lingering physical effects a migraine of that magnitude leaves on the human body was still felt. My muscles were stiff all over, my fingers tingling with a faint residual numbness.

I waddled into the bathroom, scared to move too quickly, and turned the shower to its hottest setting. The steaming stream worked to relax the aching muscles across my neck, my shoulders, my back. I stood unmoving under the lava for at least five minutes, breathing deeply, calming my brain as thoughts of the project results seeped in.

It's fine. You'll know their decision soon enough. It's out of your hands. There's nothing you can do about it now besides wait.

In, two, three, four. Hold, two, three, four. Out, two, three, four...

I dressed, blow-dried my recently cut hair, and put on makeup for the first time in at least a week. Feeling incrementally better, I took Kieran up on his invitation to come over. I figured, if nothing else, getting out of the apartment would be good for me. Otherwise, I was just going to sit and worry the rest of the day. At least at his place, I could worry *and* have some company.

It was a strange mix, being exhausted from weeks of hard work and mental strain, combined with the exhaustion of feeling unwell, and yet being so wired and anxious about the Newbie Comp results that I wouldn't have been able to rest even if I wanted to.

The only thing to do was ride the wave until it was over.

⟫⟫⟫ ⟪⟪⟪

"You're free!" Kieran's muffled voice said into the scarf around my neck when he pulled me into a hug. We'd gotten a fresh dusting of snow that morning, which cast everything in sparkling white and held a damp coldness that cut right to the bone. "How does it feel to rejoin the outside world?"

I hugged him back, but wasn't sure how to answer.

I didn't think giving my all to the Newbie Comp could be categorized as "leaving the outside world." The way he said it was as if I were trapped in thankless, unfulfilling work. Sure, it was a grueling couple of weeks towards the end of the process, but it was also a life-changing opportunity. Not just in my professional career but for my personal growth as a writer. My defensive response caught in my throat.

"I like your hair like that." He kissed my temple as he ushered me inside. "You should go shorter next time. How are you feeling?"

"Better, thankfully. Still not quite a hundred percent, but getting there."

He led me into the large kitchen, where the scent of mouthwatering Italian food in the oven hit me, causing my empty stomach to growl in response. I half expected Kieran to ask me for an update on my project submission as he helped me shrug out of my coat. An inquiry on the results? Something? Anything? But he didn't.

When he turned his back to check on the food, I spoke. "We haven't heard anything about who won yet." I turned my email notifications on earlier in the day, but it didn't stop me from opening the app and refreshing my inbox every ten minutes.

"Well, you should be proud regardless," he said over his shoulder.

I unwrapped the scarf around my neck and set it on the counter as I took a seat at his sleek counter. He closed the oven again, readjusting the timer before walking to the opposite corner of the room to the bar cart.

"I know. I *am*. I just don't think I'm going to be able to relax until we know who got selected."

He threw me a glance, scoffing. "Come on."

"What?"

"You're a writer. It's just an article. There will be others, right?"

I stared for a moment, unsure I was understanding him correctly. "It isn't *just* an article; I worked really hard on it."

"No, I know," he said, retrieving a glass from the bottom shelf of the bar cart. "I get it, your hobbies mean a lot to you, but—"

"It's more than a hobby, Kieran; it's my job."

"Right, but…" He trailed off, bobbing his head back and forth.

Defensive confusion flooded my senses, and my head throbbed. *Is he serious? I know I'm not saving lives, but what I do is hard work. It's competitive. It's culturally significant.*

"Sorry," he interrupted my thoughts. "You're taking it differently than I'm meaning it." He snagged a small vial of orange bitters from the cart. "I just mean you've been working your ass off, and I want to help you relax."

He came to stand in front of me, pressing against my bent knees, and placed the items on the countertop. Cupping my face, he gently forced me to look him in the eye. "Let me make you a drink," he said softly, reassuringly. His lips tenderly met mine in a slow, innocent kiss.

He turned his back again, opening the pantry door. "You like Old Fashioneds, right?"

I picked at the skin around my nails. "From the few times I've tried them, yes."

"It's my cheat day, so I'm going all out on the empty calories." He closed the pantry door with his foot, a perplexed look on his face. "Where the hell did my bourbon go?"

I laughed. "It's *your* house."

"I know, but I swore—oh wait." He snapped. "It's in the garage. Be right back."

I took the opportunity alone to pull my phone out again and check my email, refreshing twice before closing the app and putting it on the counter next to Kieran's.

Just as I did, his phone pinged, the screen lighting up.

A little voice inside of me told me not to look at his screen. *It's an invasion of privacy. Just look away.*

In any other scenario, I absolutely would *not* have looked. But his phone was right there, face up, with the text previews visible. I couldn't have avoided seeing it if I tried.

Kellie

> Hey, handsome! Missing you so bad. Can't wait to see you tomorrow!

Something in me glitched over and over until the screen went black. I resisted the urge to tap the screen to wake it up and check to see if I was hallucinating.

It was a good thing I didn't because right then, the door that led to the garage opened, and Kieran's muscular frame sauntered back in, a fancy bottle of bourbon in hand.

"I forgot I moved all my liquor to the garage since it's going to stay nice and cold out there for a while."

I sat in silence, watching as he made two Old Fashioneds, one for him and one for me. I rolled my lips together, debating whether to say anything. There was no way I could simply pretend I didn't see it, and I wasn't in the business of leaving things unsaid anymore.

"You good?" he asked, glancing up at me with a weary smile.

I nodded.

Chicken.

Kieran turned and opened the freezer. "I know you're nervous about the project thing"—he returned with a tray of large ice cubes—"but you really should—"

"Who's Kellie?" I interrupted, the words bubbling out of me on their own.

He seemed unfazed by the question. His hand didn't even flinch as he stirred the drinks. In fact, he looked a little confused, like he had no idea who I was talking about.

"She texted while you were in the garage. I didn't mean to look, but…" I gestured to his phone, which was still face up in its position on the counter, inches from my own.

"Oh, *Kellie*," recognition painted his expression. "Did she text?" He slid one of the glasses to me and grabbed his phone like it was nothing. He read the text and quickly typed out a reply. "She's just this girl I've seen a couple of times." He set the phone face down this time and took a sip of his Old Fashioned, like we were discussing the fucking weather.

I blinked at my glass, then lifted my befuddled gaze to him.

His brows drew together. "What? What's wrong?"

I said nothing, unsure of what to say without sounding catty, jealous, or like one of those girls in teen drama movies who were about to have a total freak-out.

Realization dawned on his handsome face, and his eyes went wide. "Oh. *Oh*. Shit. Olive, I'm sorry, I— I mean," he scoffed, the smile not quite reaching his eyes as he scratched the back of his head. "You're seeing other guys, too, I'm sure." A long pause. "Right?" He nodded like he was prompting me to nod, too, like we were totally on the same page, in complete agreement.

I gave my head a slow shake, lowering my gaze to my hands on the countertop. "Nope," I said, popping the *p*.

That seemed to confuse him further. "Wait." He reared back. "You're not?"

"No. I'm not. I should—" I rose, grabbing my scarf, my fight or flight definitively telling me to flee. "I'm gonna go." The shock was catching up to me now, my heart rate increasing, my anxiety along with it.

This is not happening.

Throwing my coat over my arm, my feet carried me to the front door. Kieran abandoned his drink and followed a few steps behind me.

"Olive, you don't have to go," he reasoned.

I was wading through molasses, not quite processing anything, focusing only on my breathing and getting outside.

"Yeah, I do," I said over my shoulder, my restraint waning. I threw the door wide and stepped out to the freezing night.

"Olive, I-I'm sorry..." He paused on the front porch, but didn't follow me farther.

Stalking to my car, I vaguely registered the sound of his oven timer beeping, adding to my overstimulation.

Breathe. Breathe.

My car was still warm from the drive to Kieran's when it roared to life. I sat in the driver's seat in silence, trying to quiet my mind enough to count to ten. My thoughts were somehow racing at lightning speed and moving in slow motion simultaneously. If Kieran was still on the front porch, I didn't notice.

One, two, three. I'd barely made it to four before my phone dinged.

Not the chime for a text. A chime for an email.

I gasped and lifted my phone, the bright screen stinging my eyes. An email from Julienne. Without thinking, I unlocked my phone with shaking fingers and opened the email.

Good evening,

We here at The Mountain would like to express our deepest gratitude to each and every one of the candidates who put forth applications for the Newcomers Competition. It is with great pleasure that we would like to announce Lee Ha-Joon as the candidate selected for this distinction. We sincerely hope you all will join in congratulating...

I locked my phone and closed my eyes, not bothering to read the rest of the email.

Dammit.

The tremble of my chin was immediate. I tried to get a grip on the wave of emotions washing over me before it crested. But it wasn't a wave. The pressure on my chest pushed harder. It was a fucking tsunami.

Again, my instincts told me to flee.

Somewhere. Anywhere. It doesn't matter, just go.

With no plan in mind, I put my car into drive and pulled away.

CHAPTER 33

One Year Ago, January

What's a word for not wanting to be social, but not having a good enough excuse to bail?

I drove with no clear direction, counting to ten over and over again. The tears sprang to my eyes, no matter how hard I tried to hold them back, spilling silently over my cheeks. The only sound outside of my deep, forcefully controlled breaths was the occasional sniffles and hiccups that snuck out. Like my tears, my thoughts threatened to spill over and run rampant, too, but I tried to force them down.

I failed miserably at both. I was going to fall apart at any second. The searing pain of rejection from all directions was too much, and it ate at me from the inside out.

My project was rejected.

What if that was the very best that would ever come from me? What if that was as good as it would get, and yet it was still passed over? What did that say about me? About my future? Am I so naïve to believe I stood a chance?

Self-doubt would do nothing but make me feel worse, but I couldn't stop it. It was already too far gone. Never mind the fact that Ha-Joon's project was probably amazing, and he probably put just as much time and effort into it as I had. My happiness for him meant nothing at the moment, not when the dismissal cut me down to the bone.

My head gave a dull thud behind my left eye.

Kieran.

Grown-up, mature, kind Kieran. Silly, wide-eyed, ignorant, unwanted Olive. I couldn't shake the image of his perplexed face, the way he was *so confused* at my reaction.

Why did he assume I was still dating around? What did I do to make him think that?

He clearly hadn't stopped seeing other women.

Embarrassed was an understatement.

Wasn't *he* the one who pursued *me*? Wasn't he the one who sought me out? Sent me food when I was stuck working long hours, unwilling to step away? Called me just because he was thinking about me? Wasn't *he* the one who went out of his way to be attentive and romantic? The one who gave me no reason to believe he wanted anything less than a serious relationship?

Did I just read the signs completely wrong?

No. I didn't read anything wrong.

But was it a betrayal if it wasn't intentional? If he genuinely thought I was dating around, too? Maybe not, but some communication would have been fucking nice. What happened to bare minimum communication?

Good riddance, I told myself. A mantra I barely believed. I wanted something real. I thought I could've had it with him. Maybe if I forced myself to repeat it enough times, the hurt would eventually go away. But in that moment, it really, *really* hurt.

More than my feelings, my ego was bruised. My pride. It clutched and held on like a vice. There was no use in pretending the hurt wasn't there. Everything in the last forty-eight hours felt so big, and it was compounding in my heart, doubling by the second. Another sob bubbled out of me.

I forced a tight lid on the pain as I drove. My head pounded in protest with every heartbeat. Thoughts raced with no regard for my efforts. I reminded myself of what I was *actually* upset about to stop my anxiety from compounding and snowballing the hurt, but *god,* it was hard. All too quickly, my mind jumped to every little thing weighing on my heart, relevant or not.

I missed Gemma. I missed my mom. All I wanted to do was cuddle up on the couch, lay my head in her lap, and listen to her hum. I'd never been good at bottling up my feelings. It was a horrible coping mechanism that tended to have disastrous results when they finally boiled over.

Being alone wasn't a good idea when I felt like it might overflow, but I kept driving anyway.

I was more than halfway to Hartwood before I realized what I was doing, like my soul knew where to go even if my mind didn't. The tears suddenly became that much harder to hold back.

When I got a few miles out, I figured I needed a plan and decided to call Gemma. It went to voicemail on the second ring, and a text followed shortly after.

Gemma

Sorry! At the movies. Everything okay?

Right. She and Grant were probably having a date night.

Pulling into the nearest parking lot—a chain family restaurant near Sumner U's campus—I found a spot and parked.

Me

Yeah, just called to chat. Love you!

Gemma

Love you too!

Letting my head fall back against the headrest, I sat in silence for a full minute. I closed my eyes, grounding myself, and actively recognized the sensation from the top of my head to the tips of my fingers to the bottoms of my feet, diligently pushing down the building anxiety. My mind wandered to anything and everything that was not my job, was not Kieran, was not the hurt I felt.

I should have known where it would land instead.

Despite two years without contact and the hurt he'd also been responsible for once upon a time, his was the voice I wanted to hear.

He probably isn't even in town. It's Saturday night; I bet he has a show.

The silence of my car was loud as I debated it.

Families piled into their minivans around me, hands loaded down with takeaway boxes from the restaurant. My stomach growled, but I didn't move.

Outside of what happened with Nate and me, outside of the sex, or whether or not we had feelings for each other, we were close at one point. Friends. I questioned a lot of things when it came to him, but I never once questioned if the connection we'd developed was genuine. I missed our friendship, regardless of how long it had been.

And I did not want to be alone.

With shaking hands, I unlocked my phone and scrolled to the number I could never bring myself to delete.

The line rang once. Twice.

This is stupid.

Pulling the phone away from my ear on the third ring, I made to cancel the call until I heard his voice say my name for the first time in two years.

"Oli?"

Air whooshed from my lungs, and I couldn't stop the ever-insistent lump in my throat from rising again at my old nickname. It took a few beats to answer.

"Nate?"

"What's wrong?"

He knew. Of course, he knew. I'm sure he knew something was wrong the second he saw my name on his phone. With the way we left things, something would *have* to be wrong for me to speak to him again.

His loaded question hit me in the chest with a fatal blow. A sob bubbled, and I couldn't hold it back before it escaped my lips. Fat tears gathered and overflowed, staining my cheeks as they descended.

God, why did I call him? Do I just have a penchant for humiliating myself?

But for a reason I didn't know and would never be able to explain, I finally let go. The tension I'd been holding since I submitted my project snapped and released. Hot tears fell in a stream of heavy droplets, the force of my sobs shaking my shoulders.

Nate didn't push for an answer to his question. Didn't panic at my emotional outburst. He didn't speak at all, in fact. He just sat with me in silence, breathing slowly on the other side of the line while I cried.

"I'm sorry," I whispered when I was finally calm enough to speak.

His voice was low and patient. "What are you apologizing for?"

"I don't know," I answered honestly. "Nothing. Everything."

He paused like he was rolling his next question around his mouth. "Are you okay?"

The gentle concern in his voice outlined the question he asked. He didn't ask me what was wrong again, and he didn't ask me what happened. He asked me if I was okay.

I tried to think of an answer, but came up empty again. "I don't know that either," I chuckled dryly, roughly wiping my nose with the sleeve of my sweater. There was another long silence, but the comforting sound of his breathing on the other side remained.

"Where are you?" he asked.

I had to laugh at that because the honest answer was truly so pathetic.

"Um," I stalled, looking out the window. "Crying in my car in the parking lot of a restaurant by my old apartment?"

"Really?" I couldn't tell if he sounded amused or not. I imagined his eyebrows pulling together and his lips tugging into a skeptical smirk.

"Yeah." Honesty was the best policy at that point. I was already in an emotional black hole. What could possibly make it worse? "I started driving and eventually ended up here. I don't know why."

The sound of shuffling fabric in the background told me he was moving around. "Do you," he said tentatively, "want to tell me what happened? You don't have to if you don't want to."

I weighed the question. Did I want to open the floodgates? Did I want to tell him about Kieran? About the project I worked so hard on? About my involvement with *The Mountain*?

A wave of rejection washed over me again.

And frustration.

And shame.

And anger.

I was grateful for the out he offered, so I took it.

"No," I told him. "I don't think I want to talk about it right now. I'll just get upset all over again."

"That's fair," he answered pointedly, patiently. More movement from his side of the line, sounds I couldn't quite pinpoint. Distant music, a door shutting, multiple voices talking. It suddenly dawned on me that he very well could have been right in the middle of something, just like Gemma was, before I called him unannounced to bawl my eyes out. I forced him to be my emotional crutch without even giving him a chance to tell me he was busy.

"Oh, god." I pressed at the dull, thudding pain in my left temple. "Nate, I'm so sorry if I barged in on your night by calling. If you have to go—"

"No. Not at all," he said, stopping me. "You're fine."

I felt guilty for pulling him away from his plans. As much as he was trying to hide it, I interrupted his night. I pictured him hanging out backstage at some music venue, lounging, having drinks with the guys. Sneaking out the back door just to take my call.

Does he have a girlfriend? Do I even care? Should I care?

Memories flashed of Nate's hands wrapped around that beautiful girl. Blair. Him kissing her in front of all our friends, showing her off in a way he never did with me—in a way I craved.

"You still there?" He broke me out of my thoughts.

"Yeah, I'm here." I mulled over what to say next, unable to continue until I knew there wasn't another girl waiting on him to get off the phone. "You sure I'm not interrupting? You're not recording? Or hanging out with a girlfriend? Or friends?"

He let out a short, dry laugh. "No, I'm, uh—" He paused a beat. "No. No girlfriend, or anything like that, Oli. I'm on the road right now, and service might be a little spotty, but I'm here, okay? I'm here."

I nodded, breathing a little easier.

He was letting me take the lead in the conversation, allowing me to offer as much or as little information as I wanted. Never pushing. Never asking for more. It was appreciated more than he knew, and I didn't want the conversation to end yet. I wanted to hear his voice, even if it was only a minute longer.

"Do you want to hear something pathetic?"

He sighed a deep chuckle into my ear, a sweet sound I didn't realize I missed so badly. Goosebumps rose on the back of my neck. "Yes," he answered. "Always."

"I went to one of your shows."

A beat of silence, and I could almost hear his blink of surprise. "Really?" he asked. "When? Which show?"

"Two months ago, in Boston. I took a friend of mine to see you guys play." I decided to leave out the details of *why* I went to their show. It didn't matter now anyway.

"Really?" he parroted like he didn't know whether or not to believe me. The noises behind him stopped altogether. "Why didn't you tell me? Or at least stick around to say 'hi' after? Now I'm trying to remember if I did anything embarrassing on stage." The smile in his voice was audible.

"I don't think you did. The show was amazing. It was nice hearing all the old songs." *And a few new ones with lyrics that sounded a bit too familiar.*

"Honestly, though, why didn't you say anything?" He wasn't going to let me avoid answering the question this time.

"Honestly?" I thought about it, tasting the truth on my tongue before saying it. It was bitter because the truth was that I was a coward. "I didn't know what I would say to you."

The empty space between our words was filled to the brim with all the things left unsaid. I was being carefully selective with my words, and if I were a betting person, I'd say he was being just as selective.

"I can understand that." He paused again, thinking. "I'm glad you called me tonight."

I took a deep breath and nodded slowly to myself, realizing that the short-lived conversation with him was coming to an end.

When would we speak again? Would we ever?

Nothing had changed, not really. He was still Nate, determined to succeed in music, noncommittal and unbothered. And I was still me, chasing stability, honoring routine, never fully at ease. I reached to turn my car engine back on, resigned and numb, when he broke the silence once again.

"Wanna get a bite to eat?"

"What do you mean?"

"There you are."

My head snapped up. Instinctively, I looked over my shoulder and behind my car, but only saw an elderly couple entering the restaurant hand in hand. A pickup truck passed in the aisle to my left, but the parking lot was otherwise empty. I peered over my other shoulder, out the back passenger windows, when movement in front of the car caught my eye. I did a double take, and when my eyes adjusted, he was there. In the stupid parking lot, striding between cars.

Nate Cassidy was walking toward me.

Long and lean, he had one hand up to his ear and the other shoved casually into a front pocket. I stared at him through the windshield, open-mouthed. He gave me a grin as he slowly rounded the front of my hood, ending the phone call.

I took a split second to close my eyes and gather my wits before pulling the key out of my ignition and gingerly opening the driver's door.

"I thought you were on the road." It was the only thing I could think to say as I climbed out of the car, knees shaking with the sudden onslaught of nerves. I didn't meet his eye.

"I lied," he said simply, holding the door open. "You sounded like you didn't want to be alone, and you weren't hard to find. There's only, like, two restaurants over here."

My chin trembled at his words. *You sounded like you didn't want to be alone.* How much did he have to know me—the real, deepest parts of me—to know to say that? Those words held more truth than he could ever know. They were the *exact* thing I needed to hear.

That was the thing about Nate. He just got it. *Got me.* He effortlessly understood. It didn't matter that we used to float into and out of each other's lives, always just shy of lovers but somehow more than friends. We were somehow tethered together, in tune, even when we weren't together at all.

"That was nice of you," I whispered, holding back a new round of tears before they could fall. I ran my fingers through my hair, suddenly feeling exposed and self-conscious about the blotchy face I was sporting.

He stood patiently in front of me, waiting for whatever choice I would make next. I didn't know what to say to him, but I knew I did *not* want to spend more time getting lost in my thoughts. There was no more capacity for self-loathing. No fight left in the tank. So, I shook the lingering negativity from my head and slowly lifted my gaze to meet his deep blue eyes.

A small, reassuring smile spread across his lips, and a warm feeling bloomed in my chest. Without a word, he opened his arms to me.

I didn't hesitate as I crossed the single step between us to close the distance. He circled me in his arms, and I gave in languidly to the comfort of being near him. Clasping my hands around his waist, I let my head fall against his chest. A long sigh escaped my lips when his arms tightened incrementally around my shoulders. I breathed in his scent. He smelled just the same as he always did: leathery cologne, fabric softener, and *Nate*.

A new wave of emotion tightened my throat, but this time it wasn't because of my shitty day. I just missed him.

"You okay?" His voice was muffled from his cheek pressed against the top of my head.

I nodded against his chest in response.

"You wanna eat and get drunk and forget about it?"

I thought about it for all of three seconds before nodding again. He huffed a laugh through his nose, placed a quick kiss on my hairline, and released me.

CHAPTER 34

Now

For a man of many words,
I'm speechless when I try to pen you.
It's impossible.
Words fail.

L etting the monotonous process of de-stemming the flowers soothe me, I worked in comfortable, lonely silence. White, pink, and champagne-colored roses surrounded me on all sides of the picnic table, filling my lungs with their scent.

I grounded myself as I worked, inhaling all things calm and exhaling all things worrisome. Inhaling stillness and silence, exhaling restlessness and scattered thoughts.

Plucking roses out of their buckets one at a time, I snapped each thorn between thumb and forefinger, clipped the ends at an angle with shears, and placed them in a pile on my other side. One after another after another, only the distant sounds of birds and the vineyard sprinkler system filled the silence. Therapeutic.

I wasn't sure how much time had passed when feet crunching against the gravel walkway piqued my attention.

Coming into view around the corner into the beer garden was Nate. He had both his hands buried in pockets, eyes trained on the ground, that black baseball cap still backward on his head. His steps were unhurried and unsure, like he would have debated turning around and walking back to the ceremony space if I hadn't noticed him.

I paused my rhythm to narrow my eyes at him, but he continued around my workstation, never looking up, and sank into the seat to my left with a sigh.

"You good?" I asked, eyebrows raised in mock concern.

He reached out to toy with the stem of a white rose, twirling it between his fingers. "Need some help?"

I hesitated. The solitude in my little pocket of the resort was too nice to pass up. But just as I opened my mouth to say *No*, the word, "Sure," came out instead. Biting my tongue before it said anything else stupid, I slid a spare pair of scissors to him.

I showed him what I'd been doing, cutting the stems of the hundreds of roses into equal lengths, picking off each thorn, and trimming the wayward leaves.

He nodded silently, plucking a rose from the pile, and set to work next to me.

We worked in silence for a few minutes, the tension building thick in the air like it had at the welcome party, like it had a hundred times before. A stillness that filled quickly with all the words that sat unsaid on our tongues.

Anxiety, nervousness, butterflies—whatever it was, it bloomed in my stomach, making me fidgety. It wasn't an unpleasant feeling, just one I couldn't shake.

Reaching for another flower, I took a deep breath through my nose, not missing Nate's imperceptible glance at me from under his lashes before looking away again. Of course, he clocked my nervous tick as if it were his own.

I stuffed the bouquet-ready roses into waiting vases of water so they could stay hydrated until they were ready to be primped and primed for arrangements. I'd done at least a hundred already, but another full bucket of untouched florals sat on the other side of the table, staring at us.

"Alright," I said, dropping a rose into a vase and standing with a wince.

His eyes followed me. "Where are we going?"

"I need you to stand and hold these. I can't sit hunched over anymore." I held two small vases out as he maneuvered his long legs out of the picnic bench.

He took them and faced me. Because of our height difference, the vases were at too high a vantage point for me to see properly to make the arrangements. I wrapped my hands around Nate's forearms, ignoring how they flexed under my touch, and lowered them gently until the vases floated chest height in front of me.

"Sorry," he mumbled.

"Hold still, just like that," I ordered softly, reaching for a stack of roses and a few sprigs of greenery from the table.

"You got it."

He swallowed thickly as I dropped green filler flowers into the vases, his Adam's apple bobbing with the movement. I was distinctly aware that he was avoiding eye contact, but then again, so was I.

I shoved a stack of the nicest-looking roses into each vase, primping, fluffing, and adding greenery to any unfilled gaps. But the stubborn flowers wouldn't cooperate. They looked... lumpy? Not at all what I envisioned, and certainly not what Gemma was hoping for. I added more greenery to the already-tight bundle and kept making adjustments, brow furrowing.

This whole flower project is taking way longer than anticipated. It's already been over an hour, and we've barely started. Who died and said I was a flower expert anyway? These are going to look like shit.

"You're going to chew all the skin off your lip," Nate teased.

I paused. Only then did I realize I'd rubbed my bottom lip raw with my teeth while we worked.

Nate regarded me, eyes scanning my face and settling on my swollen lip. Then, for the briefest moment, his eyes dipped to the neckline of my tank top before blinking back to the space over my head.

Caught red-handed.

Arching a brow, I grabbed his forearms again and raised the vases back up to chest height where they'd been.

"You're letting the vases drop lower than I need them, Cassidy."

"My arms are getting tired, McLaren."

"Bullshit. You play piano and guitar. Your arms don't get tired." I gave him a pointed look. "You're distracted."

"Can you blame me?" He eyed me with a rare cocky expression, raising his brows in question. One semi-pleasant conversation in the vineyard, and he was already back to being a shameless flirt. He always did have a talent for doing it without making me feel icky, though.

I huffed a laugh, ignoring the blush that was probably working its way up my neck.

I should not be flirting with Nate Cassidy.

"Oh, shut up."

Finally happy with how the first two bouquets looked, I took the vases he held and replaced them with two more, repeating the process and ignoring our extended proximity.

CHAPTER 35

One Year Ago, January

Is this really happening?

W hen we settled into the booth, I finally released the deep breath I'd been holding for the last three hours. The dust inside of me settled, too. One grain at a time.

I let myself take a good look at Nate as he slid into place across from me. He was calm and comfortable, as he almost always was. Unbothered, like nothing could ever be big enough to ruffle his feathers. His nose was a little pink from being out in the cold, and his hair was longer than I had ever seen it. The sides that were usually kept short were now long enough to be tucked behind his ears, but the top was just as tousled and wavy as always. As if reading my mind, he reached up to run his fingers through the length of it. The corner of my mouth lifted at the familiar habit.

"You grew out your hair," I said as the waitress dropped off two glasses of water.

"You cut yours." He leaned back against the booth. My fingers reached up to play with the ends of my now shoulder-length hair. "It looks good," he assured.

"Thanks." My face burned. Whether it was a leftover flush from crying or from being across from Nate was anyone's guess. I ran my cool hands down my cheeks. "I don't have mascara all over my face, do I?"

He grinned, dimple popping into view. "No, Oli. You look great."

I took another deep, cleansing breath, feeling incrementally better with each one, and relaxed back into the booth, shoulders falling as tension released.

What's harder to believe: the fact that I'm sitting across from Nate Cassidy? Or the fact that sitting across from him is somehow making me feel better?

I shouldn't have been surprised. It was his nature.

He had the inexplicable ability to draw you in and create a soft landing to come back to. My pride had been bruised by him before, sure, but he was somehow still a safe space.

Feeling safe didn't mean it wasn't awkward as hell, though. A massive elephant sat on the dirty table. Right between us. Impossible to ignore.

"This is bizarre," I laughed, shaking my head.

He smirked, nodding as he twisted his water glass in circles.

"Does this feel weird to you?"

He didn't miss a beat. "Of course it does. But I'm okay with it." He leaned forward, resting his forearms on the table. "It's good to see you."

My lips rolled when his eyes held mine for a beat too long. My fingers tangled together under the table.

"So, what made you come see us in Boston?"

I sighed and rolled my eyes, eliciting a brow raise from him at my huffing. Amusement and about a dozen questions danced over his handsome features.

I decided not to tell him about my project, nor did I mention *The Mountain*. It would have been trespassing too closely to what I was unwilling to talk about just yet. I couldn't bring myself to think about the rejection. Fibbing felt easier.

"A friend of mine is a fan of Crescent Light. I told her I knew you guys, but she didn't believe me. When we saw you were playing close by, we bought tickets." I shrugged, playing off my intentional concert-going as casual happenstance. "She had a great time."

"Mmhm," Nate hummed. "A fan, huh? You should've told me. I could've gotten you free tickets, or we could've gone out or something afterward." My stomach fluttered at the thought of what might have happened if I had reached out and met up with him. "I would've loved to see you. I know you haven't lost my number," he added with a teasing grin.

"I don't know, Nate." I shrugged again, looking around for anything to hold on to. "Maybe I'm a wimp. I wasn't ready. There's a lot we haven't talked about."

"I agree." He nodded, taking a long drink of his water.

Tightness gathered in my chest again, my thoughts picking up speed and racing through my mind. I shook my head and met his eye again. "Honestly, I don't want to hash all that out right now. Can we pretend things between us are good for tonight? And if we want to go back to hating each other tomorrow, we can?" My sarcasm was evident, but there was no hiding the underlying truth of my words.

He let his head drop and laughed to himself. "Okay, deal. But I don't hate you, Oli. You know that."

I didn't know, but it was comforting to hear it, despite my cowardice, jealousy, and hurt feelings, there was something congenial underneath that remained.

I raised my glass. "Truce?"

He clinked the rim of his glass with mine. "Truce."

We ordered a round of cocktails and spent the next two hours in the booth eating, drinking, and chatting like we hadn't spent the last two years as strangers. He asked me how I liked Boston. I asked him about the band. He told me about a handful of shows they had lined up for the summer on the West Coast, and how he'd quit smoking for good during their last small tour. When I asked him about Billie, the corners of his eyes creased, and he told me she was as spoiled as ever. He still had his apartment nearby, but he had to take Billie to his sister's place when he was gone for extended stints with the band.

Slipping back into this comfortable place with Nate was so easy. I thought back to the night I met him and almost laughed. I never stood a chance of not developing feelings. He was too nice, too charismatic, too handsome. He listened too well and had the uncanny ability to make someone feel like they were the only person in the world.

I tried to remind myself of all the red flags when we were together—*not* together—before.

He disappeared a lot. He was private. He wasn't a great communicator. I never knew where I stood with him. Music was the only thing that mattered, which wasn't a bad thing, but I suspected he thought he couldn't do music and anything else at the same time.

Looking back, I always felt suspended, unstable, waiting in the wings, wondering what we were.

And yet.

Being near him was just. *So. Damn. Easy.*

"So, do you want to tell me why you were so upset earlier?" he finally asked while working on his third drink. I sipped on my fourth, enjoying the weightless feeling.

With a flick of my wrist, I waved the question away.

His discerning look saw right through me.

"I—It was a lot of things at once. A lot of things that built up and up and spilled over, and now every little thing feels so..." My hands mimed a globe in front of my face. "...*big*. Y'know? Like one minor inconvenience might send me right over the edge. Does that ever happen to you?"

He nodded.

Sighing, I watched my fingers as they knotted together. "There was this... thing at work, a project that meant a lot to me. I worked on it for a long time—the hardest I think I've ever worked on anything in my life—and it got rejected." I rubbed at my brow.

"All that work. It was all for nothing, and now I don't know if I'm cut out for being a journalist. I feel stupid for saying that because rejection is part of the job; I know that. But I poured my heart into this project, and now I'm doubting everything. On top of that, I was sick in bed all day yesterday, so I'm really drained and..."

I glanced at him warily. Maybe it was the alcohol, but I kept going. "And there's this... guy I've been seeing. I found out he's basically been playing me, so that's great. The guy stuff hurts, but the thing at work... that hurts worse. It's kind of messing with my head, if I'm honest. Did I mention all this happened within twenty-four hours? Anyway, it triggered an anxiety attack, and— I— It was just a lot."

He watched silently.

The weight of my rattling and oversharing sat like a brick in my stomach. I regretted it immediately.

"So, yeah." I clapped my hands together on the table. "In conclusion, I'm bad at my job, men are stupid, and I should call my therapist."

Nate nodded again, running a hand through his hair. "You're not wrong. Not about the job thing," he amended. "You're brilliant; you'll figure it out and land on your feet. But about the 'men are stupid' thing. They really are. *We* really are."

"Yes." I pointed a finger across the table, barely missing an empty glass. "You *really* are."

He put his hands up in surrender.

Another thought jumped to the forefront of my mind, most *definitely* influenced by the alcohol. "Can I ask you something?"

He took another swig of his drink, shaking a piece of ice into his mouth. "Anything."

"Can I ask what happened with the whole suddenly-there's-Blair situation?"

He froze mid-ice crunch, staring at me a moment before burying his face in his hands.

I laughed, reveling in the sight of him being uncomfortable for once. "Come on! Not that it matters anymore, but I deserve a bit of an explanation, don't you think?"

Nate groaned, peeking at me between his fingers. "Would you believe me if I said I was just dumb? No other rhyme or reason?"

I hummed, weighing his words as I sipped my drink. "Yes, but I'm curious anyway."

"The truth is I have no idea why I did it, and I genuinely regret it." He drummed his knuckles on the table. "It only lasted for, like, two months, and it wasn't worth it."

Something stirred in my chest, but I shrugged it off, not wanting to expend more energy on negativity when I was enjoying his company.

"Fair enough. We don't have to get deeper into it. Fuck it."

"Oh, is it a *fuck it* kind of night? Because if so, I know the perfect thing to make it better. Or worse." He slid to the end of the booth. "But probably better."

"I think we're well beyond *fuck it* at this point, Nate."

"Be right back. Don't move."

I watched him saunter toward the bar and checked my phone for the first time since leaving my car, half expecting something from Kieran.

Nothing.

Good.

A minute later, Nate reappeared, holding two shot glasses of clear liquid in one hand and a small bowl of lime wedges in the other. The shit-eating grin on his face spread wider as my eyes rounded. I shook my head furiously back and forth.

"Nope. *No.* Absolutely not."

"Oh, come on!" He slid one glass in front of me and returned to his seat across the booth. "Nothing says *fuck it* like tequila, Oli. We have to!"

"No, we most certainly do not. Didn't you once tell me bad things happen when you drink tequila?"

"Probably. Now come on." He pushed my glass closer with one finger and leaned over to snag the saltshaker from the far side of the table. "We're doing this together."

Oh god.

I eyed the shot with trepidation. I caught sight of Nate's tongue as it darted out to lick the back of his hand before he poured a small pile of salt there.

Oh god.

My head was starting to swim, but his blue eyes sparkled with amusement and challenge and—

Giving up my resolve with a defeated noise, I licked the back of my hand and held my other out for the salt. His grin spread wide, dimple deepening, as he lowered the shaker into my hand.

"To shitty nights."

"To terrible, shitty nights," I replied.

Together, we took the salt, tequila, and lime, and grimaced as the perfume-y liquid went down.

⟫⟫⟫ ⟪⟪⟪

Sometime later—I'd lost track of when—Nate and I lazily approached the side entrance of his apartment building. I was in a dreamlike trance as I climbed the all-too-familiar stairs to his all-too-familiar apartment.

I'd almost forgotten the thrill of walking behind him as he led the way up, but the old sensation buzzed through my fingers and toes. It reminded me of being a teenager sneaking out of the house for the first time.

The minimalist interior of his apartment felt like something I'd seen the day before and a lifetime ago all at once. I took in the full, surreal scene.

There he was. Nate. Leaning against the same marble island, next to the same living room, with the same furniture and subtle decorations that had always been there. There were only a few changes and additions of note—an extra guitar in the corner, different houseplants, a bigger cat tree Billie lounged in. Mostly the same, yet distinctly different all at once.

Maybe I'm just different.

Memories flooded my mind, flashbacks of all the time spent together, all the things we'd done, all the places we'd done them *in*. A hot flush crept up my neck.

"Gosh," I whispered, mostly to myself, as I glanced around back to where Nate leaned.

He looked a little sheepish—a rare look—like he was recalling the same memories I was. Like he was weighing my reaction as much as I was weighing his. The tug at the corner of his lips had mine turning up, too, and we both expelled nervous, breathy laughs.

The silence that followed filled the air like a thick smoke.

"Come here," he finally said, his voice soft and husky.

On shaky knees, I closed the gap between us, each step more reserved than the last. He reached out when I was arm's length away and rested a warm hand on the swell of my hip. We stayed like that for a long minute, silently connected by only the press of his palm. His deep blue gaze said so much without saying anything at all.

I see you. I missed you. I ask nothing of you. You are safe to be whoever you need to be here.

We were at that familiar crossroads again, where the constant nagging question replayed again: *turn back now or dive in and damn the consequences?*

His throat bobbed.

Is he… nervous?

I saw the question from a mile away as his eyes searched my face, like he wanted to ask but was afraid to scare me away. Between the alcohol, the emotions, and the heady feeling of being close to him, I was putty in his hands.

"Can I kiss you?"

My nod was automatic.

The second his lips touched mine, all reason, all *thought*, all things that weren't Nate Cassidy shut off.

He cupped the sides of my face, his calloused fingers diving and weaving through the hair at the base of my neck as he sighed deeply against my lips. His shoulders folded inward, cocooning me with his towering height, and I couldn't have stopped the moan that escaped me if I tried.

He turned us until my back pressed against the island, trapping me further under his frame. When he grabbed the back of my thighs and hoisted me onto the countertop, my legs wrapped around him instinctively, pulling him closer. He deepened the kiss, movements becoming more and more frantic with each press. Goosebumps rose on my arms when his lips ventured to my neck and down the curve where it met my shoulder.

He sucked gently with each kiss. Not enough to leave a mark, but enough for me to never want him to stop.

Don't stop. Please, don't stop.

My hands found his shaggy hair, fingers tangling through the longer length of it and tugging.

When his mouth returned to mine, he took my bottom lip between his and sucked, coaxing another moan from me.

"*Fuck*, Oli," he whispered, voice low in my ear. "I've always loved the little noises you make."

He was a man starved, the way he kissed me with such urgency, down my neck and back up, capturing my mouth again and again, his tongue sliding against mine, his taste making me dizzy, his hands roaming every inch of my body.

I couldn't tell if he was pressing his hips against mine or if I was pulling them closer with my legs wrapped around him. Either way, his erection strained through his jeans, making me mad with want. He must've felt the same way because just then, he gripped my ass and slid me off the countertop, hoisting me high onto his hips as he aimed for the bedroom.

We didn't get very far.

Nate pinned me against the wall with an impatient huff, wrapping his hand around the back of my neck, forcing me closer to him. I ran my nails through his hair, along his scalp, behind his neck, dipped them below the collar of his shirt.

I wasted no time lifting my shirt over my head when he pushed up the hem. He wasted no time undoing my bra and throwing it across the hallway. He pressed me even harder against the wall, head dipping to my breasts, kissing, sucking, leaving little red spots all over my flushed skin.

When we'd slept together before, Nate usually kept some semblance of control, but now he seemed completely and utterly without restraint. It made my head spin.

"Nate?" I gasped.

He hummed a low, quick response against my skin.

"Bedroom."

He lowered me to my feet and all but dragged me into the bedroom, barely lifting his lips from mine to close the door. He backed me to the foot of the bed and eased me down. The sensation, the *weight* of him, fueled my fire that much more.

I tugged at his shirt, and he leaned back onto his heels, impatiently removing and discarding it. I barely registered the new tattoos across his chest and arms before he was scooting backward off the bed toward my feet. Grabbing my left ankle, he carefully untied and removed one shoe.

"Take these off." He tapped on the button of my jeans and reached for my other shoe. I did as he said, breathing heavily as I unbuttoned my jeans and pushed them over my hips. He dropped my sneaker to the floor and took the liberty of dragging my jeans the rest of the way, pulling them inside out in the process.

"I want to taste you," he whispered, almost to himself.

My panting was the only response when he hooked his fingers around my panties. He took a single beat to catch my eyes. With a furious nod from me, and an almost imperceptible "Yes," he slid them the rest of the way off and settled between my thighs.

His sense of urgency didn't subside.

He planted a single, soft kiss on the inside of my thigh before he hooked his arms under my legs and ravished me like his life depended on it. Running the flat of his tongue up my core, he circled my clit, sucking on the sensitive bud, and repeated the torment again and again. I gasped at the pleasure, desperately fumbling and gripping at the comforter beneath me.

He snaked one hand up to my breast to drag a calloused fingertip over my nipple while the other stayed at my thigh, squeezing the soft flesh and no doubt leaving purple marks. My brain couldn't keep up with what my body was experiencing. It was all I could do to keep breathing as his unrelenting cadence continued.

"Don't stop," I whispered into the dark, digging my fingers into his strong shoulders, his hair, anything to anchor myself to him. He hummed his affirmation against me, sending me gasping at the vibration against my clit.

The hand at my breast eased back down my body, not stopping at my thigh but continuing lower until he slid a single digit inside me, joining in the steady rhythm of his tongue. He added a second finger, twisted, and angled upward until he hit the spot that was my undoing. I came with a shutter and a cry, squeezing my eyes shut as he continued to pump his fingers until I rode out the rest of my orgasm.

He kissed the inside of my thighs again, planting his lips over and over, sucking gently as he rose over my body. I tasted my release on his soft, swollen lips.

I ogled him openly when he slid back off the bed and tugged off his jeans. His erection sprung free, and I relished in the familiarity of his naked form. I couldn't resist reaching between our bodies as he settled back over me to touch him and was blessed with a deliciously long moan from his lips. He gazed down at me with heavy lids, skating his fingers over the flushed, freckled skin on my chest and neck.

"You're so pretty, Oli."

Leaning back on his knees again, he grabbed himself and pumped once, slowly, as his eyes roved over my body—laid out, blushing, waiting for him. He didn't look away as he rolled a condom over his hard length and slid the head of his cock through my release. He teased my core in a painting motion, gliding himself up to my overly-sensitive clit, circling down to my slick entrance, and back up again, making me squirm and wiggle impatiently beneath him.

"So pretty," he murmured again.

In one fluid motion, he dipped to my entrance and pushed inside, not stopping until he was fully seated. I gasped at the exquisite pressure, adjusting myself around him as he waited, panting heavily. He hooked a hand around the back of my thigh and lifted my leg nearly to my chest, increasing the tight pleasure even more.

His thrusts were deep and unrelenting, like he couldn't wait a second longer before having me. He bent forward and captured my mouth in a fervent kiss. I cupped his face, kissing him again and again, memorizing the feel of his mouth against mine.

Long fingers wrapped around my wrist and pulled my hand away until he held it with an iron grip above my head. He shifted, grabbing my other wrist and repeating the motion, holding me hostage by both wrists at the headboard. From this angle, he had no choice but to lower his face to my neck, his unshaven scruff teasing the soft skin and adding to my hypersensitivity.

"*Fuck*," he breathed against my neck, sliding into me again. He was unyielding, pumping harder, *harder* as he chased his high.

But I was rising again.

Needing more, more, *more,* I threw my legs around his waist and hooked my ankles around his thighs, holding on tightly to him. A slew of curses tumbled from his lips, and his soft whimpers in my ear sent goosebumps rising all over my body.

"God, Nate. I'm going to come again."

I heard the change in his breathing from uneven and shaky to focused and steady. He was shifting his concentration, staving off his own release until I could get mine again. Jaw flexed, he worked his hips in a deliberate, unchanged pattern, driving into me in exactly the place I needed him to.

Considerate as always.

My fingers curled into fists, begging for purchase where he still held me tightly by the wrists. He loosened his grip just enough to lace his fingers through mine, never letting up on his pace. Tiny moans erupted from my throat as he pushed me closer—rising, nearing the edge with each thrust of his hips.

When I couldn't rise any further, I shattered apart a second time, shuttering around him, moaning his name. He chased me over the edge only a moment later.

"F—*Fuck,* Oli. Shit," he whimpered into my ear, gripping my hands so tightly I could feel blood pumping in my fingertips.

Only our shared panting filled the silence. He didn't move out of me. Instead, he loosened his grip on my hands and relaxed, burying his face into my neck. We laid, unmoving, until our breaths synced, and even then, we didn't move.

We breathed through the descent from our shared peak, breathed in each other's scent, each other's breath, and through the stillness that followed. We breathed in the moment, so familiar yet so very different, together.

CHAPTER 36

One Year Ago, January

Some things start out fun but don't end well.
Tequila, for example.

I t didn't take long to realize what a massive mistake I'd made.

Nate sprawled on the bed beside me, fast asleep on his stomach. His steady, deep breathing was the only noise in the otherwise silent apartment. Me? I lay there wide awake, staring at the ceiling for what felt like hours.

No, not felt like.

I laid there for literal hours.

When the euphoric high subsided, I expected to drift into a blissful sleep like he had. But the heady emotions only settled briefly before they started the ascent again.

It started with a nagging feeling in my gut, the all-too-familiar feeling of anxiety burning its way into my veins at an achingly slow rate. I couldn't gather a single thought before the next came in on its heels, racing quicker and quicker as the last forty-eight hours caught up with me. Through Nate's peaceful, rhythmic breathing, my heart rate rose, palms turning slick with sweat, fingers and toes going numb at the tips.

And I could do nothing but lie there.

I could do nothing but stare at the ceiling, eyes wide, chest rising and falling so quickly it's a wonder I didn't wake the man next to me. Part of me acknowledged the panic attack as it was setting in, but the other part of me was frozen. Paralyzed. Unable to stop the mental avalanche once it started.

Too much happened in too little time. I hadn't given my mind and body enough time to process any of it before I acted. The project submission, the migraine, Kieran's blindside, the rejection. Forty-eight hours ago, I was hopeful about my job, my relationship, my potential. Now?

Now, it was all a mess.

Too much. I shouldn't have come here. Shouldn't have done this. Oh god, what have I done? I should have gone home. I should have slowed down and gathered my thoughts before doing anything. Before calling anyone—Nate, of all people.

I dragged him into my mess. Two years without speaking, and I dragged him into my mental spiral. I didn't know he'd show up, and I sure as hell didn't think we'd have sex. But as soon as I saw his face, I should have known. It's what we do. Fuck now, ask questions later, right?

I'm an idiot.

I called him because I needed someone and didn't want to be alone. By that logic, I used him. I fucking used him. God, I'm a horrible person. This was not the answer.

And now I can't take it back.

Hours ticked by. My mind didn't relent. Self-loathing set in, negative self-talk, shame, embarrassment, name-calling. My mind—my worst enemy—came for the slaughter. Silent tears streamed out of the corners of my eyes and pooled near my ears. All the while, Nate's breathing, his scent, the heat of his body enveloped me, comforting and suffocating all at once.

I had to get out; I couldn't breathe.

When the sky lightened into a dull, hazy blue, I pulled back the covers with shaking fingers and slid from the bed, hastily tugging on my clothes as I collected them from throughout the apartment.

My phone shook as I called an Uber. We'd both left our cars at the restaurant since we were half-pickled by the time we left.

I need to get out of here.

Hot, new tears stung my eyes as the panic continued to rise. Everything within me was itching to run, run, *run.*

I checked my phone and peeked out Nate's living room window. *Nine minutes away.*

My teeth ripped away at the skin on my bottom lip until a metallic tang of blood spread across my tongue. I checked my phone again. *Eight minutes away.*

Fuck it. I'd rather wait outside in the cold than stand still.

My legs carried me to the front door. I didn't dare look around the apartment I would likely never see again, didn't dare give Billie a parting glance as she blinked at me from her perch. It would only twist the guilty knife in my gut to look at the kitchen island and imagine his lips on mine.

He showed up for you, my inner critic told me, *and you used him. Because you felt a little sad? You're such a piece of shit.* I was unlocking the deadbolt when I heard his tired voice.

"Oli? Are you okay?"

I froze. Squeezing my eyes shut, I slowly turned. Nate stood in only his tight boxer briefs, one hand gripping the frame of his bedroom door, the other raking his mussed hair.

Even then, he was breathtaking. Heartbreaking.

Am I okay? What a loaded question.

No, I wasn't okay. Far from it. I probably looked like shit; the physical effects of ebbing and flowing panic over the course of several hours took its toll.

I didn't answer him. I didn't have to. The mere silence as my chin trembled was answer enough. Realization washed over his beautiful face in waves.

After a weighted silence, he opened his palms to the room around us, eyes searching high and low for some sort of answer.

"So, that's it?" His eyes were soft with bewilderment. "You're leaving? No goodbye or anything?"

I tucked my shaking hands under my arms, unable to meet his eyes. Residual tears stung my eyes, blurred my vision, as I hugged my middle. "Thank you for everything, really, but I–I shouldn't have called you. I'm so sorry—"

His loud scoff halted my words. He had a disbelieving, far-away look on his face, and nodded numbly as if accepting some universal truth.

"Yeah. Okay, fine," he said flatly, his nod transforming into a shake. "See you in a year, I guess. Or two."

He looked like he was about to turn and go back to bed, but just before he disappeared through the door, he whipped back around, something indecipherable outlining his expression. Frustration? Hurt?

"What are we doing, then? I mean, what are we doing with this?" He gestured from the center of his chest to the air between us. "Is this going to be like before?"

I reared back, pulling my eyebrows together. "What?"

"We see each other once in a blue moon, we have fun, we fuck, but none of it ever means anything? Because I can't do that again."

I blinked, sniffling, unable to answer. His words rang through my head again, and still, they made no sense.

What is he saying?

Cool, calm, collected Nate, who was utterly unflappable, was *angry*. My dazed silence only fueled him further because, after only a moment, he continued.

"You didn't want me before, and that was fine. I wasn't good enough for you anyway, so I didn't push anything, didn't push *us*. I was happy to have you when you wanted me. But then... I don't know, things changed, and you left. You got to move away, start all over again, date jerks, clearly," he added with a wave of his hand and a painfully accusatory brow raise.

I found my voice and cut him off before he could say another word. "What are you even *talking* about?" There was more bite than I intended, but I didn't have the strength to hold back. "I didn't *want* you? You were the one who was always cooped up in the studio, writing, doing shows, disappearing off the face of the earth. And I never complained. Not once. I was happy to wait on the sidelines because I knew music would always come first. So don't act like you were waiting around for me." My quickly rising temper surprised me. Two years' worth of hot, burning anger.

"You went on dates with other guys—"

"I went on *one* date! One! Because *you* told me to."

"—but the second I tried to move on you were pissed," he snapped.

"That was different, and you know it. You disappeared and then showed back up with a full-blown girlfriend. It took me *completely* off guard. And you showed her off in front of everybody. I felt like a fucking idiot."

"Yeah, tell me about it," he said sardonically, bringing his hands to rest on his hips.

I cocked my head to the side. "What's that supposed to mean?"

"It means you're a hypocrite, Olive. You have a boyfriend."

We both knew that wasn't true. I most certainly did *not* have a boyfriend. He said it just to get under my skin, and it worked, twisting the guilt and shame in my gut, heating me from the inside out.

"Don't pretend like you ever wanted anything more with me, Nate. You made it crystal clear on multiple occasions you weren't interested in anything real or remotely serious. And if you've had *all* this on your mind, all these things to say to me, then you should've opened your mouth and said them a long time ago."

"Yeah, well, I'm glad I didn't." His eyes landed on mine.

My head shook. I couldn't believe what was happening. How quickly our brief truce flipped on its head. His eyes that shone with tender comfort, desire, and yearning hours before, now filled with resentment and indignation.

This was the furthest thing from what I wanted.

"Nate," I started calmly, attempting to regain a semblance of control over my emotions. "I don't want to fight. You know I care about you. You were one of my closest friends, despite everything that happen—"

"I'm not your friend."

My mouth snapped shut. He clenched his jaw as his deep sea eyes flared with an anger I'd never seen in the entire time I'd known him. Devastated, heartbroken anger.

"I've never been your fucking friend. I'm a convenient distraction for you, at the *very* best."

The words struck me in the heart, making my chest bow as I exhaled. My eyes closed against the fresh tears threatening to fall, willing this fight, our first and our last, to be over. I bit my lip in an attempt to still my uncontrollably trembling chin.

"Fine," I said, barely louder than a whisper. "I'll go." I reached for the door again and pulled it open. "Have a nice life doing—" I shrugged helplessly. "—whatever you want to do, and I'll—"

"You'll have to go find a new fuck buddy, I guess. Next time you get bored, don't call me."

My eyes crashed into his, mouth dropping open wordlessly.

A slap to the face, that's what it was. A gut punch. Sure, we were never really together, but at one point, he was an important person in my life. He was still—until ten seconds before—important to me. I thought I was important to him, too.

That's what you get.

Tears welled and spilled as I stared at him, frozen in place. He stared back at me silently, his eyes tracking my tears as they rolled down my cheek. A flicker of something like regret peeked through the hurt in his deep blue eyes.

I turned on my heel.

"Oli, wait—" He attempted a step toward me, but I was too quick as I stepped into the hall and slammed the door.

⟫⟫⟫ ⟪⟪⟪

I drove back to Boston in complete silence. Once frantic thoughts slowed to a crawl, then stopped altogether after seeing Nate's anger—the *hurt* in his eyes. I felt hollow. Empty. So devoid of energy that even my self-loathing took a break.

Back at my apartment, my feet led me straight to my bed, which was still unmade from when I was down with my migraine.

How was that only two days ago?

Sleep tugged at the corners of my mind, but as I curled under the thick blankets, I caught a whiff of a familiar scent. It was somewhere. Everywhere.

I sat up, pulled the ends of my hair under my nose, and sniffed. Nate. His cologne, his apartment, his laundry, *him*. The collar of my T-shirt? Nate. It tangled my hair as I pulled it over my head and tossed it across the room.

The tiny purple mark over my left breast? That was Nate, too.

Ignoring the stinging in my eyes, I threw back the blankets and trudged to the bathroom. He was in my skin, the aching muscles of my body. Steam bloomed on the vanity mirror once I twisted the lever to a hellish level, desperate to wash him away. I stripped the rest of my clothes and shoved them deep into the bottom of my overflowing hamper. When I returned to my bedroom to grab the discarded shirt off the floor, I paused.

As much as I wanted to wash Nate Cassidy off my skin, out of my hair, I—for whatever reason—pressed the fabric to my face and inhaled deeply one last time. Forgetting him was going to be impossible; I knew that. I'd tried before, and it didn't work. But still, I wished I could.

It'd been two years since the last time we were together. Two years, but I still remembered every detail. And last night was… different. It was the first time I'd truly *connected* with someone since… well, him. It was like reigniting the embers of a twin flame. Like curling into your bed after a long, hard day. It only made our fight feel that much worse.

Stepping under the water, I let the steam fill my lungs.

The shower acted as a catalyst for turning off my emotional brain and switching to my logical one. Everything was clearer when thought about in a shower.

I focused on what I knew instead of what I felt for once, and the facts of the matter were straightforward. Blatantly obvious.

I wasn't in a good place mentally; I didn't take the time to think things through, and I acted purely based on emotions. All sense of self-preservation and reason was dust in the wind. Now, I was paying the price for it.

Here's what I know.

1. Kieran assumed we weren't exclusive. I assumed we were. Things with Kieran are over.

2. I should have come home after I left Kieran's. I didn't.

3. If there was any chance of having a friendship with Nate, or even being indifferent acquaintances, that was long gone.

Any lingering embers of feeling for him were snuffed out. They had to be. I would make them. Sleeping together—no matter how willing we were—was a mistake of massive proportions because he was still Nate, and I was still me.

And now there was nothing.

4. He called me a hypocrite. He isn't wrong.

As pissed as I was, hurt and cut to the core by his words, there were a few that rang louder than all the others.

Some because I knew they were true. *"You're a hypocrite, Olive."*

Others because I knew they weren't. *"I'm not your friend. I've never been your fucking friend."*

This morning was the first time I'd heard him say anything that resembled ever having real feelings for me. The first time I'd heard a semblance of truth from him. Real, raw, vulnerable, honest truth.

And I was so fucking pissed about it.

I may have regretted some of my actions, some of my words, but I was glad I called him out on that part. Glad I told him he should have said all of that long ago, because he damn well should have.

Maybe things could have been different.

Who knows what could have been, what might have become of us if he'd just… if he'd just *talked* to me. If he would've opened his mouth instead of writing everything down and had a real conversation.

He doesn't get to put this on me. He doesn't get to act like the heartbroken one.

He doesn't get to make me play the guessing game for over a year and blame me when I didn't want to play anymore.

He sure as hell doesn't get to make me feel bad about it now.

"*I'm not your friend,*" he'd said. "*I've never been your fucking friend.*"

Message received. Loud and clear.

Chapter 37

One Year Ago, January

She was here. Now she isn't.
And my pillowcase smells like lilacs.

The hardest part about everything that happened was having to go back to work on Monday and act like I was alright. Everyone would be buzzing from the announcement of the Newbie Comp winner, and even though I was prouder of Ha-Joon than I was jealous, I was still so emotionally raw.

And to be honest, I was feeling physically raw, too. My legs were sore, my nipples sensitive, and the insides of my thighs sported faint purple marks that were suspiciously the size of Nate's fingertips.

In any normal scenario, I might think of the residual marks and soreness as a turn-on. But they were only bitter reminders of how badly everything was fucked up.

I picked up coffee for Wren and Ha-Joon on my way to the office, determined not to let my sourpuss mood bring me down all day. The usual: vanilla oat milk latte for Wren, black coffee for Ha-Joon, Earl Grey for me.

Shiny gold balloons that spelled "congrats" were draped over Ha-Joon's side of our three-sided cubicle. My lips quirked up just thinking about how Ha-Joon, our humble sweetheart, probably hated them.

"Congratulations, hot shot," I said as I reached over his shoulder to put the coffee next to his laptop. I wrapped an arm around his chest and gave him a squeeze.

"Thanks," he smiled sheepishly. "I don't know how I feel about all the attention, though."

"Hush," I scolded, circling around and plopping Wren's latte in her waiting grabby hands. "You deserve it."

She let out a deep moan as she drank. "Mmh. You are a goddess, thank you. You just missed Lifestyle coming in here to formally congratulate our poor Ha-Joon. They applauded and everything. He got so red I thought he would burst into flames."

"It's very sweet. But it's... a lot," he murmured, fingers flying over his keyboard, already busy at work. Maybe he didn't love the attention, but he was flying on cloud nine in his own way. His dark brown eyes sparkled, and a certain lightness immolated from his lanky form. He'd even styled his black hair differently, gelling it back so it revealed his forehead. He reminded me of a kid on school picture day, reluctantly dressed up and pretending not to be excited.

"A title on the cover of the next edition and a mention on the website's main page is a big deal, Joon," I said. "You need to let yourself bask in the bragging rights for at *least* a day."

His ears, usually hidden under his dark mop of hair, burned red as he gave Wren and me a heartfelt smile before ducking back into his work.

⋙⋙ ⋘⋘

The rest of the day was, thankfully, uneventful. We carried on, business as usual, knocking out upcoming dailies for the next week. I put my headphones in and worked silently for the most part, desperate to keep moving fast enough that my brain would stay occupied.

I was packing up my things, feeling grateful the day was over and proud that I kept my brave face on the whole time, when Julienne's voice flittered out her open office door.

"McLaren, is that you?"

My head fell back and my eyes settled on a crack in the ceiling.

So close.

I'd been doing so well at avoiding people. I was peopled out. If Julienne wasn't my boss—and terrifying, and brilliant—I might've pretended not to hear her.

Sliding my laptop into my tote bag, I slung it over my shoulder and trudged to Julienne's office.

"Hey," I said in my most normal voice, stopping in the entryway. "Did you need something?"

She leaned back in her seat, dark eyes assessing me. The barest hint of a smile graced her full lips as she extended one slender arm to gesture to the plush armchairs in front of her desk. "Come sit."

It sounded like an invitation, but she wasn't asking.

Getting fired would be very on-brand for how the last few days have been.

She must have seen the skeptical look in my eye because she added, "You aren't in trouble."

I made a show of releasing a relieved breath as I sat, and she laughed, teeth shining stark white against her dark brown skin. It was only then I realized I'd never heard her laugh before, and it eased something in me.

"Olive, I wanted to tell you personally how much I enjoyed reading your submission."

My eyes widened. A tight, politely awkward smile formed on my lips. *Lovely. It's like being rejected all over again. Only this time to my face and with an extra serving of pity.*

"Actually," she continued, "I enjoyed it quite a bit. As did the rest of the judging committee."

"Oh. I mean—thank you. That means a lot."

"And I'm not just saying that. You committed to the assignment. We asked everyone to dig deep, and you did exactly that. The level of care you put into your project was evident."

It felt a little like salt was being rubbed into my wounds. I wasn't sure what, if any, response she was looking for.

She leaned forward on her elbows and steepled her hands under her chin. "Olive, I think the idea can go even deeper."

My eyes widened further. "What do you mean?"

"I think there's more of a story to tell, another level we can explore with the artists you chose. I wanted to see if you'd be interested in taking another whack at it. Obviously, I have some notes and a number of suggestions. But if we can hone in on the research a bit, I think this could be a great piece. Not to mention the positive impact it could have locally."

Julienne paused, giving me a chance to respond, but continued when I failed to produce a sound. "The Newbie Comp is over, so the same incentives and distinctions won't be offered. You'll have to submit the piece for approval, and it'll go through the same selection process as every other article, but it's still a great opportunity for you. Something to hang your hat on if it's approved, to be sure. If you're interested—"

"Yes!" I nodded furiously. "I'm sorry, I don't mean to interrupt, but yes. I believe in this piece. I'll do whatever I can to see it through. It would mean a lot for me, yes, but for the artists, too. They—" Crescent Light flashed through my mind. The determined look Nate got when he was on stage. Muddy as things might be, my opinions on his artistry were unchanged. He was brilliant. *They* were brilliant. "They deserve it."

Julienne gave me another soft smile. "Your heart is in the right place. We can see that. Now"—she leaned back in her seat, reminding me of a queen on her throne—"let's go over a few suggestions and discuss a timeline."

⇢⟫⟫ ⟪⟪⟪⟵

Julienne and the panel loved my piece.

I said it over and over in my head because it just didn't feel real. We spent the next hour in her office going over my article. She passed along notes from her and the rest of the panel, all constructive pieces of criticism I totally agreed with.

The biggest takeaway was that they felt there was a deeper level I could have gone into with each artist, but that five groups may have been too big of a pool for the level of detail they wanted. Focusing on three artists, instead of five, would have allowed me to peel back another layer for each one.

I left her office feeling better than I had in days, with a new sense of challenge, of purpose. A fire within me reignited, determination flaring at the chance to push myself. The chance for my work to still see the light of day.

Diving back in, I took each of Julienne's suggestions to heart as I reworked. I leaned further into the details the panel liked and trimmed the fat on the sections that weren't as strong. My free time was once again consumed with the piece, and I couldn't have been more glad for it. I was on the precipice of something that could change the trajectory of my professional career, and I would not, could not, take it for granted.

While the rewrite sometimes served as a fantastic distraction from my personal life, it came with its own set of distractions. Especially when I shortened the list of artists from five to three, and Crescent Light made the cut yet again.

Only this time, I couldn't blame it on any unconscious, personal bias about them. Nope. Crescent Light was hand-picked by the goddess Julienne herself as the artist she was most interested in learning more about.

It was harder to keep my head and my heart separated. Harder to keep my love for music and my history with Nate—both ancient *and* recent—carefully divided. Harder not to allow them to influence one another.

When I re-listened to songs, Nate's soothing voice pulled me in. When I watched live performances, I got stuck watching the way Nate moved on stage. When I analyzed lyrics, I found underlying meaning in the words.

In fleeting moments, I could forget about what happened and let myself indulge in him. But the sour hurt would always return a moment later.

"I'm not your friend. I've never been your fucking friend."

The article required focus, free from my clouded judgment. So, I packed him up in a box and shoved him into the corner of my mind to be dealt with, looked at, and reconciled another time.

I needed to quit him. Fleeting promises of a sweet, gooey center lingering under his unreadable shell wasn't a good enough reason to keep holding out hope.

Like a moth to a flame, seeing him proved that all it took was one glance for me to be drawn in—for me to be burned.

I wanted to hate him. I wanted to blame him for my anger, my heartache, for taking up so much of my time, for occupying so many of my thoughts. I wanted to curse him for robbing me of a chance at ever forgetting about him, and demand answers I know I would never get.

And yet.

Crescent Light deserved to be heard by the entire world.

Maybe this could've been my way of reconciling a part of what happened so I could, at last, walk away from everything without being flooded with regrets.

Maybe this rewrite will give me exactly the kind of catharsis I need to finally quit Nate Cassidy once and for all.

CHAPTER 38

Now

*When I can see her and smell her and imagine how soft her
body is and hear her laugh, I'm a fucking goner all over again.*

Between de-thorning, trimming, and building arrangements, my "easy" flower chore took the rest of the morning and lasted well into the early afternoon.

Nate and I developed a system as we worked. He took up the task of snapping thorns off the roses one by one, cursing under his breath every time he caught a fingertip on the sharp points. Then, he would pass the thornless roses for me to snip the stems, pull off low-hanging leaves, and drop them into water.

Once we had a large enough pile of processed flowers, and our backs were aching from sitting for too long, we would stand to build the arrangements. Nate held empty vases two at a time, and I'd stuff them with flowers. Then, we would walk the finished centerpieces inside the air-conditioned building to stay fresh on a banquet table until we got the greenlight from resort staff to store them in the walk-in fridge.

Rinse. Repeat.

We kept our heads down and conversation light, centering topics mostly around roses and greenery. When conversation lulled, we worked in comfortable silence.

Thorns, stems, leaves, water, repeat. Thorns, cursing (Nate), laughing (me), stems, leaves, water, repeat.

After a long while working in silence, he cleared his throat.

"I, uh— I never did thank you. You know, for the article."

I stilled, my sheers hovering at an angle mere centimeters from a stem. There was a slim chance he never saw my article when it was first published; I knew that. A photo of Crescent Light had been used as the thumbnail when it was featured on the Online Daily homepage, for crying out loud. Not my idea. The marketing intern thought Crescent Light was the best artist to use on the homepage because they had "the best look." AKA, the charmingly attractive frontman was perfect clickbait.

It never occurred to me that I would ever be put in a position to talk about the article with Nate directly, though.

When I didn't respond right away, he continued. "It's a big deal for a band to be acknowledged by *The Mountain*. It's made a difference for us, you know?" His deep blue eyes met mine as he handed me a de-thorned rose and reached for another one. "You did us a favor."

"It wasn't a favor." I shook my head. "We were asked to write about something we cared about. I care about artists who don't get enough attention. I wrote an honest article about who I thought truly deserved it." I snipped a stem. "I didn't do you any favors. I just wrote the truth."

He smiled. My gaze drifted to his cheek, and my heart fluttered with the familiarity and intimacy of knowing his smile so well.

"Well, thank you anyway."

I huffed a laugh, dropping the rose into its waiting vase.

"Also, *The Mountain*, Oli? Seriously?" He smiled incredulously. "When were you going to let me in on *that* little secret? It's a huge fucking deal."

I laughed again, full and freeing. His eyes roved over my face like he was savoring every last drop.

"Yeah. It's… amazing. I still can't believe it's real."

"Hell yeah, it is." He grinned. "I'm so proud of you."

Something in me swelled.

The truth was, I was proud of him, too. Crescent Light was officially on the map, their fan base and attention growing internationally by the day. Seeing him and the guys shine was amazing. I couldn't take credit for it, but knowing that I might have been responsible for someone finding their new favorite artist was enough to give me the warm fuzzies.

Nate snapped the thorns off the next rose, then the next, then the next, his brows drawn together in concentration.

Silence returned, but it didn't have any of its prior heaviness. It reminded me of all the times we would sit in his apartment. Me, reading or typing away on some assignment, him with headphones on, hunched over his keyboard or his leather notebook.

Parallel play.

After a time, we stood and began the next step in the process. Nate held two empty vases and stepped closer for me to assemble. His scent overwhelmed my senses, and all the sweetest memories flashed through my mind. Then, all the bitter moments. I breathed through my mouth and continued.

Eventually, the silence grew heavier. Instead of his contended, neutral expression, his face became tight. His jaw worked as he snipped at the thorns. Twice, I caught him opening his mouth from the corner of my eye as if he was going to say something, only for him to shut it again. I wished so badly that I could read his mind, but there was a tiny piece of me that warned me not to go down that path.

Curiosity won out.

"I wish you would say whatever is on your mind," I said a half hour later as we walked a handful of vases inside.

He laughed through his nose—a confirmation of my suspicion that he'd been ruminating on something.

He breathed in, prepping to speak but hesitating all the same. I already regretted asking him what was wrong. "Your boyfriend—"

"Never mind," I cut him off, placing my vases down on the table inside, not looking at him as my walls rose defensively. "I don't wanna know."

"So, now I'm not allowed to ask questions?"

"Not if it's going to make things weird."

"What would possibly be weird about it?" He said it in a facetious, sarcastic tone as if whatever he had to ask was purely innocent. As if he was just any other friend asking about my relationship.

We both knew what his angle was.

"Fine." Annoyance pricked at my fingers and toes as I turned in a flourish to face him. "Please enlighten me with your *totally* normal, appropriate, non-intrusive questions."

He took a micro-step closer, standing toe to toe instead of backing down. "I have about a thousand. Where would you like to start?"

A small cough sounded from the corner of the otherwise empty room. A member of the resort staff stood there, giving a friendly wave as a way of announcing themselves and apologizing for the interruption all at once.

"Sorry," she said. "Just wanted to let you know the walk-in refriger-ator is all set to store the flowers in. We cleared a wall of shelves."

"Right. Thank you," I answered in the friendliest voice I could muster, even as I fought the urge to shoot daggers at Nate.

"Of course. Would you like some assistance carrying the flowers in?"

I waved my hand politely. "No, that's alright. I'm sure you have other things to worry about. We'll take care of them."

She gave a small nod with a grateful smile and disappeared around the corner in the opposite direction of the kitchen.

I waited until I knew she was gone before I turned my back on Nate, picked up the vases I'd just set down and started toward the kitchen door.

Nate picked up two more vases and followed. "So, are you happy with him?"

I nearly tripped over my feet.

What the hell kind of question is that?

I pushed open the swinging door to the kitchen with my shoulder, scoffing. "Why wouldn't I be?"

"I don't know, Oli. Maybe because he used the words 'empty calories' unironically last night? Or because he looks like he only leaves the CrossFit gym long enough to eat raw eggs?"

I juggled my vases, refusing Nate's hand, until I could pull open the heavy door of the walk-in fridge. Ignoring the sudden rush of cool air, I shoved my vases to the back of the wall of empty shelves. "So, what? There's nothing wrong with going to the gym."

My steps echoed off the metal floor as I stepped back out of the refrigerator.

"You know," he said, hot on my heels, "I've been thinking about it, and I know I just met the guy, so I could be completely off base here, but I truly cannot conceptualize a single thing you two might have in common."

"We have plenty in common," I snapped. "You don't know what you're talking about."

I grabbed four more vases and held them to my chest, catching Nate's shoulder on mine as I turned again.

"Yeah?" There was an edge of amusement in his challenge. "Like what?"

My steps faltered for a beat, but I stomped forward, my mouth opening and closing as I thought of an answer.

"Well, there's…"

We have a ton in common. We've been together for over two years. There's obviously… What?

"We like going on walks." I pulled the giant walk-in door again, nearly dropping a vase before Nate caught up with me to assist.

"Oh, well, in that case, I wish you every happiness. May all your walks be magical."

I ignored the way his chest pressed against my back for a split second before I stomped inside and slid my vases on the shelf.

"We have plenty in common. I don't have to justify my relationship to you."

"Of course not," he said, beating me out of the walk-in this time and holding the door open for me as we exited. "But, I'm curious anyway. What does he think about your job? Your friends? Your hobbies? You know, all the things you care about?"

I shook my head, buying time as I seethed. I snatched more vases, sloshing water onto the floor in the process, and turned on my heel again.

My job? Kieran had never outright said it, but I knew he didn't understand what I did. He knew I was a journalist, yes. He knew I was involved in the music industry, yes. But he didn't see how something that was one part writing, one part interviewing, one part going to concerts, and keeping up with pop stars was a sustainable career.

My hobbies were so closely knit to my job that they almost felt like one and the same. He didn't appreciate music like I did, but that wasn't a deal-breaker on its own.

Everyone is entitled to their own likes and dislikes. It doesn't really matter, right?

And my friends? His general disdain for Gemma's social media-centric lifestyle aside, the only person he'd hit it off with this weekend was Gemma's football player brother. And while I loved Michael like a sibling, he wasn't one of my actual friends. Come to think of it, Kieran hadn't said much about *any* of my friends. If I had to guess, I'd say he was generally unimpressed by them. Bored, even.

I was far ahead of Nate when I reached the walk-in and tugged the heavy door open. When I slid the vases into place on the shelf, I leaned my forehead against it, focusing on the cold metal against my skin.

The door opened again behind me, but I didn't move. It shut with a thud as Nate reached my side, but he wasn't done.

"And another thing," he pressed, relentless in his grilling. He carefully slid his vases into place and faced me, propping an arm on the shelf over his head. "*Why* are you drinking red wine? You *hate* red wine."

I ground my teeth. I started drinking red wine more when Kieran and I got together because he insisted it was the only thing to drink with red meat. Then he started ordering it for me when we would go out, and I never asked him not to. I didn't know why.

"Come on, Oli," he pushed. "What are you doing with him? I mean, really? What are you *doing* with a guy like that?"

I pushed off the shelf and faced him, squaring my shoulders.

"Why the *fuck* do you care?" I felt the venom in my words, saw the look in his eyes as he blinked back his surprise, but I didn't care. It was my turn to ask the questions. "Why the fuck do you care about my relationship? Why do you care about who I'm with or what I'm doing? You've never cared before."

I made to push past him, but he stepped in my way, brow furrowed. "You think I don't care? Really? You honestly believe that?"

I met his eye. "Yeah, Nate. I do."

I didn't.

There was a piece of Nate that did care about me, just like how there was a piece of me that did and always would care about him. It was impossible to ignore, though life would've been easier if it went away.

My body shivered as I passed him, but before I could open the refrigerator door, he stopped me again. "What makes you say that?"

"Because you—" Blood boiling, I whipped around to face him again, hair arching with the force. "You *had* me, Nate! You had me. For a long fucking time. And you didn't care enough to do something about it! You kept us quiet and in limbo when I deserved to be loved out loud."

I stared at him, shaking my head. This man. He frustrated me, vexed me, consumed my thoughts. He was the one thing I could never shake, no matter how hard I tried. Suddenly, I understood his smoking habit more than I wanted to.

"And you know what the funny part is?" I should've shut up, but I pushed on. "I would have done that for you. I would have loved you, and supported you, and been your biggest fan. I never would have taken too much or asked to be your everything—I know where your priorities are, and I respect that. I only wanted to believe that I had a fucking place in your life. And *you* couldn't do that."

He focused on me, brows drawn together, jaw tense.

He was still my favorite thing to look at.

"You want to know what I think?" I asked, placing a hand on the door. "I think that when things started to get a little too real for you, you fucking ran."

I gave the door a push, but it didn't budge.

Huh?

I placed my other hand on the door, bracing against it, and pushed again. Nothing. Before, the door had been heavy, yes, but it still swung open with relative ease.

"What the hell?" I whispered, shoving it a third time.

Nate closed in behind me, his chest again pressing against my shoulders, as he reached over my head and gave the door a push.

"Shit," he mumbled.

"Do you have your phone?"

"No, it's out there on the table."

Fuck.

"Mine, too." I glanced over my shoulder at him, the column of his neck only inches from my face, as he reached up again to give the door a sharp push.

Wiggling away, I imagined all the words I said to him scattered on the refrigerator floor like a layer of sand. I'd said too much, and now there was no taking it back.

A small stack of empty milk crates sat in the corner. Grabbing one and flipping it upside down, I sat, burying my head in my hands.

I'm locked in a fridge with Nate Cassidy.

We don't have our phones.

I left my sweater outside.

Amazing.

"At least it's a balmy forty-two degrees in here," he snarked, taking a step back. "Someone's bound to open the door in a few minutes."

I counted to ten in time with my breaths, then counted again. I heard Nate settle somewhere in front of me, against the opposite wall of the fridge.

"You okay?"

"Don't." I pushed the heels of my palms against my eyes. "Just… don't talk for a minute. Please."

He said nothing, but I sensed his nod.

We stayed frozen long enough for the motion sensor in the fridge to shut the lights off, and even then, we didn't move.

My thoughts swam and stilled all at once, still hung up on Nate's questions.

What do Kieran and I have in common?

What is one thing? Just one thing?

What did Kieran think about my job, my friends?

I knew the answer to those, but I'd spent so long overlooking them that I convinced myself the answer didn't matter. Now faced with saying it out loud, it felt like they did.

As angry as I wanted to be at Nate, I was angrier at his questions because they forced me to take a closer look at something I hadn't realized I'd been sweeping under the rug.

The lights flickered back on as Nate moved, and a moment later, I felt the warmth of his hoodie being draped over my bare shoulders.

I blinked up at him. "Thanks."

He reached up and laid a palm over his backward hat as if miming the movement of running his fingers through his hair, despite it being tucked away.

"Remember earlier when I said I never thanked you for the article?" He didn't meet my eyes as he leaned against the shelves behind him and shoved his hands into his front pockets. "There was something else I never did."

I eyed him, fishing my arms through the sleeves of his hoodie, bracing myself for whatever he was about to say. His tongue darted out and rolled over his bottom lip like he wasn't sure what exactly would come out of his mouth, either.

"I never gave you the apology you deserved."

My stomach bottomed out, and I closed my eyes in a singular, slow blink. "Nate—"

"Let me get this off my chest. Please."

He rolled his tongue over his lip a second time and bit down on it. I met his helpless stare and tried to place what was behind it. Nervousness? Apprehension?

"That night," he paused, taking a deep breath. "The last night we…"

"I've never been your fucking friend."

He looked down at his shoes, swallowing, weighing his next words. "I said some shit that night that I'm not proud of. Horrible things that should have never even come out of my mouth because they weren't true, and they weren't fair."

When I didn't move a muscle, he took a step forward, crouching in front of me.

"I *hate* that those were the last words I said to you. I thought about it for a long time, but I didn't know how to make it right, so… I didn't. The way you left… I figured I was the last person you'd want to hear from, so I gave you space. I stood there while you walked out my door—watched you walk away without making it right because I was hurt. And I was a coward. And you didn't deserve that—you *don't* deserve that. I don't know if I'll ever be able to fix it, but I am so sorry, Oli."

He pressed his lips together, eyes meeting mine and lingering there, reading my face. Studying. Waiting for my response.

What was there to say?

A million things.

Nothing at all.

I took a steadying breath and leaned forward, resting my elbows on my knees.

"We both did and said things we probably shouldn't have that night. I wasn't in a good place, and it wasn't okay for me to call you like that. I'm sorry I put you in a position to do something you regret. If I could go back and do it differently, I would."

That small crease between his eyebrows returned. "I don't regret anything we *did* that night." He shook his head, running a hand over his hat again like his fingers were begging to get to his hair. "Never that. I just regret the things I said before you left." He didn't regret the phone call. The drinks. The sex. Never the sex. "I regret causing the look on your face before you slammed my apartment door. I haven't been able to stop thinking about it for almost two years."

A new mix of emotions washed over me with every heartbeat as I stared into his eyes. Consolation from hearing what I didn't realize I needed to hear. Relief that some of the tension between us could finally untie itself. Heartache that any of it happened in the first place. Trepidation of what to do or say next.

My chin trembled.

A tear spilled over my lashes and slid onto my cheek.

He tracked the movement, dropping from his crouch to lean on one knee, his eyes softening. As if he couldn't help himself, he gingerly grazed my jaw with his calloused fingertips and wiped the tear away with the pad of his thumb.

His voice was strained as he said, "I'm sorry. I didn't mean to make you cry." His hand didn't leave my cheek as he leaned closer. Instead, he slid it to the back of my neck and ran his thumb over my jaw, back and forth, soothing. I leaned into his touch, our noses only an inch from touching.

"…Nate."

"Oli."

He was so close. I should've pulled away, but I didn't. Couldn't. His lips, only a breath away, were so near my eyes fluttered to a close, welcoming their touch.

A featherlight graze of his top lip on mine, then—

Whoosh. The seal on the walk-in door released and the door swung wide.

"You two have about three seconds to get your shit together," Gemma hissed as I jerked back from Nate and met her wide-eyed gaze.

"Is she in there?" a voice behind her asked.

Kieran.

Shit.

CHAPTER 39

One Year Ago, March

Nobody hates me more than me.

Kieran

> I'd really like to talk to you. Can you meet me somewhere?

Kieran

> Will you answer the phone?

Kieran

> Olive, come on.

Kieran

> I respect that you clearly don't want to talk, but I would at least like the chance to explain myself.

I read Kieran's last message again.

He first texted me two days after The Incident. I hadn't responded, too swept up in the falling out with Nate and the news about my article. He tried to call a few days later, and again a day after that, which

I ignored. I didn't have the brainpower to deal with anything that wasn't work-related.

Well, I had the brainpower. I just wasn't willing to spend it on anything that caused me more stress, anxiety, or generally didn't spark joy. I Marie Kondo'd my text messages.

A week of silence passed before he texted me his latest message.

A chance to explain what? You're seeing other girls, and I was naïve and hopeful enough to think you weren't. What else is there to explain?

I left his texts unanswered. Not so much out of spite, hurt feelings, or the sake of my sensitive, bruised ego. No, it was good ol' fashioned avoidance. It wasn't a conversation I was willing to have. Simple as that. I didn't want to look Kieran in the eyes and feel stupid. I didn't want to admit to myself that I was the common denominator.

Healthy, long-term, adult relationships were apparently impossible. Which, for some reason, probably attributed to the patriarchy, felt like a failure on all fronts.

Not to mention, I was just plain *sad*. I liked where things were going with Kieran before it all went belly up. I missed his company.

A month had passed since the night with Nate, and I was finally beginning to see the light at the end of the tunnel. Not just with my feelings about him, which seemed more manageable and distant the more I looked at him purely as a subject of my article and not as my ex-situationship, but also with the article itself.

Pride bubbled inside me as I worked through my last round of edits before submitting again for consideration. Even if my article made it through the selection process, it could still be months before it ever saw publication. But my piece was better, stronger, more impactful now than it ever was before my rejection.

I leaned closer to my laptop screen, scanning for the millionth time, looking for any last-minute edits, when a knock at my apartment door nearly made me jump out of my skin.

"What the hell?"

My fuzzy socks slid across the kitchen floor as I shuffled to the door and squinted through the peephole.

Kieran's hulking frame stood on the other side, an anxious look painting his face. His light green eyes were unfamiliar and wary with nervous anticipation. I took a step back, staring at my closed door, unable to decide what I wanted to do.

I didn't have time to think about what plan of action to take, what the possible outcomes might be.

He knocked again. My instinct was to unlock the deadbolt and let him in, lean into him, feel the weight of his arms around my shoulders. But my stubborn pride kept me bolted to the spot.

"Olive?" his muffled voice called behind the door. "If you don't want to answer the door, that's fine. I just thought coming down here to talk to you in person would be a little less pathetic than calling and texting over and over again. But, now I'm thinking…" He trailed off. "This feels kind of pathetic either way."

He sounded like he was about to completely deflate on the dirty floor of the landing.

I took pity and opened the door before he totally lost his nerve. His eyes snapped to mine, and he stood there, mouth agape, for a moment before he tentatively crossed the threshold into my apartment one careful foot at a time.

"Olive," he said, his voice hoarse. "This sucks. I've missed the hell out of you these past few weeks. Please believe me when I say this is a huge misunderstanding." He ran a hand over the stubble on his chin, shaking his head slightly. "I know this probably sounds like a sorry fucking excuse, but I promise you, I genuinely did not realize you wanted to be exclusive. Saying that out loud makes me feel like a dick, I know, but that's the truth."

He laughed humorlessly. "If I knew you wanted to be exclusive, I would've jumped at the opportunity. I'd be an idiot not to. I guess I just assumed you were dating around, too. That's just how most people in the dating world are. Everyone's on the apps; everyone has multiple people they're talking to at a time."

I wasn't on the apps, but I'd heard how nightmarish it could be. My arms stayed crossed over my chest.

He took a small step toward me. "I was talking to Kellie and very, *very* casually texting another girl, too. But things are over and done with both of them." He took another step closer, stooping his head to catch my eye.

Dammit, Olive. You're supposed to be mad at him.

"I'm sorry for catching you off guard. I don't want those other girls, okay? I want to be with you."

Dammit, dammit, dammit.

He assumed I was seeing other guys. Could I blame him? Aside from finding out he was dating around, Kieran had never done anything wrong. On paper, he was the kind of guy anyone would be lucky to have. And here he was, communicating and telling me exactly how he felt.

He wasn't talking to anyone else. He didn't want anyone else. He wanted me.

And I didn't realize it, not consciously, but more than anything, I wanted to be wanted.

His expectant eyes still bore into me, waiting for a response. The silence drug on, making me want to crawl out of my skin. But his nervous, patient expression was so hopeful.

"That was very nice," I said quietly, matter-of-factly, hoping the tension would dissipate.

It worked. He let out a short bark of a laugh, his chest falling as he released a long breath.

"God, I hope so. I rehearsed it the whole way over. You're a hard woman to get a hold of." Kieran reached a hand out as if to wrap around my waist, but stopped short and righted himself. "Tell me you forgive me."

I nodded, looking down at my feet, and took a single step to close the gap between us.

"I think we can talk about it."

Realizing what that step meant—concession, showing that I was willing to work things out—Kieran closed the space between our bodies and lifted me off the ground in a crushing embrace.

CHAPTER 40

Now

Don't go.
Just stay.
A little while longer.
With me.

I stood in a flash, nearly knocking over the milk crates I was sitting on as I shot for the door of the walk-in. I barely made it to Gemma before Kieran appeared behind her, looking confused as all get out.

His confusion transformed when his eyes shot over my shoulder to what I'm sure was a very strapping musician emerging from the walk-in right behind me.

"Thank god you found us," I explained, trying my best to sound graciously casual. "We were bringing the flower arrangements in here for the night, and we got locked in." It was the truth, but even I thought it sounded like a load of bullshit.

Gemma jumped right in. "Oh, I forgot to tell you! My uncle mentioned the door can stick sometimes. It doesn't actually lock from the inside, but if the pressure and temperature are just right, the seal can stick so tight you'd think it is."

Gee, that would've been nice to know twenty minutes ago.

Kieran's eyes darted from me to Nate, his posture all rigid lines and tight agitation.

The industrial kitchen was muggy and too warm compared to the fridge. Nervous sweat gathered under my arms.

"How long were you in there?" Gemma asked, attempting concern as she led us away from the walk-in. I started to follow, but was engulfed by Kieran's frame as he guided me in the opposite direction with a stern hand at the back of my neck.

"What's wrong?" I asked.

"We need to talk," he said in a clipped, hushed tone, closing me off from the others when we reached a wall. "Now."

From my periphery, Nate's steps slowed to a stop, followed by Gemma's when she realized nobody was following her.

"Is everything okay?" Nate called.

Kieran ignored him, instead grabbing my wrist and ushering me farther away. "Come on, let's go." His pull on my arm wasn't aggressive, just insistent. Even without the smell of liquor on his breath, I could see on his face that he was wasted and most certainly angry about something more than just finding me in the walk-in.

As I opened my mouth to tell Kieran to let go of my arm, Nate was there in front of him with both palms out, attempting to defuse whatever bomb was about to go off. "Hey, man. Chill out, okay?" His jaw jumped as he clocked Kieran's hand around my wrist.

Kieran must not have liked Nate's proximity because he dropped my wrist and took a sure step forward, shoving Nate in a sharp push to the shoulder. It wasn't enough to knock him off balance, but it forced him to take a step backward.

"Woah, woah, woah!" Gemma shouted distantly, stomping closer.

"I'd like to talk to *my girlfriend* in private." Kieran took another intimidating step toward Nate. "So, back off."

Oh, fuck.

A calm mask slipped over Nate's face as he raised his eyebrows at Kieran. Straightening, he slipped his hands into his pockets, unbothered by the drunken outburst save for the focused, stoically enraged look in his eyes.

Kieran didn't stand down. "You had your chance, rockstar."

I found my voice as Gemma reached us. "Okay, that's enough." Putting my hands on Kieran's broad shoulder, I attempted to steer him away before he did anything else stupid. "Let's go."

He refused to move at first, an immovable force, but then he turned and stalked out of the kitchen, leading me like a child from the scene. Gemma shot me a look that said, *What the fuck?* as I passed her, but there was nothing I could say back.

As we rounded the corner, I glanced over my shoulder to where Nate stood. He was still rooted to the spot where I'd left him, jaw working, eyes tracking me until I was out of view.

The realization of what happened hit me like a ton of bricks. Kieran got in Nate's face—shoved him. Physically put hands on him. I didn't always have the best judgment, but I did know, as well as any kindergartner, that violence was never the answer. There had to be something else Kieran was upset about, because there was no way he saw what Gemma saw in the walk-in.

Whatever that was.

He stalked with me closely behind all the way to our cabin suite. By the time we shut the door, Kieran rippled with anger. It painted every inch of him, but it painted me, too.

"Care to explain what the hell that was all about?" I snapped. "You are *clearly* upset, I can see that, but you didn't have to beat your chest and haul me away like some kind of—"

"Do you have any idea how embarrassing it is to find shit out about your own girlfriend by some random people you don't even know?" he interrupted.

There was only one thing he could've been talking about, but my stubbornness wanted to hear him say it. Wanted to hear him say the thing that was making him act like a raving lunatic. I put my hands on my hips, raising an eyebrow. "And what might that be?"

"That you apparently used to go out with that loser fucking musician."

There it was. The thing I only kept from Kieran because it didn't seem worth bringing up. The thing I thought didn't matter—*wouldn't* matter—especially to someone as kind and confident as Kieran. But there it was anyway.

"Then," he continued, stepping closer to me, "imagine my surprise when I try to find you to talk about it, and I find you with him. Alone. And wearing his fucking jacket. Or at least, I assume it's his because it sure as shit isn't mine."

I looked down at Nate's black hoodie and shook my head. Kieran didn't see us in the walk-in. For all he knew, we were on opposite sides of the fridge before Gemma opened the door. And besides, nothing happened. *Almost* happened didn't matter. What mattered was what happened—and nothing happened.

"We were locked in a fridge, Kieran. Did you expect him to let me freeze to death? And I told you we didn't date." *Because we didn't.*

"Maybe not." He rolled his eyes, the movement delayed by his drunkenness. "But you guys *were* together. At least long enough for your friends to remember it."

"What exactly did you hear?"

"I overheard some of those… people you went to school with. They were wondering where he was. And when they put two and two together that he stayed behind and you were both *here*, helping do Gemma's wedding shit…" He made a face and shook his head. "They laughed like it was the funniest thing in the world. They were talking about how you guys used to hook up. They didn't know I could hear them, but that doesn't matter. I still look like a fucking idiot for letting you stay behind."

I ran a hand over my face, unsure of where to start.

Saying he "let" me stay behind is messed up, for starters.

I didn't have a chance to respond before Kieran took another unsteady step toward me and continued.

"Tell me the truth, Olive. Is there anything I need to worry about with that… fucking *nobody?*"

"Don't call him that." The words were out of my mouth before I even thought of them.

He staggered back. "What, you're defending him now?"

"No. Not just him. It isn't cool to call anyone a 'nobody,' Kieran. What the hell?"

"Just answer the question."

"Fine," I said, taking a steadying breath. My heartbeat pulsed in my ears. "When Gemma and I met all of them back in school, we were both very, *very* single. Yes, Nate and I have hooked up—"

Kieran threw his hands in the air as if to say, *See, Your Honor? She's guilty.*

"But it might as well be ancient history. It wasn't worth bringing up."

"You're serious?" his voice rose. "You *actually* slept with that guy? Really, Olive?"

"Why do you say it like it's supposed to be some kind of insult? You don't see me grilling *you* about every person you've hooked up with. We can have a conversation, but what's with the interrogation?"

"I just never thought you'd stoop so low."

My blood boiled. Not just because of the attitude he had going on at the moment, but because of the implication that Nate was some kind of lowlife.

I blinked at him. "What the fuck is that supposed to mean?"

He smirked back and shrugged. "What do you think?"

I knew what he meant. Maybe I'd chosen to look past it all this time, but Kieran didn't have a shred of respect for anything even remotely related to the arts. He may not have said it directly, but he didn't have to. To him, musicians were deadbeats who didn't have real jobs and were going nowhere in life. People who made their living designing or creating content on social media, like Gemma, were air-headed, stuck-up narcissists. My job must have come with just enough bragging rights to be palatable for him, but even I had to take a share of backhanded comments from time to time over the years. To him, it was still a hobby. Not a real living.

He thought we were all beneath him, and he was finally acknowledging it. It left an acrid taste in my mouth.

I'd never been less attracted to Kieran than I was at that exact moment.

"You know what?" I turned on my heel. "You're drunk. I don't know what this alpha male bullshit is, but it isn't cute. I'm going to go back out there and finish helping Gemma because she is my best friend, and she is getting married tomorrow." I clocked the roll of his eyes. "She asked for my help. Which, for your information, is what I've been doing the whole day. Despite your attempt at slut shaming me, or whatever this is. If you want to have an actual conversation, we can have it later. You need to sober up."

I kept my head down as I walked back to the beer garden to finish my task alone and clean up our workstation. I vibrated with anger, irritation, and embarrassment. There were only a few more vases left, and I'd lost track of what else Gemma needed help with.

In a perfect world, I would bury my head in the sand for the rest of the day.

My feet crunched to a halt when I got back to the beer garden. The area was completely cleared. The flowers, the vases, the tubs of water and flower scraps, everything. It was all gone.

Like we hadn't been there at all.

CHAPTER 41

Now

Selfishness and clarity
A clear perspective I've known for so long
I want it all

I stayed out of our suite the rest of the evening, needing space to think about what my relationship with Kieran had become in a matter of days.

Something had shifted, changed in a way that was irredeemable. He showed a side of himself I never wanted to see again. But now wasn't the right time to face it, not when emotions ran so high and he was so far gone. All I wanted to do was get through the rest of the night unscathed.

After finding my flower workstation tidied, I trudged to the walk-in—careful to prop the door open with a milk crate—and spied a few new arrangements with sad, lopsided-looking flowers inside. A soft smile tugged at my lips at the thought of Nate attempting to build the flower arrangements by himself, just to make sure the job got done. I toyed with flowers, sprucing them up a bit and plucking stems from the others until they looked somewhat uniform.

I searched the ceremony space for Gemma or Grant, but it was vacant, save for the rows of empty seats and the giant wooden archway at the end of the aisle. A rogue hammer lay discarded on the ground, and a handful of empty cardboard boxes were piled atop a chair in the last row.

Making myself busy, I set about cleaning and organizing all the boxes left around the ceremony space and inside, stacking everything into the designated storage room. I milled about until the sun began to set, and there was nothing left to do but trudge back to my suite.

Gemma found me before I found her.

"Oli!" she shouted distantly from an Adirondack chair on the outskirts of a brick fire pit. Around her sat Grant, Martinez, Jared, Miles, and Leo. The whole gang, except one.

My heart warmed at the sight of my friends huddled around the fire. I was greeted with a chorus of hellos as I took the remaining empty chair closest to Gemma. Martinez and Miles roasted marshmallows on long metal sticks as Jared and Grant bickered over something on Jared's phone. Leo simply stared into the flames, transfixed.

As much as it felt somewhat incomplete without him, I was grateful Nate was missing from the group. I was still a bit shaken by what happened with Kieran, and being near him would confuse my emotions more than they already were.

"Hey, babe," Gemma said, untucking the blanket wrapped around her legs and tossing half of it to me. Her eyes lingered on Nate's zip-up I still wore, but she said nothing about it.

"Hi," I replied, settling in. "I took care of the boxes that were left outside."

"Thank you. The resort staff were supposed to come pick them up, but I guess they haven't made it over there yet. I appreciate you." She leaned closer and offered her hand.

I took it, looping my fingers with hers.

She squeezed softly. "Do we need to talk about what happened earlier?"

It was a multilayered question. *Do we need to download about what happened in that walk-in? Do you need to vent? Do you need a come to Jesus about your relationship?*

I sighed through my nose, momentarily transfixed by the fire, then met her baby blues and shook my head. Half of me didn't want to talk about it because the other half of me already knew what needed to happen. There was no coming back from it.

She gave my fingers another gentle squeeze. "Got it."

The group of us sat around the fire, talking, laughing, and spending time in each other's company. Martinez tracked down a server inside the main building to bring us all glasses of wine—white for me—along with more marshmallows for him to char. We didn't talk about our jobs or the weather. Nobody asked where Kieran was—or Nate, for that matter. We didn't focus on anything in particular at all. We simply hung out, like old times.

Eventually, the sky grew dark, and the fire died out. One by one, our little group dispersed until Gemma and Grant declared they had to part ways until it was time to say *I do*—my cue to head to bed. With a yawn, I gathered Gemma in my arms and hugged her tight.

"You are a perfect angel goddess," I murmured into her hair. "You sure you don't need me to slumber party with you tonight?"

"My mom already called dibs on my last sleepover before the wedding. Trust me, I wish it was you instead. She doesn't understand that a facemask will ruin my spray tan."

We both laughed.

Grant pulled me into a hug. "Thanks for everything, Olive."

"Call me if you need me in the morning, okay? I'm happy to help with whatever."

"You've done enough already! Tomorrow is the easy part." Gemma slipped her freshly manicured hand into Grant's. I gave her a look, making her amend her statement. "I'll let you know if I need anything, okay?"

"Good."

The walk back to the suite was a long one. Exhaustion settled into me, my brain shutting down little by little with each step.

I changed into pajamas in silence, ignoring Kieran in the corner of my eye. He lay awake in the bed, watching me, saying nothing. I didn't have the energy to talk to him.

Instead, I crawled into bed with my back to him and closed my eyes. A few minutes later, he rolled closer to me, kissed my bare shoulder, and fell asleep.

⇝⇝ ⇜⇜

Sleep gripped me, making me snooze my alarm three times before I bothered to open my eyes.

When I stretched, my arm landed on an empty pillow. A quick glance around the room revealed Kieran's tennis shoes and headphones were gone. Probably a morning run.

I'd only had one glass of wine at the firepit the night before, but I might as well have had the whole bottle. My stomach roiled, my body ached, and a dull headache pressed behind my eyes.

Pulling on a loose-fitting pair of jeans and a sweater, I made my way down the hill to breakfast. I kept my head down as I spooned a heaping pile of fresh fruit and a piece of toast onto my plate. My social battery was dangerously low, and I needed to charge it again before the ceremony.

Sitting at the only small table left empty in the dining room, I picked at my fruit and opened my email on my phone. Luckily, there wasn't a significant change from the day before. Only one notification caught my eye. I'd set up alerts a while back to flag any new posts from artists I followed for work so that I wouldn't miss anything important, like album drops or new music videos. Opening the alert, I studied the official announcement for Crescent Light's European tour. My eyes lingered a few extra moments, as they always did with Crescent Light, before I locked my phone again and put it face-down on the table.

Kieran was still in his running clothes, huffing deep breaths when I opened the door to our suite.

"Hey," he said, cracking a handsome smile. "There you are."

I said hello back but didn't feel inclined to say much else as I knelt next to my suitcase to dig through my toiletry bag. I felt him behind me as he leaned down to kiss the top of my head. Like nothing was wrong. Like nothing at all out of the ordinary had happened.

"I was going to see if you wanted to get breakfast, but you were already gone."

"Yeah, I already went down," I said, standing. "I'm going to take a shower."

He followed me, leaning against the bathroom doorframe just as I turned the water on as hot as it would go.

"Can I join you?"

A crossroads. Asking to join me in the shower was his form of apology. An effort, an invitation for closeness, for intimacy, in hopes everything was forgiven and forgotten. Saying yes would smooth things over amicably until we could have a real conversation.

Did I want to continue fighting? Not really.

But did I want to give in? Move on and push our issues aside just to keep the peace? Pretend like everything this weekend didn't happen?

With a gentle hand to his chest, I urged him out of the bathroom. "No."

Everything was clearer when thought about in a shower.

Nate's questions from the night before rang over and over again in my head like a mirror held in front of my face.

Was there anything Kieran and I had in common? Did he care about any of the things I cared about? Our hobbies, our friends, our lifestyles, the things we liked: was there nothing we were aligned on?

Were the red flags just so subtle that I never looked at them all together? Was it that I didn't want to see them until now? It seemed I always had a justification to excuse the little things that bothered me, a reason behind the edits I'd made to myself to better fit his mold.

This weekend didn't reveal anything new at all. It only shined a spotlight through the holes in our relationship that I didn't want to see.

Then there was Nate.

How was it possible to be so weak around someone? How was talking and laughing with him after everything so easy, so natural?

No matter how much I wanted to be able to stay away from him, I never could. From the day I met him, he had occupied a spot in the back of my mind, a place in my heart, and no amount of time had made him go away.

The second I set eyes on him, no matter how long it had been, I got sucked into his gravitational pull. I couldn't resist it if I tried.

Fighting with Nate in the walk-in had shifted something. I hadn't realized how much I needed closure. How much I needed to tell Nate I was sorry and hear it back from him. How much I needed the release of having it out, to say every unsaid thing.

He could still read me like a book, even after all this time. Was that dangerous? Or was I just uncomfortable with being that deeply known?

Maybe that was the reason I was scared to see him this weekend. Because at my core, I hated that someone had the power to look right through my façade.

At one point in my life, it might have scared me to know that someone *knew* me. That someone could give me butterflies while simultaneously cutting me open and revealing parts of me I didn't want to look at. The parts I wasn't proud of.

But it didn't anymore.

We were bound to each other. It was as if there was some subconscious part inside of me that saw and recognized the complimentary piece inside of him. Hurting each other in the past didn't undo that, and neither did distance.

I was certain now that while time had done both of us a world of good and gave us space to do some growing up, it would never change that inexplicable spark.

It would never change the fact that I was in love with Nate Cassidy.

Oh my god.

I'm in love with Nate Cassidy.

Turning off the hot water, I wrapped myself in a huge fluffy towel and stepped out of the shower. I watched myself in the mirror, staring deeply into my eyes.

This woman. From the top of her head to the soles of her feet, every dip and curve, every soft, dimpled contour, every freckle and scar, she was exactly who she was meant to be.

She knew who she was. She was a hard worker. She was intelligent and capable and artistic and creative. Worthy of the best friends anyone could ask for. Worthy of unconditional happiness and support and success.

Why would she settle for someone who didn't cherish, support, and accept every single part of her?

Why would she settle for less when someone like Nate existed in the world?

CHAPTER 42

Now

Even in a crowd
the one I want to find is you.

Kieran was sitting on the bed when I emerged from the bathroom, streaming a football game on his laptop, which he muted the second he saw me.

The look on his face was an unfamiliar mix of trepidation and expectation. I'd denied him the opportunity to "make it up to me" in the way he wanted. He knew something was up.

I'd thrown on a pair of leggings and a sweater when I got out of the shower, not wanting to get ready for the ceremony until this conversation was had.

"Hey," he said, stretching his long legs out.

"Hi."

A beat of silence. "Everything okay?"

"Not really."

"Look." He leaned forward, resting his forearms on his knees. "About last night."

So, he's willing to accept that he crossed a line. Good. Even if it won't change the outcome.

"You don't have to beat yourself up for not telling me about what-shisname. So you slept with him in college. It's okay to be embarrassed about it; you fucked up. I wish you had told me, but I forgive you."

My eyes widened in genuine disbelief. I never said being with Nate was a fuck up, and I never apologized for it. Sure, I should have given Kieran the heads-up before this weekend—I accept that—but did he really think that was the only issue here? Did he forget he put his hands on Nate and dragged me around the property like a rag doll?

And that wasn't even including his snide comments, overdrinking, and possessiveness the last two days. Of course, he wouldn't acknowledge those things. In his mind, none of that mattered.

He doesn't know me. He'll never be able to understand me on a soul-deep level, despite how good he is on paper.

It only encouraged me to say the next part with more confidence. "Kieran, this isn't working."

His eyes met mine. "What's not working?"

"This. Us. I don't know, I just…" *Don't back down now, Oli. This is the right decision.* "I don't feel good about this anymore. We can talk about it more later, but for tonight, it would be best if you didn't come to the wedding. We're only here for one more night, so it is what it is, but when we get back to Boston, we should go our separate ways."

The words landed with finality, and a small bloom of pride appeared in my chest, even as I nervously studied his reaction. He looked like he was trying to solve a math equation in his head, eyes far away, darting left and right.

He must have come to some sort of conclusion because he suddenly sat a bit straighter.

Pulling his running shoes back on, he said, "You're right. Let's take some time, and we'll talk later."

I opened my mouth to respond, to tell him that taking time wouldn't change my decision, but within a matter of seconds, he stood on stiff legs and was out the door.

Silence filled the suite.

Okay, not how I pictured that going, but I guess I'll leave him to cope however he needs to?

I didn't have time to dwell on what he was doing or how he was taking the news; I had a ceremony to get ready for.

⇝⇝ ⇜⇜

The golf cart came to a halt at the base of the winding path to the ceremony space. The valet offered his hand to me as I maneuvered off the cart, and I held on to it for dear life until I regained my balance. Not rolling my ankle in these heels was perhaps going to be the biggest struggle of the evening.

A refreshing breeze gently blew through my hair, a perfect complement to the warm sunshine that poked through puffy clouds. This was it. Gemma was about to get married to the love of her life in the most beautiful venue on the most beautiful day, and I was lucky to witness it.

The ceremony space overlooked the sprawling vineyard hills. Rows of white garden chairs lined either side of the aisle, so covered with champagne-colored rose petals you couldn't even see the muted green grass underneath.

At the end of the aisle, the massive wooden archway was equally cloaked in roses of white and champagne, orchids, and whimsical greenery. It was breathtakingly perfect. Much of the seating had already been claimed by the time I arrived, but luckily, I spotted a half-empty row toward the front and slid in.

Sitting alone was a little humbling, but I didn't dwell on it as I did a quick once-over of the crowd, admiring everyone's wedding attire. My eyes caught almost immediately on a familiar figure.

Nate stood across the aisle from me and a few rows back, glancing around like he was looking for someone—Jared, probably. He looked a little out of place, standing tall and lean in a navy-colored suit. His hair was swept back off his forehead—a style I'd never seen on him before, but it looked good. Some might say too good. His eyes caught mine as he combed the crowd, and my heart flipped when he did a little double take, holding my gaze for only a second before giving me a close-mouthed smile and continuing his search.

He always did have a way of making public situations still feel intimate. Even if for only a moment. I faced forward again before a blush had the chance to settle in.

"Sorry I'm late," a voice behind me said, sliding onto the seat next to me.

Kieran was done up in his suit, looking fresh out of a GQ photoshoot. I watched him get comfortable, my eyes growing wide.

"What are you doing here?"

He looked sidelong at me, adjusting his sleeves under his suit jacket. "I flew out here to attend a wedding. I'm attending the wedding."

How he managed to shower, dress, and still be there in time was beyond me. He was still gone when I left the suite.

I scoffed incredulously. "But, I—"

"You look hot, babe." He eyed me from head to toe, or as well as he could while sitting.

Am I in the freaking Twilight Zone or did Kieran totally ignore me telling him not to come to the wedding?

My stomach went into knots as the first notes from the string quartet filled the air.

Being dumbfounded and frustrated would have to wait.

I'll be damned if anything spoils this memory.

A second later, Grant, the handsome devil, emerged from the side of the building behind us. He was led by Gemma's uncle, who was officiating, and I couldn't take my eyes off his sweetly anxious face as they took their places in front of the floral archway. He smiled nervously, searching the crowd. When his face lit up, having found who he was looking for, I followed his gaze to the other side of the aisle. Jared grinned broadly up at his brother from his place next to Nate, shooting him a thumbs-up.

"You didn't wear the yellow one?" Kieran whispered into my ear.

I bristled. I almost wore the yellow dress I'd packed, the one that he liked best, but when I was getting ready, I remembered I liked the black one more.

Shooting a glance his way, I shushed him.

All too quickly, Gemma's uncle instructed the crowd to stand and turn to await the bride's arrival. A quick glance to the right and my eyes connected with the same deep blue gaze for a fleeting moment before we both looked away again. Nate's profile showed off his flexing and unflexing jaw.

Maybe he's struggling to focus as much as I am.

In an empty space between wedding guest bodies, I caught a glimpse of the bride, and my breath caught.

She. Was. A. Goddess.

Gemma's golden hair was perfectly placed in thick, old Hollywood waves around her shoulders like an angelic halo. Her dress was timeless, sculpted to her body in all the right places, and flared modestly at the bottom. The train ruffled the rose petals at her feet as she glided down the aisle. Surely, she was a deity of some sort, an otherworldly being of unspeakable beauty and grace. The kind of woman that men of myth and legend waged war over.

Grant's face told me he thought the exact same thing as it took on a dreamlike expression, and silent tears streamed onto his cheeks.

Damn right, you better cry, I thought, silently threatening him because that's just what best friends do. The sight of him reaching out to take her hand, a single tear still streaking down his cheek, was enough to make me choke up as well. When Kieran took my hand and squeezed, I didn't squeeze it back.

The ceremony was absolutely perfect, just like Gemma deserved. There was no bridal party, no special readings or songs, no extra frills or dedications. Just two people who were completely, madly, ridiculously in love with each other, vowing to love each other for the rest of their lives. That was all they needed.

The look on Grant's face after he kissed her rivaled that of someone who'd just won the lottery, an Olympic Gold Medal, and the Super Bowl all in one. I thought for sure he was about to scream, "I'm going to Disneyland!"

I wouldn't have blamed him if he had, but he settled on a triumphant punch to the air instead.

CHAPTER 43

Now

What is it about a black dress?

The herd of weddinggoers made their way to the cocktail reception, which was being held in the same tasteful courtyard where the welcome party was. Yet again, the space was transformed. Its chic, Italian, rustic look was now covered in white, pink, and champagne-colored roses and lush greenery that matched the flowers Nate and I worked on the day before. It felt like weeks ago that Nate and I sat pruning and arranging those damn flowers, weeks since we fought in the walk-in, since our almost kiss...

Kieran followed closely behind me, hovering as if nothing was wrong. I was caught between wanting to whip around and scream at him to go back to the suite and ignoring him altogether.

To make a scene, or not to make a scene, that is the question.

I opted for the amiable approach and ignored him. *Let him loiter around if he wants to. It won't change anything. What's done is done.*

He went straight to the bar, which was somehow already occupied by a mile-long line of guests. I spied Leo, Miles, and Martinez circling together in one corner and took up a position in their huddle.

Martinez and Leo seemed deep in conversation about how much a weekend like this would have cost if Gemma's uncle wasn't the co-owner versus how much they think was actually paid. Miles and I ignored them, instead *ooh-ing* and *ahh-ing* at the decorations and the view.

"Hey, guys." I heard Nate's smooth voice behind me. He and Jared must have B-lined to the bar right after the ceremony, and they took the liberty of grabbing drinks for everyone by the collection of beers in their hands—six in total.

"Have I told you I love you today, Nathaniel?" Martinez gratefully took one of the outstretched beers from Nate's hands while Jared distributed his extras to Leo and Miles. Nate wordlessly handed one to me, leaving the last for himself.

Kieran would probably be annoyed when he came back from standing in the long bar line to find me with a drink already in hand, but I was having a hard time caring.

"Thanks."

"Of course."

I took a long slug of the beer, unsure of what else to do with my hands, and eyed Nate over the neck of the bottle as I chugged. Coincidentally, he was doing the exact same thing, causing us both to nearly choke with laughter when we made eye contact.

My first laugh of the whole day.

"Sorry," Nate coughed, a giggle bubbling from his throat.

"You were staring," I accused, wiping foam off my lips and chin, careful not to smudge my lipstick.

He took a micro-step closer, tilting his head in that *Nate* way. He kept a respectful distance, but only I could hear his next words.

"It's just hard for me to see you look this pretty and not stare. Even harder to not say anything about it."

I was grateful my face was downcast because I wasn't sure what expression overtook it before I gathered my wits about me.

Huffing a nervous laugh, I mumbled my thanks and smoothed a hand over my black dress. It was tighter than my typical wardrobe, and the front dipped a little lower than usual, too. But it had a timeless simplicity that could flatter anybody. It was the prettiest thing I owned.

"Sorry if I shouldn't have said that," Nate added, glancing behind us conspiratorially.

Bullshit. He isn't sorry.

"It isn't a come-on or anything. I mean, unless it's working."

I wanted to play back, tell him it *was* working. Continue the conversation we'd started in the walk-in. Tell him how I felt. But I settled on scoffing as I hit his shoulder with the back of my hand.

"I'm kidding!" he said, dramatically staggering back a step to humor me. "But you do look really pretty."

I bit back a smile, finally meeting his eye as I raised my bottle to my lips again. "You shouldn't say that kind of stuff to me, Cassidy." Not because I was taken anymore—nobody knew about that but Kieran and me, or apparently just me, since Kieran ignored it—but because it might've sent me into cardiac arrest.

"I know, I know." He tipped back his beer and took another swig, raising his eyebrows as if to say, *It's true, though.*

A few minutes later, Kieran and Michael joined our little group, a beer in Michael's hand and a gin and tonic in Kieran's.

The power trip started almost instantly. Even though Nate—in an attempt to not put me in an uncomfortable position, I'm sure—had moved to stand next to Jared on the opposite side of our huddle, Kieran still placed himself between us. Then, in a grand spectacle of alpha male dominance, Kieran leveled a stare at Nate as he draped a heavy arm around my shoulders.

Poor thing. Nate knew exactly what he was doing and ignored him completely, casually sliding a hand into his pocket and continuing his conversation with Jared without a care in the world. I, on the other hand, rolled my shoulders about as aggressively as I rolled my eyes and stepped out of Kieran's hold.

Just ignore him, Oli. Enjoy the evening.

"Hey, wasn't there supposed to be appetizers?" Martinez asked, pinning me with a look. "Gemma was telling me to try the bruschetta. Olive, wanna help me track some down? I'm starving."

I agreed all too eagerly.

He wasted no time looping his arm through mine as we turned away from the group and disappeared into the crowd.

"This is better than TV," he whisper-shouted as we walked through the crowd.

"No, it isn't," I groaned. "I want to die."

"I know we've been playing it cool, but what is going *on* with you three?"

"Do you want the context first? Or just the juicy gossip?"

"Juice first, always."

"I broke up with Kieran this morning."

His steps faltered. "Shut the fuck up."

I urged him along, laughing. "Kieran overheard you talking on the boat yesterday. Thanks for making my sex life a topic of conversation, by the way."

He grimaced and mouthed, *Sorry.* I waved him off.

"Kieran went all macho man, marking his territory, and he may or may not have gotten into it with Nate."

"No judgment, but he's also been wasted the whole weekend," he added.

"I *know*. Add that to the list of things that have upset me. Anyway, I ended things this morning and told him not to come to the wedding, but he still showed up and is acting like nothing happened."

Martinez gave me a look, clearly feeling sorry for me despite the entertainment value. "Do you need me to run interference? I know I just met him, but I'm happy you broke up. I don't like that guy. Not for you, anyway."

I laughed humorlessly. "Thanks, but I'll be fine. My plan is to just ignore him. We fly home tomorrow, and I can figure things out then."

He nodded. "It's going to be a fun night. We'll make sure of it."

We camped out by a table littered with salted meats, cheeses, grapes, strawberries, and bruschetta—which really was to die for—until the cocktail hour ended and the wide double doors into the reception space were opened. The DJ called everyone inside, and we all herded in like cattle.

Thank god—and also Gemma—that Nate was not sat at the same table as Kieran and me for dinner.

Kieran sat next to me, drinking two more gin and tonics while we ate, and kept a heavy arm permanently around the back of my chair. When his fingers inched onto my shoulder, I sat up straighter, leaning away from his touch. And when he slid a hand over my knee, I subtly plucked it away and returned it to his lap.

How am I supposed to ignore him when he is suffocating me?

As our plates were being taken by our servers, Kieran leaned in so close his lips touched my ear.

"If he looks over here one more time, I might lose it."

I was so sure I'd misheard him. "What?"

"You know what." He jerked his chin in the direction of Nate's table. "He's looked at you, like, three times since we've been eating."

I ground my teeth together. "You are unbelievable. I told you not to come because today isn't about any of this bullshit. You need to stop." I dabbed my mouth with my napkin, hoping I wasn't being loud enough for the others at our table to hear. "And he's probably looking over here because *you* are staring at *him*."

"Or because he wants to fuck you," Kieran mumbled, leaning back with a painfully unattractive, cocky look on his face, sizing up the room as I shot daggers at him.

This is going to be a long night.

CHAPTER 44
Six Months Ago, April

I read the words on the page, but all I saw was your face.

"Do you think you could proofread my article before I send it over to Julienne? She's going to butcher it to smithereens either way," Wren deadpanned. "But, you know."

"You mean to tell me you haven't already proofed it a thousand times?" I switched hands to hold my cell phone between my ear and shoulder as I opened the door to my apartment building. After landing a co-writing credit on a blog piece that went viral a few months back, Wren was finally getting her breakthrough piece put to press. I couldn't have been more excited for her.

"I mean, yeah, of course I have. But I need a fresh set of gorgeous hazel eyes to look at it."

"Those can be expensive, you know. I heard the market for new eyeballs is kind of tight this time of year." I turned left down the narrow hall to the mail room.

"Har har har. I'll send it over to you now. Oh! Did you get the new issue today?"

I swung open my mailbox and grabbed the small pile inside, rolling my eyes when I saw this month's new issue of *The Mountain* folded hotdog style around the rest of my mail. It was a good thing I had a fresh, crisp copy I bought from the bodega down the street nestled—nice and protected—in the bag slung over my shoulder. Apparently, the words *Do Not Bend* doesn't matter to the postal service.

"Yep." I couldn't help but smile as I slid the rubber band off my stack of mail and unfolded the magazine. "Looking at it right now."

On the front cover of *The Mountain*, in the bottom right corner, under the chin of a close-up shot of the newest teen actress turned all-grown-up pop star, was the title of my newest piece.

A sequel—a sister—to my first print piece. The piece I poured months of my life into a year and a half prior. I flipped open the magazine, desperately balancing my phone, my bag, and my mail, and beheld my newest article.

Three (More) Artists You Should Know: Another Look Into New England's Underground Music Scene
By Olive McLaren

"It's so pretty. Your name looks great on the cover, babe."

"Thanks, Wren. Your name will look even better."

"Eh, I'll get there eventually. I gotta go. My article should be sitting in your inbox, okay? Let me know what you think."

I folded the pile back over and locked the mailbox. "Will do. Love you!"

"Love you, too."

The smell of garlic and onion and savory, wonderful things hit me like a wall as I ascended the stairs to my apartment door.

"Hello?" I said as I fished my key out of the lock.

"In here!" Kieran called from the kitchen. I rounded the corner to see him pouring a modest dose of chianti into a pot of tomato sauce. I'd given him a spare key a few months back. It felt like the natural next step in our relationship. "I let myself in. Hope that's okay."

I laughed, circling the island to peer over his shoulder at the enormous pot of spaghetti sauce. "It is when it smells this amazing. What are you making?"

"Zucchini spaghetti."

I gave him a tight, sarcastically teasing smile. "*Yum,* my favorite."

"You will like the zucchini someday, I promise. It'll grow on you. Plus, it's way healthier than regular noodles." He put the wine bottle down on the counter and leaned in to kiss me, careful not to let his tomato-splattered shirt touch my white top.

"Wanna see the new issue?" I practically bounced with excitement.

"Uh, in a minute, yes. I need to keep an eye on this."

I deflated an inch and pulled my bag off my shoulder, shrugging out of my jacket and fingering through the rest of the mail.

"You're on the cover, right?" he asked.

"*I'm* not on the cover, but my title is."

"Same difference."

I shook my head to myself as my phone began to ring. An incoming FaceTime from Gemma.

"*Ugh,*" Kieran groaned. He knew Gemma's ringtone by heart by now. "Can you tell her we're about to eat dinner?"

I giggled. "It'll probably be quick."

"So? Can she not make a decision without calling you?"

Laughing again, I swiped to answer the FaceTime.

"I'm reading your article as we speak," Gemma said by way of greeting. "I'm like a proud parent."

"I just picked up my fresh copy. Remind me to write a strongly worded letter to the postal service."

"Does that mean you've already checked your mail today?"

"Looking through it now, why?" Propping my phone against the bottle of chianti, I flipped faster through the junk mail. I paused when a fancy-looking, champagne-colored envelope caught my eye. It was addressed to *Ms. Olive McLaren and Guest,* with the return address being Gemma's mom's house.

I gasped. *This must be it.*

Gemma squealed as I tore open the envelope and pulled the pristine, embellished cardstock from inside. The invitation was complete with useless scented tissue to keep the papers from sticking, and a stamped return envelope.

"They look even better in person! The pictures you sent me don't do them justice."

"Right? They turned out so good! Oh shoot, gotta go. Mom's calling me."

"Bye!" I glanced at Kieran's back once the call disconnected. "See? Quick."

"Hmm."

I roved over the invitation, giddy with excitement for my friend at first, then excited to see all our friends. Then, like an unwelcome guest, someone else's face popped into my mind.

Will he be there?

I swallowed and turned back to Kieran, who was busy at work stirring the bubbling sauce. "You don't happen to have anything going on the weekend of October nineteenth, do you?"

He snorted. "Considering that's six months from now, I have no idea. Why?"

Together with their families,

Gemma Allison Clark

&

William Grant Christensen

request the pleasure of your
company to celebrate their
joyous union.

CHAPTER 45

Now

I shouldn't hold out so much hope...

"Could you slow down?" I broke my silent treatment when Kieran downed another gin and tonic shortly after dinner.

"I'm just getting a good buzz going. Wanna make sure I'm getting the most out of Gemma's party."

"Yeah, well, I think you have the buzz you were looking for. Slow down." Then, for emphasis, though he didn't really deserve it, I added, "Please."

I left Kieran somewhere near Michael in hopes that he would stick close to him while I attended to Gemma.

She'd hunted me down the second she had to pee and recruited her mom to assist as well. We got her into the bathroom and team-lifted her skirts while she did her business, laughing hysterically the entire time.

"I love you guys," Gemma said as her pee filled the acoustics of the bathroom.

"I've never felt closer to you," I responded in earnest.

I fulfilled my duties diligently. When toasts were made, I held up my champagne glass. When the cake was cut, I made sure drunk guests—Kieran included—were out of the way. I even stood in the middle of the room with the rest of the unmarried ladies when the bouquet was thrown, though I barely participated. I stayed in the back of the small crowd and made a less-than-abysmal attempt at catching it.

Nate shot me an amused smile when he caught my eye over two of Gemma's cousins as they wrestled over the bouquet. I flipped him the bird, to which he burst into a proper belly laugh.

I got a fresh look at just how wasted Kieran was when he hovered over my shoulder again twenty minutes later, and I nearly lost it.

"What the hell?" I hissed. "I asked you to slow down."

He didn't say anything; he just leaned closer to me.

"If you get sick, I'm not taking care of you. You're on your own."

"I wish you would take care of me." His attempt at a hungry, sexy look only made me cringe. "You haven't all weekend."

Don't make a scene, don't make a scene, don't make a scene.

I didn't see him leaning in until he was giving me a sloppy kiss on the cheek. Wrong. It felt wrong. "I'll slow down. I promise."

Apparently, promises only last an hour because when I came back from the bathroom to a crowd of line dancers, I spotted Kieran leaning against the bar top for the thousandth time that night. The bartender slid a gin and tonic across the counter, and the second Kieran's lips touched the glass, I finally snapped.

The final fucking straw.

Broken up or not, I got to choose what kind of behavior I accepted. And I did not accept this.

The lack of awareness, the disrespect, how flippantly he disregarded me and my boundaries, it had to stop.

No more pushing the conversation aside. No more being nice. This was going to get ugly, and it wasn't waiting until tomorrow.

I stalked to the bar, grabbed Kieran's hand and turned, pulling him out into the hallway, out of the reception hall.

I found a small meeting room and shoved Kieran inside. A long boardroom-style table sat in the middle of the room with high-backed rolling chairs evenly spaced around it.

This will have to do. I'll be damned if I spend another second tonight biting my tongue.

"What?" Kieran said defensively. The sheer attitude in his voice reminded me of that of a fifteen-year-old boy getting scolded by his mother. It made my simmering blood finally reach its boiling point.

"What the hell is wrong with you, Kieran? You've been acting like this all weekend. I barely even recognize you."

"Funny," he slurred. "I could say the same about you."

"What does that even mean?"

"Everyone here knows you as a completely different person than the girl I know."

"And? Who doesn't change after college? If you're looking for an apology for anything I did before I even met you, you're not going to get one."

"How come I've literally *never* heard about him before this weekend?" Kieran's voice grew louder with every drunken word. He swayed where he stood. "Other than the fact that you used to be friends with 'Grant's brother's-fuckin-band,' you've never mentioned him."

Technically, I had. Kieran knew Crescent Light was one of the bands I'd researched for work. He just didn't know Crescent Light *was* Nate's band.

"How many times did you fuck him?"

I reared back. "Excuse me? Why does that matter?"

"I just would like to know how many times my girlfriend spread her legs for losers going nowhere in life."

What the fuck?

As much as his words shocked me, it suddenly occurred to me that I didn't have to do this. I already broke up with him. He wasn't entitled to a second of my attention. But he continued talking before I got the chance to tell him where to shove it.

"You know, I'm really starting to question your judgment, Olive. Not just for who you get hard-ons for, but your fuckin' friends, too."

"That's *enough*. This is ridiculous."

But he ignored me, pressing on, puffing out his chest. "I want to marry you one day. This weekend made me realize that I want all of you to myself. I don't want to share you anymore with anybody."

Oh, god. "It's too late for that."

"I'm serious." He swallowed a belch. "I don't want to share you. Not with that fucking nobody. Not with your dumb ass friend or her dumb ass wedding—"

A loud, humorless laugh burst out of me. "You know what? That'll do it! We're done here. You need to leave."

He blinked, swaying again and gripping the back of one of the leather chairs next to him. "Yeah, whatever," he mumbled.

"I'm serious. Go back to the suite and go to bed. And in the morning, pack your shit and go."

I could see the words register in slow motion across his smug face, the cocky façade fading into the insecure little boy hiding underneath.

"You don't mean that."

I raised my eyebrows, having never been more serious or sure about something in my whole life.

"Oh, yes, I fucking do. You have done nothing but disrespect me and my friends this entire weekend. I understand I kept something from you, and I shouldn't have done that, but it doesn't excuse your behavior. And as if that wasn't enough, you disrespect my best friend on her *wedding day?* Are you actually crazy?" I shook my head in disbelief. "I'll figure out how to get back to Boston on my own. I am fucking done."

Turning on my heel, I threw open the boardroom door to find Jared leaning against the opposite wall of the hallway. *Shit.* The last thing I wanted was an audience, but thankfully, it was just him.

"You good?" The question was for me, but his eyes were trained over my shoulder on Kieran.

"*Christ,* do you guys ever leave her the fuck alone?" Kieran pushed past me like he was going to rejoin the party.

I pressed my hands to his chest, stopping him. "I'm not letting you go back in there."

He shook his head like a defiant toddler. "No. I'm not leaving."

"Yeah," Jared said, shouldering between me and Kieran like a protective brother. "You are."

"Dude, mind your own fucking business," Kieran slurred.

Suddenly, I was worried things might get ugly. Jared was scrappy; I wouldn't put it past him to throw a punch if needed. But he had a European tour coming up, and he kind of needed his hands to play the drums. Not to mention, Kieran outweighed him by at least thirty pounds of solid muscle.

"Kieran, just go," I begged.

His bleary eyes landed back on me. "Why are you being such a bitch?"

"What the fuck did you say?"

My heart stopped at the sound of Nate's voice. I'd been so focused, I didn't even notice him round the corner with Martinez, and the two were now closing in on where Jared and I stood in Kieran's way.

Nate's steps didn't slow. He pressed closer until Jared abandoned his hand on Kieran's chest and placed it against Nate's instead.

"What did you just say to her?"

Nate's face was a mix of fury, challenge, and dismay. Like he was *daring* Kieran to repeat the word while simultaneously refusing to believe he was dumb enough to say it in the first place.

"Jesus Christ," Kieran groaned, rolling his eyes as he slumped against the wall. "This fucking guy." The fact that he hadn't passed out yet was a miracle.

Jared tried his best to wedge between Kieran and Nate, but Nate didn't even see him, wild eyes trained on Kieran like he was using all the willpower in his body to not come unglued.

"Do you have any idea how good you have it?" he spat. "Any idea how *lucky* you are? Or are you just stupid?"

I was stunned silent, even as I balanced Kieran's unsteady body.

"Martinez," Jared called, both hands now on Nate's chest, urging him backward, "jump in anytime here."

With a shake of his head, Martinez snapped into action, wrapping a tattooed arm around Nate's middle and tugging him back with ease.

Kieran's eyes slipped closed as he struggled to stay upright. I caught him under the arms just as he tumbled forward, but was saved by Jared, who pulled him upright and looped one of Kieran's arms over his neck.

"I'm sorry," I whispered to my friends, mortified by the spectacle.

"Are you okay?" It was Nate, ignoring Martinez's hold as his concerned eyes turned from Kieran to me.

I nodded.

"We need to get him out of here," Jared grunted under Kieran's weight.

Releasing Nate, Martinez crossed to Kieran's other side and mirrored Jared, hooking an arm around his shoulders. "Olive, do you have the key to your suite?"

"It should be in his wallet."

Nate's eyes were a hot brand on me as I stepped closer and fished Kieran's wallet out of his back pocket. I didn't miss the way Nate positioned himself closer, just in case Kieran did anything stupid. Well, stupider.

After retrieving the key and returning the wallet to Kieran's pocket, I wordlessly led Jared and Martinez toward the exit.

"We got it," Martinez called after me.

I turned, taking in the spectacle in front of me. Martinez and Jared each with their arms looped around Kieran's torso. Kieran held like a ragdoll, too drunk to stand upright. And Nate, lingering behind them, focused solely on me. "What do you mean?"

"We'll get him back," Martinez said, extending his free hand out for the key. "Go back inside and enjoy the party."

I eyed him and Jared. "I'm not sure that's such a—"

"Nate, take Olive back inside. We're going to handle this."

Nate didn't move. With an expression that was half concern, half pleading, he didn't say anything. It was my decision.

They clearly weren't going to let me leave the wedding to babysit Kieran, but my emotions were still running too high. Not knowing what else to do, I washed my hands of the whole thing and stomped away.

Instead of turning down the hall that led back to the reception, I kept going until I met a pair of double doors that led to an unoccupied patio.

Then, I turned on my heel and paced back to where I started. I knew Nate was behind me, silently offering his support by his presence alone, but the adrenaline and anxiety pumping through my system didn't allow me to stop walking until I paced up and down the empty hallway a few more times. Embarrassed didn't begin to cover what I was feeling. Jared, Martinez, and Nate had to be furious with me.

Heels slowing on the marble floor, I shot a glance at Nate a minute later. He'd taken up a spot against the wall and was studying his shoes, hands in pockets, waiting.

Defeated, I came to a stop in front of him.

He met my eyes over his lashes, keeping his chin tucked toward his shoes.

"Are you mad?" I asked.

He pulled his brows together, the wheels in his head turning for a beat. "Yeah. I'm pretty pissed."

I swallowed. "I'm sorry."

"What are you apologizing for?" he asked, standing up straighter.

My palm pressed against my forehead. "I don't know. I ended things with Kieran this morning and asked him not to come tonight. And I should've told him to go back to the suite when he showed up to the ceremony, but I didn't want to make a big deal out of it, and—"

"Hey…" Nate soothed, taking a small step forward.

"—I didn't mean for it to become a whole thing. You guys have the right to be pissed. You shouldn't have to clean up my mess."

"Let's back up," he said, shifting his weight. "What happened?"

My shoulders rose slowly with my inhale. "Turns out, spending the whole weekend drunk off your ass, being a possessive jerk, and talking shit about my best friend doesn't bode well for keeping a relationship alive. Also, someone pointed out the fact that Kieran and I don't have very much in common, and… they were right."

A million questions painted his face, mingled with a look of pride. "You told him not to come to the wedding?"

I nodded. "I broke up with him this morning. Told him he shouldn't come, but he did anyway."

Nate shook his head, running his fingers through his hair. "You should have told somebody."

"And what? Make a big scene? Have him escorted off the property?"

Nate bit back a smile and nodded, almost to himself. "Would have loved to see that."

I laughed dryly. "When did you get so vengeful?"

"You really wanna know the answer to that?"

The bass of the distant reception music bumped as I waited.

"That night when you called me crying." He sucked his teeth, shaking his head. "I'm not a violent person, Oli, you know that. But when you said a guy was partially responsible for you crying like that?"

My eyes fell to my feet.

He moved a lock of hair out of my face and pushed it over my shoulder. "Are you okay?"

I nodded, smiling softly. "Yeah."

"Let me be clear," he said, keeping his hand resting gingerly on my shoulder. "Nobody is upset with you. You don't have to apologize for anything. In fact, I should be apologizing. I escalated things."

I leveled a look at him. "You're not sorry, are you?"

His head shook as he cracked a smile. "No, not at all. Fuck that guy."

A laugh bubbled out of me, echoing off the walls.

"Nobody else saw, Oli. Nobody has to know anything if you don't want them to."

Shaken and embarrassed as I was, another feeling washed over me in equal measure.

Relief.

It was like I'd finally set down a heavy weight I'd been carrying around for days, weeks, perhaps even months. And it was over. One thousand and ten percent totally fucking over. Dead and buried.

I didn't have to settle. I didn't have to keep the peace. I didn't have to bite my tongue. I could be my true and authentic self with the people who loved me for exactly who I was.

Meeting his eye again, I wanted to say it. That I loved him, and not a day had gone by since we met that I didn't think about him. Now that I'd realized it for myself, the floodgates were opened. It wouldn't be ignored.

Dropping his hand from my shoulder, he said, "You wanna go back inside?"

I took a deep, cleansing breath. "Yeah. Let's go."

CHAPTER 46

Now

...And yet?

I stayed close to the reception hall doors, unable to breathe easily until I knew Martinez and Jared were back. When they finally returned ten minutes later, they looked like they'd just stepped outside for a quick smoke and nothing more.

"All good," Jared said when he reached me, raising his voice over the music.

"Really?"

"Yep. He's all tucked into bed. No worries."

"How did you even know where we were?"

Jared shrugged. "I saw you pull him into the hall. Wanted to stay close in case things got ugly."

Martinez came to my other side, hanging an arm over my shoulder.

I sighed, closing my eyes. "Thank you, guys. Please don't say anything to Gemma or Grant. I don't want this to cause any more of a scene than it already has."

Martinez winked. "We got you, girl. Now, go have fun."

Jared Christensen and Jaden Martinez. My heroes.

The opening notes of The Killers' "Mr. Brightside" rang through the reception hall, and the dance floor surged with a fresh wave of wedding guests.

Pushing through the huge group, I wedged my way to the center until I located my beautiful bride. Her eyes lit up when she saw me, and I wrapped my arms around my best friend in a spine-crushing bear hug. Grant was there a second later, picking Gemma up by her waist and spinning her, scream-singing, "It was only a kiss, it was only a kiss!"

Words couldn't express how happy I was for them. Had there ever been a more perfect couple in the entire existence of the world? *No*, I thought. *I don't think so.*

I deserved what they had. I deserved something great. Really fucking great. Not just good enough.

I was finally present and in the moment. There was no regret. Not even a shred. In fact, I wasn't sad at all.

I felt fucking great.

My friends and I crowded together as the song rounded out its final chorus—Grant and Gemma sharing a comically long kiss, Martinez, Jared, and Miles singing at the tops of their lungs. Even Leo took to the dance floor. The only one missing was…

I spotted Nate on the perimeter of the dance floor, smiling as he bit his lip and bobbed his head to the music. His brows rose when I approached him.

"Why aren't you out there busting a move, Nate Cassidy?" I took up a spot at his side, nudging his arm with my own.

"Because I'm not sure they could handle me out there, Oli McLaren."

I laughed at him and shook my head, letting my eyes linger on his dimple for an extra second.

A late 1990s alternative rock ballad faded in, the lighting shifting to a moody blue, and on the dance floor, friends and couples alike paired up.

"Do you wanna dance?" He tilted his chin to the center of the room.

I hummed, pretending to weigh the question. "I do love this song."

Goosebumps rose over my arms at the first contact of his hand with mine. "Let's go then."

Surrounded by couples, Nate eased me closer and inched a hand around me until it rested modestly on the middle of my back. His other held mine aloft, my fingers resting in the crook between his thumb and index finger. We swayed with middle-school level stiffness, and I suffered middle-school level nerves when he stepped closer.

It only took a second before a melody of broken giggles bubbled up my throat, shaking my shoulders even as I held them back.

"What?"

I shook my head, another round of giggles escaping.

He cracked a smile, steering us to sidestep a passing couple. "Come on, what? Tell me."

"I'm just thinking about the night we met. When you asked me to dance."

"Oh god." He laughed, a full burst that I eagerly drank in. "How could I forget? I was so nervous about it."

"Whatever." I rolled my eyes. "You don't get nervous." *You're a rockstar, for crying out loud.*

"Oh yes, I do. And I was very nervous that night."

"Why?"

A sweet smile tugged on the corners of his mouth. "Because you terrify me, Oli."

I snorted. "Is that a bad thing?"

"No."

I hummed contentedly and leaned into him, resting my head against his shoulder. Nate's arm encircled me further, lowering to rest comfortably on my waist. With the hand he was holding, he ran his fingers around the back of mine and held it against his chest. My heart squeezed, and I closed my eyes, relishing in the sound of him humming along to the song's second verse.

Another laugh flew from my lips a second later.

"What now?" he asked, exasperated but grinning down at me as I lifted my head from his shoulder.

"Nothing. It's just... surreal."

He swallowed, nodding slowly.

Surreal was one word to use. I could have also said nostalgic, heart-warming, gut-wrenching, tender, sentimental—but as usual, words escaped me when it came to him.

The song crescendoed and slowed again to the end, and we took an extra beat together before pulling away, even as the DJ mixed in the next pop song.

When the rowdy crowd returned, he scratched his eyebrow, half-turning in place.

"Come on." I pulled at his sleeve. "It's still a party."

And party we did. For the next hour, we sang, we ate cake, we watched as the crowd macarena'd, chicken danced, and cha cha slid.

Jared and Martinez owned the dance floor, making fools of themselves with the bride and groom, and I twirled right along with them.

When Gemma announced she needed a refill, I volunteered to get it.

Nate was already at the bar, dropping dollar bills into the bartender's tip jar as I approached. I grinned when his eyes met mine.

"Drink duty?" he asked.

"Of course. A white wine and a water, please," I said to the bartender, then propped an elbow on the bartop. "It's my honor to keep the bride both tipsy and hydrated."

"Very thoughtful," he said with a casual sip of his beer. "Don't think I haven't noticed what you're drinking, though."

I scrunched my eyebrows. "Vodka soda?"

"Vodka soda *with lime.*"

My eyes closed in recognition as I bit back a laugh.

"Are we in a celebrating–slash–'fuck it' mood, Oli?" Nate challenged with a twinkle in his eye. His hair had returned to its usual messiness throughout the evening and now hung over his forehead in that stereotypical *Nate* way.

The bartender slid Gemma's drinks to me, and I shook my head at Nate, breaking into a full smile that mirrored his own. "Something like that."

I peer pressured him into joining us on the dance floor, and when we returned, the whole group was finally accounted for.

We tore up the dance floor together, all of us celebrating, laughing at each other's ridiculous dance moves, and living in the moment. When Neil Diamond's "Sweet Caroline" started, every remaining wedding guest flooded in, squeezing together shoulder to shoulder.

I let myself fold against Nate, the movement so natural and familiar, and we sang at the tops of our lungs, lacing our fingers together as Neil Diamond belted, "Reaching out. Touching me, touching you."

Is there anything better than a room full of drunk people screaming *Bah! Bah! Bah!* in unison while Neil Diamond serenades them? Probably. But in that moment, I couldn't think of anything.

I'd missed this—the joy and levity of being surrounded by my friends. The goofiness, the freedom from judgment, the love we all shared.

The desire to want nothing but the best for each other. There was something special about when we were all together. Like weird, jagged, mismatched pieces of a puzzle that shouldn't fit together, but somehow do.

⤜⤚⤙ ⤛⤚⤛

"It's starting to clear out," I said to Nate late in the evening as the crowd thinned. The room went from being packed only twenty minutes prior to being about a third full as soon as the bars made their last call and liquor stopped flowing.

"That it is."

He watched me with that ever-perceptive, deep blue gaze. Studying me, like he always did. Always had.

A familiar fluttering started up in my belly.

I nudged his side with my elbow. "What?"

"I have a proposition for you." Nate rested his forearms against the high-top table where we stood and leaned in.

"Oh gosh," I sighed. His arm rested against mine, his body so close I could smell his intoxicating leather and laundry scent. But I couldn't resist the urge to give him shit. "I'm tempted to say *no* right off the bat."

He scoffed, rolling his eyes but inching closer. "Look, Oli…" My heart never failed to thump harder when he used my nickname. "You need a room to stay in tonight, right?"

I rolled my lips together.

Crap. There's no way I'm going back to the suite with Kieran there. Not tonight. I was so busy thinking about a game plan for getting home tomorrow, I didn't consider where I would stay tonight. I can't exactly crash with Gemma.

"Uh, yeah. I guess I do."

"Well, between you and me," he said in a hushed tone, looking around conspiratorially, "I have a mighty large, very *comfortable* bed in that fancy-ass suite they gave me."

I gave him a doubtful look, even as my pulse quickened.

Is he doing what I think he's doing?

"Get that look off your face!" He stood straight, holding his hands out in front of him as if this was a well-prepared sales pitch. "Just hear me out, okay? There aren't a lot of people I would trust not to murder me in my sleep if we shared a bed. And we've shared a bed lots of times, so."

I raised my eyebrows at him, blinking once, twice. "Nate."

"Oli."

Can I be alone with him without doing something rash? Without making the same mistakes again?

"This—" I shook my head slowly. Unconvincingly. "This is a bad idea."

He faced me head-on and put both hands on my bare shoulders with a sigh. "I know."

"Like, it's a *very* bad idea." I swallowed.

He nodded. "I know."

"It's never worked with us, Nate. Never."

He took a small step closer, letting his hands fall from the tops of my shoulders, gently pressing his thumbs into the bend in my elbows. "I know."

"And it's not going to start magically working now." I tilted my chin up to look him in the eye. "You do realize that, right?"

His grin widened, revealing a brilliant, full smile. "I know."

When he took a step back, I watched as he downed the rest of his drink and placed the glass delicately on the table behind him.

Circling me, he reached out a hand for me to take. "So, are you coming or not?"

I stared at it for a long moment, shaking my head in disbelief and biting back the ridiculous smile spreading over my face. But then a rightness settled in my gut. A surety. I loved him. And I was willing to bet he loved me back.

My heart thundered in my ears; butterflies took flight in my chest, and without another thought—without a *single* doubt—I put my palm in his waiting hand, and followed Nate Cassidy out the door.

CHAPTER 47

Now

Like a scar from my childhood, you are a part of me.
I don't know what I look like without you.

The door to Nate's suite closed behind us, and suddenly, I was surrounded by the still silence of being alone with him. He had given me his suit jacket on our walk back to his suite, and it hung loosely over my shoulders. His suite was an exact mirror image of mine, but it felt smaller somehow. Like all the air was being sucked up, and the room itself held its breath.

He led us further inside, absentmindedly loosening and untying the tie around his neck. Maybe it was the jacket, but I was dizzy from the intoxicating scent of him that filled the air.

My eyes roved around the room—from his open suitcase spilling clothes onto the floor, to the black hat he wore the day before hanging on the handle of the balcony doors, to his leather notebook on the bedside table—and finally settled on his shoulders, the back of his head, the hair hanging lazily over his forehead as he turned to face me.

There it was.

That static electricity. That feeling of weightlessness and grounded-ness that existed all at once when he looked at me.

We both knew what was supposed to happen next.

He took a step closer, and I expected him to invade my space, to say something, but instead, he dropped to a knee. I stepped back instinctively, confused.

"Wha—"

"Here." He motioned, encouraging me to lift my leg. Tentatively, I lifted my left foot. He wrapped a hand around my ankle and began undoing the buckle of my heeled sandal. I had to brace a hand on his shoulder to stay upright as he tugged at the strap, gently guiding it free.

"You don't have to do that," I whispered, feeling childish.

"Hush," he whispered back, easing the heel off my foot and motion-ing for me to give him my other ankle.

I obeyed.

"Thank you," I said when he rose to his full height.

Every time I looked at him, it was like the very first time. It was as if I hadn't been looking at him all night, all weekend. Suddenly, I was back at that packed club in Hartwood, surrounded by college kids in ugly Christmas sweaters, heart racing because a cute guy's knee bumped mine under a sticky table. He stole my breath.

"I'm not having sex with you," I blurted.

He froze a moment, then laughed through his nose, flashing that dimple with his close-lipped smile. "Who said anything about sex?"

"It's kind of what we do in these situations. We have it down to a science, I fear."

He toed his shoes off without untying them. "Believe it or not, I don't always show up with an agenda."

I chewed on my lip, eyes darting away from him and back again, my paper-thin willpower threatening to break with the slightest pressure.

"We don't have to do anything, Oli."

I sighed and paced in place, shrugging out of his jacket and handing it to him. "I don't have anything to wear," I thought aloud.

"Do you want me to go to your suite and get some things for you?" Nate asked, bending to rifle through his suitcase.

"Oh, god no," I protested, then laughed at the thought. "He might *actually* kill you if you showed up and packed an overnight bag for me. Maybe I can text Gemma and..."

Nate gave me a look over his shoulder and held up a black lump of fabric. My words died in my throat.

No way.

I took it from him and unfurled the lump—a ratty old band T-shirt.

"You sure?" I asked. Jim Morrison's faded face looked up at me from the fabric.

Hello, old friend.

He shrugged. "Figured it would be more comfortable than the dress."

Five minutes later, I emerged from the bathroom in his T-shirt and a pair of boxers. Feeling hilariously sheepish and out of place, I made quick work of crossing the room and hiding under the covers on the far side of the bed.

Nate watched me with a laugh, probably feeling just as funny as I did about what was happening. He disappeared into the bathroom, returning a minute later in just a pair of boxers.

Willpower, Olive.

I only allowed myself a quick, savoring look before averting my eyes as he peeled back the covers and lay on the other side of the bed. "So, are you going to try and get on another flight to Boston tomorrow?"

I sighed. "I guess. Though, I do have a few more days of PTO. I'm tempted to just hide out here for a while. What about you? Going back to Hartwood tomorrow?"

"I actually live back in Connecticut now."

"You do?"

"Yep. Moved about six months ago. I'm closer to my mom and Paige now."

And closer to Boston, my squirrel brain noted.

"But to answer your question, I'm not going home tomorrow. I'm planning to go down to San Francisco for a few days."

"Really?" I turned onto my side to face him, tucking my hands under my head. "I've never been."

He lolled his head to the side and propped an arm under his neck. "Me neither. I figured since I'm here, I might as well check it out."

"Don't you have a European tour to prep for?" I teased.

He laughed through his nose. I barely caught a glimpse of his dimple, half hidden by his pillow. "We don't start rehearsals until January. I have some time."

I hummed my reply. When he turned his gaze back to the ceiling, I did, too, letting the still silence wash over us once more.

It seemed like neither of us was eager for the night to be over, desperate to stay in this moment just a minute longer but having no clue what was safe to talk about. For the next few minutes, Nate's breathing slowed. Were it not for the nervously twitching fingers I could see out of the corner of my eye, I would have thought he'd fallen asleep with the lamp light still on. My fingers tangled together under the blanket.

"Oli?"

"Yeah?"

"Would… would you want to come with me? To San Francisco?" He cleared his throat. "It's, uh, it's already planned. I mean, I have a hotel already sorted out. Three nights near the wharf. You don't have to if you don't want to. But… I'd like you to. If you want."

I studied the tiles above the bed. "I'm not going to invite myself on your vacation, Nate."

"You aren't inviting yourself. I just invited you."

"I don't know." I hesitated. Three nights alone with Nate. *What would that mean? Are we just hitting restart on a movie we both already knew the ending of? Or could it be something else altogether?* "I'd like to think about it, if that's okay."

He nodded, swallowing. "Of course."

Nate turned over, and I caught a glimpse of The Fool tattoo on the back of his arm as he flipped off the lamp, surrounding us in darkness.

He settled back down and got comfortable, and I mourned the loss of being able to see his face as I turned my head back toward him. At least he couldn't see me staring.

Throwing an arm behind his head again, he said, "I'm really glad I got to come this weekend."

"Yeah?"

"I didn't know if I'd be able to. I had to sort some stuff out for the tour, and Paige needed help moving, and… I didn't want to miss it for Grant, but…" I didn't have to see his face to know those blue eyes were on me when he turned his head. "I'm not going to lie and say I didn't think about you the whole flight here."

Glad to know I wasn't the only one.

"I'm glad you came this weekend, too."

He nodded, and we fell into silence again for a beat, staring at each other through the darkness.

"I really am sorry," he said quietly.

"For what?"

"For all of it. Everything."

I pressed my lips together in a sad smile. "Me, too."

His nod shook the pillows slightly, and he turned his face back toward the ceiling. Pressure built behind my eyes as I kept them trained on the faint outline of his profile.

How sad. And silly. And paradoxical.

I tried so hard for so long to let him go, willed myself to forget my feelings, begged to be rid of the memories of his smile, his eyes, that stupid dimple. And now I didn't want to sleep—didn't even want to blink for the fear that this moment might disappear forever.

I wasn't ready to accept a life he wasn't in. I never had been.

Was I willing to jump into the unknown with both feet, even if I couldn't guarantee happiness was at the bottom?

But what if it is?

The old Oli would have questioned if the risk was worth it, but I was learning to say the things on my mind—to ask for the things I wanted.

A warmth bloomed in my chest, a calmness.

Fuck it.

"Nate?"

"Mmh?"

"There's a conversation we need to have. And I think I need to have it before the night is over."

Wordlessly, he flipped the lamp back on and twisted into a sitting position facing me. The blankets fell away from his body, leaving him with only one leg covered as he rested a hand on a propped-up knee. I sat up, too, crisscrossing my legs, looking at him face-on. His chest rose and fell almost as fast as mine when the weight settled around us.

I closed my eyes and took a deep breath.

"I can't let another day go by without knowing what we are… what we mean to each other. I've always been too scared to say it out loud because deep down, I didn't think you'd feel the same. It felt easier to stay quiet so I could protect myself, but I know now that wasn't the right decision. So, I'm just going to say it."

My eyes caught on his throat as he swallowed. Looking away, they settled on my lap, on my fingers picking at the thick duvet. This was brave, but I wasn't quite strong enough to keep my thoughts straight when he was so close.

Steeling myself, I met his deep blue gaze again.

"I love you, Nate. I tried to run from it; I tried to ignore it. I tried to pretend it wasn't there, but it's never gone away. Not really. And I want something real with you." I shrugged. "It's as simple as that. I know deep down, you don't think you can juggle Crescent Light and be with someone because I know you. But I still want it. Late nights at the studio, writing sessions, going away on tour—none of that matters because I will still be there wanting you. And… and if you don't feel the same, I need you to tell me now because—"

"I want it."

My gaze snapped to his. His expression was awestruck bewilderment laced with pure, bone-deep yearning.

"I want it," he repeated. "All of it. More than *anything*. I want you."

I studied his face, knowing it almost as well as I knew my own. As easy as it would have been to toss my arms around him and throw caution to the wind, there was more I needed to hear first.

"What exactly does that mean to you, though? I'm sorry, I can't depend on assumptions anymore. I need complete transparency. Total honesty."

He ran a hand through his hair, his thoughts visibly catching on something, before stretching an arm back to the bedside table. For a split second, I thought he was going to flip off the light and roll over, effectively pretending my confession didn't happen. But when he faced me again, he was opening his leather notebook.

I watched as he leafed through the pages, feeling the familiar urge to be a voyeur over his shoulder just to catch a glimpse at his inner thoughts. He flipped to a page toward the back of the book, a recent entry. Then, to my shock, handed the book to me.

My heart thudded in my chest, suddenly worried that the words would lose their magic if I touched them. He held it closer, urging me.

Slowly, I lifted the book from his hand, running my fingers over the soft leather, combing over Nate's black, scrawling writing.

He pointed to the bottom of the open page.

> *Maybe at one point, when I didn't know where she was, what she was doing, who she was with, when I could tell myself she hated my guts and wanted nothing to do with me, I could have pretended I didn't want her so badly. But now? With her mere feet away from me? Within arms' reach? When I can see her and smell her and imagine how soft her body is and hear her laugh, I'm a fucking goner all over again.*

"This isn't the same notebook I had when we met," he said, "but it goes back about a year." He took it back, flipping to an earlier passage before handing it to me again and pointing.

> *Almost sent you a song*
> *Just to see what you thought*

As if that was normal
As if I forgot

He took it again and turned to another passage further back.

There's a piece you have
A piece of me
Don't want it back
It's yours, it's yours, it's yours to keep

Then he flipped to another, this time at the very front of the book. The first entry, dated over a year before.

Somewhere out there in the stars, when all time ceases and the earth fades to dust, a tiny part of what remains of me will still be there, loving you

I read it twice, my chin trembling as tears blurred my vision.

Nate shifted closer. "You asked me what I meant by saying I want you." He reached tentatively for my hand, his fingertips trembling slightly as they closed the gap to mine. "I mean everything, Oli. I want your face to be the first thing I see in the morning and the last thing I see at night. I want to call you just to hear your voice. I want to spend all day doing nothing but existing beside you."

I leaned in, folding over myself as his words settled into my system. He dropped his forehead against mine and I closed my eyes, breathing in his scent.

He swiped a tear that had fallen onto my cheek. "I used to think wanting you so badly was selfish, and maybe it is, but I don't care. I don't want to go another day without you being mine. Because I am yours."

Cupping my face, he gently lifted it until I met his eye. "I love you. I have loved you for a long time. And I'm all in, Oli. I want it all. Titles and anniversaries and anything else I can get. Whatever you want, I want it, too."

My breath hitched with the soft sob that bubbled out of me. My heart swelled and burst in my chest, flooding me with a truly indescribable feeling. Like something had finally shifted and dropped into place so perfectly, it was as if it had always been there. Like I was full, overflowing with something so pure I didn't know it existed.

I wiped at my eyes, my sobs mingling with quiet laughter, which only grew louder when I met Nate's eyes. He was biting his bottom lip, holding in chuckles of his own as he watched me. He caught stray tears as they ran down my cheeks, his own eyes looking glossy and full of emotion.

"Can I kiss you now?" he asked with a laugh.

"Please."

In a movement as natural as breathing, Nate cupped the back of my neck, thumbs rubbing along my jaw, and kissed me. Long and slow and savoring, I leaned into him and sighed against his lips, in no rush for the moment to be over.

He pulled away only an inch, rubbing his nose against mine, leaving light, lingering kisses on my cheeks, my brow, my jaw, the corner of my mouth before melting against my lips again.

The first few of a million kisses to come.

When we finally pulled apart, he stayed close, not letting me out of arms reach as we settled back under the covers.

He circled me in his arms, kissing me again and again, moving his lips against mine with languid, adoring leisure, whispering honey into my ears.

I missed you.

I'm sorry.

I love you.

I love you.

I love you.

I was drifting to sleep against his chest, my hand resting over his sunrise tattoo, the next time he spoke.

"Does this mean you'll come to San Francisco with me?"

My voice was barely above a whisper. "I think I'd like that."

He didn't respond. He didn't have to. He just squeezed me tighter, planting a kiss on my hairline.

We lay in still, peaceful silence. Two people, two friends, who always seemed to barely miss each other on the pendulum of their lives—bound inexplicably together for a reason neither understood.

Only this time, finally, they met in the middle.

Epilogue

*Whoever said they couldn't have their cake and eat it too
clearly has never been in love with their best friend.*

My eyes darted to the clock on the microwave again. Only three minutes had passed since the last time I checked.

Ten minutes, I thought, *only ten more minutes*

I wondered if I would always feel like this. If the shock and excitement and anticipation of seeing him would ever fade. So far, it hadn't, and I didn't foresee it changing anytime soon.

It'd been that way ever since we left San Francisco. After the wedding, we spent three days in the Bay Area, exploring, eating, drinking, and doing all the touristy things that we'd never gotten to do before. While in some ways it was like nothing had ever changed, in other ways, it couldn't have been more different. Developing a steady rhythm with Nate Cassidy was the easiest thing in the world. It always had been. But it was different this time. We were together. Really, truly, *finally*, together.

And it seemed that we were on the same page without even having to discuss it. This was new. This was a clean slate. We needed to treat it with care.

Nate and I kept things modest in San Francisco, which was different for us. Soft, tentative touches were as far as we went physically—hooked ankles under the table at dinner, an arm around my shoulders as we rode the ferry to Alcatraz Island, interlaced fingers over the duvet as we drifted to sleep. And on our final night, we spoke more honestly with one another than ever before.

"In my eyes, this is the greatest opportunity I've ever had," he'd said. "I'm just thankful that you're here with me, after everything. I'm sorry if I'm laying it on thick, but…" He met my eye, shaking his head with the conviction of his words. I'd never seen him so earnest. "You're it for me, Oli. I don't plan on fucking this up again. You mean too much."

This time around was liberating. No more guessing games, no more uncertainty, no more wondering what the other person was thinking, how they were feeling. Complete and total honesty in everything.

In the month that followed San Francisco, my stomach fluttered with every text message from Nate, every phone call, every late-night FaceTime. He came to Boston to visit in early December and stayed the weekend with me, and during that visit, he invited me back to Connecticut to spend Christmas with his mom and sister. It was quite possibly the best Christmas I'd ever had.

And now it was February, and he was two minutes away.

I'd never been so happy.

Footsteps sounded in the hall outside my door, and I swung it open before he had the chance to knock. I was greeted immediately by his wide, close-lipped, dimple-popping, *Nate* smile.

"Hey," he said easily, taking a step into my apartment.

"Hi," I beamed back, already breathless.

I waited patiently for him to set his guitar case down and sighed into his neck when he folded me into his arms. My fingers went to the dark hair at the nape of his neck, and his palms spread wide across my back like he was trying to take in as much of me as possible. We breathed each other in.

"I missed you," he muffled into my hair after a beat.

When I pulled away, he cupped my face to keep me close and planted his lips against mine once, twice, three times.

He lived just over an hour away now, but sometimes it felt too far.

"I'm glad you made it," I said, holding his hands and easing him further into the apartment with another kiss.

He hummed, pressing his lips to mine again, taking another big step toward me, forcing me backward. In an easy motion, he shrugged off his denim jacket without pulling away from me.

"Are you hungry?" I asked breathlessly. "I was thinking we could order something in tonight."

Another big step forward from Nate and his chest pressed against mine. "Starving."

"And Jared?" I asked, dipping a hand under the hem of Nate's T-shirt, running my fingers across his abdomen. I hooked a finger into a belt loop at the front of his jeans and tugged gently. "Did you guys get everything sorted for your meeting tomorrow?"

"Oli?"

"Mmh?"

He met me in another dizzying kiss as we crossed the threshold of my bedroom. "I love you."

I smiled against his lips.

I'll never get tired of hearing him say that.

"I love you, too."

He eased me onto my bed and crawled on top of me, pushing my lavender sweater to my chest as he climbed his way up. Calloused fingertips smoothed over my soft stomach.

"Good. So, let's not talk about Jared right now, okay?"

My laugh was cut short when he dipped his head to kiss the top of my breast. His teeth scraped against my nipple through the thin fabric of my lace bra, and I arched toward him, sighing.

"Is this new?" he breathed, dragging his tongue hotly over my nipple through the lace.

"Maybe."

A second later, he slowly peeled the sweater off my body, taking his time to kiss and run his mouth over every inch of my exposed skin.

This was what I needed. What I craved, always. His touch, his kiss, the weight of him against me, his presence, his company. Even if we sat in silence, doing nothing but existing together, I wouldn't trade it for the world. There was a *rightness* to the world when we were together.

I buzzed from head to toe.

No, just on my ass, actually.

My ass physically buzzed from my phone shoved into my back pocket.

Nate sucked gently on the sensitive skin at the pulse point of my neck. "Should you get that?"

"Um." Resetting my brain to process anything that wasn't his hand on my thigh or the one tangled in my hair was an impossible task. "Yeah, maybe."

He laughed through his nose and rose to all fours, hovering above me as I wiggled my phone free from my back pocket. I had to blink at the screen twice to make sure my brain wasn't playing a trick on me.

"My sister is calling." Concern laced my words.

"Which one?"

"My older one." I slid my thumb over the screen to answer. "Lily? Everything okay?"

By the time I hung up, Nate was sitting back on his heels, watching me with his brows pulled together. He knew my siblings rarely reached out to me, and it was highly unusual for Lily to call out of the blue.

"What's wrong?" he asked, drawing circles on my knee with a thumb. His hair was adorably disheveled, a sweet contrast to the blush staining his cheeks.

"I'm not sure. She said she needs somewhere to stay for a few days and that she'll explain later."

"Is that… normal for her?"

I snorted. "Not at all. I mean, I'd be less surprised if it were my brother, River, but Lily?" I shook my head, thinking. "No, something is definitely up. She'll be here in a few hours."

Nate nodded and ran his hand from my knee to my ankle, making no move to continue the fun we'd started before we were interrupted.

I pushed up to a sitting position, angling my head back as I met his eye. I put a hand on his T-shirt and tugged him forward until his lips met mine in a slow, lingering kiss.

"We still have plenty of time," I whispered.

His contented sigh was answer enough.

Acknowledgments

What a surreal feeling to be writing this. I told myself I would save the acknowledgments for last because I needed to be sure this thing would see the light of day. But here I am. Days away from sending the manuscript off for line edits, days away from the cover reveal and opening pre-orders. Mere months away from sharing *Not a Friend* with the world.

So I guess it's time to write the acknowledgments.

Here we go.

To the Bad At Books writing group. This book literally would not exist without you. You gave me a sense of community at a time when I felt like I had none. Your encouragement, knowledge sharing, critical feedback, and overall cheerleading has and continues to mean the world to me. Also, thank you for thirsting after Nate with me for well over a year.

To my amazing alpha and beta readers. Your honest feedback and constructive criticism made *Not a Friend* better in so many ways. Thank you for the time you dedicated and for always talking through improvements with me.

To all the friends and family who loved and believed in *Not a Friend*—even when you didn't know much about it—simply because you loved and believed in me.

To the incredible artists who helped bring Oli and Nate to life: Stacia (@stacia_grace_designs), Ian (@lis_photoart), and Chelsea (@chelzd_art). And a special shoutout to Liz Parkes (@eklixio), who is responsible for *Not a Friend*'s gorgeous cover. Obsessed doesn't even begin to describe my feelings about it!

To my editor, Allison. Thank you for your endless professionalism, positive attitude, and for bringing *Not a Friend* through the finish line!

To Half Moon Run, for striking the match that inspired Oli and Nate's story.

Here's where I start crying.

To my beloved sister, Samantha. You've listened to me nerd out, fangirl, and talk about my delusions for our whole lives. It's only fitting that I've gabbed to you about this story since the beginning. Thank you for loving and supporting me unquestionably, and for providing tie-breaking decisions as the story unfolded. I love you. Life would be boring without you.

To my sister's wife, Sara Cassidy. Thank you for letting Nate share your last name!

To my husband, Christopher. Thank you for your unyielding belief in me. Unyielding support. Unyielding faith that I could see this through, even when I doubted myself. Thank you for keeping me fed and watered (like the house plant I am) during the long days holed up in my office. Thank you for encouraging me to keep going and for never getting jealous over my love for fictional men. I love you, I love you, I love you.

And finally, to myself.

Specifically, an eighth-grade version of me, daydreaming constantly, head full of ideas and characters, hyperfixating on the thousands of stories you were dying to tell. You snuffed out that flame because you never thought you would be able to actually do it. Writing a book was a faraway dream that would never come to fruition. So you kept a Pinterest board titled "Writing career that probs won't happen" saved for over ten years, secretly filing away prompts, tips, and FAQs with no plan of ever acting on it.

Spoiler alert: it happened.

And here you are at the end of it.

The best part is, it isn't the end. You have more stories to tell, more lessons to learn, more book boyfriends to fall in love with, more genres to explore, and a seemingly ever-growing list of ideas begging to get out of your head and onto paper.

Hold *Not a Friend* near and dear because it's the first, your labor of love. Oli and Nate will always have parts of you that no other characters ever will. Be proud of yourself, because you've earned it.

It's just the beginning.

I am so proud of you.

About the Author

Taylor Hannah is a music-loving midwestern nerd currently living in Appalachia. When she isn't writing, traveling, or daydreaming about fictional men, you can find her either at home watching trash television or drinking a sour beer at her local indie bookstore. She loves canceled plans, strong female friendships, warm blankets, and her pets: Chance the chocolate lab, Dublin the tuxedo cat, and Ivy the fluffy tabby. Oh, and her husband Chris, who keeps her fed and watered dutifully.

www.authortaylorhannah.com
Instagram: @authortaylorhannah
TikTok: @authortaylorhannah